Normans Cay

A novel

by

Paul Boardman

authorHOUSE™

1663 LIBERTY DRIVE, SUITE 200
BLOOMINGTON, INDIANA 47403
(800) 839-8640
WWW.AUTHORHOUSE.COM

© 2005 Paul Boardman. All Rights Reserved.

First published by AuthorHouse 08/15/05

ISBN: 1-4208-6522-6 (sc)

Library of Congress Control Number: 2005905305

Printed in the United States of America
Bloomington, Indiana

This book is printed on acid-free paper.

This book is dedicated to Neoma and Zak.

Prologue

August 1825

The trip from London had been refreshing. The worst part had been the first twelve hours in the English Channel but as "jolly old" dipped below the horizon the seas settled into a comfortable roll. The hundred and fifty foot brig carved its way south, past Spain to the Canary Islands off Morocco.

There it stopped briefly and took on water, fresh fruit and salt fish before beginning its journey across the Atlantic. The next port of call was Nassau, the largest port in the Bahamas.

Rebecca Outerbridge was the only woman aboard the vessel. She was thirty-five years old and still slim. She had never been a raving beauty. Nor was she unattractive. Perhaps it was her manner, too severe, too determined, which gave off an aura that many shied away from. The Captain however had found her to his liking. She had never complained even once about the food, the accommodation, or even the intense sun. On a few occasions he had warned her about being out too long but she had merely replied that she intended to live in the Bahamas and the sun would have to get used to *her* presence. Her choice of words amused the older gentleman and he had invited Mrs. Outerbridge to dine with him, in his cabin, in the evening.

That evening had begun a solid friendship between the middle aged woman, of her era, and the elderly captain who was approaching sixty and who had crossed the Atlantic as many times. Over the next two weeks they had shared supper every night but one, when the Captain had been busy taking a shot with his sextant and doing the tedious calculations to determine his position.

So when the heavy weather hit, only a hundred miles from their destination, the Captain took extra care of his sole female passenger. He tried to keep her in her cabin but she insisted on appearing on deck every few hours to view the water. The seas were making the final leg of her journey a nightmare, instead of the pleasant dream she had associated with sailing up to now.

Her cabin was atrociously small. It contained enough room for her trunk beneath a berth barely two feet wide and six feet long. Its only redeeming feature was a porthole that let in a bit of daylight. There was a stool where she could sit to take her meals and a chamber pot. It was small wonder that even such a determined woman had graciously accepted the Captain's offer to sit at a table, to dine.

After her second trip topsides the Captain had sent a seaman's hat and an oilskin coat, the smallest he could procure, to Rebecca's cabin.

Rebecca appeared on deck an hour later wearing the oilskin and hat. She also wore a self-conscious grimace that may have covered a smile.

"The sea's best left alone when she's in this kind of a mood", the Captain stated, "but if you insist on watching her, you might as well dress for it."

Despite her trepidation, as the powerful walls of water glided toward the ship, she preferred the openness of the bridge to the confines of her cabin.

It was daylight when they first sighted Highbourne Cay. Indeed, there was not a living soul on the small island and the Cay would have been almost invisible after dark. Had they suspected approaching land at night, the Captain would have turned back seaward, to avoid the shallow water.

The Captain was familiar with the cut, and with plenty of daylight, and the storm appearing to ease, he forged ahead. Standing directly beside his two helmsmen who controlled the wheel, with Rebecca braced in the corner of the bridge, he skillfully directed his crew as his ship passed from the Atlantic to the Caribbean. The ship had cleared the cut and was well into Exuma Sound when disaster struck. The lull they had just experienced had been the edge of the storm's eye. The Captain sensed the approaching blast of wind before he saw it, tearing up the sea into a black shadow, which bore down on the ship, a rippling, moving wall, approaching at a steady, ominous speed.

"Brace yourselves, lads", he shouted to his helmsmen.

He moved to Rebecca's side. "This is going to get bad. I wish you were in your cabin," he shouted in her ear. "Hold on. Don't let go, no matter what!"

Rebecca braced herself against the rail and the Captain stood behind her with one hand on the rail on her right and the other on her left. When the wind hit he squeezed her body tight against the bridge. The wind hit with such an overwhelming force that it sucked the breath from Rebecca's lungs. She remembered looking up and watching in awe as both huge masts snapped like matchsticks. The chaos that ensued was worse than anything she had ever imagined. Thousands of feet of rope that held the masts upright crashed to the deck. With it came booms and stays and spreaders. Much of the rigging fell into the sea, barely missing the bridge where the Captain braced himself and Rebecca. One of the helmsmen was knocked off his watch. He landed against the cabin, back broken and dead within a second. Rebecca watched as the two men who had manned the crow's nest plummeted gracelessly into the sea. Half a dozen seamen were soon caught on deck, in fallen rigging and dragged, screaming, into the foam that covered the surface of the water.

The Captain called for a second man on the helm. He then recruited a brave soul to stand guard over Rebecca and give his life, if necessary, to protect her. Arming himself with a cutlass he made his way down to the deck, ordering his seamen to cut the rigging and let the fallen masts slide into the sea. The deck was impossible to walk on. The sea breached the gunwales with every wave. Nothing that had been secured on deck remained so. Objects skidded across the deck often crushing men in the process or toppling them overboard. Brave sailors hacked at rigging trying to free the ship from the colossal timbers that pinned the boat broadside to the waves, aggravating the already dangerous list, the starboard gunwales only a few feet above the raging sea.

The Captain directed his remaining crew skillfully and from Rebecca's perspective, braced against the bridge rail by a hearty seaman, he seemed to be gaining ground. It took over an hour of indescribable horror and loss of life but one mast was floating away from the ship. The men were working furiously to set the second mast free.

Rebecca thought she heard the winds abate when the ship groaned and the mass of wood and rigging shifted five feet across the deck. She watched as seamen hacked at newly snagged lines. The timber mast shifted again, tilting the entire ship to starboard as it eased its way off the deck, snapping the remaining rigging in procession.

Had it broken all the lines the ship might have been saved but the sea was hungry and luck was against the brave warriors. The mast slid off the deck on the starboard side, the lee side of the ship. Fatefully, it was not set free but remained attached by a tangle of ropes. The ship righted but as it did the tangle of lines tightened and the broken spur of the mast was dragged back toward the hull. The Captain and crew thrashed at the rigging with their cutlasses trying desperately to free the mast but each wave jammed the hull against the ragged spur increasing the size of the hole the mast had punctured through the hull.

At first Rebecca had cheered when the mast slid over the side but now she felt a new sluggishness to the ship and an increased list. The last of the rigging had been severed and the mast inched away from the ship but it was simply too late.

The Captain was beside her again. "We will soon go down. I'll do what I can to save you." He dismissed the seaman who had been Rebecca's bodyguard with "Save yourself, Seaman. Your duty is done here. God bless", and turned his attention to Rebecca.

For a minute or two he watched as his men abandoned ship or clung frantically to whatever they could find. He helped Rebecca out of her heavy coat and holding her arm, jumped overboard. The poor man couldn't swim but nevertheless somehow dragged Rebecca toward the broken mast. Rebecca, who also couldn't swim was only semi-conscious when they reached a crosspiece still attached to the mast. She didn't remember the Captain lashing her wrists to the crosspiece. Nor did she remember the way he had kissed her hand and blessed her before he turned to help another drowning soul. He never reached his helpless seaman. It wouldn't have mattered anyway. Two miles off shore with night approaching, well, it was hopeless.

Part One

Chapter 1

Phil Harrison reached for a screwdriver with his right hand while holding the monitor bracket in place with his left. The screw was already on the tip of the driver, held in place by the magnetic shank. As his fingers touched the handle a gentle vibration began, next to his heart. It was followed by a shrill series of bells that had been muted to a fiendish annoyance. Phil let the bracket drop and placed it upside down on the console. He reached into his shirt pocket and extracted the vibrating, squealing device.

"Hello".

"Phil, its David. Got a minute?"

"When am I going to learn to turn this damn thing off?"

"Well, if you leave on schedule, that should be about seventy-two hours from now. Right?"

"You have a point there, David. So what's up? Tell me you're on your way over with a case of beer and I'll forgive you".

"Not exactly, sailor. I am sending someone over to meet you. Should I tell her to pick up a six-pack"?

"Not now Dave. I'm just hooking up a hanging monitor. Getting the wires over was a bitch. The boats a mess, I'm a mess".

"Sorry, Bro. No choice. Expect her in half an hour. Hold on. Forty-five minutes and she'll bring beer. Bye!" When he said goodbye it was a poor imitation of Wolfman Jack saying goodbye to Cornelius.

Phil found himself staring at the screen on his phone that indicated "call terminated". His immediate reaction was to call back and demand that David cancel whatever he was planning, but the situation tweaked his curiosity gene. Although it annoyed him to admit it, he found himself grinning as he put down the phone and reached for his tools. In forty-five minutes he could finish this job, tidy up and still have time to wash his face. He checked the brass clock, shaped like a ships wheel. Returning to the bracket he muttered, "This time you go up straight and you stay up straight!"

The half-hour gong sounded on the brass clock. Forty-five minutes had expired. Phil had just finished washing and was drying his face when there was a polite knocking on the cabin roof followed by a cheerful, "Ahoy, Zara".

"Be right up", shouted Phil as he glanced at himself in the eight inch round mirror.

As he climbed the companionway to the cockpit he caught a look at the back of a shapely brunette standing on the dock. She still had her back to him, looking out the harbor entrance, as he stepped down, into the cockpit. Phil took in a better view. She certainly did have a nice shape, but it was also her clothes. Casual, practical, bright colors. Boating shoes … well worn, too. A six-pack of beer dangled from her fingers. At least her outfit looked friendly.

"Hello".

She turned. Her hair blew away showing a beautiful face. Dark eyes, prominent cheekbones. Not much make-up other than a bit of lipstick.

"Hi, I'm Judy. David sent me". She paused, "Sort of ….." She smiled brightly, showing off lots of teeth. Anyway, I brought a dozen beer".

"Hello Judy, I'm Phil." Phil looked around clumbsily. He spotted a second six pack at Judy's feet. He regrouped quickly. "Well you're far too attractive to be left on the dock with so much beer. Welcome aboard Zara." Judy handed the beer on board and then accepted Phil's hand as she stepped onto the deck. She immediately plunked herself down in the cockpit on the side of the boat shaded by the canvas sunroof.

"It must be a hundred degrees in the city. It's cooler here by the water". Judy waved her hand in front of her face in a motion that was homey and girlish, natural and sexy all at the same time.

"What can I get, to help you cool off?"

"I'd kill for a gin and tonic, but my second choice is beer", said Judy, smiling with teeth showing.

"Coming right up. No need for nasty dead bodies."

Phil descended to the galley grinning, and wondering what the hell was going on. As he returned, drinks on a tray, he had not had a chance to place them on the cockpit table before Judy blurted out, "Bet you are wondering why I'm here, hunh?

Phil sat down, grinning but then tried to be smooth. "Nope, this sort of thing happens all the time".

"You wish!" laughed Judy. "Well I'm going to tell you anyway, since you were kind enough to get me a drink."

Phil sat, still grinning, not knowing what to say.

"You are a treasure hunter. Just starting. Good career choice! Stable income, group benefits, weekends and holidays off. Perfect! David told me all about you. I had a P.I. do a quick check, too. Then I did a bit of observation of my own from that parking lot over by the hotel. I even rented a room one day but I got bored staring out the window with a pair of binoculars. You have been working hard on the boat …. Very dedicated and methodical."

Phil's grin disappeared in a hurry. Being spied on didn't suit his often borderline, sometimes hermit-like, existence. "Well I'm glad to hear you got bored. It indicates a lack of professional training. So you're not CIA, FBI, GRU or MX6." Phil's voice was caustic. He was just starting to get angry.

Judy, however, was still smiling girlishly. "I'm not NBA, NFL, WWF or MP3, either. I did make the swim team in high school …. But that doesn't really matter".

Phil opened his mouth to speak but Judy ignored him and reached for her drink. "Good mix", she said cheerfully, ignoring any of Phil's anger.

Phil closed his mouth, reached for his beer and regrouped. He looked up at Judy who met his eye directly. After a second she looked out over the harbor, looking truly content. Phil was glad she wasn't looking at him because he could feel his armor melting in the humid Boston sunshine.

"O.K. Let's start again. You've been watching me ….. At some expense. Who are you and why such interest?"

Judy turned to him with enthusiasm bubbling out of every pore in her body. "You're not going to believe this. Well, eventually you will, but at first you'll think I'm a bimbo, nuthouse fruitcake. Right?"

Judy was unnerving. Phil was having a real problem being angry. Suppressing a smile he calmly said "Go on."

"O.K. From the beginning ….. In chronological order …. Without undo embellishment or "irrational exuberance".

Phil wondered how tough it would be for Judy to avoid "irrational exuberance". He was reminded of Greenspan's warning in 1997. He suspected he would have to ignore Judy's warning for about as along as the market had ignored Greenspan … which was about three years. He hoped he could avoid a "crash". It seemed impossible but he was already beginning to like this strange, forthcoming woman.

"Three years ago I got divorced. At least that's when I started a divorce. David was my lawyer. A year after that my mother died".

"I'm sorry", interjected Phil.

"You didn't say you were sorry about my divorce?" The quick reproach caught Phil by surprise but he was quickly learning to expect the unexpected. "But thank you about my mother." The smile disappeared from Judy's lips. "It was her time. She had been sick for five years, although she still lived in her home. I'm glad … bad choice of words … relieved … that her suffering is over.

"Anyway". Judy paused for a second, before continuing. "David helped with the estate so between the divorce and the estate settlement we got to know each other a bit. He asked me out a couple of times and I said 'yes', but on our first date he mentioned you.

That was about a year ago. You were his crazy friend who was selling his house, buying a boat and going off in search of sunken treasure".

That made Phil wince.

"I kept prodding him about you. I found out lots before he caught on", Judy continued proudly.

"So much for client confidentiality".

"Yah, right! Oh it was innocent enough. David figured out I wasn't interested in him, and at that time I didn't know your last name. Then, about three months ago, I moved into my apartment. I had moved into my mother's house near the end. After she died, I did a lot of the clean-up, you know, got rid of old clothes, outdated furniture and old kitchen stuff, slapped on some fresh paint, did a few repairs, and listed it. Eventually, the house sold. When I moved I kept and old trunk, sort of a hope chest, that my mother always had at the foot of her bed. I knew there was some private stuff in it. I had gone through it quickly but none of it affected the estate so I just left it as it was. I guess it was just too soon to actually look at it. I took my time getting set up in my apartment, back in my own space. One rainy weekend, when there was nothing good on TV, I opened the chest and started going through the contents."

Judy looked up and found Phil listening intently. There eyes met and for a brief second and held, each gazing directly at each other, looking for a deeper understanding.

"I found an old letter", Judy continued. "The letter was so sad. I read it every night for about a week. Then it finally dawned on me what that letter really was. I called up David and asked for your name. He tried to fend me off but I was persistent. Finally I had to show him the letter. That's when he relented. Once I had your name, I hired a P.I. and started my CIA, FBI, GRU, MP3 surveillance."

Judy paused, looked up and smiled brightly. "So here I am! Your drink is empty." She took a gulp of hers. "Woops, mine too! Want me to get refills?"

Once again Phil found himself being set to explode, and being defused with equal dexterity. All he managed was a grunt as he climbed below for more refreshments. But as he poured drinks, his stomach growled and he threw a bag of tortilla chips on the tray.

Before the tray had touched the cockpit table, Judy had snatched away the chips.

"You're not eating those. I bet you haven't had a thing to eat yet today. I'm buying lunch …. Over there". Judy pointed to a seaside restaurant located not far away. "You probably have some questions."

"You're damn right I have some questions but what makes you think I want to have lunch with a spy?" Phil stared hard at the adorable smile and watched his resolve disappear like the mirage it was. "Give me those chips".

"No way, Jose! Get it? …. Tortillas! …. Jose!"

Phil pretended to lunge around the table but Judy was nimbly jumping up and climbing over the life rail on the seaward side of the boat. She was clutching the chips to her chest.

"I'll jump. If you won't have lunch with me, I'll jump ….. And I'll take the chips with me. Then if I drown someone will probably sue you."

"You told me you were on the swim team".

"That was before I got amnesia and forgot how to swim".

Phil gave up and slumped laughing into the cockpit cushions. He watched in wonder as Judy slid the hatch boards into place and closed the sliding hatch cover. She sat down beside him, handed him the beer from the tray and took her own drink. Then, switching hands she fanned her face quickly with her right hand in a mannerism that was already becoming familiar. She sat back in the cushions close to Phil and without any indication that it was not the most natural thing in the world, dropped her hand into Phil's.

"I'm not really a spy, you know. I just had to confirm that you weren't a criminal or a real schmuck or something."

"You mean, perhaps, that I'm not a bad criminal", teased Phil. "Only the bad criminals get caught … the good ones get away without a record".

"Well I don't think you're a good criminal or a bad guy. After all, you didn't let me drown a minute ago".

"I reserve the right to reconsider … but I am starving so let's eat and I'll listen".

Judy smiled and stood up. "You don't get that from most men". With that she was downing her drink and already stepping onto the dock.

Chapter 2

Phil and Judy sat on the veranda of the seafood restaurant overlooking the harbor. They both ordered sandwiches and beer and waited until everything had arrived before discussing business.

"OK, where was I? Oh yeah, the house is sold, I'm in an apartment with an old chest and I find a letter. The letter was written by a Rebecca Outerbridge to my great, great, great grandmother, give or take a great. I have a copy of it in my purse. David has the original. Well here. Why don't you just read it? We've already established that you are either not a criminal, or at least a good one."

Judy extracted an envelope from her purse and handed it to Phil. The letter inside was a single page long, with perfect borders, written in a beautiful but difficult to read script, which gave the letter an appearance of a work of art, rather than a letter. Phil began reading but the handwriting was so old he had to read many parts two or three times. Judy sat calmly at first. Then she took a sip of beer and a bite of her sandwich. She stared out at the ocean. She dusted off a crumb and fidgeted. Finally, exasperated, letting out a gush of air, she snatched the letter from Phil's hand and began to explain it.

"The letter was sent to my great grandmother by Rebecca Outerbridge, who was some relation to my great grandmother. I think we can assume that Rebecca died shortly after sending the letter because of what she says about the chest pains. But we're not positive that she didn't recover.

"Rebecca was en route from England to her husband's estate on New Providence, or in other words, Nassau. I had an old title search done in Nassau and sure enough the Outerbridge's did own a sugar plantation on the island. I also checked some old records. The way I understand the story, Rebecca sailed from England, in a merchant ship. There had been smooth sailing until they were almost here. Then suddenly a storm hit. The captain decided to make the cut into the protected waters of Exuma Sound at Highbourne Cay".

"It's amazing how well the old sailors knew the sea routes", interjected Phil. "That's the same route used by the mail boat to this day."

Judy looked up. "Really, hmm. I didn't know that". She continued, "It was after making the cut that disaster struck! In terrible winds the masts snapped and the ship was adrift. It was blown south of the channel where it ran aground on the rocks and coral heads off Normans Cay in an area known as Normans Spit. I checked the charts and Normans Spit extends out about five miles. The ship went down and everyone was lost. Everyone, that is, except Rebecca Outerbridge. She must have bumped into a large spar, which she assumed was a piece of the broken mast. Clutching onto the log she somehow drifted ashore. She was sure she would have died on the spot, had it not been for an old Negro, living alone on Normans Cay. He had found her on the beach, the next morning. Although she had been delirious, over the next couple of weeks, in his small cabin, the Negro had nursed her back to health. She had started to improve but then severe chest pains developed. It was probably her heart giving out, or pneumonia, or something. The pains grew worse and although she could walk around a little she felt certain that she was going to die.

"One day she asked the Negro ... you know she never referred to him by name...only "the Negro"... Strange hunh?"

"There was still slavery in those days. If she suspected him of being a runaway, it may be that she didn't use his name to protect him."

"I never thought of that," said Judy. She continued. "One day she asked the Negro to tell her if he had seen the shipwreck. He had pointed out the cabin door and said ... look its right here. Judy's finger pointed to a paragraph;

"Just over that bluff of white rock I saw the ships lights. I knew it must be on the rocks. Soon the lights went out. The next morning I found you, Miss Outerbridge, all tangled up in the rigging from the broken mast."

The last paragraph of the letter told of her sea chest that she was bringing from London. Judy read from the copy;

"Perhaps, when my sea chest holding the bars of gold and my jewelry sank to the bottom of the sea, it was God's wish that I should die too. I doubt that my dear husband, who has been five years building our estate, will be able to continue without his gold. The Negro tells me we are only one day's sailing away from each other and urges me to get better, promising to find me a boat in which to sail to New

Providence, though I don't know how he would do that. Each day the pain in my chest grows worse and I feel that God is calling me. I have written both you and my husband and made the Negro promise to deliver the letters to Nassau. He has been kind to me and I wish no harm might come to him. There is no more paper so I must say goodbye, and God bless.

Your dearest friend, Rebecca Outerbridge."

Judy looked up, beaming. "So …. What do you think? Isn't it great! I mean it's sad, but great!"

She stared directly into Phil's eyes. Her own, became moist but she was in total control. She spoke very softly but with excitement oozing out of every pore. "I know almost exactly where a ship went down in 1825. The bars of gold. The jewelry. Don't you get it? This letter is a frigging treasure map."

Phil looked away and lifted his glass. He rolled his beer around without taking a drink. "Wow, that's quite a story. Why me?" he asked.

"I don't know ….. Karma ….. Coincidence. Look, I don't know many treasure hunters. Well, a couple of dozen or so", she kidded. "There are probably lots of you guy's out there but I just haven't met them. Then David tells me about you. A genuine treasure hunter and you even come with a reference. Can you beat that?"

Phil was starting to grin again. Judy seemed capable of turning any situation into a joke. Nor did she display any ability to slow down once she got on a roll.

"So here's the deal. Fifty-fifty partners. My treasure map …. Your boat. We each pay one half of expenses and I'll indemnify you for half the cost of the boat, or repairs or any of that stuff. David put it all in a contract."

Judy dove into her purse. "Here, I've got it. Just sign on the last page". She finished by handing a manila envelope across the table, putting her hands in her lap, and smiling brightly. Phil stared directly into her eyes but Judy just smiled and said nothing.

Finally to break the ice Phil mumbled, "Maybe I should read this over. Do you mind if I take that copy of the letter and go over it myself".

"No, I guess not." Judy paused and considered the consequences. "Sure, it's OK", she said.

"Are you nuts? Don't give him the letter …. It's all you have, you idiot!" said an inner voice. Judy picked up the letter and handed it to Phil.

"Look Judy, I'm due to leave in three days. This comes as a big surprise and I need a bit of time to get my head around it. What say we have dinner tomorrow night and I'll give you my answer, then?"

Judy looked dismayed at the delay but she rallied her courage and smiled, tilting her head, "I didn't really expect you to sign the contract without reading it. Tomorrow night would be fine. Give me your cell phone and I'll put in my address.

Phil reached into his pocket and extracted the wicked device. "Wouldn't a piece of paper and a pen work better?"

"I always lose pens. This is easier". Judy's two thumbs flashed over the keypad for thirty seconds. "There, done. See, that's me … Judy Simpson …. That's my phone number, my email and my address. I'll be ready at seven. You know you have a calendar on this phone. Do you want me to put me down for dinner?"

"No, it's OK. I think I can remember", said Phil sheepishly.

"Bet you didn't even know you had a calendar. Do you know how to use the address book?"

"I have the manual on the boat. I'll figure it out."

"David told me you hated that sort of stuff".

They rose from the table.

"That's my car over there". Judy pointed at a ruby colored Mustang convertible. "See you at seven, tomorrow." A wet kiss landed on Phil's cheek and Judy was gone. Phil turned back toward the table and reached into his pocket for a few bills. The waiter appeared at his shoulder.

"It's all taken care of, sir. The lady got it on her way out."

"Oh ….. Great! ….. How did she do that? ….. It doesn't matter." Phil collected the contract and the letter and headed back to his boat. He felt a bit dazed. When he sat down in the cockpit he pulled out his cell phone. It took him about three minutes but he finally found Judy's address and phone number. "Amazing", he muttered to himself. He was already looking forward to tomorrow night.

Chapter 3

Phil retrieved his tools and continued to install the computer at his navigation desk. His array of instruments was impressive. With his chart plotter attached to its GPS exterior antennae forming the nucleus, the various other gear including radar, underwater video, depth sounder, magnetometer and various communication equipment surrounded it. Having full computer capability on board, as opposed to dedicated navigation screen which he had at the helm, meant that from the cabin he could plot his course, send an e-mail play a videogame or watch a movie on DVD. He was happy that he had bought equipment that could all be screwed into place, instead of regular laptop technology. In strong winds not many things remain on table tops. Nothing was going to fall off this desk no matter how nasty the weather got.

With the job finished Phil kicked back in the salon and began to read Judy's letter. It was tough reading and after a while he gave up and turned on his new computer. Sitting at the nav station, he attempted to type the letter, inserting the underscore mark each time he missed a word or a letter. It took an hour but now had the letter fully typed with only a few missing words, which he assumed were idioms that had disappeared, over the years, from the English language.

Now he sat back and read it at normal speed and with a better understanding.

"Judy, you might just have a treasure map", he mumbled. Then ignoring his high tech capabilities, he dug out a chart book of the Bahamas and looked up Highbourne Cay.

"You were right about Normans Spit extending out five miles. That's a shipwreck waiting to happen. I bet more than one ship has gone down there", he thought out loud. "Normans Cay …. The name is familiar …. Let's check the guide".

Phil reached for his Yachtsman's Guide to the Bahamas and flipped through the pages until he found the Exumas. He scanned a few more pages until he found the description for Normans Cay. He read for a few minutes and then let the guide fall into his lap. A slow and drawn out "Oh shit", escaped almost silently from his lips.

"David", he muttered to himself. "First you set me up with a spy …. Maybe I could forgive that because she's a good looking spy …. But this! You just lost all your brownie points, buddy".

Phil reached out for the keyboard and found a document he had saved. He inserted Judy's letter onto the last page of the document. "There you go, baby. Hidden from prying eyes!" He folded Judy's photocopy and inserted it into the envelope.

⊰❧⊱

Judy's apartment was in an older, but still classy part of town, a block away from a main avenue that was lined with restaurants, book stores and flower shops. Phil rang the doorbell at 7:10 and Judy answered by opening the door, already wearing a light jacket over a summer dress.

"Ready! Let's go. I'm famished!" Judy passed Phil on the steps and somehow a quick kiss brushed his cheek, followed by a whiff of intoxicating perfume as she bounded down the stairs to the sidewalk. "Where's your car?"

"I don't have one. Came by cab. I sold my car yesterday. Didn't your spies tell you that?"

Judy was unphased by the rebuke.

"Besides, I like convertibles", Phil added.

"OK. Follow me. The garage is around the back." Judy reached in her purse and tossed Phil the keys. "You drive", she commanded breezily.

꧁꧂

The restaurant Phil had selected seemed to have more tropical plants than patrons. The couple sat in a booth, screened from other tables by the dense foliage.

"Ooh. Very private", exclaimed Judy. "I bet you're going to have a New York steak, since you'll be living on seafood for the rest of your life".

"Good idea", said Phil putting down the menu.

"I'll have the same ….. Same reason", said Judy.

"OK Judy. We have to talk. You seem to have a plan all worked out but maybe I should add a bit of input."

"Sure. I can handle that."

"First, I'm returning your letter." Phil reached into the breast pocket of his sports coat and handed Judy the envelope. "Thanks but no thanks to your offer of a partnership. I've been doing research for three years on another ship and that's the one I'm going after".

Judy's face took on a pained expression and for once she remained silent. Phil's resolve began to crack in several places at once.

"Look. You don't know what you're getting into. Searching for shipwrecks is like looking for needles in haystacks. The problem is, the haystacks are hundreds of years old and covered with sand."

"So you think I'm not tough enough to help. Better think again, buddy!" said Judy angrily.

"That's not it. You don't know, do you?"

"Know what?" asked Judy.

"Do you know about Normans Cay?"

"Sure I do. It's a little island with this big dangerous reef called Normans Spit, all around the side of it. Of course I know that. It's dangerous …. That's why Rebecca's ship sank. Because it's dangerous!"

"It's dangerous all right. But not because of a coral reef. Jude, I'm sorry I have to be the one to tell you this but you are never going to be able to reach your Grama's, girlfriend's gold."

"Nice alliteration! … And why not!" demanded Judy in an angry whisper.

At that moment the steaks arrived giving Phil a moment to collect his thoughts. As soon as the waiter left Phil looked up and found himself in an eyeball duel with a very upset female.

Finally conceding, Phil began. "I knew something was wrong as soon you mentioned Normans Cay. I just couldn't remember what it was."

"Well what was it, Captain Highliner", snapped Judy.

Phil snorted at the rebuke and continued. "Normans Cay is a private cay. Very private! The Yachtsman's Guide is very specific about it. It is protected, around the clock, by armed guards in cigarette boats. They probably have "Do Not Enter" signs posted all over Normans Spit." Phil looked up but saw no amusement in Judy's eyes. "Just kidding. You simply can't park and dive, anywhere you want on the spit. The guide suggests avoiding Normans Cay by about five miles."

"So who owns this *very private cay*? Some movie star or something?"

"Not quite. I wish it was that simple. Normans Cay has one humongous house on it. It also has a substantial private harbor and an airstrip. All very nice. This is the bad part, so brace yourself. It is reputed to be the drug center in the Bahamas. When they say armed guards they mean guys in cigarette boats with Uzis and M16's."

Judy deflated like a rag doll. Her shoulders slumped, her hands went limp, her jaw dropped slightly. Phil felt genuinely sorry for her and reached across the table to take her hand. For a good twenty seconds Judy sat there, almost comatose.

"Wow ….. That's a bummer", she finally mumbled, making a feeble attempt at humor.

Eventually she took her hand out of Phil's and made a noble effort to carve off a piece of steak. "Wow!" she said again. "I didn't see that one coming".

Phil began to poke at his steak. Neither one had taken a bite.

"So much for our partnership", said Judy dejectedly.

Phil looked up but Judy's eyes were cast at the plate of food. It was odd, he noted, that she had said "our partnership" and not "my gold".

It took a few minutes, but Judy regained her composure. The rest of the meal was filled with banal conversation and another half liter of wine. Still, there was a closeness between the couple that belied the fact that they were on their first date. They left the restaurant holding hands, comfortable with the arrangement. Phil drove Judy home but when he reached her townhouse Judy seemed to wake up from her daze.

"Hey, you think I'm going to let you into my apartment while you phone for a cab. Forget it, sailor. Take me to your boat. I can drive home myself".

Phil performed the mandatory objection but relented to Judy's logic. He was glad that she was recovering from her shock with a bit of her normal bravado. "Sure, why not? Thanks."

Phil parked the mustang and leaving the engine running unfastened his seat belt, preparing to let Judy take the drivers seat. Judy reached over and shut off the engine.

"Come on, Phil. At least offer me a nightcap on your boat. It's the least you can do after ruining the plans I started months ago."

Phil grinned. "Sure Jude. Would you like a night cap?"

Judy smiled brightly, though the sadness in her eyes remained.

"I'd love one, kind Sir".

Phil watched Judy walk down the dock in her evening shoes and was pleased that she slipped them off before stepping on board. "You've been around boats before, I see."

"My uncle has an older thirty-five footer in Chesapeake Bay. I can use it whenever I want. He taught me to sail."

"Let's go below. I'm too lazy to dry all the dew off the cushions, just so you can sit down".

Judy waited patiently as Phil unlocked the cabin and descended the companionway and turned on a light.

"Say, this is nice", admired Judy. "Lot's more room than a thirty-five. And it's so modern. Are you sure this condo floats?"

Phil appreciated the praise. Like most boat owners, he was very proud of his. Judy wandered around, passing the galley and standing behind the swivel chair at the nav station. "Good set up. Looks like you have all the toys, almost." She turned toward him and admitted, "Of course I knew that … but it's still nice to see it all put together."

Phil swallowed. He hated the fact that he had been spied upon. But he directed his anger mostly at David Windrow, his lawyer and, especially in the last six months, an occasional drinking buddy. Judy saw the flash in Phil's eye and assumed that he was angry with her.

"Sorry".

"Some how I'm not so upset with you. You had a reason to spy … well, sort of. At least as soon as we met, you leveled with me. That's OK. David, on the other hand has been playing me like a fish …. And that pisses me off, royally."

Suddenly Judy was in his arms and crying gently on his shoulder. Phil stood like a rock, occasionally stroking her long brown hair, doing what men do when women cry, mostly just feeling helpless and wishing it would stop.

Finally, Judy pulled away, and dabbed at her eyes. "About that nightcap, better make it a strong one".

Phil mixed the drinks and sat down in the comfortable settee. Judy joined him but snuggled right up close, curling her feet up and half closing her eyes.

Phil found himself with his arm around her, playing with her hair, curling it around his finger and then straightening it out.

For fifteen minutes Phil and Judy rested together on the settee, saying little, occasionally sipping on their drinks.

"Don't send me home tonight, Phil".

Phil awoke to an empty bed with the sounds and smell of coffee brewing in the galley. For a minute, he adjusted to wakefulness, reviewing in his mind the previous night. He found himself smiling. "Just my luck", he thought to himself. "I meet the most gorgeous creature I've met in years, the day before I'm set to leave town." He swung his legs over the side of the bed and pulled on a pair of shorts.

Judy was sitting at the table, wearing an oversized shirt that Phil had given her in the middle of the night.

"Coffee's ready!" she said.

"Looks like you found everything."

"Wasn't hard … you're a pretty neat guy."

"Have to be that way on a boat".

"Tomorrow's the day, hunh?"

"Yup".

"I had a great time last night."

"So did I".

"Want some company, sailing to Florida?"

"What?" Phil questioned. Then he realized how his reply must have sounded.

"Just kidding", lied Judy, convincingly.

Phil paused for a second. "What if I said OK? … Is what I was about to say".

"Liar".

"What if I wasn't lying?"

"I'd say OK".

"I wasn't lying", said Phil, cautiously.

"Liar! Liar! Pants on fire!" teased Judy. "OK, I'll come, since you offered."

Both people found themselves staring hard into each other's eyes and stayed that way for half a minute.

"Wow! May I sit down and have some coffee? I can't quite believe what just happened", admitted Phil.

Judy patted the bench beside her. "You can't seal the deal with a kiss until I've brushed my teeth."

Phil sat down and sipped on his coffee. "We never talked about you. Can you really just take off on a day's notice? No job … no commitments?"

"Nope! I need about ten minutes to pack. That's all. Lock the door. No pets. Someone will take care of the plants if I'm gone too long. How long will it take to get to Florida?"

"A couple of weeks. I planned a couple of stops along the way. The calendar on this boat doesn't work too well. I think the sea air messes it up."

"I thought everything was ship-shape?"

"Everything is. Except for the calendar."

"OK. You need my car for any last minute errands?" questioned Judy, casually. "You passed the driving test last night."

Phil grinned. "Didn't your PI tell you I got a speeding ticket last year?"

"I knew that … but I got two, plus some parking tickets. One's OK".

"Have I been totally set up?" asked Phil, still grinning.

"Just a little bit. I started to get the hots for you that day I spied on you from the hotel window. It was kind of erotic being a "peeping Tom". If you drive me home so I can change, I'll buy you breakfast, then you can have the car for the rest of the day."

"Do you always plan things?" asked Phil.

"Yah. Most of the time. I'm a computer programmer, you know".

"No, I didn't know. That does explain how you knew how to program my cell phone, though."

Judy grinned. "Kid's stuff. Let me out so I can get dressed."

Chapter 4

David Windrow arrived at his office a half-hour before his secretary was due in. He closed his private door behind him and tried to read the morning paper. It didn't work. He was unable to concentrate. He heard Ginny enter the reception area and begin her morning routine. He paced back and forth on thick carpet trying to collect his thoughts. Finally he stabbed the intercom button.

"Good morning Ginny. Come into my office for a moment please."

He sat down and composed himself. The door opened and a beautiful young lady entered.

"Good morning, David."

"You're looking lavish this morning. Another successful shopping spree on the week-end?"

Ginny smiled. She knew she spent half her paycheck on clothes but she had no intention of changing her ways. David liked her cheery disposition and her smart appearance. A lawyer's office could get drab sometimes and she knew David preferred his office to those of his fellow lawyers whose offices showed less flair. She had been with David two years now. A few months after she started, David had remarked on her sense of color and style. He had asked her opinion about some carpet. She had, after a little diplomacy, up-graded it. Her decision had been accepted and David had been pleased with the results. Before long she had been given almost a free hand in re-decorating. Her taste was excellent but she had not wasted money. He had started by giving her five hundred dollars to buy a couple of chairs and a coffee table for an empty corner of the reception area. A week later she had delivered, one chair, a small table, and a plant. David had been surprised, even a bit ticked off, at first, but it soon became evident that the odd corner became the favorite spot for clients who came alone. It wasn't long before David was financing a few more changes. Ginny was proud of the job she had done and knew David was too.

"Mrs. Gibson is coming in at ten o'clock. In the meantime would you please bring in the Simpson file."

Ginny started to turn away when David finally said what was on his mind when he called her in. He really just wanted to talk. "I wonder how Miss Simpson is doing. She left me a message over the week-end saying she was leaving with Phil on Saturday, Florida bound."

"She's doing well. I like Judy Simpson", Ginny said with confidence. "We have chatted from time to time while she has been waiting for you. David. Is that letter really real?"

"I think it is, Ginny." David turned toward the window to cover the shadow of a smile that was forming. Ginny knew the entire file except for the content of the letter.

"Will it really lead to sunken treasure?" Ginny asked. Her eyes sparkled at the thought.

"Who knows? It's a helluva big ocean. But I'll tell you a little secret. Judy still owed me some money from the estate. I agreed to write off my bill and carry the rest of her legal expenses for ten percent of the find... if anything is ever found."

"So that's it! I noticed we had stopped invoicing. I thought you might be sleeping with her, so I didn't ask. Now I find out my boss goes starry over sunken treasure just like any normal human being would."

David laughed at Ginny's candid summation. Once again she had proved herself to know a lot more about his office than she pretended to.

"To be honest I couldn't get to first base with her", he confessed. "What the hell.... I made out well on her divorce and so did she. We managed to stick it to her ex-husband pretty good and Lord knows he deserved it! The estate stuff was easy."

"So the conquering hero didn't get laid", teased Ginny. "You expensed her for at least three dinners."

Again David realized how well a secretary and bookkeeper, in a small office, could know more about you than you did yourself.

With mock sternness that Ginny saw right through, David asked. "Don't you have something to do this morning?"

Ginny snapped to attention and despite high heels and thick carpet, clicked her heels, stuck her ample breasts forward, saluted and replied, "Aye, aye Captain."

As she headed through the door David called after her, "Ginny, pull that letter from the safe and let me take another look at it."

Ginny nodded over her shoulder but as she passed through the door acknowledged, "It is exciting isn't it."

David was sitting back in his chair reading the Gibson file when Ginny returned carrying the Simpson file with an oversized sealed envelope protruding from it. Balanced on top was a cup of coffee.

"Thanks." David folded the Gibson file shut. It was a nothing estate case that he would have passed to someone else in a larger firm, but cases like that paid the bills in his solo practice. "Want to see the letter?"

"God yes".

Ginny sat down opposite David in the client chairs. He broke the seal on the envelope and extracted the letter which he had encased between two pieces of rigid clear plastic. Ginny knew the contents of the letter were not hers to read, by the stamp on the sealed envelope, so she remained a respectful distance from the document. But her heart fluttered at the thought of being so close to the equivalent of a treasure map.

Suddenly she became quite serious. "I think I know why you took your fees in futures."

"It gives you gold fever, doesn't it? But I never thought I would be involved in a treasure hunting expedition."

Ginny rose to leave. "Who'd have thunk it!"

⟨⟩

An hour later there was a soft knock on David's open door.

"Mrs. Gibson is here. I have a ten minute errand so I'll take the phone across the hall to Joan".

"That's fine. Just give me a second and bring Mrs. Gibson in".

A minute later Ginny was escorting an elderly woman through the door.

"Good morning Mrs. Gibson."

"Good morning Mr. Windrow".

Windrow came around the desk and helped the elderly widow into a chair. Then, as he sat down, he decided to avoid small talk and get right down to business.

"I believe we have the paper work in order and we just need a few signatures to finalize it." He began to pass copies to Mrs. Gibson explaining what she was signing as they worked through the various documents. Twenty minutes later they were completed but as David reviewed the checklist at the front of the file, he realized that he had omitted a standard declaration.

"I'm sorry Mrs. Gibson. There is a single page standard form I don't have in the file. Would you mind waiting a moment and I'll get one from next door." His checklist said "out of stock" but there were a number of lawyers in the building most of whom were co-operative with each other. David walked into reception and although Ginny was still on her errand he noticed she had prepared a tray with a silver thermos of coffee, milk, sugar and cups before leaving. David carried the tray in and poured a cup of coffee for Mrs. Gibson before he went next door. "I'll just be a minute", he assured her.

When he arrived in the reception area of his fellow lawyer's office, the receptionist was taking a message on the phone and David had to wait.

Mrs. Gibson added sugar to her coffee and sipped it from the china cup. Her eyes wandered around the room but settled, as they had once or twice during the signing process, on the obviously very old letter on the corner of Mr. Windrow's desk. Mrs. Gibson had a passion for old pieces of paper... letters, wills, land transfers... and she had been collecting them for years in an old scrapbook. The letter intrigued her...

not the content, which she rarely read in any of her collection... just the beautiful handwritten script and the artistic way the letter was balanced on the page with wide margins and a perfectly spaced header and footer. Moving spryly for an older woman, she got up, moved around the desk and picked up the letter. She knew immediately that it would be the prize in her collection it was so beautifully formed. Without hesitation she moved to the photocopier. She placed a piece of paper that she had inadvertently picked up under the copiers lid and pushed the green button. The copier worked just like the one at the library, she thought. She removed the paper and carefully placed the letter in its plastic case under the lid of the copier. A second later she had a perfect reproduction of the original.

Her aging heart was pounding but she had done it...pulled off the caper ... like they said in the movies. She felt like a heroin in an Agatha Christie novel. Moving quickly, she returned the original to the desk and slipped the photocopies into the folder of papers she had brought with her. When David returned she was sitting as he had left her, sipping her coffee and waiting patiently.

"I'm sorry about the delay," said David.

"Not at all", said Mrs. Gibson. "After signing all those papers its pleasant just to sit and relax for a while." Mrs. Gibson hadn't had so much fun in years and the adrenaline in her aging system was a potent stimulant. She enjoyed telling the "little white lie" almost as much as she had enjoyed the rest of her caper.

"One more signature and we're all done". David made a little small talk before standing. He helped with Mrs. Gibson's chair and walked her all the way to the elevator where he pushed the button and waited for her to get on. He always made a point of being very courteous to older women.

"You're such a nice young man," said Mrs. Gibson as she stepped into the elevator but it was not until the door closed that she let loose a little of the excitement that was bubbling inside her. When she disembarked on the main floor she was smiling brightly. She passed Ginny in the lobby but didn't notice her at all.

Back in the office Ginny stepped into David's doorway. "Flirting with older women again, I see."

"What?" questioned David.

"Well Mrs. Gibson was positively glowing when she stepped off the elevator", teased Ginny, affecting an accent from the Deep South.

David laughed. "She's probably spending some of the insurance money her husband left her. It should be in her bank account within the month. It's not very much."

"The way she was moving I wouldn't be surprised if she bought a Ferrari."

David looked up at Ginny. She was always a pleasure to work with, not to mention to look at. Although he had avoided asking her out socially he had often considered the possibility.

"Work," he ordered.

"Yes, boss."

❧

The forty-two foot Hunter sliced through the open water south of Martha's Vinyard, where they had spent the previous night. Judy was a competent helmsman, which left Phil in charge of the sails.

"Everything's set. Put her on autohelm and let's have a coffee. If this wind holds, and we don't have to dodge ships headed for New York, we could hold this course all the way to Virginia Beach."

"That would be the longest tack I've ever held", said Judy. "Did I tell you how much I like this boat?"

"Yah, about twenty times." Phil took a last look at the horizon and then peaked over Judy's shoulder at the radar/chartplotter screen mounted at the helm. "Nothing close by, at all. Come on, coffee."

In the cabin both of the couple peeled off their Gortech wind breakers. "It's warmer down here. That's for sure", said Judy.

"You'll be begging for cooler temperatures by the time we get to Florida. Or at least, after we land."

"I'll cross that bridge when we come to it", answered Judy. "Basically, I'm a sun worshiper!"

"Good religion", laughed Phil.

"Think you'd be lonely out here, all by yourself".

Phil laughed. "Lonely, not a chance. I'd be too busy. Now that's not to say there aren't times when a second pair of hands wouldn't be useful, or it would be nice to have someone else on watch, so I could get some real sleep. And a bit of company does add to the enjoyment … sometimes", he added. "The trouble is, when you have bad company on a boat, you can't just ask them to leave. But if you are fishing for a compliment, the last twenty four hours have been great. And you really do know how to sail. Big bonus!"

Judy beamed. "I'm having fun, too! Thanks for letting me come. I bet the sex is better when I'm on board. You didn't mention that!"

"That too," admitted Phil.

Chapter 5

FLORIDA

Amidst the hustle an bustle, the underlying muted roar of the sea breaking on the sandy shoreline, the salt smell of the ocean, mingling with the rot of seaweed, dead fish and shellfish, the tropical smell of fruit ripening and flowers blooming, there hung a state of melancholy.

Phil and Judy walked along the beach, hand in hand, trying not to say goodbye. The arrangements had been made. Judy was booked into a hotel. The boat was docked in the hotel marina and the couple had eaten an expensive meal that neither had tasted. Phil was prepared to leave the marina a couple of hours before dawn with the hope of reaching the Bahamas before sunset.

"It was one helluva sail!" said Judy. "Longest I ever made".

"You were great".

"You, too. You never even yelled at your crew", joked Judy.

"Maybe once, when we almost lost the winch handle".

"OK. Once ... still ... not bad".

"It was a good crew".

There was a short pause in the conversation.

Judy broke it, saying, "I guess I should head back to my room. I might even have another shower". Judy's hand fanned the air in front of her face.

"Did Captain Bligh ration the water too severely?"

"You figure", laughed Judy, hugging Phil's arm. "We still had half a tank when we arrived here. OK, that's it! I'm outa here! Got to go. Good luck. Bye for now. See you later".

Judy reached up with both hands and drew Phil's face toward hers for a long, heartfelt kiss. Turning abruptly, she trotted across the sand, without turning back.

It was three o'clock in the morning. Judy was awake, crying softly. She had moved the lounge chair along her balcony so that she could watch the harbor. She saw the hatch being opened and watched Phil climb into the cockpit. Suddenly a light came on in her mind. Grabbing a pair of shorts and a sweatshirt she stuffed the rest of her belongings into the soft duffel bag she had packed for the trip. Without combing her hair or brushing her teeth she raced for the elevator, stabbing repeatedly at the "down" button. She raced through the lobby and down toward the dock. Phil's boat was purring away contentedly but it was still tied up. Judy threw her bag on board and scrambled over the lifelines. Phil heard the commotion from below and felt the movement of the boat.

"Phil", called Judy, quietly.

Phil smiled a crooked smile then closed his eyes and tried to summon a bit of anger. They had both reached a decision. Of course he could have let Judy stay. But this was not a pleasure cruise. Not exactly, anyway. He had some pretty solid information about an ancient shipwreck off Long Island. He had spent the last three years organizing for this trip … this expedition. Now Judy was interfering at the last minute. She was already coming down the companionway.

"Phil … We have to talk … I have an idea".

Phil looked at Judy. She looked wonderful. Her eyes were puffy, her hair and clothes were disheveled, and she wasn't wearing a bra. "You look a bit like you've been run over by a Mack truck", teased Phil.

"Forget the way I look. I ran all the way here carrying that damn duffel bag. Meanwhile you're planning on running out on me like some damn, seafaring cowboy. Well look here, buddy. I haven't slept a wink, so you had better watch out. We have to talk. Is the coffee made yet?"

Phil motioned toward the counter. "I thought we talked about this, already".

"I'm not here for romance, asshole". Judy's anger dissipated. "Sorry, I didn't mean that". She smiled sheepishly and waved her hand in front of her face to cool off. "I'm here on business".

Phil grinned at her. "I see you're wearing your best Gucci business suit and shoes".

"Go to Hell!"

Phil raised his hands and took a step backward, still grinning.

"I have an idea. Are you going to listen or are you just going to be a jerk!"

"Coffee's already made".

Phil covered up his smile and sat down on the settee. Judy straightened her clothes and sat primly at the table.

"OK. Hear me through. Promise?" Phil motioned in acknowledgement. "Say it … Do you promise?"

"I promise".

"Good. Go shut off the engine. We can leave in an hour, after we discuss this".

Grudgingly, Phil climbed the companionway, shut down the engine, returned to the cabin and poured himself a coffee. Judy had run a brush through her long brown hair and looked surprisingly different.

"Here's my thought", started Judy. "Suppose you find your treasure ship and a horde of gold and jewelry. What are you going to do with it?"

"Sell it and live happily ever after", shrugged Phil.

"You're not going to run to the Bahamian government with it and spend years in court trying to figure out who owns it?"

"I might try to avoid that, if I could", admitted Phil.

"How would you avoid that?"

"I don't know. I think the trick is to get your booty to New York. I've never had a treasure trove, so I'm not really sure. To tell the truth, I thought I might find treasure first, then, deal with that side of it".

"Poor planning! Well suppose you already had it. How would you get it to New York"?

"Bring it into Florida, first. I don't know".

"I'm looking for a magic word. You would blank, blank, blank it into the States".

"I don't get you. I would ….. blank… it into the States. What? Smuggle? Is that what you want me to say?" said Phil, confused. "I suppose I might smuggle it … If that's what you're driving at. If that is a crime, it's certainly one with no victims", answered Phil, a bit angrily.

"Good choice of words. Now who are the best smugglers, say, in the Bahamas".

"Damn near everyone. Bahamians have been smugglers for five hundred years!"

"OK. But who are the best!"

"The drug runners. They do it for a living. They're the best equipped".

"And suppose we did find gold off Normans Cay. Think we could get some help getting it States side".

"Are you going where I think you're going with this?"

"Sure, it's worth a try".

"You mean we go right up to Normans Cay and say "Hi, we're here to find some gold and when we do, we'd like you guys to take it to Florida for us".

"Pretty much so. What do you think?"

"I think you really might be a bimbo, nuthouse fruitcake … But you might be onto something, too. In fact it might work to our advantage. There would certainly be a total security net around the area we were exploring."

Judy now sat cross-legged on the bench, at the galley table, with a wide grin on her face. "See my point?"

Phil stared into Judy's dark eyes for a full fifteen seconds, saying nothing. "I'm beginning to come around", answered Phil. "You're not just another pretty face!"

"My bag is already on board. Let's give it a whirl".

"Now hold on! Let's think this through. We might be dealing with some pretty unsavory folk."

"Oh I'm sure drug smugglers are all really nice people.... They're probably just misunderstood." Now, she was being flippant but neither was she giving an inch.

"You are really serious about this aren't you?"

"It's begun to be kind of an obsession. If anyone has a claim on that gold, it's me. It's my letter. Right?"

"I suppose you have a point there. Mind if I digest this for a minute?"

"Sure you can, all the way to Normans Cay. Let's rock and roll."

"You're out of your mind!"

"They're just businessmen, Sweetheart .... Looking to make a profit."

"Businessmen who would as soon deep six us after we found the treasure as look at us again."

"We don't know that.... Not until we try. I didn't come this far just to give up. We could arrange some insurance."

"Like in the movies. Leave an envelope with someone not to be opened until we're found dead!" Phil was incredulous but Judy was still way out ahead of him.

"Like with David. He has the original letter in his safe."

"As if I'd trust that bastard, any more." Phil regretted saying that as soon as it had crossed his lips, but thankfully, Judy remained stone-faced, appearing to ignore it. "Sorry", he added. "OK. You're on board to Nassau. I'll make up my mind there", said Phil with a finality in his voice.

Judy was smiling broadly. "I'll take the wheel. You cast off".

"Nassau … Not Normans Cay. Right?"

"Aye, aye, Skipper". Judy climbed topsides humming the tune to Gilligan's Island.

Chapter 6

Mrs. Gibson hurried into her small house. Without taking off her coat she rushed into the kitchen and prepared a pot of tea. Carrying the tea into the living room she sat down on her threadbare couch. Her cat sprang up from the floor and crawled into her lap.

"Tessy", she said to the cat, "I have something wonderful to show you." She reached into her purse and pulled out the photocopy of the letter. "Isn't it beautiful? I was so lucky to get it. I was very clever too!" she boasted to her willing listener.

For a few minutes she admired the letter and sipped her tea. Then, putting on a pair of glasses from her purse she began to read. The script was difficult as was some of the wording but Mrs. Gibson was familiar with both and made her way through it on the second reading. She read it another time out loud to Tessy. Along with the letter she had a second piece of paper which she had also photocopied just to be sure the page was inserted the right way. Curiosity proved a potent poison. She now realized it was a copy of the letter, neatly typewritten in Italics. She almost threw it out but decided to read it, just to check her "translation", and to pass the time.

She read the typed version catching two small mistakes. But reading it the fourth time gave her a better understanding of the content.

"Oh that poor woman!" she said. "She was only a few miles from her husband when she was shipwrecked and almost drowned. She was saved by the Negro only to become ill again. I believe this is the last letter she wrote before she died. That's the saddest thing I've ever read." She petted her cat with one hand while her other hand with the two pages dropped into her lap. She sat there for a full ten minutes, trying to picture poor Rebecca. Finally she poured another cup of tea from the pot.

"I know what I'm going to do, Tessy. I'm going to mount one letter, the old one, on the right hand page and the other letter, Mr. Windrow's version, on the left. Just in case someone wants to read the letter and can't get through the old script.

A few minutes later she got up and went upstairs to her bedroom where she had been viewing her scrapbook. She pealed back the cellophane on the hard pages of the scrapbook. Making sure the letters were straight, she pressed the clear plastic back in place. When she looked at the scrapbook the original took up the whole right page and the printout rested on the left page. Pleased with the job she had done she carried the book downstairs and left it on the kitchen table. A little tired from the trip downtown and the excitement of snitching the letter she decided not to go shopping as she had planned and spent the rest of the day watching television and doing a bit of housework.

Just after the news at six she walked over to the telephone and placed a call to Florida reversing the charges. The phone rang in Florida and young female answered.

"Harry's Bar."

"Collect call for Harold Gibson. Will you accept the charges?"

"Just a sec, operator. Harry there's a collect call for you. Do you accept?"

Harry Gibson checked his watch. "Sure, I'll take it in the office."

"He'll accept operator. Hold on a minute while he gets the phone."

There was a click; "This is Harry Gibson."

"Harold, this is your mother."

Harry Gibson experienced a mild shock but recovered enough to say, "Hi Mom, how are you? Is everything alright?"

"Everything is fine dear. I just called to see how you were doing."

"Doing fine, Mom", Harry Gibson lied. "Did you see the lawyer today?"

"Oh yes, everything went fine at the lawyer's. He's such a nice young man. There are a few things we should discuss, though. Do you think you could drive up here, tomorrow?"

Harry was now totally surprised. First of all his mother had never before, called him at work. Usually, she called him at home on Sunday nights to get the discount phone rates. Secondly she seldom asked him back home except on holidays which he usually, though often grudgingly, accepted. Still it was early in the week and he would be back for the weekend when he was really needed.

"Sure Mom, if it's important."

"I'll expect you for dinner then, tomorrow."

"O.K. Mom, I'll see you then and I'll take you out for Chinese food."

"That would be nice," said Mrs. Gibson sincerely. "Goodbye dear."

There was a click and the line went dead. Harold grunted to himself, laughing at the way his mother was so abrupt whenever she was talking long distance. "Silly old woman", he thought.

He did up the night receipts after closing hour and climbed into his Buick. He was not tired so he decided to go back to his apartment, only a block away, pack a bag, and drive until he became weary. He figured he would be at least half way to Boston before that happened.

Mrs. Gibson was sitting in her favorite chair so that she could see the street when Harold drove into the laneway. He greeted her with a kiss and a small box of cheap chocolates. She took his jacket and after hanging it up bustled off into the kitchen to make him a sandwich.

"How was the drive, dear", she called from the kitchen.

Harold grimaced. His mother always asked the same questions and did the same things, the same way. Still, she was his mother and he cautioned himself to be polite. Maybe the lawyer had finished and he might go back home with some money. He assumed that was why his mother had invited him to come.

"The drive was fine. Just the usual traffic."

While Harold waited for the sandwich he looked around the living room noticing how shabby the carpet and upholstery were. Someday he would buy her some new furniture. Someday .... If business ever improved. Mrs. Gibson arrived carrying a tray with sandwiches and a soft drink.

That evening, Harold took his mother to a Chinese buffet restaurant. He disliked it but it pleased his mother who thought it was an affordable place to go to. Afterwards they went home. Mrs. Gibson turned on the TV but Harold decided on going to bed. Up in his room with the single bed, he looked around at the furniture and decorations. It was the same room, with the same things in it that he had owned when he was in high school. Nevertheless he soon fell asleep and for the next five hours, slept peacefully.

A sharp pain in his stomach woke him. He got up and took a package of Rolaids from his toilet kit. Within a few minutes the pain had subsided but he was thirsty and decided to go to the kitchen for a drink. He trundled downstairs in his shorts and pulled on the handle of the ancient refrigerator. He decided on a glass of milk and sat down at the kitchen table. Half way through the second glass he opened the photograph album. He was surprised to find it filled with old deeds and letters. He flipped through until he came to the last page. The book lay open revealing both the left and right page. He sipped on his milk. The name Windrow on the letterhead on the left-hand side caught his attention. Recognizing it as the lawyer handling his father's estate he read the letter hoping it would reveal information about his inheritance. After finishing the typed version of the Outerbridge letter his eye drifted to the original. He re-read the letter comparing the two. Finishing the letter for a second time the contents he sat in shock at what he had just discovered.

"It's a fucking treasure map", he mumbled to himself. "In a photo album. My mother is keeping it because she likes the dumb writing. I bet she doesn't even know what she has here. I can't believe it. Hot damn!"

He closed the album and gulping down his milk wandered back to bed. Finally he fell asleep again but this time he was dreaming of new wealth and how he would spend it.

When he arose in the morning he could hear his mother puttering around in the kitchen. He decided to shower and shave first, then go downstairs. He was greeted at the kitchen door by the smell of pancakes. It seemed like years since he had eaten pancakes for breakfast and for a moment he had a genuine feeling of warmth for his mother, but it passed so quickly it failed to register. He had a job to do and that was all he was going to concentrate on.

"Morning Mom" he said jauntily. "Smells good!" Mrs. Gibson beamed at the compliment about her food.

She had everything prepared and was pouring coffee even before he sat down. Mrs. Gibson was drinking tea with a bit of honey in it but she had made a full pot of coffee for her son. She served him three huge pancakes. Her own plate was noticeably empty by comparison, with one small pancake, looking lonely in the center of the plate. She sat down to eat, but Harry knew that she would be up doing something before he was half finished. He looked around the room. There it was! Sitting on the counter. The photo album with the red plastic cover, greenbacks pouring out of it, covering the counter and falling to the floor. Harry blinked and the album appeared normal again.

"You make good pancakes," he said between bites.

Mrs. Gibson beamed. When he had finished and she had cleared the table, she sat down and poured another cup of tea.

"Mr. Windrow asked to see you. It's about the will. Your father left the house and most of the savings to me, until I die" she added, "but he had a special account that he had set up for you. It's not very big but I'm sure you will be pleased that he was thinking of you."

"Sure Mom, I'll phone Mr. Windrow and set up an appointment."

"It's already set for two o'clock this afternoon. I spoke to his secretary after you said you were driving up."

"That's good."

"Now that that's taken care of, I'm going to have my bath." Mrs. Gibson got up to leave. When she was half way up the stairs Harry called after her.

"I'm going to the corner for cigarettes. You want me to pick up anything?"

"I don't think so, dear."

When Harry was sure his mother was in the bathroom he hurried over to the photo album and extracted the last two pages. Not bothering to lock the door behind him he hurried out to his car, jamming it into gear the second it started. It stalled, he swore, and cranked it over again. Minutes later he was in the drugstore at the mall ramming a quarter into the photocopier. The copy came out a little crooked but it was clear. Harry was a little more particular with the second page. As he walked through the door he could hear his mother pull the plug in the bath. He turned to the last page of the album and reinserted the photocopy pages. He didn't notice that he put the slightly crooked copy back in the album. After all, they were all photocopies. The other set he pushed deep into his pants pocket. In the bottom of his pocket his fingers touched the small silver box. Quickly he took it out and sprinkled some of the fine white powder onto the glossy cover of a cooking magazine. Rolling up a dollar bill he snorted the white crystalline substance deep into his nostril.

Pouring another coffee and went into the living room where he switched on the morning shows on the TV. The bad jokes on the morning show seemed particularly funny today.

At two o'clock Harry strolled into David Windrow's office. The first thing he saw was Ginny sitting sideways at her desk typing away on her computer. She looked up immediately.

"Good afternoon".

"Hi there. I'm Harry Gibson". Harry had already skimmed a lecherous eye across Ginny's body and came close to the desk to get a better view of her legs. Ginny was used to having men look at her but there was something peculiar in the way Harry did it that immediately sent a small shiver up her spine. She glanced at her telephone.

"Mr. Windrow is on the phone but he is expecting you, Mr. Gibson. I'll let him know you're here." Ginny was about to offer him a coffee but on impulse decided he didn't deserve one and resumed her typing. Harry sat down opposite her in the sofa. She could feel his eyes undressing her and tried to ignore him. Harry picked up a magazine, looking over the top of it frequently.

"Beautiful day outside", he commented. "Cooler than Florida."

Ginny smiled sweetly. David was off the phone. She rose and went to his door. Knocking once, she walked in and closed it behind her. She spoke softly almost mouthing her words. "There is a creep outside who say's he's Harry Gibson."

David chuckled. "One of those."

"I thought his eyes were going to pop out of his head."

David chuckled again, cocked his head to one side and looked over Ginny himself. "Can't blame him at all."

"Next time I bring you coffee I suggest you put a towel in your lap...just in case it spills." With that she turned and opened the door.

"Mr. Windrow will see you now", she said across the reception area. She held the door until Harry had passed through. Then as David glanced up to thank her, she stuck her tongue out at him behind Harry's back and smartly closed the door.

David sized up Harold Gibson as they shook hands. Ginny was right. At first glance he immediately distrusted this man in front of him. It was his eyes.... They seemed extra bright. Dismissing personal feelings David went to work explaining the will and the progress that had been made in clearing the proceeds. He had a file of paper in front of him with little sticky plastic arrows tabbed onto the side of various pages that said "Sign Here". Fifteen minutes later he was shaking hands with Harry at his office door. Then, in a manner that appeared totally natural and businesslike, he walked Harry through reception to the outer door. Harry glanced back at Ginny who refused to look up from her typing. As Harry exited and the door closed Ginny looked up at David.

"O.K. you're forgiven."

David winked and said nothing but as he returned to his office his stomach growled and he remembered that he had skipped lunch. He returned to reception and leaning over Ginny's shoulder said "Shut that damn thing down for ten minutes and I'll buy you an ice cream cone in the park."

Ginny looked up, batted her eyelashes, and feigning a southern accent said "Why Sir, I'd be honored."

With lightening speed, despite her well-manicured fingernails, she saved the document and exited the computer. She plugged up two phone lines and picked up the cordless phone, which she would hand off to her friend on the way out.

Ginny sat on a park bench as David bought two cones from an ice cream vendor. As he handed one to her his stomach growled loudly again.

Ginny looked up into David's eyes reprovingly. "Lunch?" she asked.

David said nothing and sat down beside her.

⊰⊱

It was 9:30 in the evening when Harry walked his mother to her door. They had eaten chicken at a small restaurant. She handed him her key and he took it, the way he had been taught, and inserted it in the old fashioned lockset.

"It's a fucking skeleton key," he thought. "I should tell her to get a proper deadbolt installed but this lockset is so old no modern crook would know how to pick it anyway."

"I already loaded my bag. I'm going to hit the road right away", he said politely.

"Why don't you rest a few hours before driving back to Florida, son", Mrs. Gibson asked knowing full well her offer would be refused.

"I'll drive part way and get a motel, Mom. That way I'll break up the drive." Harry thought about his room at the top of the stairs, unchanged at all since the day he had moved out fifteen years ago. Rock and roll posters were still stuck to ratty wallpaper. A high school photograph of him sat on the dresser. The scruffy little desk he had done his homework was still under the window. The narrow bed was still jammed against the wall. It was all spotlessly clean and the sheets smelled of Fleecy fabric softener but to sleep there another night would be a lousy re-run of a boring childhood. A Boston breeze, much cooler than Florida, sent a shiver through his spine.

Harry pushed open the door and stepped in first so that he could find the light switch. Instinctively his hand reached out in the dark and touched the plastic knob. The old-fashioned hall light came on. For a second he squinted as his mother stepped across the threshold and closed the door. He was trapped.

"Well at least I'll make you a pot of coffee, dear."

This was inevitable. She would make coffee and put it in an old pickle bottle that she would have previously scoured clean. She would wrap the bottle in paper towels held tight with elastics that would serve as insulation. A Styrofoam cup would appear out of a leftover tube from some church bazaar and everything would be placed in a brown paper bag, neatly folded along the top edge.

"Now be sure to keep it right side up" Mrs. Gibson would say. "I put in a few cookies too."

⊰⊱

"Thanks, mom." Harry gave her a hug like he always did. As he put his arms around her he slid a folded fifty-dollar bill half under the kettle on the kitchen counter. He begrudged this act, knowing it stemmed from guilt instead of love.

"Drive safely, dear."

"Yes, Mom. Bye."

Finally he was back in his car with the brown paper bag, right side up, on the transmission hump, leaning against the seat. He waved, smiled, tooted his horn and was gone. His artificial smile disappeared immediately.

He headed toward the turnpike but before getting on the ramp pulled into a drug store parking lot. He parked well away from the store. Reaching under the front seat he pulled out a small plastic bag. Then he filled up the little silver box he always kept in his trousers pocket. On the back seat was a Newsweek magazine. Gently dumping some of the contents of the plastic bag onto the glossy cover of the magazine and pushing it into a line with a paper match he snorted the cocaine into his nostrils through a rolled up dollar bill.

For a second he stared rigidly at the neon sign above the drug store holding his breath. Only when he was sure he wouldn't sneeze, did he let it out. He had a broad grin on his face as he stuffed the plastic bag back under the seat and threw the Newsweek into the back of his car. He lit a cigarette and started the engine. There was a sudden stirring in his loins. As he pulled onto the turnpike he had a full erection just thinking about a strip joint bar and whorehouse in Georgia. He thought about the letter he had photocopied. He should be able to sell it for enough to pay off his cocaine debt. His bar was making good money and he was making five hundred dollars a week selling coke to a few regular customers but he never seemed to have enough to pay off his bills at the end of the month. It almost crossed his mind that he spent a thousand dollars a week on cocaine. But as long as he kept moving a little powder out the back door of his bar, Prince and his friend didn't seem to mind that he owed them money.

"Shit" he thought. "There will be something for me from the old man's estate. Not much, but something for sure. And that letter is a fucking treasure map." He had already decided to sell it for ten thousand dollars. That would wipe out his cocaine debt. Maybe he'd ask for fifteen.

Driving with his knees he poured himself a cup of coffee from the bottle and settled in for the five-hour drive to Georgia. The coffee tasted good. He wondered if there would be any new girls at the strip joint.

"Fuck, there are always new girls!" he said aloud as he reached between his legs.

Chapter 7

Phil and Judy sat huddled together in the cockpit as the morning sun began to inch its way over the horizon. The winds were steady, the waves were a constant three foot swell and Zara glided along at a steady six knots.

"I'm ready to go back to bed", admitted Judy.

"Getting up at three AM does throw your system out of whack", agreed Phil. "Just let the wind hold and we'll be in Freeport by suppertime".

"Lobster …. I want lobster".

"I'll buy you the biggest one in town", promised Phil. "Go below and get some sleep".

"After the sun rises". Judy paused for a few moments watching the sun, already a half circle on the horizon. "Phil, tell me about your computer".

"Hey, I thought this was a romantic sun rise".

"It is", said Judy snuggling closer. "What do you have in the way of software?"

"Off the shelf stuff. Map and track, using the GPS. Marine charts. I've got underwater video using a "fish" that runs through the computer.

"A fish?"

"Yah. It drags behind the boat on a downrigger and films whatever it passes over. I can see the images on a monitor but I have to watch the entire film or I could miss something important. I have a magnetometer so if there is metal I hear the beep and can rewind the video. Why do you ask?"

"Mind if I play with your computer later".

"The computer? Of course not! It's all yours."

"OK. I think that's the most beautiful sun rise I ever saw".

"No kidding".

"I'm going back to bed. You want anything …. Coffee … A sandwich?"

"I'm coffee'd out. You rest now and I'll grab an afternoon nap."

Judy tilted her chin up, for a kiss, before climbing down to the cabin.

Phil scanned his instruments and checked the horizon. There was nothing in sight but ocean and sky. No other vessels. Land was far out of sight, beyond the horizon. Phil breathed out a sigh of contentment. All the world's troubles seemed very far away.

"Catch me if you can", he mumbled to himself.

Judy rose around nine thirty, feeling a bit groggy but reasonably fit. She joined Phil in the cockpit and took over the watch while he went below to make breakfast. It was a simple meal of fresh fruit and a cold drink but somehow it had taken nearly an hour to prepare. Judy suspected that Phil had closed his eyes, while waiting for the fruit to ripen.

"That was quick", she teased, as Phil re-appeared.

There was really nothing to do, other than maintain a watch, so Phil and Judy set up the cockpit table and chatted about nothing. Finally Judy said she was going below to play with the computer.

Two hours later she had not returned.

"Are you still alive down there?" asked Phil, poking his head down the hatch.

"Let me check my pulse". Judy mocked feeling a throb in her neck. "Yup! I think so", she called. Without another word she was back on the keyboard.

Half an hour later she appeared in the cockpit wearing shorts and a halter top and drinking a bottle of water.

"What were you doing down there? You've been stuck on that computer for nearly three hours."

"I'll show you when we get to Nassau", was her cryptic answer.

"I vote we spend a day in Freeport. R and R".

"No problem, mon", teased Judy. "I got some sleep but you must be exhausted. I'll take over for the next three hours, if you want."

"I wouldn't mind that at all. You OK with everything?"

"Sure. I checked our position at the nav station ….. Just to make sure you weren't abducting me to some strange hide-a-way of yours. I'm worried you might have a bit of pirate in you."

"I do. But even pirates need sleep. You have the helm, Miss Simpson".

Judy laughed and moved behind the wheel to check the position and the radar. Nothing but ocean. She shuddered slightly but fought off the trepidation of being so alone on such a vast ocean. She checked the course, the speed, the depth, the wind and realized she had nothing to do for the next twenty minutes. Then she would check everything again. "Tough job!"

she muttered and sat back in the cockpit starring out at the waves.

⛤

It was close to midnight when Harry pulled into his parking space behind the bar. He stretched, patted his breast pocket and using a key on his key ring entered the bar from the back door, past cases of empties and green bags of garbage. The bar was busy enough that Harry knew he would do better than break even tonight. That was good. He hated having to rely on Friday and Saturday to make the weeks profit. He wondered how much his staff had ripped him off while he had been away. If it was over five hundred it would show. Below that it was hard to confirm. If it hit a thousand a few of his staff would be out on the street, looking for new jobs!

His manager was the first to notice him. "Harry, you're back."

Harry wondered if she was saying it loud enough to warn other staff members who were skimming. He smiled weakly and sat down at his favorite chair at the end of the bar and ordered a rum and coke. "Everything OK while I was gone?" he enquired.

"Yah. Lewis overloaded last night and we had to throw him out. Told him not to come back for a month."

"God damned drunk. You should have left it at 'Don't come back' …period. Everything else OK?"

"Everything else was normal. How was your trip, boss?"

"Saw my mother. What can I say? Has Prince been in?"

"I think he's in the back playing pool, right now."

"Good". Harry picked up his drink and wandered to the back of the bar. He nodded and said 'hi' to a few regulars. There was Prince, playing pool with a gorgeous black girl who had had at least a dozen tequilas. Her blouse was open below her breasts. She was lifting her leg and showing white panties as she leaned over the table for a shot. Harry grinned and sat down at a table to watch the show.

Eventually Prince noticed Harry and walked over to his table after giving his girlfriend a big squeeze on her ass.

"That bitch is hot for me tonight", Prince bragged, by way of introduction.

"That's if she doesn't pass out first," said Harry.

"You know me man", countered Prince. "I got something to keep her up as long as I'm up". Prince admired the girl from a distance. "That bitch is Hot!"

"Prince, you know that guy in the Bahamas. The one you get your dope from."

"You crazy man? I don't know nothin' bout the Bahamas. What's the matter with you, man?"

"Cut the shit. I got something that dude will want. And I want my debt cleared off plus a couple of thousand," he added.

"What you got that's worth that kind of money?" demanded Prince.

"A treasure map, dude. A fucking treasure map!"

"Man, you must have had a joyous trip up north to come back with a story like that." Prince was laughing now and getting up to leave. Harry grabbed his sleeve and pulled him back down.

"I know it sounds crazy but it came right out of my lawyer's office. He must be organizing a syndicate to go after it or something. Anyway, this is legit."

"Man, I'm going back to my bitch. At least she's got something I want."

"Hold on, Prince. Take a look at this." Harry reached in his pocket and pulled out the photocopy of the letter.

Prince stared at it for a minute and shoved it back across the table.

"That ain't no map. It's a letter. And it's so old I can't read it".

Harry reached into his pocket a second time and pulled out the translation. "Read that".

Prince studied the letter. He looked up at Harry and stared him in the eye. He looked back at the letter and read it a second time. This time he took both pieces of paper and slipped them into his pocket. "I'll talk to him. You OK for tonight."

"Yah, fine", answered Harry. "Enjoy your babe with the boobs".

⚛️

Phil and Judy were tied up at the Nassau Yacht Club. They had just eaten a marvelous dinner of conch steak and were walking back to the boat hand in hand.

"How much wine did we just drink?" asked Judy.

"Just one bottle. Are you feeling tipsy?"

"I feel OK but I can't walk a straight line".

"I know what you mean. It feels like the dock is swaying." Phil looked at Judy's legs. "I have to admit, though. They're about the best looking sea legs I've ever sailed with".

"What do you mean, 'about'?"

Phil pretended he didn't hear that and got a poke in the ribs for it.

"It's time, you know".

"Time for what?"

"Time to tell me what has kept you glued to my computer for the last two days".

Judy pretended nonchalance. "Nothing much. Pour me a glass of wine and I'll show you."

"You're on", said Phil. His curiosity was truly peaked.

Judy led the way down the companionway and sat down at the computer. She turned it on and let the program load. She turned up the volume and clicked the mouse.

"Rebecca's Gold" appeared across the screen in gold letters over a deep blue background. There was a picture of a treasure chest, overflowing with gold coins. A couple of fish glided by.

"After I discovered I had a treasure map, of sorts, I read a couple of books on the subject. Duncan Mathewson's 'Treasure of the Atocha' and 'Ship of Gold' by Gary Kindler."

"Good books! I've read both of them".

"So what I learned is that searching for a shipwreck is a bit like following a trail of bread crumbs. If you catch the trail you can follow it, from artifact to artifact, that were lost as the ship began to sink. The most important thing, is to record each artifact, carefully, trying to determine the course of events that led to the ship sinking. Eventually the trail should lead to the motherlode".

"So far, so good", stated Phil.

"Well you know I'm a programmer. So what I did was take the whole process and turn it into a game. You told me you would have to watch hours of video of the bottom. I just made it a bit more interesting. Here, watch this. It's a kind of demo or simulator of what we'll really find."

Music began to play in the background and a picture of a sailboat named 'Zara' appeared, bobbing along. Suddenly, over the music was a sound like a Geiger counter. "Magnetic Reading" flashed on and off in the corner of the screen. Judy clicked her mouse. A picture of the ocean bottom appeared as the "fish" was dragged over the area where the magnetic reading had occurred. A cartoon image of a slice of bread appeared in a pop-up. A cartoon hand tore off a crumb and let it sink to the bottom. The hand and slice of bread disappeared. A fact menu popped up in the top right corner.

"Here's the known information", explained Judy. "You have time and date, depth, GPS co-ordinates, strength of magnetometer reading already recorded. The artifact is given a number. If you want to view the video you can view it for as long as you want, either before or after discovering the artifact. Just go to 'view' and set whatever time frame you want.

"Now suppose you decided to dive the artifact." Judy pressed 'dive' on the menu and two cartoon divers appeared. One was a bare breasted mermaid with long flowing hair and the other was an antique hard hat diver in a full suit and weighted boots. "That's me … That's you!" explained Judy.

"Thanks a lot! I'm a bit old fashioned, don't you think?"

"I think you're kind of cute", said Judy, playfully.

A comic book dialog cloud with the arrow pointing toward the mermaid appeared.

"What have you found?" asked the mermaid.

The hard hat diver held up a writing tablet. It said "steel box". The words 'steel box' appeared in the pop-up. Beside it a question formed. "Is this an artifact? Yes. No".

"Say no", said Phil.

Judy clicked on 'no' and a garbage scow, towed in by a tugboat, sailed across the top of the screen. It stopped over the debris on the bottom and a crane with a double jawed excavator, like the kind that pick up kids toys at county fairs, was lowered. It clamped onto the steel box which was lifted and dumped on board the garbage scow. Puffing black smoke the tug boat towed the scow away. The artifact's number was changed to G 1 and a place for a description appeared.

Judy typed in 'twenty year old steel tackle box … empty. "Get the idea?" she asked, proudly.

"This is great!"

"Watch this".

Judy clicked away and a map of dummy island appeared in an enhanced version of the electronic charts. All of the information was identical to a typical chart, including depth in different colors of blue and green. The only real differences were the cartoon palm trees on the island and a pirate ship harbored in a lagoon. Judy clicked and a series of numbers appeared in a pattern, off shore.

"Those are all the artifacts that led us here". Phil looked closer. There were icons beside the numbers indicating wood, jewelry, coinage. Everything pointed toward the 'motherlode'.

"Woops!" exclaimed Judy. Phil noticed that she had moved up the menu to the word 'game'.

"The pirates saw us! Look out. They are firing their cannon." Judy continued to play, explaining that they had only six cannon balls left. "We can't retrieve the treasure until we sink the pirate ship but we can send mermaids to search the bottom for more cannon balls.

Good thing we picked up some shipwreck survivors and earned 'mermaid points' hunh?"

"You're crazy!" exclaimed Phil. "You did all this?"

"It was really pretty easy. I just had to make the video and the magnetometer talk to the chart plotter. The rest was just fun stuff! I did some of it the day you borrowed my car. You like it?"

"I love it, it's great".

"Good. Now that you see how useful I am I guess you want me as your partner. Right?"

Phil backed up a step. "So that's what this is all about?" he said warily.

Judy was completely unphased. "Want half my gold, sailor?"

Phil looked directly into Judy's eyes. Their gaze held for long moments until finally Phil replied, "Yah, I guess I do".

"I knew you would say that. Let's celebrate with a glass of wine."

Phil stared at Judy in silence for another half minute before he moved into the galley and thought through what had just happened. "Do you always get what you want?" he asked, as he handed Judy her wine.

"Most of the time", said Judy, brightly.

Chapter 8

The owner of Normans Cay sat on his patio looking over the ocean and enjoying a late breakfast of fresh fruit. He saw the sloop lower its sails as she prepared to motor around the outer edge of the spit.

"Isn't that the same boat I saw yesterday?" he asked casually of one of men on the patio. A thin black man put down the book he was reading and sat up straighter in his chair. He picked up a pair of high power binoculars from beside him and focused in on the sloop.

"Sure is.... They came in through the main channel day before yesterday. They're moored out at Highbourne Cay."

"They're probably divers. Can you see anyone on board?"

"There is a man and a woman in the cockpit, Mike", answered the young black.

"Better keep an eye on them. They're probably just tourists."

Victor continued to watch the sloop through the binoculars until the squawk of a seagull distracted him. He looked up and then focused on the gull. Suddenly a flash caught his eye and he caught a glimpse of a plane coming in from the direction of Nassau.

"Are you expecting a visitor, Mike" he asked politely. ·

"No. Why?" answered Michael Farris.

"There's a small plane.... No... It's a chopper coming toward us."

Mike Farris stood up and walked to the edge of the patio and leaned against the stone wall that surrounded it. He squinted up at the sky, then reached for a second pair of binoculars. "Turn on the VHF", he said quietly. Another man on the patio moved over to a doorway off the patio. It opened into a small room that had been added to the original house. Inside was a collection of electronic equipment including radar, CB, short wave, VHF and automatic scanning devices. It appeared that everyone in the area was maintaining radio silence. The man turned on a tape recorder and stood at the communication room's door.

The chopper was much closer now. It changed course and headed toward the sailboat. It hovered five hundred feet above the boat for a minute and then suddenly swung back toward Nassau.

"God damn it, that's Ricky!" swore Farris angrily. "What the hell is he doing here and why is he interested in that sailboat? Something is up! Was there any communication George?"

"I didn't hear any but I can double check the tape."

"Victor, take the cigarette boat out and get a better look at those tourists. George, go with him. Keep your guns out of sight but be ready just in case."

The two black men sprinted down the stairs and path to the dock. Moments later the sound of twin four hundred horsepower engines could be heard. The motors warmed up for half a minute, then the sleek craft eased away from the dock. Once clear, the bow lifted and the boat surged forward out of the natural harbor and into the spit. Phil and Judy were about five miles out. It took only five minutes before the cigarette boat was alongside them.

⊰§⊱

"We seem to be attracting some attention," said Phil as the helicopter hovered overhead.

"You're not kidding" answered Judy. There was a distinct nervousness in her speech.

"I think the helicopter is leaving," she added.

Phil looked up and offhandedly, waved goodbye. On shore Michael Farris saw the wave and cursed under his breath. Four minutes later Phil saw the cigarette boat approaching.

"More company's arriving. Take a peak over there. Jude, maybe you should go below for a minute or two."

"Phil, should we have a gun?"

"We have three of them, wrapped in oiled sheepskin, but I suggest you leave them that way."

Judy started down the companionway but stopped with her head and shoulders still out the hatch. The cigarette boat pulled closer and slowed to idle speed thirty feet off the port side. A black man with a wide white smile called out.

"Hello, Zara"

"Hi there", answered Phil. Judy waved from the hatch.

"Mind if we pull along side?" It was a rhetorical question. The cigarette boat was already maneuvering.

Phil hesitated for a moment. He had not wanted his first encounter with Normans Cay to take place in open water with no one else in sight. He was equally reluctant to appear anything but friendly.

"What can I do for you?" Phil asked.

"We're out of matches, mon. Thought we could borrow some." Without waiting for a reply the cigarette pulled right alongside.

"I'll toss some over to you," said Phil.

"Relax, mon" said Victor. "This is a friendly visit." His manner was casual and believable.

"Are there other kinds of visits?"

Victor grinned again. It would have been a likeable grin under different circumstances. "Yah mon, some visits are not friendly. Did you know that chopper that was just overhead?"

"Don't have a clue who he was", said Phil. "Are you fellows from Normans Cay?"

"Yah, mon. That's where we're from."

"Do you know that chopper?"

Victor was a good judge of character. He was aware that the man in the boat was asking as many questions as he was. He decided to answer. "Yah mon. The chopper is from Nassau." He noticed a bit of surprise in Phil's eyes. Phil had assumed the chopper came from Normans Cay.

Judy spoke up for the first time. "We would like to meet the owner of Normans Cay."

"It's a private cay, ma'am. There are not many visitors."

"You did come out to meet us, perhaps to find out why we're here. We would like to have the opportunity to explain that to the owner of the cay." Judy's voice was in total control. Both Victor and Phil were favorably impressed by the manner in which Judy had spelled out her request.

"Let me see what I can do for you, pretty lady." Victor gave an almost imperceptible nod and George handed him the radio headset. No one said anything during the call. Victor spoke too quietly for anyone to hear what he was saying and the other end maintained privacy through the headset when a speaker would have been normal. Victor put down the headset and smiled up at Phil and Judy. "Mr. Farris would like to invite you to dinner. We'll pick you up at six o'clock at Highbourne Cay and bring you back afterwards."

Phil looked at Judy. There was no indecision in her eyes. "Please express our thanks", he said.

George began to put the cigarette boat in gear when Phil raised his hand. George stopped, reversing just two feet.

"Your matches." Phil reached into his pocket and pulled out a book.

Victor grinned broadly and reached out his hand. George gee-hawed the cigarette boat expertly until Victor could reach them as Phil leaned over the rail.

"Thank you, mon. Chill", said Victor. The cigarette boat eased away until the distance allowed for adequate safety and then with a rumble of eight hundred horsepower lifted and took off like a shot.

When Phil and Judy were alone again Judy turned to Phil and said sharply "That was interesting. But who in the hell was in that helicopter?"

Phil was equally curious. "Maybe we'll find out at dinner. Now let's make a couple of passes and head back early. By the way, you were good!"

"So were you. I need to pee." With that Judy ducked below.

Phil sat down in the cockpit and waited for Judy. Things were developing quickly and there already appeared to be an "unknown factor". Phil was not surprised by the cigarette boat, but the chopper was a mystery. When Judy returned topsides the two made an honest attempt to eliminate a piece of the grid that they had marked on their chart indicating highest probability of discovering Rebecca's ship. However, the sun was hot and they were both thinking about their upcoming dinner. They both lacked concentration.

Finally Judy spoke up "Let's go for a swim".

Phil jumped at the opportunity and reached immediately for the scuba gear. Minutes later they jumped in over the side of the boat. The next forty-five minutes literally seemed to "float away". Phil tapped Judy on the shoulder, then pointed at the console dangling from his tank and now in his left hand. He held up an extended palm toward her indicating that he was down to five hundred pounds of pressure and pointed toward the surface.

As they clamored back aboard and pulled in their diving gear they noticed a sport fishing boat anchored out a little over half a mile away. It had a tall fly bridge that made it quite distinctive. Phil kept a loose eye on it over the next half-hour. He was sure someone was watching them with binoculars.

⚜

Outwardly Michael Farris was calm. He sat on the patio and sipped a fruit punch.

"Victor, when you invited our friends to dinner and suggested picking them up at Highbourne Cay, did they ask you any questions?"

"No questions, Mike. They seemed anxious to meet you... the girl especially."

"So what in the Hell is Ricky's chopper doing buzzing them and then we see his boat arriving an hour later. You don't suppose they could have rendezvoused on Ricky's boat."

"No mon, they were back on their boat five minutes after Ricky arrived. They would have to be half shark to swim that fast."

"Any ideas?"

"None boss. It's as strange to me as it is to you."

"O.K. Victor. Be a little early to pick them up. I don't want them searched but check them over visually. Try to get a feel of the lady's handbag but don't make it obvious. If they are armed stay very close when you get back here. If you drift away I'll know you think they're clean."

Ricky remained seated in the swivel chair on the fly bridge, forty feet above sea level. One of his men had a fishing line out and was casting from the rear deck. Fishing was a long way from Ricky's mind. He reached into a vial with a small golden spoon and snorted the white powder. He buzzed for a few seconds and then resumed staring at a notepad he was holding. On it he had printed "Zara" in large letters. He had traced over those letters a dozen times.

He collected his thoughts. He had purchased a letter, which was supposed to be a treasure map, for fifteen thousand dollars. It was a dumb thing to do but he was a bit drunk at the time and the idea seemed like fun. When he went out to look at the site, there was a boat, perched right over the area. And scuba divers! But the really odd part was the location. Right off Normans Cay.

"Damn" he thought. He tried again to focus. "Why did this mysterious letter lead him to a location just miles from Normans Cay? Do they know about the gold? Did Michael Farris set up this part of an elaborate trap? It must be! Assume it is! After all, Farris is your only serious competition within a hundred miles."

His mind drifted. The letter had been found on some little old ladies kitchen table? His head began to ache. He began a conversation with himself.

"Fuck! It's too confusing".

"She couldn't have been a part of the plan. Work backwards. Prince... Gibson... His mother! No way! That's too far back! But what was the plan?

"The lawyer on the letterhead. He's part of the plan! He has to be! He has to be working with Farris. I must have intercepted something. What else is in the lawyer's file?" He resolved to fly to Florida and visit Prince that evening. It was still early afternoon.

His thinking was making him angry. There were too many variables. He hit the starter button. They had been drifting, not anchored. He threw both the powerful engines into gear and jammed the throttle forward. The man fishing nearly fell off the stern. He grabbed a rail with one hand, stumbled and sat down hard on the deck but managed not to drop his fishing rod. The man glanced up at his employer and shook his head.

"That coked up asshole needs a rubber room!" he muttered from the stern deck.

Ricky looked down at Gino, now sitting on the floor, still trying to reel in his stupid fishing line. He laughed but his eyes drifted to the nearest piece of land and his mind returned to the problem at hand. What was the connection to Normans Cay? It didn't make sense. Other than a couple of minor incidents

Farris and Ricky had kept at arms length and neither
had interfered with each other. Until now!"

Judy was dressed in a bright orange pant dress
that was tight at the ankle, pressed flat at the knee
where it was buttoned together with a single button
that held together a long slit up the leg. The neckline
plunged and the waist was tight and tied with a sash.
It was sleeveless. She wished she had a full-length
mirror as she tried to look at herself in a twelve inch
by eight-inch shaving mirror. She gave up and looked
at her face.

"At least I'm saving money on rouge", she thought.
Her cheeks were brown but with enough pink from
the sun to need little touch-up. She decided on a little
more eye make-up and lipstick than she usually wore.
She tried on a few pieces of jewelry and decided on
gold earrings, a gold chain and bracelet.

Phil dressed in a pair of light blue slacks, a dark
blue shirt and a beige sports coat. He knew that Judy
would prefer to be alone while dressing but life on a
boat meant that turning your back often constituted
being alone. He couldn't even glance at her in the
mirror because she had removed it from the door in
the tiny bathroom and had it propped against a pillow
on the bed. He decided to mix a couple of drinks while
they waited but at quarter to six he heard the rumble
of the powerful cigarette boat and hurried topsides to
secure the bumpers. He took the bow line that George
handed him while Victor lashed onto a cleat at the
stern.

"Judy's not quite ready yet. Come aboard and
have a beer while we wait." Phil knew that sooner or
later the boat was going to be seriously looked over

and decided that it might as well be sooner rather than later. He heard Judy close the cabin door to the forward stateroom.

Victor climbed aboard but George waited in the cigarette boat. Phil went below to the refrigerator. Victor sat in the cockpit where he could look into the cabin. He noted immediately the computer and unusual amount of equipment on a pleasure craft. Phil came up the companionway carrying three beers in bottles. He handed one to Victor and passed one over the side to George. Victor's well-trained eye continued to take in everything. The bright work was immaculate, every line was neatly coiled and the working equipment shone. He knew he was in the company of an experienced sailor. He noticed a sheathed fishing knife strapped neatly to the binnacle and knew it would be razor sharp.

"I like your boat, moan" he said sincerely. "You're well equipped."

"Thank you", said Phil, matter of factly. He hesitated for a moment. "Would you like to see below?"

"Yah mon."

Phil led the way deciding that he might as well do everything he could to get what was obviously a survey of the boat over with as quickly as possible.

Victor was surprised and showed it when he saw the nav station with its extra monitors. "What are these for?" he asked politely.

"She's equipped with an underwater camera and metal detector", answered Phil directly.

"You looking for sunken treasure, mon?"

"Something like that", answered Phil.

Victor laughed showing all his teeth. "Good luck, mon." He turned back up the companionway.

A minute later Judy made her appearance. All three men admired her. She looked stunning. Victor climbed aboard the cigarette first and offered his hand to Judy. She switched her small purse to the other hand and accepted his. She had a second bag of soft silk. There was something lumpy in it. When Phil came aboard he was carrying a small carry all. Victor directed Judy to the front seat while George untied the bow. Phil loosened the stern which had been tied with a quick release slipknot. He glanced forward just in time to see George give a quick tug and release the bow. He had not tied on with a slipknot when the cigarette boat arrived. George must have retied the knot when he and Victor were below. He felt a knot begin to form in his own stomach.

Victor started the powerful engines. He was carrying on a conversation with Judy, acting the perfect gentleman. Judy was laughing. "Victor is a charmer," thought Phil, with just a tinge of jealousy. The cigarette boat eased out of harbor through the channel but as soon as it was clear of leaving a wake in the harbor Victor accelerated fast. When the speedometer hit sixty he eased off and held it there. Phil had never experienced such acceleration in a boat. Judy, her heart in her mouth but obviously enjoying the exhilaration smiled and gave up on the fact that she had just spent fifteen minutes on her hair. Phil looked behind at the huge rooster tail the cigarette left behind. The waves were not small and once or twice the cigarette left behind a large spray on either side but the passengers remained dry. In minutes they were entering the private harbor at Normans Cay. The house itself was high on a hill and not clearly visible because of palm trees and vegetation. The dock was concrete and steel. Victor helped Judy out of the boat. Immediately she undid the string bag on her wrist and changed out of her flat shoes into a pair of heels. Victor watched as the string bag flattened before she put her boat shoes back in it. Then she opened her purse and extracted a compact and a hairbrush. The purse contained little else other than lipstick and the like.

Victor had watched Phil carefully as he had reached to untie the cigarette boat as they left the "Zara". There was no bulge under his jacket that he could discern. Only the carry all contents remained unclear and it was zipped shut. Victor led the way up a cut in the rock that had been landscaped with paving stones. George trailed behind.

Both Phil and Judy were awed by the splendor of the private harbor. Tied to the dock was a second, identical cigarette boat. Along a seawall at right angles to the dock was a forty-foot cruiser equipped for deep-sea fishing. The harbor was surrounded with palm trees, banana trees and other fruit trees that Phil did not recognize. A boat house which was an unlikely cross between a Spanish style hacienda and a modern Californian design lay beside the pier with a slip going under what must be a swing bridge in front of it's oversized boat door. The balance of the structure was obviously accommodation, and no small room at that. Curtained windows appeared to be second story bedrooms overlooking the slip in which a boat was or could be housed.

Michael Farris watched from the patio as the cigarette boat pulled into harbor. Then he lost sight of everyone as they climbed the path and stairway to the patio. He remained standing in the center of the large patio as Victor mounted the stairway first. Fifteen feet separated the foursome from Michael as they all ascended the steps. Farris quickly appraised the couple. Phil was a handsome man, well dressed and with a capable air to him. Judy was stunning. Victor glanced at Phil's carry all and Michael noticed the eye movement.

"Welcome to Normans Cay. I'm Michael Farris." His manner was that of a gracious host.

"I'm Phil Harrison and this is Judy Simpson. Thank you for inviting us."

Phil's carry all was on his left shoulder still zipped shut. He extended his right hand to Michael Farris while holding the carry all with his left. Farris moved forward and shook hands. He then turned to Judy and gently squeezed her hand.

"You look ravishing, Judy. Victor told me how lovely you were but his words were inadequate."

Judy blushed at the compliment. There was a slight clink from within the carry all. Phil felt the air stir as Victor and George tensed behind him. Farris slowly released her hand and stood straight.

"We brought some wine to thank you for your invitation", said Phil as he unzipped the carry all. He extracted a bottle of red and a bottle of white, both French, and handed them to Farris.

Michael Farris accepted the two bottles while Victor and George watched the unzipped bag.

"My thanks to you. It is a pleasure to have guests on the island. Now, may I offer you a cocktail?" Farris waved a hand toward a portable bar sitting on the patio.

The bar was an intricate affair on large but graceful wooden wheels that appeared to be refitted bicycle wheels judging by the rims and tires. There was a canopy over the whole contraption. The back end was in fact, a bicycle, but with the same wooden wheel. The handlebars were oversized and must have come off a motorcycle judging by their thickness and the handgrips. A variety of liquor bottles were arrayed on top but on the side and front were pictures of ice cream cones, skillfully hand painted.

"I love your bar", cried Judy and walked over to it fondling the gold fringe around the canopy.

The four men followed Judy and Michael Farris moved behind the bar. Phil removed the carry all from his shoulder and placed it on the patio beside a chair.

"This is a work of art," he said admiringly. He stepped away from the unzipped carry all but it did not escape his eye as Victor positioned himself so that he could peak inside it. Victor caught Farris' eye for a split second and moved away.

"We have anything you like but I have been told I make an excellent dry martini", Farris volunteered.

"That sounds wonderful," said Judy.

Farris looked at Phil. "Perfect" Phil responded.

Michael Farris removed a glass pitcher from a compartment on his side of the ice cream cart.

"I confess to buying a kid's ice cream business in San Diego", he laughed. "He was a university student working his way through engineering. He built this cart himself. Frankly he was a better carpenter than he was an ice cream salesman. When I told him why I wanted the cart he volunteered to convert it, himself. He built a new top better suited to hold bottles and added a little hand pump for water. See!" Farris pulled a lever repeatedly and a small tap squirted water into a bar sink. "He cut the cooler in half and added shelves for glasses and mix leaving enough room for ice." Opening a door he reached in and put two large scoops of ice in the pitcher, which he placed on top of the bar. He liberally sloshed in white vermouth. Then taking a tumbler from a shelf he poured the vermouth out of the pitcher into the glass leaving only the residue of the vermouth on the ice. "Bartender's prerogative", he said downing the vermouth in one gulp. Next he half filled the pitcher with gin and began sticking olives on toothpicks.

"The kid spent four weeks on the refit and finished just before school started. I think he really hated selling ice cream. Judy, give the motorcycle grip a turn."

Judy cranked the gas on the handle and a bicycle bell tingled. "Now try the clutch."

Judy reached over to the left handlebar and pulled the clutch. From speakers hidden somewhere came the sound of a nickelodeon playing. Everyone laughed. As the music played Farris handed Phil and Judy their drinks.

Phil was trying to size up Farris but had yet to form any opinion other than he was beginning to like the man. Victor and George had disappeared after they had determined that the carry all was empty. Farris had a Mediterranean look to him, square jawed with a dark complexion made darker by a deep tan. His hair was black and curly with just a touch of gray. He was not as tall as Phil and a few years older but he was obviously in excellent shape without a hint of fat. His eyes were clear and he was most certainly a ladies man, charming and sophisticated in a natural way that attracted women without upsetting men. Over drinks they talked and joked about everything and anything. Farris kept their glasses filled until the pitcher was empty. An hour after they had arrived he suggested that soon they should go inside for dinner. He then excused himself and went in to see if everything was ready. A few minutes later he slid open a patio door and called out;

"Dinner's on!"

Phil and Judy stood and walked across the patio. A planter overflowing with tropical plants screened the dining room itself from the patio. The table was cherry wood with a heavy black ebony border. Between the cherry and ebony was a narrow strip of brass. The buffet at the far end of the room was a built in cabinet of cherry and ebony with brass highlights and etched glass doors. The ceiling over the table, that was large enough to seat fifteen people, was a huge coffered mirror, the same size as the table, with two chandeliers hanging over the table. Looking up, the crystals in the chandeliers reflected from both the coffered part and the flat part of the mirrored ceiling. The effect was a dizzying array of crystals reflecting only a few dozen, candle shaped bulbs. The walls of the dining room were Californian redwood with cherry cornice and baseboard highlighted by the same thin brass strip. The floor was a highly polished parquet inset with ebony squares. There was an array of silverware laid out on the table, with each of the casserole dishes being kept warm with a small Sterno flame. Farris moved gracefully around the table and held the chair for Judy. Phil was directed to sit opposite Judy with Farris at the head of the table. Farris filled their wineglasses with a sparkling spritzer.

"To good food, good wine and good company."

The wine was very light and following the martinis it could not have been a better choice.

Two pretty, young Bahamian women appeared and began serving from the silver casserole dishes a variety of fish, lobster and fresh vegetables. After serving the meal they disappeared again.

"Bon Appetito!" said Farris imitating an Italian accent.

The meal was excellent and one of the young ladies returned to serve seconds but was unanimously declined. Over dinner Farris told an amazing fish story that had Phil and Judy rapt with attention until he offhandedly finished with a punch line that proved the entire story bogus and sent Judy into such a fit of laughter that tears started to flow from the corners of her eyes.

Following the meal, Farris suggested they have coffee in the living room. Once seated one of the girls brought in a tray with three desert plates containing rum cake, so laden with rum that it oozed out at the bottom. Coffee was served and conversation continued. The desert dishes were removed and Farris sat back in his chair sipping his coffee.

"So, what brings you people to this part of the world?" he asked casually.

Phil looked directly at Judy and nodded almost imperceptibly.

Judy shifted in her chair toward Farris and said, "Sunken treasure."

Michael Farris almost coughed but tried his best to maintain a poker face.

"Interesting."

Phil studied Farris' face for a full minute during which no one said another word. "For a second" he thought, "you could have knocked Farris over with a feather."

"Unfortunately, Michael", said Phil speaking slowly and carefully, "Our trek has brought us to the front door of a very private island."

"Are you telling me that you believe you will find pirates gold on Normans Cay?"

Phil's eyes locked on Farris. The reference to pirate's gold disturbed his thoughts. Farris was, after all a modern day pirate himself. Was this reference meant to mock Phil and Judy or was there a double entendu in the phrase?

"The 'pirate's gold' is not on Normans Cay but very possibly on your doorstep," said Phil.

Farris relaxed a bit and his eyes shifted to Judy.

"On the spit?" he asked.

Judy had watched as Phil's eyes met Farris'. She was not averse to meeting a man's stare head on when she thought someone was trying to put her in her "female" place.

"Not necessarily, Michael." Now her eyes bore into Farris'. "Possibly on the split but definitely somewhere between Highbourne Cay and Nassau."

"But the spit is your first choice?" countered Farris.

Judy said nothing. Her eyes remained locked and unblinking on Farris. She could feel the mental energy. It was powerful ...intimidating ...but somehow not distasteful... not yet, anyway.

Farris blinked, smiled broadly, then as if remembering his role as host he got up hastily and went over to the bar in the corner of the room. He returned with three liqueur glasses and a bottle of Tia Maria. He poured three drinks and passed two of them to Phil and Judy.

"A toast" he said. "To sunken treasure!" He polished off the drink in a quick gulp. His face radiated pleasure.

Phil and Judy both took a sip of their drinks. "We're being laughed at" they both thought. Farris glanced at their almost full glasses and frowned at his empty one. He poured himself another, looked up directly at Phil and Judy and added quietly;

"And to great success!"

Phil watched the change in Farris' face. It had gone from bravado to something quite different.... Sincerity, perhaps. Or was this just another form of poker face.

Farris stared at his glass swishing the thick liquid around in a circle. "If it wasn't for Ricky's presence I'd be tempted to believe these two adventurers," he thought.

Farris got up and going over to an entertainment center with a wide screen TV he plugged in a videocassette.

"Have you ever played the video version of "Clue"?" he asked.

It was nearly midnight when the game concluded. All intimidation had vanished with the beginning of the game and the night had been full of honest laughter.

"I could ask Victor to run you back to your boat but he's probably asleep. Why don't you spend the night in the guestroom? You'll find it very comfortable."

Phil was about to speak when Judy's laugh interrupted him. Judy was not drunk but "tipsy" was as good a description as any.

"Is it bigger than a boat's cabin?" she giggled. She reached over and gave Phil a hug. "I love the boat, but with all I've had to drink this evening...."

Farris chuckled and completed the sentence, "you will accept my invitation and sleep in a bed that doesn't rock."

If Phil had any objections it was pointless to voice them. He shrugged and accepted graciously. Farris escorted the couple down the hallway and stopped outside a closed door.

"You will find everything you need. Goodnight Phil, Judy." He retreated with a wave of his hand.

The guest suite had everything a penthouse apartment should have including a doublewide Jacuzzi. Phil and Judy collapsed on the king-size bed.

"Michael is quite a guy," said Phil.

"He sure is", answered Judy.

For a second Phil felt a touch of jealousy but Judy snuggled up against him and soon all thoughts of Michael Farris disappeared.

❧

Michael Farris was up before seven. He showered and wandered into the kitchen where he made a pot of strong Brazilian coffee. At seven thirty he stabbed the third button on his telephone. Victor answered on the first ring.

"Morning, Victor."

"Good morning, boss."

"O.K., shoot."

"Nothing boss.... Nada"

"Come on Vic... You must have heard something."

"They screwed like crazy and fell asleep."

"Cut the crap, Vic."

"No kidding, boss. They said a few nice words about you like they never figured a dope dealer could be such a nice guy and then they screwed like crazy. That was it!"

"What about this morning?"

"They're not up yet."

"O.K., keep listening."

"Mike, it's on tape... You can listen." Victor hesitated before expressing an opinion. "I don't think they were faking it... About you being a nice guy."

"What are you saying, Victor?"

"I don't think they're in the business, mon....they're too naive. They don't know the room is bugged."

"How do you know?"

"The way they made love, man. If they were acting they're the best actors I've ever heard. Way better than the porn channels!"

This time Michael Farris hesitated. Victor usually kept his opinions to himself...unless he was sure.

"All right, Victor, keep the tape running and get some sleep."

"That's a 10-4, boss." The line went dead.

Farris looked around the kitchen for a cigarette. He had quit smoking a long time ago but right now the urge was strong. He poured another coffee and headed out to the patio. George smoked. Maybe the communication rooms. He opened the door. Bingo! There was half a pack of Marlboros on the desk.

"I know I shouldn't be doing this." He reached for the cigarettes.

Chapter 9

The buzzer rang incessantly. It stopped for a second and started again. It had stopped twice before. Harry Gibson finally roused himself making no attempt to do so quickly.

"Who the fuck is it?" he muttered out loud letting out stale breath that stank of last night's cigarettes and whisky. "Jesus Christ, its eight o'clock in the morning." he said scowling at his alarm clock. He stumbled out of bed and stabbed at the intercom. He missed and stabbed out again.

In the lobby "Talk" appeared in red letters on a miniature screen.

"Wake up, Harry."

"Christ, is that you Prince?"

"It sho is, you lucky mother."

"What the fuck do you want at this time in the morning?"

"I need to do business. Open the door."

Harry was too hung over to argue. He pushed the "Enter" button and struggled back to the bedroom to look for a bathrobe. On the way past the door, he unlocked it and left it open just a crack. He couldn't stand the thought of someone knocking on it. When he came out of the bedroom there were four men standing in his living room and the door was closed. He recognized Prince but the other three men were unfamiliar to him. A sudden bolt of fear brought him to full attention. He looked at Prince about to speak but stopped abruptly as he recognized a strange attitude about him. The tall, wiry black was afraid. Harry had never before seen fear in Prince's eyes. His sense of foreboding doubled.

Two men walked toward Harry. Before Harry had even the chance to move one man laced out with a fist to Harry's solar plexus. Harry simply doubled over and vomited on the carpet where he stood. The two men grabbed him, one of his arms each, to keep him from buckling at the knee. When the dry heaves stopped the two men dragged him with his bare feet pointed backwards through his own vomit and tossed him into the couch as if he was a feed sack. The slimy feeling on the top of his feet made Harry want to throw up again but some inner strength prevented it. From his position on the couch, his mouth opened to utter a protest but a hairy hand with a large ring on the middle finger slapped him hard, backhand, across the jawbone. Pain shot through his body as the ring tore at the flesh on his cheek jamming it against his teeth. He tasted blood and felt it running down his chin and dripping on his chest. He looked up again but this time kept his bleeding mouth shut.

Harry glanced at Prince. He was hovering in the background. He looked at the other three.

"They look Puerto Rican", he thought, "or Italian.... Christ ... not Italian ... who the hell is Prince linked up to ... not the fucking Mafia?"

The third man walked up to him. "This is the boss," thought Harry. He was so frightened he thought he was going to piss his pants. The man reached inside his sports coat and withdrew the largest automatic Harry had ever seen. He moved slowly with the gun bringing it closer and closer to Harry's face. Then the cold steel touched his nose and inched sideways into the left nostril. The touch was gentle at first but the pressure kept building until Harry's neck was plastered to the pillow backed sofa. The pressure continued until Harry could feel the nostril tear and begin to bleed. Harry stared in fear at Ricky's eyes.

"The guy's fucking insane," he thought. He whimpered as he felt his underwear dampen as he lost control of his kidneys.

"Hello, Harry. My name is Ricky. I'm the guy who bought your letter and I'm not happy with it."

Spit and blood drooled from Harry's mouth. He wanted to speak but couldn't.

"Where did that letter come from ... asshole?"

"My mother", squeaked Harry. He jerked back convulsively as the automatic pushed farther into his nose tearing more flesh. He threw himself into the corner of the couch drawing his knees up in front of his body as if his knees would protect him from the huge gun. He felt a prick behind his right ear.

"Holy Jesus" he whimpered as he realized one of the other men held a knife, which was being drawn down to rest directly under his right earlobe. "Listen ... I'll talk ... my mother got the letter out of her lawyer's office in Boston. That's all I know!"

"And she gave it to you.... Right?" said Ricky, straightening up.

"No ... I took it ... she doesn't even know I took it ... I made a copy. The prick of the knife increased just slightly drawing a thin droplet of blood. Harry wanted to scream but held it back. He felt another warm sensation on his testicles as his kidneys gave another squirt.

"Tell us about the lawyer... asshole?" Ricky sounded like a high school bully mimicking a scared shitless runt.

"I don't know anything. He's just a lawyer."

"Have you met him?"

"Yah, once. So what."

The prick of the knife disappeared to be replaced by a dull ache as a fist slammed into the back of his head behind his right ear. Harry's mouth drooped open and his eyes rolled but he didn't quite lose consciousness.

"Papers ... the kitchen drawer ... the letterhead."

Ricky waved the gun at Prince who gratefully headed for the kitchen. Dirty dishes lay on the kitchen counter and the smell of stale garbage made his stomach, already weakened by the carnage he had just witnessed, turn. He yanked open the kitchen drawers until he found one containing bills and letters. He thumbed through the envelopes until he found one that looked like a lawyer's. He tore it open. This was it. He hurried back into the living room. The room stank of urine and Prince's stomach rolled again.

"Here, Ricky" he said handing over the letter and stepping back quickly.

Ricky scanned the letter.

"Your old man die, asshole?"

"Yah, my mother was in the guy's office when she found the letter." Suddenly it dawned on him that his mother was now in danger. "She collects old letters and shit.... She likes the handwriting or something.... She doesn't even realize what the letter means."

"David Windrow.... He's the lawyer, right?" demanded Ricky.

"Yah, that's right." Harry was trying his hardest to please this maniac.

"Who owns the "Zara"?"

"The what?" mumbled Harry.

The hand with the ring on it seized Harry's right wrist and forced it down on the arm of the couch. Another hand grabbed two of Harry's fingers and pushed them backward. Everyone in the room heard the snap as Harry's fingers broke. Harry screamed and then began to cry, rocking forward on the sofa. The toe of a leather shoe slammed into his kidneys. Harry went back into a fetal position sobbing.

"The Zara, asshole. Who owns the Zara?"

"I don't know. What the fuck is the Zara, anyway ... a nightclub?"

The barrel of Ricky's gun slammed into Harry's bare shins. Harry curled up tighter.

Prince couldn't take any more. He had beaten up a few deadbeats that owed him money and once even broken a guy's arm but he had never witnessed this kind of punishment.

"All right Ricky, the motherfucker is telling the truth. He doesn't know shit. Let's go!"

Ricky was also convinced. This time he took out his anger on a telephone sitting on a table beside the stinking couch. He yanked the wire out of its wall socket and heaved the phone directly at Harry's bent over head. He missed his mark hitting Harry on the kneecaps. Then, he slipped his magnum back into a shoulder holster and straightened his clothes. One of the two men went into the bedroom and cut through the telephone wire beside the bed with his razor sharp knife. He paused to check his appearance in the bedroom mirror. All four men ignored Harry blubbering on the sofa and left the apartment carefully locking the door behind them. Prince was the last to leave. He glanced back at Harry, who sat curled up in urine, vomit and blood, whimpering on the couch. His stomach turned again.

❧

"Well let's see", Judy cooed. "The bed was just a tiny bit bigger and a shade softer than the forward cabin. Of course, you could sit up in the morning, without worrying about banging you head. And it was nice to swing your legs over the side of the bed without having to crawl first. The Jacuzzi with the gold handles in the shape of little fish was a tad more luxurious than the rubber hose in the fiberglass shower stall. It was nice be actually standing up to get dressed...oh and the full-length mirror was an improvement on a little brass trimmed shaving mirror...."

"O.K., O.K! " mumbled Phil dejectedly. "Some people just require more creature comforts than others...." He glanced up at Farris "I enjoyed it too."

"The confession of a saint", said Farris and everyone laughed.

"Well, are you hungry for breakfast? We have eggs, sausage, fried plantain, papaya or almost anything else you might desire. Normally I don't have champagne with my orange juice except on Sundays but we could always break tradition."

For a moment Phil and Judy were embarrassed by yet another grandiose display of hospitality. Farris sensed their reaction and as if he had planned for it continued;

"And it's all in the refrigerator awaiting a crew of chefs. This way please."

The kitchen was another sumptuous room with light oak cabinets and a granite counter top. The

Jen Air barbeque and stove sat in an island. On the counter top, rested a bowl with six, unbroken eggs. Fresh oranges, mangoes and papaya had been placed in a fruit bowl with a cutting board and a stainless steel knife beside it. A glass top round table had been set for three with a bottle of champagne on ice in the center of the table. Resting on the ice around the champagne heads of hibiscus flowers floated. A fresh loaf of bread, un-sliced, sat on a breadboard with a knife laid out carefully in front of it beside the toaster. Six extra oranges sat beside a Braun juicer. Three mugs sat in front of a freshly brewed pot of coffee.

"I thought you said everything was in the fridge," said Judy.

"I lied", answered Farris winking at her. "Phil, you and I will attack the eggs and leave the fruit to the young lady, still dressed in evening attire."

Judy caught Farris' eye and thought how sweet it was of him not to put her on sausage and egg detail, which would have surely splattered her pantsuit. Folded on the counter in front of the fruit was an apron.

"Michael is being awfully nice," thought Judy. "I wonder if he's lonely living here.... And yet I'm sure by the decorating that there's a woman's touch in this house..." She put on the apron and started peeling and slicing plantain which she handed to Phil. Farris handed Phil another skillet with a big blob of butter plunked cold in the middle of the pan and moved over to start slicing bread for toast. When the papaya was prepared Judy slipped outside and pinched a few more flowers from the bushes adding to the centerpiece another vase of flowers.

⚜

"That was delicious," said Farris as he put his knife and fork down on his empty plate. "Are you planning to continue your search today?" he asked casually.

Phil answered. "We have broken the outer perimeter of Normans spit into a grid pattern. Our first job is to work the grid with a metal detector and try to find some trace of wreckage."

"Then you are fairly convinced that the wreck lies on the spit?"

Judy spoke up. She sensed that giving away too much information would meet with Phil's disapproval because of the obvious danger. Ultimately though, if all went according to plan, they would have to trust their new partner with smuggling the contraband into the USA. Judy's intuition was working overtime searching for a crack in the Farris armor. She was leaning toward bringing in Michael Farris sooner, rather than later.

"We have reason to believe the ship got through the channel at Highbourne Cay. After that we don't know what happened, other than it went down before reaching Nassau."

"Then the spit is an excellent place to start" responded Farris. "Would you like to set up base camp here at Normans Cay for a couple of weeks while you work the spit?"

Judy's eyes met Phil's. They had planned to make contact with Normans Cay and even enter into a partnership of sorts but they had never anticipated a close tie.

"We really have no idea how long it might take" said Phil. "Perhaps its better that we stay at Highbourne Cay."

"As you wish, of course" said Farris. "May I ask if anyone else is on the same trail as you?"

"No", said Judy. "Our information has been kept very private."

Farris had sensed no hesitation. Judy's reply had been in an almost conversational tone. Judy, at least, believed what she had just said.

"That's good ... well my offer remains open. You would of course save a lot of travel time going back and forth from Highbourne Cay...." He paused. "There is also the matter of security should you find the treasure." Once again he searched for words. "I assure you that both your personal safety and that of your treasure would not be compromised by accepting my invitation." He sat back in silence. He thought, "My reputation has preceded me. Well it's up to them now."

Phil looked at Judy. He could feel her assessing both the benefits and the dangers of the offer. Finally he spoke up.

"Michael, your offer is both generous and tempting. Would you be offended if we went back to the Zara, discussed this, and called you on the VHF at say three o'clock this afternoon."

Farris looked at Phil. He respected the businesslike manner in which Phil had avoided a direct answer. He did not want eye contact to become a contest so he reached for his coffee mug and took a small sip.

"Of course, whatever you wish," he said without looking up. "Please understand that I am not trying to pressure you but it is necessary to get you back to Highbourne Cay before low tide or you will be unable to leave the harbor and you will miss a day's search. And yes" he smiled warmly "I will be pleased to hear your call at three on, say, channel 27." He stood up abruptly.

"I'll do the dishes", volunteered Judy as she started to stack plates. Phil and Michael joined in but when they had brought everything into the kitchen Farris insisted on just putting the dishes into a large commercial tray similar to those used in restaurants. "The two girls come in at three to clean and prepare supper. They would be offended if there was no work. If they had their way they would cook breakfast too, but I won't let them."

Judy returned to the guestroom to get her purse and Phil and Farris wandered ahead to the dock. Farris hopped in the cigarette boat himself and after carefully checking things over started the engines. When Judy arrived they cast off and Farris jockeyed the boat away from the dock expertly.

"Would you like to drive, Phil?" Phil grinned and moved behind the wheel.

"Men and their toys!" quipped Judy in a good-natured fashion. Both men grinned at her and then at each other as if to say, "What is it that women don't understand about toys?" Farris pointed out the heading and Phil swung the powerful boat around with skill, if not with finesse. Almost unconsciously he checked the compass bearing.

"Hold on, Judy. Go ahead Phil."

Phil eased the throttle forward and immediately felt the surge of power. The bow lifted gently and then slowly dropped as the speed increased. In seconds they were skimming along at fifty miles per hour. They hit one bad wave that sprayed the boat but the low windshield deflected most of the spray. The speed was already exhilarating yet Phil realized that he was still a long way away from full throttle.

❦

Within an hour Phil and Judy were entering the grid. The amplifier was turned up on the metal detector, the computer was turned on, tracking their course and there was little to do other than to motor slowly and avoid coral heads.

"What do you think, Phil?"

"In a way it's exactly what we planned" he answered.

"Not that.... Do you trust him, I mean?"

"You can't help but like the guy", responded Phil.

"You just like his boat, silly, ... or boats, I should say", she teased.

"And you just like the king-size bed and the Jacuzzi."

"True ... and he is good looking."

Phil ignored the last comment. "I think I would trust him. He's either O.K., or the smoothest operator I've ever had the pleasure of meeting."

"Or both!" added Judy.

"I can't think of any reason to say no unless we think he's going to wait for us to find the treasure and then rip us off."

"Me neither, and somehow I don't take him for a thief...do you?"

"No, he doesn't seem the type but he's not what I expected of a drug smuggler either", admitted Phil.

"Same here! I guess I was expecting Al Pachino, AKA Scarface."

"Hey, looks like we've got company."

"I thought most people stayed clear of here," said Judy.

"It looks like the boat we saw yesterday. Maybe he just likes this fishing hole."

Ricky's sport Fisherman eased off as it entered the spit. Half a mile away Phil and Judy watched absently as one of the men threw out a hook and two divers with sleds jumped into the water.

"Must be a charter fishing and dive boat," said Judy.

"Must be" answered Phil but for some indefinable reason his stomach growled. Judy heard the rumbling.

"Drink too much last night, dear."

Phil responded with a "Humph".

⹅⹆

On the patio at Normans Cay Farris swore out loud. Both Victor and George looked out the door of the communication hut.

"Any radio contact, George?"

"Nothing boss."

"Victor, now how do you feel about what you said this morning?"

"Like I should have kept my mouth shut."

"Could they be talking on walkie-talkies?" asked Farris.

"Don't think so ... I would hear static."

Fifty miles away, but well out of sight, a storm cloud broke open. One flash of lightening, a little thunder, and a ten minute downpour over the ocean. The isolated cloud drifted away.

"Now I'm getting static," said George as he played with his dials.

"Shit!" said Farris. "Victor, I want that boat searched for a walkie-talkie as soon as possible...without being discovered."

⹅⹆

Phil was now well onto the spit. "Judy, mark this position as too much coral for a tall ship to penetrate. I'm going to swing back closer to Normans Cay."

"I thought we were going to take a shot at deeper water."

"That's where the dive boat is. Let's leave that area for another day."

For two more hours Phil and Judy surveyed another section. During that time the sport fisherman weighed anchor and headed back to Nassau.

"It's nearly three", called Judy.

"O.K. Gorgeous", answered Phil. "What's your verdict?"

"I'm going to let you make the decision this time." She smiled shyly, "I think I might be overly influenced by creature comforts."

Phil grinned realizing, not for the first time, that he was with one hell of a woman. "Come here and give me a kiss then get up on the bow. We're on a bad part of the spit right now."

The Zara motored slowly into the spit for a quarter mile. They finally reached a part with fewer heads.

"O.K., we are going to turn."

Suddenly a cool breeze began to blow. Instinctively Phil looked skyward.

"Judy, look over there!" The storm clouds were approaching fast from the Atlantic side of Normans Cay. They were now visible over top of the small island. Suddenly the radio crackled on the call channel;

"Zara, Zara, Normans Cay."

Phil looked at his watch. It was five minutes to three. "Judy can you get that, please."

Judy gracefully slipped through the forward hatch and reached for the radio.

"This is Zara, switch to twenty seven."

Judy switched from the call channel to a more private channel. "Go ahead Michael."

"Judy, get off the spit immediately. A storm is approaching fast." There was a pause.

Judy pressed the transmit button "We just noticed it ourselves." she released the transmit button and turned to Phil through the main hatch. "What do I say now?"

Phil had already made up his mind. "Any port in a storm."

Judy giggled with obvious delight and pressed the transmit button. "Phil says "any port in a storm"."

She heard Michael click his transmit switch followed by a chuckle. "Smart decision, you two. Get off the spit A.S.A.P. and I'll meet you to escort you into the channel. Batten down the hatches. These isolated storms don't last but they do get nasty. Out."

Judy remembered the forward hatch that she had left open and moved quickly to dog it shut. Then she checked the portholes making sure everything was secure. She grabbed two tee shirts for herself and Phil and raced up the companionway closing the main hatch behind her. Already the sky had darkened and the temperature had dropped significantly. A lightening bolt flashed in the darkening sky. Judy began to count out loud "one thousand and one, one thousand and two, one..." There was a deafening clap of thunder.

"That's getting close" called Phil.

Judy tossed him a tee shirt. "Do you want me on the bow?" The wind picked up as she spoke.

"Think you'll be O.K."

"I'll be fine." Judy started forward. A wave came from nowhere and swamped the bow. The rain was just beginning. Phil reached for a locker in the cockpit.

He yelled at Judy. "Put on a harness" and tossed it forward. Judy put the belt around her waist and clipped the loose end to the lifelines as she inched her way forward. Finally she was on the bow and climbing onto the bowsprit, holding onto the pulpit with both hands. The lifeline was now clipped to the pulpit.

The lack of sunlight, the rain and the waves, which had gone from, slow easy rollers to choppy whitecaps made seeing bottom from Phil's vantage point impossible. Standing on the bow and looking straight down gave Judy a distinct advantage. All Phil could do was to trust Judy's eyes. The fish finder and depth meter couldn't project what was ahead of the boat. Judy waved forward and Phil maintained course. Suddenly Judy began frantically pointing to starboard and Phil responded hard on the wheel. Judy now lifted her left hand and pointed forward at a forty five-degree angle. Again Phil responded in the cockpit. Two minutes later Farris could be seen approaching. He stopped a hundred feet off the bow and swung his boat around. Phil gave the O.K. signal to Judy and began to follow Farris. He increased speed until he realized he was drenching Judy on every wave and backed off. He wished Judy would return to the cockpit but surmised that she did not want to risk the twenty feet across slippery deck. By now the winds had increased to gale force but the entrance to Normans Cay was coming into sight. Inside the harbor the wind and seas calmed but the rain continued as hard as ever. Farris backed off until he was alongside.

"Tie up to the main dock" he called then throttled hard in reverse to drop behind. The cigarette boat was far more maneuverable than the keelboat. Phil could now see Victor and George on the dock waiting to receive the lines. He saw Judy was preparing a bow line already. "Good girl", he thought. As he cut the engine he watched Judy throw a line to George who immediately wrapped it around a bollard. Phil scrambled to get a line to Victor from the stern. It took two tries but finally the Zara was tied off. Meanwhile Farris jockeyed back and forth in the harbor, waiting for George and Victor to assist him. Both George and Victor stood a few feet apart each grabbing one of Judy's arms as she half stepped, half jumped onto the dock. Victor paused only long enough to grin broadly at Judy and offer a "Welcome ashore, mon", before assuming the same position to receive Phil. The boat pitched just as he was about to step and he was grateful for the assistance to maintain balance as he landed. Victor repeated his reception with another grin and identical greeting. Then both George and Victor left at a slow, careful run to bring in Farris, on the breakwater dock.

Phil put an arm around Judy and gave her a warm hug. "You did good, sailor."

"So did you, Captain."

"Come on, let's go thank Michael."

Michael Farris stepped out of the cigarette boat looking as fresh as a man could look despite the torrential rain. He was wearing a broad brimmed hat laced below his chin and an orange flotation jacket. The others looked like drowned rats in soaking wet tee shirts and with wet, messy hair.

"Congratulations on the way you handled yourselves out there", said Farris heartily over the din of the storm. He looked directly at Judy. "If you had been under the bowsprit instead of standing on it I would have taken you for a magnificent maidenhead."

Judy blushed at the compliment and grinned. "It was wet enough over the bowsprit. I'm really glad I wasn't under it!" Her hand waved in front of her face.

"I think we are wet enough. Let's get back to the house", Farris commanded.

"I'll grab some dry clothes and meet you up there", shouted Phil as he headed back to the Zara.

Farris had Phil's boat in his own harbor. Victor would have no trouble searching for a walkie-talkie but as much as logic dictated that Ricky's presence was connected to Phil and Judy, his heart told him the exact opposite. He was tempted to cancel Victor's orders but resolved not to.

Ricky's sport fisherman was half way back to Nassau when he saw the storm. He was well ahead of it and would be tied up before it hit. Suddenly the radio crackled on channel 16; "Zara, Zara, ...Normans Cay". Ricky stabbed the volume control to full and listened. He switched to twenty-seven on Judy's command and continued to listen.

"That settles it!" he thought. "The Zara is definitely out of Normans Cay. But maybe that little prick Gibson didn't know that! He's just a dupe. He had to be telling the truth. He was so scared he even pissed himself!" At the thought of Gibson cowling and pissing Ricky actually laughed aloud. Gino looked up at the fly bridge but said nothing. Ricky continued thinking aloud. "So what... the letter comes from the fucking lawyer in Boston. He must be working for Normans Cay. That's it! But the letter.... Is it real or is it some sort of trap?"

"Gino" Ricky yelled "get your ass up here."

One of the other guards moved to the controls in the main cabin and Gino climbed the ladder to the fly bridge.

"What's up, boss?"

"Just sit down and shut up."

Gino did as he was told. He was good at that.

"That letter... it started out on some lawyer's desk. The little prick's mother steals it, cause she likes old shit, and shows it to her little boy. The little prick copies it and sells it to Prince. Prince sells it to me. Right?"

"Right, boss."

"It's too fucking complicated to be a set-up. You know how we know for sure?"

"Sure, boss. If the old broad really has a copy in her house?" For a second Gino thought Ricky was going to hit him but nothing happened.

"Yah, that's right. If Momma has the letter, then we know the little prick was telling the truth." Ricky pretended that he had thought it through and was just testing Gino. He did that a lot! "Somehow I figure the letter is real, and the lawyer works for Farris."

"I'll take a couple of boys and check out the old broad", said Gino.

"Yah, do that!"

"What about the little prick. Prince says he's into coke pretty good".

"You think he might blat about something?" spat Ricky.

"He'd say anything to anyone who put pressure on."

"Yah I was thinking that," said Ricky. "I'll decide after we check out the old broad."

"Sure." Gino stood up. "Anything else, boss."

"Yah, fuck off!"

Gino climbed down the ladder. He didn't mind the way Ricky treated him but he hated that fly bridge, forty feet in the air. Overall, though, he was content. He made good money and he liked the work. Plenty of fringe benefits too!

Chapter 10

Farris said goodnight to Phil and Judy and wandered to the edge of the patio, which was still wet from the storm. He leaned against the stone wall and looked out over the sea. Moonlight from a quarter moon glistened on the water where it lapped against the shoreline. Sometimes, never far from shore, a moon beam caught the top of a wave illuminating it, only for a second. A few droplets of water in a vast expanse that stretched as far as the eye could see. Out where the horizon should have been was total blackness. There lacked even a hint of where the water ended and the sky began. If you could ignore that void, and look higher, the stars appeared arranged in their familiar patterns. There was Orion, the warrior, with his sword hanging neatly from his waist. He had not yet climbed high in his nightly trek across the heavens. Farris admired him for a moment, deciding he should have reached his present position by about ten thirty. Reaching over with his right hand he pressed the button on his watch that illuminated the digital display. Ten twenty-five.

He walked down the steps toward the dock. At the bottom of the stairs he followed a pathway to the living quarters of the boathouse where Victor and

George resided. He knocked on the door and Victor opened it. Farris wandered in and went directly to the fridge where he found a couple of beers. He handed one to Victor.

"Let's have it?" he asked, tiredness seeping into his voice.

"They're clean, Michael."

"Did you find anything?"

"Yah man, I found a walkie-talkie all right. A pair of them in fact, only they're still hermetically sealed in the box they were bought in. He probably figured he might need them sometime but didn't want the sea air to get to them."

"O.K., what else?"

"He's equipped all right, mon." Victor ticked off the items on his fingers as he talked. "Radar, sonar, satellite navigation, chart plotter, metal detection equipment that even has a video camera attachment. His computer is top of the line with everything from a printer to a mouse ball. He's got hardware too.... a twelve gauge, a thirty-eight and a Remington thirty OT six, all neatly wrapped up in oiled sheepskin. He's got diving gear, fishing gear and everything is stowed neat as a pin. His diesel glistens and everything is shipshape."

"Good" said Farris finishing off his beer.

"Mike, that static we picked up might have been the storm."

Farris' eyes flashed. "Hadn't thought of that! Good thinking. Have you picked up anything from their room?"

"Nothing...they went straight to sleep. They did say something about a letter once."

"A letter, eh. Well Victor, I might be a fool but they don't seem like the kind of people who would be connected to Ricky. Is there any way they could have transmitted to him?"

"No man, I don't think so. I even checked their VHF to see if a special channel might have been added but no one has touched that radio since it came out of the box."

"O.K. Victor. Shut off the surveillance. Linda will be back tomorrow and my guess is she'll go for Phil and Judy in a big way. If they pass that test they're good enough for me. Better remove the bug too. If Linda finds out we've been listening to them screw, she won't talk to me for a week."

"Should I keep the tapes?"

"No, erase them."

"Hey boss, they don't know anything about Linda do they."

"No, why?"

"They think you may be lonely, boss."

"Nice", Farris drawled sarcastically as he left the boathouse.

The next morning Phil and Judy were out on the spit early. With no other boats in the area they decided to search the deeper water on the immediate outside edge of the coral heads that formed the spit. They scanned the bottom where the sport fisherman had been anchored and continued along the outer edge of the reef.

"That boat with the divers bugs me," said Phil.

Judy was pouring some of Michael's excellent Brazilian coffee from a thermos. She looked up as Phil spoke and spilled a few drops on her leg. When she jumped she spilled more coffee on the deck.

"You O.K.?" asked Phil.

"It's hot but not scalding." Judy paused to collect her thoughts. "Phil, did you get the feeling that we were being watched by that dive boat."

"Sure did", answered Phil without hesitation.

"Follow my train of thought on this. This cay is supposed to be private. Victor and George came out to visit us in an awful hurry.... So how come the dive boat anchors here and no one bothers him?"

Phil rested against the wheel. "Maybe they know him. We could ask Mike."

They were half a mile from where Ricky's boat had anchored when the metal detector started to whine. Immediately Phil cut the engine and dropped the anchor.

"Let's check the video" he suggested.

"Let's go for a swim", countered Judy. "I'm hot already."

Phil grinned when he saw the sparkle in Judy's eyes. "Gold fever?" he asked. Judy was about to respond when the radio broadcast;

"Zara, Zara .... Normans Cay."

Phil reached for the radio. "Zara, going to twenty seven." He switched channels.

"Good morning, you got out early today."

"Morning Mike, thought we would get a head start on that dive boat."

"Good idea. When do you plan to come in?"

"Probably around eleven." said Phil.

"See you then. Good luck! Out."

"Hey", said Judy. Isn't that Michael on the patio? I think he's waving." Judy stood up and waved back. Phil was already beginning to prepare the dive gear.

As they jumped off the dive platform a Cessna 172 approached Normans Cay from the east and landed on the private airstrip.

Phil followed Judy towards the bottom. Her brown hair seemed longer when she swam. The muscles in her legs rippled gently as she moved her fins back and forth. They had been together just two weeks but Phil could not help but realize how serious he had become about her. There was no pretence ... no innuendo. She looked back over her shoulder and saw Phil.

As if she too had been thinking gentle thoughts, she reached back. For the next few hundred feet they swam together holding hands in their private underwater world. Silence abounded.... Hadn't Jacques Cousteau called it the silent world? Only the murmur of bubbles broke the stillness but even that sound seemed in fitting with silence. A school of hundreds of fish swam by oblivious to the divers. A colorful, translucent needlefish passed. Phil reached out to try and squeeze its tail. Although he had come within inches, hundreds of times he had never managed to touch a fish's tail. Inevitably they would dart ahead, usually just a few feet, each time he tried.

Phil and Judy swam to the anchor and Phil checked his compass pointing out the course the Zara had sailed as the metal detector sounded. They swam in that direction for a few minutes over a coral head that came to within fifteen feet of the surface. Phil calculated he was very close to where the detector had sounded. Beyond the first lay another head, bigger than the previous one. He tugged gently on Judy's hand and pointed. They separated so that each one could pass on either side of the coral. Fan coral waved at them, beckoning them forward. Brain coral, so called because each piece, regardless of size, could easily be taken for a human brain, rested serenely, appearing to emit a great wisdom.

A green line in the sand caught Judy's eye. Something seemed out of place. A shape.... Nothing more ... a brown and green line draped over a piece of coral. Maybe it was only a fissure in the rock. She reached down toward her calf muscle and unstrapped the buckle on her diver's knife. Its blade was an inch wide and quite dull but its point was sharp. She prodded at the line on the rock hardly knowing why she did so. Whatever it was, was so encrusted in barnacles that its shape was still indiscernible. A large chunk of growth broke off revealing something brown and dirty.... It was rust. Whatever the line was, it was made of iron. Now she followed the brown green line. It draped off the rock and disappeared into the sand, then reappeared draping over another rock. Excitement gripped her as she followed the line over another rock and down into the sand again. Judy followed the line and once again it ascended over another rock. She reached back and tapped on her tank with her knife. Phil who was thirty feet away turned and saw her. He swam leisurely toward her. All he had seen was an interesting cut in a rock with a moray eel's head hidden in the crevice, protecting his home and catching the odd snack if something came close enough. As Phil approached Judy pointed at the line prodding it with her knife, then pointing in the direction it was headed. Together they followed it through a six-foot miniature ravine after which it dropped five feet towards the bottom. Beyond the ravine was a thirty-foot wide stretch of sandy bottom. Something protruded from the sand. Phil and Judy swam toward it. It looked like a barnacle-encrusted piece of pipe. Phil pulled a divers knife from his own leg sheath and began to chip at the pipe. As the barnacles fell off the outline of a round ball began to form on the top of the pipe. Phil let most of the air out of his buoyancy vest and sank until he rested on his knees on the bottom. He began to dig with his hands in the sand stirring up clouds of dirt in the water so that Judy could not see what he was doing. Finally he stopped digging and seemed to be feeling his way around a few feet from the pipe. He seemed satisfied and moved away letting the cloud of dirt settle. Judy moved in closer and Phil took her hands helping her feel her way. Phil had found the chain again where it ended in an iron ring. The anchor would be buried in the sand with only the iron bar, which sat at right angles to the flukes of the anchor, exposed. The makeup of the iron ball at the end indicated that this was definitely the anchor of an old ship. They moved together about six feet from the iron bar in the opposite direction and began to dig again but succeeded in only stirring up more clouds.

Judy checked her air gauge and realized that most of her air was gone. No doubt that with the excitement of finding the anchor they had both been breathing harder and faster than normal. She tapped Phil on the shoulder and showed him her gauge. He immediately checked his own and realized he was even lower. Checking his compass he pointed back towards the Zara. Then he carefully set his watch back to zero to determine the time it would take to get back to the boat. Then, looking at Judy through his mask he touched his regulator at the mouthpiece and reached over and touched hers in the same location. At first she thought he was low enough on air to require buddy breathing but both sets of equipment had an extra regulator for that purpose. Suddenly she realized that he was passing over a kiss and grinned so much at the thought that her mask began to fill with water. Phil pressed one more button on his watch and the two started swimming on the bearing Phil indicated. Four minutes and twenty seconds later they saw their own anchor rode stretching upwards from the bottom. With almost no air remaining in their tanks they followed the anchor rode upward to the surface.

When they reached the surface they tried to hug each other but their equipment got them tangled up and laughing, they settled for a high five while holding onto the swim platform.

Michael Farris was sitting with a truly beautiful brunette wearing an indeterminable amount of fine jewelry tastefully highlighting casual slacks and a blouse that must have come from Rodeo Drive. Phil's only reaction was a silent, well-masked "wow". Judy caught her breath and smiled as her eye evaluated the exceptionally good taste of the expensive outfit. As Phil and Judy ascended the steps to the patio Farris politely stood up.

"Allow me to present my wife, Linda." There was a broad smile on his face. "Linda, this is Phil and Judy."

Up to this point both Phil and Judy had assumed that Farris was a bachelor. For a moment there was an awkward silence. Linda broke it with a quick laugh.

"I bet he never mentioned me!"

Farris grinned and looked at Phil who spoke next. "I'm afraid he didn't. I'm glad to meet you."

"He does things like that." There was no accusation in her voice, merely an acceptance of an idiosyncrasy.

"I bet he hasn't told you a single personal thing about himself either."

Phil and Judy smiled awkwardly again.

"My loving husband is the most secretive person I have ever met." She reached up and tugged his sleeve to sit down. "But I love him anyway. It's just a game he plays."

Farris sat down and waved Phil and Judy to do the same. One of the girls who served dinner arrived carrying rum punches. If Farris had been the perfect host then Linda surpassed him. She knew most of what had happened since Phil and Judy's arrival and it became equally obvious that she was an active participant in prolonging the visit. They chatted for a while about Phil's boat, about the dinner the first night and made small talk about the luxurious home.

"Is Ricky still around?" asked Linda, with only a hint of anxiety.

"Who's Ricky?" asked Judy.

Suddenly the patio became as silent as the underwater world Phil and Judy had just left. All eyes turned to Linda.

"Oh, oh" she said, her eyes taking in Judy, then Phil and finally Michael where her gaze rested and remained as fixed as stone. Farris did not look back at her.

"Perhaps the time has come for a little pow-wow", he answered, before making eye contact with his wife. There were another few seconds of intense silence, which Phil interrupted, cutting through any preamble.

"Who is Ricky?" he repeated dryly.

The game of wits continued for another few seconds between Michael and Linda. Finally, almost simultaneously, they both smiled at each other. Farris knew with certainty that Linda had already assessed their visitors. Victor trusted them too. Farris had, as patriarch, and as was fitting in that role, reserved judgment, although his gut instinct was totally positive about Phil and Judy. Now the decision was made. It was a relief.

"Ricky is...." he paused dramatically, "the enemy."

"Michael...." cautioned Linda. "Don't beat around the bush". Farris reached over and took her hand.

"Have you noticed the sport fisherman out on the reef?" he asked.

Now it was Phil and Judy's turn to stare into each other's eyes.

Judy spoke. "We were going to ask you about that."

Farris sat in his chair completely pokerfaced. "The owner of that boat and the man seen most frequently on the fly bridge is Ricky. He is Nassau's biggest drug lord and persona non grata in these waters".

"Then what is he doing here. Phil and I both have the feeling we are being watched when he is out there", commented Judy.

"That, my friends, is the question we all would like answered! Perhaps, should you wish of course, it would be a good time to discuss exactly what trail led you to Normans Cay?"

Linda spoke up abruptly. "Michael, Phil and Judy might not want to divulge that."

Judy looked at Linda and made up her mind. She glanced at Phil who nodded.

Judy began her story by telling of the dinner she had had with her lawyer, David Windrow, and how she had been, gradually at first, then later consumed by, the lure of sunken treasure, as Windrow had told her about Phil's dream. She said she had evidence of a shipwreck and had arranged to meet Phil. Avoiding mentioning the letter directly, she described a ship coming in, off the Atlantic, into Exuma Sound between Normans Cay and Highbourne Cay, then floundering and being driven onto Normans spit.

"That's a story that is easily credible but what makes you think it really happened?" questioned Farris.

Judy turned toward Phil and then slowly turned back to Michael and Linda; "I have a letter from the sole survivor of a wreck, whom I believe spent her last few months before she died right here on Normans Cay."

The silence was thick with anticipation. Judy leaned slightly forward and after a long pause, began to tell her story in greater detail. She described Rebecca Outerbridge being washed ashore, the old Negro finding her and nurturing her back to health. How she began to fail as her heart petered out. She recounted the letter Rebecca had written and finding it in an old trunk at her parent's home and how she had read it, sometime later.

Then she explained the excitement that had come to her as she listened to David Windrow's story about Phil.

When she had finished the foursome sat in silence until Linda said, almost wistfully, "I feel like one of the listeners in "The Ancient Mariner", as the old man spooled his yarn.

"So do I", added Farris. "I can't believe you two met just recently". He was genuinely shocked that they had not been intimate for years. He wasn't usually wrong about that sort of observation.

"Since we are putting the cards on the table" said Phil "I might as well add that I previously knew the reputation of Normans Cay." No one said anything that might help or hinder what was to be said next. Phil searched for words. "Should we be successful in tracking down the wreck, selling the gold in the States could pose a small problem. Ownership claims and taxes. With the possibility of finding the treasure on your doorstep, it occurred to us that some sort of partnership would be appropriate."

Farris grinned and winked at Linda. She returned his wink with a scowl.

"If Ricky is aware of the letter, then you would never get an ounce of gold out of Bahamian waters without help", said Farris. It was a plain and simple statement.

"How could Ricky be aware of the letter?" demanded Judy. "That's impossible!"

"Then how do you explain his boat? Something has brought him here," asked Linda modulating her voice in an attempt to keep the discussion in line.

"Judy has never shown the contents of the letter to anyone other than Windrow and myself, as far as I know", said Phil, defending Judy's position.

"No one", confirmed Judy.

"Are you sure the only people who are aware of the letter are the four of us, and David Windrow?" asked Farris politely.

"I'm totally positive of that!" said Judy adamantly.

"Then, if our line of thinking is correct, the leak is David Windrow", Farris surmised.

"David?" Judy could hardly believe she had acknowledged this train of thought. "Hold on".

Phil thought suddenly of the dinners in the sports bar he had had with David in the last three months. David was certainly capable of deceit. That was clear. Then he thought about the dinners David had had with Judy. Phil's mind raced. He was searching for motives for David's treachery. Certainly money... or perhaps his motives were more complex. Judy had rejected him. Jealousy?

Linda poured another round of drinks from the pitcher.

"I can't believe David sold us out. I won't," Judy said dejectedly. "Phil, I never told you this but David is already a partner.... Part of my share.... We agreed on ten percent of my share. Call it a finder's fee for putting us together and for the research he did on you. I didn't mention it because it didn't affect you directly."

"Maybe he decided ten percent of half wasn't enough". Phil's voice was caustic.

Judy's head lowered and she stared at the patio stones.

"Michael", said Linda pointing out to sea.

"Shit!" uttered Farris reaching for the binoculars.

"Is that Ricky's boat?" asked Judy.

"Looks like it is" answered Farris. A few minutes passed. "It looks like he is close to the area you were in this morning. Two divers are going in. Ricky is sitting on the fly bridge probably coked up to the gills."

"Michael", said Phil, "We might have found the first piece of the wreck today."

Farris lowered the binoculars and stared at Phil. "No kidding!"

"We definitely found the anchor to an old ship."

"Whew", whistled Farris.

"I can't believe it. I go to Florida for just a few days and look at the excitement I've been missing. Congratulations!" Linda was determined to maintain a low key. "Ricky or no Ricky, this calls for a celebration. Judy, come on inside with me while I make some sandwiches."

The four made an attempt at celebrating while Judy told about their find, but their concentration was focused on the sport fisherman. It seemed to be almost exactly where Phil and Judy had found the anchor. The divers with their underwater sleds worked the area for two hours before boarding the boat. Everyone waited to see when Ricky would leave. As Ricky's boat pulled away Farris spoke the question they had all been asking.

"Do you think they found it?"

"Want to take a look?" questioned Phil.

"Sure, let's go! Is this OK with you, Judy?"

"Fine by me."

Judy and Linda seemed content to stay home so Michael and Phil headed down to the docks.

Phil and Michael loaded the diving gear into the cigarette boat and Phil, using a hand held GPS, gave Michael a compass bearing to the site.

When they reached the co-ordinates they dropped anchor.

Farris tried to concentrate on his gear but he was feeling an excitement he hadn't experienced in years. Phil led the way using his underwater compass and followed the direction he and Judy had followed earlier. He pointed out the chain and continued onto the anchor. There was no indication that any thing had been disturbed which probably meant that the divers had not found it. There was no way to be sure. Farris was acting calmly but Phil could see the pleasure in his eyes.

After examining the anchor Phil reached into a string bag dangling from his belt and extracted a tape measure on a plastic spool. Working methodically he made a few measurements around the anchor including the size of the ball on the end of the crossbar. Then, tying off the tape to the ball he swam back along the length of the chain writing down on an underwater writing tablet the distance from the ball to exposed chain. About seventy-five feet were visible periodically as they draped over rocks and disappeared back into the sand. Then the chain disappeared and could not be found again. Next Phil checked the compass bearing on the chain going back to the anchor and jotted it down. After untying the tape Phil and Michael swam the length of the chain again and then continued in the same direction for about two hundred yards before deciding to surface. They saw nothing that indicated any sign of a shipwreck but Phil was aware of how long it could take.... Years, in fact.... To locate something underwater. Recognizing a thing, when it was encrusted with barnacles was an art form in itself. The sea was adept at playing hide and seek.

Back on the boat Farris heaped praises on Phil and Judy. "I don't know how Judy recognized the chain. I would have swum right over it."

"I think she noticed a straight line and was smart enough to investigate further," said Phil.

"She's quite a girl."

"I'll drink to that. Is their beer in the cooler you brought?"

That night the four had dinner together with Farris pouring more champagne than any one needed and toasting everything from the anchor to Judy's sharp eyes. After diner Judy suggested that they all go down to the Zara and as Phil poured a round of drinks from his bar Judy switched on the computer. Taking the underwater slates that Phil had dropped off she entered the information on the computer. She showed everyone how they would map out each find they would make, until the "motherlode", the sea chest containing the gold, was located. When they returned to the house Farris took everyone into his office where they poured over charts, that Michael had made, of the spit, indicating coral formations in much more detail than could be found on commercially available charts.

Returning with the charts which they spread out in the living room. Phil theorized that the Captain, after the mast had gone down, dropped the hook as the last line of defense against the reef. The lay of the chain, therefore indicated the direction of drift of the ship or in other words, the wind, on the night the ship went down.

"We know the direction of the current. The chain gives us the direction of the wind. The question is "Did the ship break up while it was still attached to the anchor? Or, did the anchor break free? Or, did the Captain order the chain cut and attempt to sail out when he realized the anchor was itself, pulling the ship apart?" surmised Phil. "We know Rebecca made it to shore so that puts the wreckage somewhere along this line." Phil took a straight edge and drew a triangle between either end of Normans Cay and the projection of the anchor chain."

"That's a big expanse of coral and ocean", commented Farris.

"Where's the white rock on the chart", asked Judy.

"You mean the white bluff on Normans Cay?" asked Linda.

"Yes, the one you see from the spit."

"Its right here", said Farris pointing at the chart. "Why?"

"The Negro's house, where Rebecca Outerbridge died, was near the white rock."

"Then I think I know where the house was," said Linda. "There are only a few stones left but it could have been a house or a shack. It's near the white rock. There is a beach nearby. That must be the beach Rebecca drifted onto. There aren't many places where she might have washed up that she wouldn't have been killed by the waves crashing against the rocks."

"Let's explore the beach in the morning", suggested Judy. "Who knows? Then I would like to input Michael's chart into the computer. You know, marry his chart with our chart of findings. If that's OK."

"No problem", said Farris in Bahamian dialect.

They all went to bed late but not before deciding that breakfast should be delayed until ten the next morning, after which they would go exploring.

Chapter 11

Phil was the first to stir around nine. He stumbled into the shower and let the fine spray shake loose the cobwebs the previous nights drinking had left behind. The sound of the shower roused Judy and they passed in the bedroom exchanging groans.

The magnificent view from the patio made no impression as Phil doggedly passed through the door to the kitchen and proceeded clumsily toward the coffee maker. The noise of the coffee grinder made his teeth clench and his eyes squint shut but he bore the pain until the pitch of the sound indicated that the coffee was ground. He took a filter from beside the coffee maker and dumped in a quantity of coffee without measuring. He added water and leaned against the counter listening to the gurgle and drip. Mugs hung from a mug tree and he had one waiting on the counter as the last few drops of coffee splashed into the pot. He poured the coffee spilling only a small quantity on the counter. After a small sip that burnt his lips he looked around for a dishrag to clean up.

"You made the coffee, I'll clean up the mess", said Farris cheerily.

Phil looked around and saw Farris standing in the door. Without saying a word he sat down at the table and stared into his muddy brew.

Farris hummed a tune as he poured himself a coffee and wiped down the counter. "Sleep well? Mmm, good strong coffee," he teased politely.

When the women wandered in Phil put on a brave face but no one was quite as chipper as usual. Except for Farris. As punishment, all three voted Farris chief cook while they held their heads in their hands.

By the end of breakfast everyone was feeling much better and agreed to meet on the patio in half an hour dressed for a walk.

⛄

The path beside the house was wide enough for a small vehicle and old tire tracks had carved shallow ruts in the sand and stone lane. Walking was easy enough and there were no steep hills. It was only half a mile to the white rock and Linda steered them to the left just before that. There was a square shape rising two feet above ground. The ruins of an old building with a doorway facing the way they had come.

"This is it", called Linda. "I always wondered what kind of a building this was. I guess now I know."

The others wandered around like tourists at the Parthenon, wondering what secrets the rocks might reveal. Phil walked across the path and stared at the water and a small beach below. Small waves broke over coral beyond the beach. Further out, lay the water where Judy had discovered the anchor.

"Rebecca must have been a tough old broad to have survived being washed from Judy's anchor to this little beach", mused Farris.

"She's the only one who made it", shot back Linda. "Be a little more respectful of the dead."

Farris held his comments after that.

Judy reached into a small pack and handed fresh fruit to everyone. They sat on the stone foundation and stared out to sea. Phil stood and slowly turned around.

"Is that where your runway is?" he asked pointing to what appeared to be flat land beyond the white outcrop of rock.

"That's it", answered Linda. "Usually I can land over there and taxi right over to the hanger by the house. I love this little cay but I need to know I can be in a real city when the spirit moves me."

"Best of both worlds", added Judy.

"Shall we head back and do an afternoon dive?" asked Farris.

"Fine by me", answered Phil. The two men started walking back but the girls lingered behind.

"Michael was right," said Judy. Linda looked her way as if to say "What?"

"Rebecca must have been a tough old broad. She stayed on in England while her husband tried to carve out a farm in the colonies. Finally she sails across the ocean on a sailboat with no bathrooms. She survived a shipwreck, and finally she died in the bed of an old Negro, just a few miles from her destination."

"When you put it like that you're right, she must have been tough. But I bet the two of us could run her ragged on a shopping spree in Miami." The two women laughed and started back to the house.

Chapter 12

The next two weeks were grueling and repetitious. Each morning Phil and Judy sailed to the anchor site and dived the area in an ever-widening grid pattern. During the afternoon, Judy sat at a computer she had set up in the house and calculated and recorded where each dive had occurred. Using Michael's chart of the bottom she had created a large scale, homemade map. She then printed out individual pages of computer data and carefully glued them together to create a four foot by six foot chart.

Phil and Michael usually spent their afternoons either underwater or scanning the area with a magnetometer, searching for a piece of iron that would lead them toward the motherlode. Each blip from the magnetometer, many of which were too small to warrant immediate investigation, was stored in the database and recorded on Judy's map.

By the end of the second week tempers were beginning to fray. Phil took charge and called a meeting after supper.

"We have spread out a good distance from the anchor and found nothing". He unrolled Judy's map over the dining room table. "This is the anchor. The red lines indicate areas where we dived. The green lines indicate the area covered off by the magnetometer. As you can see we are beginning to get further out in the sound.

In the last two weeks we have been running on adrenaline after finding the anchor. We haven't taken a day off. Well guess what folks. That's treasure hunting. Mel Fisher searched for fifteen years before he found the 'Atocha's' motherlode. So," he paused dramatically, then grinned, "I propose working through to Friday but quit at noon and not going back to work until Monday."

"Fantastic idea", piped up Farris. "I haven't had a weekend off since I retired".

The other three stared at him for a minute, dumbfounded. Finally Linda started to laugh and in seconds all four were laughing hysterically. The tension dissipated like a morning mist.

"So what about Ricky?" asked Linda.

Phil looked toward Farris, letting him answer. "Ricky, or should I say Ricky's boat, has hovered around daily. Ricky lost interest after the first couple of days but his henchmen continue to do the job. My guess is that eventually his boat will disappear, too. He has never come in too close. At first he stayed for the entire day. Now it hangs around for an hour or two, at most."

"I would still like to know how he managed to be here in the first place", said Judy with just a touch of pout in her voice.

There was silence as no one had an answer worth repeating.

"One last item" said Phil. "On Saturday, dinner is in Nassau, on me." There was a chorus of acceptance from Michael and Linda. Phil glanced toward Judy.

She was grinning but mouthed a large 'us'. Michael and Linda caught on before Phil did. "On us", Phil mumbled eventually.

"Accepted", agreed Farris, pointedly directing his thank you toward Judy, then Phil.

⊰§⊱

The next morning Judy begged off the morning dive saying she wanted to work on a drift pattern on the computer. Michael quickly volunteered to dive with Phil.

Once out on the Zara Michael spoke up. "I have my own drift pattern to check out".

"OK. Explain", answered Phil.

"Let's set up over the anchor. Shut down the engine and drift for as long as it takes to brew another coffee. When we finish the coffee we dive."

Phil grinned. "Einstein suggests that the Captain of his sinking ship cut the anchor line, drank a cup of Java, and sank."

"Of course not. When he realized the anchor was pulling his ship apart, more than it was helping, he realized he was doomed, drank a cup of rum and then sank. The force of the storm was far greater than the wind today so we'll substitute a slowly consumed coffee for a hastily consumed rum. Then, we should be right on target."

"Impeccable logic. It's a plan we'll adopt. We'll record this dive like all the others. All it really means is a hole in the grid."

The coffee was almost finished and the Zara had drifted nearly a mile further than it had previously explored when there was a faint beep from the magnetometer. Phil immediately released the windlass and the anchor plunged to the bottom sixty feet below. At the same time he stabbed a hand held GPS.

"Well Einstein, if this dive produces so much as a plug nickel I'll..."

Farris cut him off. "Pedal my bicycle bar around the patio, selling martinis".

"Right. Now finish your coffee and gear up. We'll probably find a trash can growing brain coral. Which will exhibit more intelligence than a coffee pot drift theory."

Ten minutes later the two men were slipping beneath the surface beneath the spot Phil had recorded on the GPS.

Once below the surface, the cares of the land world evaporated. Time slowed. The gentle movement of fish and plant life relaxed and refreshed the tired gray cells of the mind. An unqualified need to observe replaced the need to perform, that was so prevalent above.

A thought began to form slowly in Phil's mind. Something about this place was unnatural. He stopped swimming and let his body drift. The bottom was sand. Greens and browns were the predominant colors. The seaweed hung in quivering folds over the rocks.

The rocks ended in jagged spires, rounded out by crustaceans, clinging on for life. Colorful fish swam lazily along the edges. That was it! The edges. Beneath the layers of sea life that had lived and died, and still remained encrusted on the formation, the edges were more uniform than they should be.

Curious, but far from convinced, Phil drifted over and after removing his dive knife from the sheath on his calf, poked at the formation. His knife penetrated a bit and stopped. He pried but the crustaceans broke off revealing nothing. He moved over to the end of one of the spires and tried again. Farris drifted over to see what Phil was doing. The end of the spire broke off with a snap leaving a fresh jagged edge.

Wood! The spire was wood instead of rock. This formation was man made. Excitement surged through Phil and he spun around to beckon Farris closer. Farris did not understand until Phil pried off a splinter of wood and handed it to him. Dropping the broken end in his mesh bag Phil swam slowly around the formation. It gave away no more secrets. He swam further afield with Farris following behind. Nothing. The air supply indicated low on his console, when Phil indicated it was time to surface.

He gave the thumbs up to Farris indicating the end of the dive.

Neither man spoke until they were back on board and had removed their tanks.

"Forgive me for doubting your coffee drift theory, Einstein" said Phil.

"What set off the magnetometer?" responded Farris.

"Lord knows. It could be any hunk of metal. It's not likely the keel because the keel would set the fish (referring to the drag behind magnetometer) to squawking like crazy."

"What is the next step?" questioned Farris.

"We now have a new area to dive. Judy will chart this on the map and as we find more pieces of the puzzle we will slowly close in on the treasure. When the debris gets close enough together we'll need a sand pump. Right now let's put on some fresh tanks and go back with the digital camera. At least that way we can give the girls a show. Then Jude will input the photos into her computer. Might as well bring the hand held magnetometer down as well. Maybe we'll find what made the fish go bleep."

The second dive did reveal a small fragment of metal. Phil carefully photographed it and measured the distance from the timbers before picking it off the bottom. It was impossible to identify it at first glance.

⊰❦⊱

Judy catalogued the timbers and the unidentified piece of metal and tried to collate her computer generated drift patterns with "The coffee pot drift theory". There did seem to be some common denominators. Finally she gave up and joined Linda in the kitchen where she was supervising as the young Bahamian girls prepared the food.

"The boys are back at it again," said Linda.

"That was a pretty big find this morning".

"I haven't seen Michael so happy in the last five years... and I've only known him for seven."

"It is exciting!"

"You bet it is... imagine all that gold. I wish I could be more help but I become frightened in a swimming pool. I'm not afraid of boats, but I'm not much of a swimmer."

Judy sensed that Linda wanted to tell her something else but couldn't get it out. Right now it didn't matter. Their friendship was just beginning.

"I can't wait to go to Nassau this weekend", said Judy.

"I can't wait to show you some of Nassau's shops and boutiques."

⊰❦⊱

On Friday afternoon everyone was hurrying around Normans Cay like a bunch of school kids who were just let out for summer holidays. Linda had decided she wanted to fly to Nassau and Judy agreed. Michael decided it was a good day for a fast boat ride and Phil agreed. The plan was set. Everyone would meet at the hotel on Paradise Island for supper before hitting the tables at the casino.

Judy had only been in a small plane once before and was excited, nervous and thrilled at the prospect as Linda ran up the engine on the Cessna. Once airborne the nervousness evaporated and Judy was awed by the view as Linda took her on a guided tour of the Exuma Islands, at five hundred feet, before making the run to Nassau.

"I never thought flying could be so much fun", laughed Judy through a headset that Linda had provided. "It's nothing like commercial jets!"

Her nervousness rebounded as they approached Nassau International and traffic increased but Linda communicated expertly with the tower and pointed out other traffic that Judy could barely see.

On landing Linda taxied to a row of private hangers. Two young black men appeared in coveralls as the plane coasted to a stop. Linda handed one young man a set of keys and both men sauntered over to the hanger doors. They unlocked the padlock and slid back the huge doors as Linda finished shutting down the plane. The hanger was dark inside after the brightness of the Bahamian sun and it took a few seconds before Judy realized that Linda kept a Jeep Cherokee in the hanger. The SUV started immediately and in minutes Linda was maneuvering down the left-hand lane toward Nassau.

"I don't think I'll ever be comfortable with left hand drive," cried Judy over the sound of the vehicle's air conditioner.

"That's what I said when I met Michael. We adapt", stated Linda with a broad smile. "You are going to love where we're going."

⚜

Phil and Michael had taken a more direct, high speed run to the hotel dock on Paradise Island and by four o'clock were sitting in a bamboo bar overlooking a well stocked swimming pool and drinking Heineken. Happy hour had just begun.

With Phil and Farris in the bar and Linda freshening up in her room, down the hall, Judy found herself alone in her hotel room. She glanced at her watch. It was quarter to five. "Friday afternoon …. No way David is still in the office". She reached for the phone and dialed his number.

Ginny answered, "David Windrow's office".

"It's Judy Simpson. May I speak with Mr. Windrow, please?"

"Miss Simpson! David just mentioned you this morning. Are you still in the Bahamas?" Ginny caught herself. "Woops, sorry, I'll put you right through."

"That's OK," she hesitated "It's Ginny, isn't it?" she questioned, not absolutely sure.

"That's right".

"Yes, I am still in the Bahamas."

"It must be gorgeous … all that sand and sea." Ginny was bubbling with enthusiasm. Judy understood David's choice in a secretary. "I'll put you through now but I hope you are really enjoying yourself. It's pouring rain here right now."

Judy laughed. "Here it's eighty degrees, sunny and happy hour is well underway. Thanks, Ginny."

There was a pause, a click and David Windrow's voice. "Judy! How are you? Every thing OK?"

"Hi David. Yah, everything's great. I just called to fill you in. Ginny said it's raining up there." Judy let the small talk flow.

"Cats and dogs, and no sign of it letting up. If it had been nicer I'd be golfing at this very moment. I cancelled my tee-off."

Judy laughed. Here she was, calling because Phil, and certainly Farris, thought David had sold her out but she heard nothing but sincerity on the other end of the line.

"So fill me in … did you link up with Phil?"

"You could say that … a bit more than we envisioned."

"Oh ho! Well good for you! Phil is a great guy. I really do like him. Did the business deal work out as planned?"

"Oh yes, that part is excellent and we have made significant progress."

"Wonderful".

"David, there is another reason I'm calling."

"Shoot".

"It seems as if someone else has knowledge of the letter. We have been diving, Phil and I, in the area. But we are being watched. Can you tell me anything?"

David leaned back in his chair as he absorbed what he had just heard. "No. Nothing, Judy. You've taken me totally by surprise. Tell me the details."

Judy hesitated. Perhaps David was lying to her. If he was he was doing a good job of it … but that was, after all, his profession. She admonished herself. "Not all lawyers are crooks". Suddenly a flood gate opened.

"Nassau's biggest drug lord seems to be watching us, every day. He arrived on the scene the same day we arrived."

"Judy, that's impossible!" David was adamant.

"I know it is David, but its happening. I probably shouldn't say this but Phil thinks you sold us out."

David was incensed "You tell Phil ..." He caught himself. "Judy, there is no way anyone got information about you or the letter from this office. I can understand Phil being a bit upset with me, doing work for you when he was my client, but as you said, it worked out better than expected."

"What about Ginny? Is it possible she let something slip?"

"No way, Judy. I would trust Ginny with the Hope Diamond. Besides, she never saw the contents of the letter. I kept that sealed, in my safe."

"I believe you David. I just wish Phil did, too".

"Look, I'll talk to Ginny". Windrow paused, "You say that a drug lord is on your trail. That's pretty bizarre ... and it could be dangerous."

"You don't know the half of it, David." She then decided she had said enough. "I better go, now."

Windrow had a dozen questions but sensed this was not the time. "OK Judy. You be careful".

"OK David. I'll call again." Judy hung up the phone and sat down on the bed. She was still sitting on the edge of the bed when Linda knocked on the door.

⊰§⊱

David slowly hung up the phone. Ginny came through the doorway and sat down in a client's chair on the other side of the desk. She had overheard part of the conversation. She waited while David collected his thoughts.

"Judy say's some drug lord seems to be following them. What the Hell is going on? Phil Harrison thinks we sold a copy of Judy's letter to a drug connection."

"But we don't have a drug connection. You have never had a drug case since I started working here," stated Ginny.

"I have never had a drug case. I've referred a few cases to others." Windrow stared into space and tried to make a connection.

"The closest I've seen to a drug case is that idiot Harry Gibson. You know, the guy who wouldn't keep his eyes in his head. I'm sure he was on some kind of enhancer." Ginny frowned at the thought and let it pass.

David groaned. Both sat silent for a full minute, just thinking. His thoughts led nowhere. Finally he sat up. "By the way. Did you finish that Gibson jerk's bill? We can deduct fees and send him a check before he starts calling. Close that file for good."

"Already done. I did it this afternoon when you cancelled your golf game and made me work overtime. The check is ready for your signature."

"OK Ginny, I'll make it up to you. It's past five. I'll buy you a drink across the street."

Ginny bounced out of the chair. "The office will be closed in three minutes."

She sat down at her computer, where she had been working on billing, and scrolled back to make sure everything was in order before she shut down. Suddenly a name slid by and a cog turned in her mind. She scrolled back going nearly a month before she found what she was looking for. She stood and walked to David's doorway. He was still at his desk writing a memo to himself.

"David I might have found something".

"What's that?" He didn't look up as he hurried to finish.

"Do you remember the day you showed me Judy's letter?"

That made Windrow look up. Ginny's posture and face screeched out for attention. David focused on Ginny's eyes.

"You were working on her file when I came in that day".

"Yes".

"The next client you saw was Mrs. Gibson."

It still took a minute for the thought process to register. "You don't think Mrs. Gibson saw the letter, do you?"

"I know it's far fetched but it's possible, isn't it."

David rose from his chair and walked over to his safe. He opened it and extracted the file while Ginny waited in the doorway. He opened the file on his desk. Relief flooded over him as he saw the Outerbridge letter, in its plastic cover, resting peacefully in the file. He turned it over. The page underneath was a printout of the "translation" he had made on his own computer.

"Everything is OK here," he said.

"That's good", answered Ginny. She didn't sound convinced. "I'm almost finished shutting down."

"T minus two minutes and counting". He returned the document to the safe and tidied up his desk. His office may be closing for the weekend but Windrow's mind was racing. A drink wouldn't hurt. Still, there was something nagging at him. He was sure that he was missing some connection. The interesting thing was that Ginny felt the same nag. Could she be right? Was it possible that Mrs. Gibson saw the letter? Come to think of it he had left Mrs. Gibson alone in his office.

Saturday morning started lazy, like a Saturday morning should. Windrow rose an hour later than usual, showered and, after retrieving the morning paper, he headed into the kitchen where he brewed fresh coffee.

He opened the paper on the kitchen table, put a plate holding a Danish pastry on one side of the page and a mug of coffee on the other. He scanned through an article, shuffling his breakfast around what he was reading and flipped through the paper for half an hour.

Still, he was restless. It just didn't feel right. In truth he had slept badly. He had downed two drinks with Ginny and chatted with her about something inane until she finally put on her jacket and left the bar. He had offered her a lift but she said she was going shopping. He immediately paid the bill and left too.

At home he had watched a good action movie, eaten a sandwich and gone to bed. Every two hours he had awoken. Each time he had thought about Judy's phone call.

Finally he muttered a curse, gulped down the last of his coffee, snapped open his brief case and extracted his laptop. He went to his client list and there, exactly where it should be, was Mrs. Gibson's address. He made a point of changing into new jeans, an expensive, casual sweater and a pair of designer walking shoes. He went down to his garage and slid into his BMW Z3.

As he pulled up to Mrs. Gibson's door he thought he saw the curtains move. He barely finished knocking when the door opened.

"Mr. Windrow, what an unexpected surprise. Please, come in."

David glanced around the living room. It was so old he wondered if Mrs. Gibson called it "the parlor". But it was not unfriendly.

"Let me make some tea", Mrs. Gibson said and immediately disappeared through a full size, swinging door. David, who definitely didn't want tea on top of the three coffees he had already consumed, gritted his teeth and smiled. He wandered around the room taking in the old knick-naks. The furniture was middle class antique. "It's not the best but I do have some friends who would pay good money for a few of these pieces to tastefully display in their condos" he thought. He knew he was being cynical but he didn't care. "Not me!" he added as if to confirm his dislike of it all.

Mrs. Gibson breezed though the swinging door. A cat followed, barely clearing the door with its tail.

"Do sit down." Mrs. Gibson placed the tea tray on a table and sat primly at one end of her sofa. David sat at the other end.

"I was in the neighborhood and it occurred to me that I had a small question to answer in order to settle your husband's estate."

Mrs. Gibson was no fool. "You're here about the letter aren't you?"

David was dumbfounded. His courtroom training automatically clicked into gear. He managed a nod and maintained a poker-face.

"I'm so sorry. It was just so beautiful. Did you notice the way Rebecca made her "R's"? I really meant no harm but I have felt so guilty since then."

"Where is the letter now? Mrs. Gibson."

"Right in front of you". Mrs. Gibson pointed to a scrap book on the coffee table. David picked it up and thumbed through it. The album was full of old documents. The Rebecca Outerbridge letter was the last page. David began to extract it when he saw the 'translation' on the second last page. He removed both, and being copies, folded and placed them in his breast pocket. He wondered if any of his other papers were present. The rest of the scrapbook was old letters, deeds and one old will, none related to his practice.

By now David had collected his thoughts. He looked up.

"When you went out to get that extra page for a signature. That's when I copied it. It was just so beautiful. How did you know? You must have a counter on your photocopier. I thought about that after I left. I really am sorry."

David was struggling to catch up with the facts but luck had been on his side. "Yes, it was the counter", he lied. "Who else has seen this letter?" he asked.

"Oh, just my neighbor, Doris. My son was here for a day but I doubt if he saw it. He doesn't like old things like I do."

David got up to leave. He knew he should say something to scold the elderly lady but words totally escaped him. Embarrassed, and not understanding why he did it, he smiled and said, "I may have an old, handwritten deed that would interest you".

Mrs. Gibson saw him to the door and then peaked out the living room window as he drove away. She looked at his cup of tea. He hadn't touched it. "He's such a busy man, Tess. That's probably how he can afford such a nice car", said Mrs. Gibson to her cat. The old fashioned, rotary dial phone rang. "Yes Doris, come over. The teapot is still full."

※

David could hardly believe his luck. Mrs. Gibson must have been consumed by guilt. He thought about some clients he had, whom he was sure would murder the Pope and never admit to it. "Poor, sweet lady." He was convinced that her motivation for copying the letter had nothing to do with treasure hunting.

He felt the need to tell someone what had just happened. He reached for his cell phone and using speed dial called Ginny.

"Lunch is on me", he said by way of introduction. He caught himself " …. If you're free".

Ginny grinned. "Richard Gere is with me but I'll send him home. Pick me up in half an hour?"

This time David grinned. "See you soon, and tell Richard he's too old for you, anyway."

He was about to hang up when he heard Ginny call out, "Richard, honey. My boss say's you're too old and have to go now." The phone went dead. David was still smiling when he pulled up in front of Ginny's apartment.

Chapter 13

At three o'clock on Sunday the two couples met in one of the casino's many bars.

"I'm down three hundred", admitted Phil.

"Seven", growled Farris.

"About a hundred", chimed Linda.

"Up, twenty seven", bubbled Judy.

"Twenty seven bucks, not bad. At least you're positive," said Farris.

"Twenty seven hundred, darling", drooled Judy, in a stage voice.

"Twenty seven hundred … when did you do that?" asked Phil, incredulous.

"About an hour ago". Judy was grinning ear to ear and talking normally again.

Linda flew into Judy's arms and gave her a big, big hug. Phil kissed her while at the same time she managed to get a quick peck from Farris.

"Come on, let's buy 'the lucky one' a drink."

Phil and Farris drank beer, Judy had a huge pina colada and Linda, who was soon going to be flying, drank a coke. The foursome broke up with the girls heading to the plane in their vehicle while the men loaded the suitcases into the boat.

The boat trip back to Normans Cay was subdued. Having put on brave faces in front of their women Phil and Farris both agreed that it was not fun being shown up by them at the tables. They accelerated out of harbor grumbling and making lame excuses. As the noise grew, the conversation subsided.

"I'd probably be much better at blackjack if those dealers didn't wear such low cut dresses."

"You probably wouldn't even be at the tables if it wasn't for those dresses", Farris answered. "Beautiful cleavage makes losing almost bearable. If it wasn't for the dealers you would probably just play the slots."

"You've got me there."

"I think that's why women seem to win more often than men. They play the cards, not the cleavage."

The moment of quiet confession and introspection was broken as Linda buzzed the cigarette boat from behind, at fifty feet. "That was close", stammered Phil as Linda lifted, waggled her wings and continued on.

They continued to bounce over the waves at fifty miles an hour. A few minutes later Farris asked, "Phil, I never saw the letter. Would you mind if I took a peak at it."

"Hell no, Judy has it in our room. What are you thinking?"

"Don't know. But one thing I am sure of … Rebecca *was* a tough old broad if she stayed alive from where we're diving now all the way back to the beach."

"You can say that again, but she was the only survivor."

"I know, and people have drifted a sea for a lot longer than five or six miles. Nevertheless, something is stuck in my craw. I can't put my finger on it. Something is not right."

"You're welcome to look at the letter. But I don't know what it will tell you that we don't already know."

No one said another word until their boat was tied up at Normans Cay.

It was only an hour after sunset and the four made a light supper of sandwiches and headed off to their bedrooms. On the way Phil handed Michael the letter in an envelope but Michael didn't even bother to open it. The next morning Farris was the first up and brewed a pot of coffee. Then he leisurely opened the envelope and carefully read the translation of the letter while glancing at the copy of the original which he held in his other hand. He was sitting like that with one page in each hand when Phil walked in.

Suddenly Michael's face went ashen.

"What's wrong Michael? You look like you just saw a ghost."

"Perhaps I did. Phil, go get Judy right away. I'll get Linda. And be back here in three minutes." Farris rushed off the patio. Phil looked longingly at the coffee but when he saw Michael hurrying decided it would be appropriate to hurry as well. Just before entering the house Farris called Phil from across the patio. "Put on good walking shoes ... no sandals."

Judy had fallen back to sleep.

"Come on Jude, wake up."

"Hummm"

Phil shook her. Her eyes opened and blinked. "Michael wants all four of us on the patio in hiking shoes in three minutes."

"Yah, right." Judy rolled over and put a pillow over her head. "Michael is a gentleman. He allows his guests time to wake up. Go away."

"You're right" said Phil, puzzled. "So why is he acting like this?"

That brought the pillow off Judy's head and brought her up to her elbows. "Are you serious?"

"Deadly serious" said Phil reaching for his running shoes.

"O.K. I'll be out soon."

"Wear hiking shoes, not sandals", ordered Phil over his shoulder as he left the room.

When Phil returned to the patio Michael was already there, wearing lightweight hiking boots, a hat and sunglasses. He was emptying the pot of coffee into a thermos.

"Judy was still in bed. Don't put all the coffee in the thermos", said Phil.

Farris poured out a cup and put the thermos into a small pack that contained a half a dozen oranges. A machete in a leather sheath was strapped to the side of the pack. Phil reached for his cup of coffee and held it protectively knowing he better finish it before the women arrived. Linda was next, looking like she had been up for hours and dressed in a well pressed safari outfit. Judy arrived last, in bare feet but carrying her runners.

"Is anyone going to tell us what this is all about?" asked Linda.

"Not on your life, my love! You'll see soon enough." Farris turned and carrying the pack led the way off the patio onto a stony path that led up along the highest ground on the island. Judy hurried to put on her shoes and then had to jog to catch up with the others. To the left you could see the airstrip with the Cessna tied down under an open hanger. Looking back she could see the magnificent architecture of the house. As they reached the peak of the small hill, only sixty feet above sea level they could see the dark blue Atlantic on the left and the turquoise Caribbean on the right. Farris set a quick pace for about half a mile before stopping.

"See that!" he said.

"It's the white rock. Those are the ruins of the Negro's house," answered Judy.

"Exactly. Now where did you find the anchor?"

Phil looked across the spit, took his bearings on the house and pointed. "Over there. Roughly north-west."

"Now look below us," instructed Farris.

"That's the beach," said Linda.

Phil and Judy looked down the hill and saw nothing but the beach where they assumed that Rebecca had landed. The hillside was sparsely covered in the same low bushes that covered the rest of the island. Farris was already descending the rocks along what might have been a goat path years ago. The others followed.

Without pausing he strode purposefully the length of the beach walking quickly in the wet sand along the water's edge. He strode the length of the beach and mounted a small outcrop of rock at its end while the others lagged behind. He climbed back down over the ancient coral bluff of the seashore and picked his way over the razor sharp coral to the extreme end of the cay and then rounded the corner before stopping at a dirty bit of sand beach. The others followed silently. Driftwood and flotsam lay pushed up to the high water mark. Piles of dead seaweed clung to the debris and dead sea-life covered the sand, giving it an eerie appearance. There were rock outcroppings jutting out of the sand. Above the beach the vegetation was rugged and knurly.

Farris picked his way through the bushes until he found a small piece of flat land above the seaside vegetation. There was a scattering of rocks but the vegetation made it difficult to discern a pattern. Farris rooted around, kicking at dead bushes. The others watched, confused but fascinated. Finally Farris straightened up, shed his pack and pulled the machete from its sheath. He slashed at some bushes and threw the brush into a pile a few feet away. Slowly, as the vegetation was stripped away, a shape emerged, revealing a crude, ninety degree, stone corner, less than a foot high. Without comment Phil began to tear out vegetation and Linda and Judy soon joined in. Two other corners slowly unfolded although the fourth had disappeared forever. Another pile of rocks, on closer examination, might have been a stone fence at one time but it was now covered in bushes and was left as is.

"This was the Negro's house." said Farris with a quiet smile. He pointed toward the sea. There was a small outcropping of pale rock in a southerly direction. Perched on the rock were a dozen egrets. The birds must have lived on that rock for generations. One portion of the rock was distinctly white from years of droppings. Farris hacked away at a few bushes and opened a path to the water. He returned to the stones and stood in the center of the front wall. "And there is your white rock!"

Farris extracted the letter from a pocket and read from it to the others.

"Just over that crop of white rock I saw the ship's lights. I knew it must have sunk because the lights went out. The next morning I found you, Miss Outerbridge, all tangled up in the rigging from the broken mast."

Farris looked up at the others. "We have been looking in the wrong spot."

Farris gave them a moment to let it all sink in.

"If this is the Negro's house and that's the white rock then this is the beach that Rebecca was washed up on. That puts the wreck off the south west tip of the cay. You found the anchor to the north-west. Now, watch this." Farris took a stick that was lying nearby and sketched out the cay in the sand.

"Suppose that the ship ran into trouble near where we found the anchor. For that matter the anchor may not even belong to our ship! Let's suppose it does. The Captain, his ship disabled, throws out the hook, but the anchor itself is already too close to the reef and the ship is being held on the reef by its own anchor. What does the Captain do?"

"He cuts the anchor free and drifts away from the spit."

"Right! But the wind pushes him this way. The ship must have already been in the lee of the island when it finally sank.

"He had cleared the spit but must have hit hard enough to be sinking anyway. The storm died out shortly after the ship went down. We know that because Rebecca was washed ashore instead of out to sea. The wind would have driven her out but the tide brought her in." Michael paused savoring the moment.

"The wreck lies in line with that rock." Once again he pointed at the gwana covered rock.

The four stood staring at the crude sketch and the rock.

Finally Linda broke the silence. "Michael's right! Follow me and I'll show you."

Linda led the way down to the beach. It was short, only a few hundred yards long, forming a small bay. The sandy bottom made the water turquoise and incredibly picturesque but the beach was a mess.

Above the tide line were huge pieces of drift wood. A few coconuts lay washed up on the wet sand. Closer examination of the high water mark showed various kinds of man made litter and flotsam, glass and plastic bottles, a couple of fenders from boats, odd pieces of wood and even what was once a guitar. Along the line of the high water mark lay a six foot wide strip of dead and decaying seaweed.

"This is the dirtiest beach on the cay. Everything washes up here. We even had a fire here a couple of years ago to try to clean it up but every tide brings in more seaweed and junk."

"Maybe that's why the Negro lived so close to it rather than up on the higher ground by the big white rock. You could easily live on what the tide brings in, especially coconuts and shell fish", suggested Farris.

"That means Ricky is looking in the wrong spot, too", said Judy.

"Ricky must have a copy of the letter and is making the same assumption you did about the large white rock."

"I don't think so", said Phil. Everyone turned toward him. "Ricky has been anchoring almost exactly where we were the previous day. I think he's locating our position on radar and simply playing copy cat until we find something."

There was a hiss of air as Farris sucked in a breath, between his teeth. "That would be Ricky's style. Its just like a hyena, moving in for a share of a lion's kill".

"That means he'll soon find the anchor."

"I'd bet a hundred dollars on that," answered Phil.

"I'll pass on that bet. Let the girls do the gambling from now on," said Farris.

Judy stole a glance at Linda who smiled and turned away.

Linda could see the hatred in Farris' eyes whenever Ricky's name was mentioned. "Let's go back and eat those oranges. I'm thirsty."

They started back toward the Negro's house where they rested on the stone foundations. Linda passed around the oranges while Michael passed out plastic cups which he filled with coffee.

Phil spoke up. "What is the reef like, if we follow your line of reasoning?"

Michael pointed over the white rock. "It's as bad out there as anywhere but it doesn't go out far, no more than a mile, and the bottom is deeper although the coral heads still reach just below the surface. The difference is the current. It swoops around the cay, especially when the tide flows, and pushes anything that's floating right onto this beach. I think that's what was stuck in my craw. Next to nothing ever washes up on the other beach."

"So why not just move our search to this end of the cay?" asked Judy.

"I have an idea" said Phil. "That bastard Ricky keeps following us. Let's play him. We'll continue to dive the north end but we'll sneak some diving in at this end as well."

"Phil, your boat has an aluminum mast with a radar deflector, right" asked Farris.

"Yes. That's how Ricky pinpoints our previous dive sites. "

"Think we could re rig some of your treasure hunting equipment into a rubber Zodiac?"

Phil and Michael grinned at each other.

"Time for a little deception?" asked Phil.

"If things go the way I think they might we might even put a marker buoy on that anchor".

⋛⋚

For the balance of the week Phil and Judy worked the grid near the anchor but having convinced themselves that they were in the wrong spot their dives were more pleasure and less work. Phil dove with a Hawaiian sling, more interested in lobster and grouper than gold.

Michael worked with Victor and George in the shop. They constructed a wooden, waterproof, box and installed it in the front of the Zodiac. Much of the equipment that Phil and Judy had installed was transferred to the box and wired to a bank of batteries.

Keeping the power to the machinery was problematic. The alternator on the Zodiac's outboard was puny compared to the oversized alternator on Phil's diesel.

"We'll just have to run the batteries until we can charge them up at night," said Michael.

"Let's supplement it as much as we can with solar battery chargers," suggested Phil.

Soon the top surface of the wooden box was covered with the smoked glass solar panels. They tested the equipment at the dock and determined they could keep the batteries alive for four hours at a time. "It's not perfect but it's not bad either", commented Phil.

The next morning Phil and Farris left the dock at dawn and began a grid pattern at the southern tip of the cay. They were back home by eleven, had lunch and Phil and Judy took the Zara out to the old dive site for the afternoon. They were down below watching a movie on the DVD player when Ricky's boat showed up on the radar screen. They shut off the movie and donned diving gear. They were sure Ricky was watching as they slid off the dive platform.

Chapter 14

Mrs. Gibson had been out grocery shopping. She liked to go to the store a couple of times a week but each time she spent less than ten dollars. She told herself it was so she wouldn't have to carry too much but if the truth were told, it was all she could afford. Once a month, the day her pension check came in, she took her two wheeled shopping cart and bought a months supply of cat food for Tessy.

She was only one house away from home when a familiar voice called from an open window.

"Tea's already made".

Mrs. Gibson smiled and turned up her neighbor's walk. She was a bit tired and knew the tea would soothe her. A few minutes later she was sitting comfortably, sipping tea and enjoying a cookie when her ever vigilant neighbor said, "There is a man going up to your door". That made Mrs. Gibson look around. She could see clearly enough through the shears to realize he was a big man, in an expensive overcoat. She glanced toward the road. There was a big dark car, "probably a Buick", she thought, pulled up in front of her house with someone still behind the wheel.

The man was knocking on her door and she reached for her own coat that lay, folded neatly, on the sofa beside her. She was just slipping it on when her neighbor gently touched her arm. She followed her neighbor's eyes. The big man had gone back down the steps and was walking around the far side of the house. That was odd. If she didn't answer the front door why would he go to the side door? Her neighbor's hand remained resting gently on Mrs. Gibson's forearm. Suddenly the fingers tightened. A shadow passed by the side window of the Gibson house. Whoever it was, had entered the house and was walking right into Mrs. Gibson's kitchen.

"But the side door was locked", stammered Mrs. Gibson.

Her neighbor guided Mrs. Gibson into the next room where the view of Mrs. Gibson's kitchen was better. But rather than looking out the window directly, the neighbor hung back on the far side of the room, clutching Mrs. Gibson's forearm firmly, remaining still, and watching the Gibson kitchen window.

The man in the house looked around and then went directly to the kitchen table. Without hesitation he picked up the photo album and thumbed through it, perusing each page quickly, but carefully.

"Old stuff" he thought. Gino was on a mission. His job was to find a letter that looked like the one Ricky had. But there was no letter in the book that looked like the one Ricky had paid fifteen thousand dollars for. Gino paused for a moment, thinking back to the morning that he had broken Harry Gibson's finger. Harry had specifically said the letter was in the photo album.

In a voice that was barely audible Gino whispered to himself, "Harry Gibson lied". This would undoubtedly be very bad for the bar owner. Nevertheless, Gino would do nothing until Ricky confirmed it. Besides, Gino liked the States. It didn't seem logical to take the first plane back to Nassau. He leaned back in the kitchen chair and decided to return to Florida before calling Ricky. He could always say he had returned to Florida to off Harry Gibson. That story ought to buy him a week at least.

Gino carelessly tossed the album back on the table and exited through the side door. He had barely closed the door of the Buick when it accelerated away.

There was another movement in the kitchen. Tessy, who hid behind a chair when the side door had been broken, now sprang on top of the kitchen table and, back arched, walked slowly around the album.

Mrs. Gibson let out a gasp of air. Her right hand closed over her friend's hand that still clutched Mrs. Gibson's left forearm. Her neighbor seemed in a state of shock. Mrs. Gibson took control. She led the way back to the sofa where they sat down together, still holding on to each other.

Mrs. Gibson tried to rationalize what she had just witnessed. First, she had found the letter in her lawyer's office. She supposed that made it valuable somehow. Second, David Windrow had realized, somehow, that she had a copy of the letter. Third, Windrow had come, on a Saturday, no less, and taken the letter back. Fourth, some strange, well dressed man in a Buick, had broken into her house, gone directly to her photo album, looked for the letter, and, when he didn't find it, left.

Doris was sitting staring blankly into space. Mrs. Gibson poured more tea, adding an extra spoonful of sugar to her friend's cup, and handed it to her. The frightened old lady smiled weakly. They both sipped tea and said nothing. The color slowly returned to her friend's face. It had never left Mrs. Gibson's. In fact, Mrs. Gibson was, once again, enjoying the adrenaline.

Chapter 15

As the sun rose over the horizon it reflected off the sea, turning the sea itself into a mere backdrop, behind a gigantic circle of fire. Ricky looked out his massive windows and almost appreciated nature's glory. Morning was always his best time although he never recognized that fact himself. Within an hour, or two at the most he would reach for his nose candy and his life would accelerate into a whirlwind of crime, sex, fear and anger. For the time being, he drank his orange juice and smoked a cigarette and did his creative thinking.

Last night Gino had called. "The fucker took two weeks holiday before he visited the old broad", he thought caustically. "Then he wastes another week casing out Harry!" Gino had filled him in on the absence of the letter at Harry's mother's house. At least Gino was competent. Ricky would never admit it out loud but he felt safer when Gino was nearby.

"Where the fuck did that little prick, Gibson, grow the balls to concoct that letter and sell it to me?" continued Ricky in his solitary musings. "It's too big a coincidence that the letter takes us to the spit off

Normans Cay. The letter *is* a ruse to get me set up on Farris's doorstep.

"Gibson is too stupid to come up with a letter like that. That means Gibson got the letter from the lawyer and made up the story about his mother. He got that idea from her scrapbook, which he probably grew up with. That means the lawyer wrote the letter but it all comes back to one thing. Farris must be working with the lawyer and he wants us, for some reason, parked on his doorstep. That's where it goes off-track and crashes. What in the name of Christ does Farris want me hanging around for? It's been nearly a month. For all the diving, Farris hasn't brought up doodley squat. But how could he? If the letter is a fake? So why is he going to all this trouble scuba diving in the same spot every day".

Ricky's mind began to draw his action plan. "That's it. I'm done going out there again, unless something big develops. I'll arrange to keep an eye on things with the boat but I'm also going to put a plane over Normans Cay until I figure this out."

Ricky reached for his orange juice. He called out to one of his henchmen. "Hey Fred, get one of the broads from last night to make me a toasted western for breakfast. Make sure you find one that can cook".

Fred retreated to the house, ten thousand square feet of gaudy luxury. "Hey, can you cook eggs?" he asked the first girl he passed. She was dressed in a bathrobe and didn't look half as good as she had the night before.

"If you want something hot, try out my pussy. Otherwise forget it", was the coarse reply.

Fred moved on. "Ricky should have ordered fried brains", he called over his shoulder. "There's plenty of those around this dump".

⊰❦⊱

Phil and Judy, Michael and Linda, sat at the breakfast table. This had become the norm. It put structure to the day and gave everyone a chance to talk about the search and express ideas and opinions. Today was visibly different. There was a tension in the air and it was obvious that something was wrong between Michael and Linda. Sensing a domestic problem, Phil and Judy had said little, and breakfast turned into a silent meal, unlike anything they had become accustomed too.

When everyone was finished eating Michael coughed quietly and said, "I hate to tell you this but I'll be tied up for the next few days. Sorry. You'll have to continue the search without me."

Linda glared at Michael showing unabated anger but saying nothing.

Judy spoke up, trying to sound casual. "No problem. Phil and I were talking last night about a swim between the anchor and the timbers. There must be something there. We thought we would take the hand held magnetometers".

"Good idea. Do you plan to dive the new site?" Farris asked.

"First let's keep up appearances. Jude and I will take the Zara out around the anchor daily and waste a bit of time. In the afternoons we will cruise the grid at site two, with the Zodiac. We will keep the fishing rods baited and work the grid until the magnetometer picks up something", answered Phil. "We won't dive the new site until we have some data from the magnetometer. That way Ricky will believe the gold is somewhere close to the anchor. If we play it right he won't have a clue about the second site."

"That sounds fine with me. Anybody else have a comment?" said Farris as he rose from the table. "Good, that's settled." Linda continued to stare him down and Michael continued to retreat toward his study.

⋧⋦

Finally, Phil and Judy were back in their room with the door closed.

"What was all that about?" said Judy.

"Beats me, lieutenant." Phil was fully prepared not to discuss it but Judy wanted to talk.

"Look, we know what Michael's business is. It's obvious that he's bringing in a shipment. All of a sudden I'm not so comfortable around here. What if something goes wrong? We are here, living in his house. We could end up in jail as accessories".

"Jude, when I told you about Normans Cay, it was your idea that we partner up with the gang that lives here. We sure as hell didn't anticipate people like Mike and Linda. The original plan we made is working. Don't get cold feet now," countered Phil.

"Why was Linda so pissed off?"

"I don't know. Think of it this way. Michael has been in this business a long time. He must know what he's doing. Right?"

"I bet that is supposed to make me fell better?" quipped Judy.

"The less we know, the better. We'll keep on diving and searching. If things get bad we pull the pin. But not yet. OK?"

"Didn't Michael say once he was retired"?

Phil snorted and grinned. "He said 'I haven't worked so hard since I retired'. It was a joke."

"I know. I just like Michael and Linda so much I don't want to believe they are drug smugglers".

Phil put his arms around Judy and she buried her face in his chest. "Well they are. At least Mike is. I'm not so sure about Linda." Phil held Judy's shoulders and pushed her out to arms length. Even then, he had to tilt up her chin with one gentle finger until she looked up at him with moist eyes. "One thing we agree on is this. Michael and Linda are our friends. Despite Michael's profession, I trust him. And I trust Linda too. I vote we maintain the game plan. Are you with me on this?"

"I'm not so sure about the game plan…. But I am with you on this." Judy wiped the tears from her eyes. "I love you." She buried herself against Phil's chest.

Phil stroked Judy's hair. "I love you, too".

Judy looked up grinning mischievously through her tears. "I knew that", she sputtered.

Phil broke away. "Come on, let's go find Rebecca's gold."

"Men" said Judy. "You say the L word and all of a sudden they want to change the oil in the car".

Phil was headed to the door. He glanced back over his shoulder with a sheepish grin but kept on moving.

🙖

Michael was on the dock when Phil arrived. He had a wrench in his hand and the cowling of his cigarette boat was raised.

"Linda asked if she could join you today."

"Yah, sure. Of course" answered Phil. "What you doing to your boat?"

"Nothing much. Just changing the oil". Farris looked up and saw Phil grinning. "What's so funny?" he asked.

"Nothing, just something Judy said," answered Phil as he climbed aboard the Zara.

Chapter 16

The Zara moved quietly through Normans spit to the GPS coordinates that marked the anchor. Phil was at the wheel, Judy down below turning on the computer or what remained of it. The brains stayed behind in the waterproof box on the Zodiac. Linda was in the cockpit with Phil, but she stood with her back to him and her arms crossed. Phil considered small talk, ruled that out, and concentrated on avoiding coral heads. He had crossed here enough times to feel confidant that he knew his way without Judy on the bow.

Judy came up the companionway and sat down in the cockpit. "I have some good news and some bad news", she announced.

Phil grinned. He knew the routine. "Give us the bad news, first."

"The bad news is there isn't enough equipment left on board to do what I wanted, to map our dive."

Linda turned, smiled weakly, and asked, "What's the good news?"

"The good news is I found a pencil and we can write down anything important."

"That pencil didn't have a half chewed eraser, did it? I lost one like that a couple of years ago". Phil maintained a reasonable poker face.

Finally Linda snorted a reluctant little laugh and the ice was broken.

"Look guys", she said. She sat down in the cockpit facing Phil and Judy. "Do you remember that Michael didn't tell you about me when you first came to our cay." Phil and Judy exchanged glances at each other and then back to Linda. "I told you, right then, that Michael was the most secretive person I ever met." Linda looked up and waited for confirmation. Phil nodded. "Well it's true." She paused. "Whatever you are thinking right now, don't be too sure. Things are not always what they appear to be where Michael is concerned."

Linda met Phil's eyes first and then Judy's. "It's OK to trust him. He really, I mean really, likes you guy's. It's just that every now and then he throws a wicked curve ball".

No one said another word and the silence seemed to permeate the boat, the sea, and the people aboard. After a minute of discomfort Phil decided it was time to change the subject. "Want to come with us for a dive".

"You know I can't swim", answered Linda.

"You could follow us in the dinghy and watch through the glass bottom bucket", Phil suggested.

Linda's face visibly brightened. She smiled. "I could do that", she agreed.

An hour later, Phil and Judy were performing underwater antics while Linda watched from the surface. Phil even pinched Judy's bum. Judy turned dramatically and with a slow, full arm pretended to slap Phil across the face. Phil did a complete back somersault and deflating his BC, sank, apparently knocked out, to the sand below. Afterwards Judy swam over to him, offered him a helping hand. The two held hands, high above their heads and proceeded to bow majestically to their fishy audience. Linda was leaning over the bow of the inflatable dinghy with her face rammed into the glass bottom bucket, laughing like a child.

When Phil determined that the fish had stopped clapping he looked up at Linda and then pointed directly at a lump on the ocean floor. Linda watched, perplexed. Phil pointed to another lump and then another. The lumps were in a straight line. Phil followed the line while Linda took the oars and caught up to his position. She looked back into the bucket, which dragged along beside the boat, suspended in a ring buoy. There was Phil, with Judy beside him. They were both pointing grandly at what looked like a piece of pipe with a ball fixed to one end.

A sudden realization swept over Linda. She was looking at the anchor. Then, in her mind she could see it all. Not just a piece of iron and a ball but a complete anchor on a massive anchor chain. Then she saw more. Half buried in the sand, with its lid hanging open lay a treasure chest containing millions of dollars in ancient coins and magnificent jewels. There were crosses, amulets and gold crowns. Gold glittered and jewels sparkled in the turquoise water. She reached out trying to touch it but suddenly it was gone.

She raised her face from the bucket and took a deep breath. "Linda, darling", she said to herself, "you have just experienced your first attack of gold fever."

Linda had grown up in a wealthy family. A rich family. She had never wanted for anything. She knew how to shop and enjoyed spending money but the amount she spent was far less than her annual allowance from her trust fund. Michael was also rich, by any standard. Linda never really thought about money. Her accountant, lawyer and investment broker did that. Yet suddenly Linda saw herself surrounded by piles of gold and jewels.

She tried to deny the feeling but it persisted, overwhelming her. "This can't be happening.... Not to me", she thought. "Oh yes it is", she responded, feeling more than a bit giddy.

When she looked back into the glass bucket Phil and Judy were swimming along what must be the chain, almost out of sight. She shipped the oars and pushed the starter button on the dinghy's motor. It started immediately. Linda could see the bubbles from the divers breaking the surface. She flipped the lever into forward and followed the bubbly trail.

Over the next three days Linda became an inseparable part of the team. At first she questioned Judy about the equipment on the Zodiac but she grasped the concepts at once and was soon pounding away on the keyboard and compiling information flawlessly. By the third day Phil had convinced her to abandon the glass bottomed bucket and taught her how to lie over the edge of the dinghy, wearing a mask and snorkel, and watch the bottom. Suddenly the fish that had always frightened her seemed more friendly. The first time she saw a shark, even though she suspected it was a nurse shark and harmless, she had been terrified. Now, she could even keep her face in the water and watch sharks, admiring their grace, and controlling her fear.

She had even promised Judy that she would accept a snorkeling lesson in a shallow lagoon, where the water was never over her head, though she had yet to fulfill that commitment.

That night, shortly after midnight, Phil was awakened by the low rumble of powerful engines. He quietly slipped out of bed and stepped out on the unlit patio. Looking down at the docks he watched as a pair of cigarette boats pulled up to the docks. George was the first on shore and he tied Michael's boat off before opening the boathouse doors and standing by as Victor entered his slip.

The three men worked quietly and efficiently until the boats were organized. When they said goodnight they shook hands, Bahamian style, before Farris mounted the stairs to the patio.

Phil, dressed only in his shorts, reentered the house and crawled back into bed. Judy murmured something and Phil whispered that Mike was back but Judy was already asleep again. Phil recapped the last three days. Tension had been high when Mike left, but during that time Linda had grown much closer to Phil and Judy. She had also truly become part of the hunt. Taken slowly enough, Phil thought they could teach Linda to scuba dive. "Wouldn't that be something", he thought, smiling, before he too fell asleep.

Chapter 17

Farris was obviously happy as Linda proposed they all go out together for the first dive of the day. Whatever conflict had transpired before Mike's departure was now forgotten. Linda couldn't wait to show Michael how she had learned to snorkel, despite the fact that she remained in the inflatable while she did it. But for dramatic effect the three had promised to reveal nothing about her "diving" before she actually did it, in front of Farris.

They agreed to dive a shallow area only a few hundred yards from where they had located the timbers while pursuing their "coffee pot drift theory". They had already recorded a couple of minor blips from the "fish". Linda had nicknamed the "fish" Blipper and the name seemed to be sticking.

Phil was steering in the general direction of the timbers with Mike resting in the cockpit. He was tired from the past three days and said little. Judy and Linda were in the cabin below leaning over a laptop.

"Blipper says we dive at 25 degrees, 37 minutes, 14 seconds North, and 76 degrees, 50 minutes, 30 seconds West. I already plugged in those coordinates down here, so just follow the bearing on the screen", called Judy from the companionway. Phil glanced down at his chartplotter and altered his course by a few degrees.

Farris poked his head into the hatch and answered "Roger that, Blipper". He then turned to Phil and said "I've been gone three days and we're now taking orders from Blipper?"

Phil bit his tongue, remembering his promise to say nothing about Linda's "diving".

"You ain't seen nothin' yet!" was all he answered.

⛥

Phil and Judy suited up while Farris said he'd watch the boat. He was mildly surprised when Linda appeared in a bikini without her usual blouse over top but when she climbed into the dinghy carrying a mask and snorkel he couldn't believe his eyes. He was even more amazed when Linda untied the dinghy and after drifting twenty feet from the Zara proceeded to spit in the mask, slosh it around, rinse it out and put it on. He watched in awe as she lay down in the inflatable with her torso stretched over the side, put her face in the water and began to breathe through the snorkel. She looked up, waved at Phil and Judy and put her face back in to watch as Phil and Judy jumped in off the dive platform.

"I'll be God damned", Farris muttered to himself.

For the next hour Michael puttered around the boat like a lost puppy. The only reason he had stayed on board was to keep Linda company and she had barely looked up in the last forty minutes unless it had been to either row or motor after Phil and Judy's bubbles. He had noticed, however, how attractively displayed Linda's bottom was, as she stretched over the inflatable's side. By the time Phil and Judy surfaced Farris was thinking about proposing a siesta when they all got back to the dock. The dinghy was a hundred yards away from Zara when Phil and Judy surfaced beside it. Farris was day dreaming and was too far away to notice the excitement. Linda dangled a couple of dock lines off the dinghy's stern and towed Phil and Judy back to the boat using the dinghy's motor.

Farris tossed Linda a line as she pulled up to the stern. "I can't believe what I just saw", he grinned.

"I can't believe what we just saw!" responded Linda. Phil was already on the dive platform handing his tanks to Farris and helping Judy with hers.

Phil peeled off his wet suit before he spoke. "We found bones!"

Linda and Judy were climbing into the cockpit.

"Human bones?" questioned Farris cautiously.

"No silly", answered Linda, the new, overnight expert, "ship's bones". She sounded like a floozy cheerleader.

Farris sat down, overwhelmed. "How long was I gone for?" he questioned. "I feel like Rip Van Winkle".

"Not that long, but too long, dear", answered Linda reverting to her normal, serious voice.

Everyone sat down in the cockpit. It was time to bring Farris up to speed.

"By the way, Hun. You looked great out there. Who taught you that?"

"Both Phil and Judy" answered Linda. "At first I just looked over the edge of the dinghy with a glass bottomed bucket but once I got the hang of the snorkel, I began to realize what a beautiful world I was missing. Then I saw the anchor. Suddenly I was imagining treasure chests and eerie wrecks. That was when I suddenly realized why you and Phil and Judy were so excited. All of a sudden this became a wonderful adventure instead of a silly pastime. Now I want to be part of this in a real way. I've even started to do stuff on the computer, logging our finds."

"Linda is no slouch on the computer either", praised Phil. "She understands the programs better than I do and types about a thousand times faster."

"I didn't know Linda could write programs until I saw her do it", added Judy.

"I knew that she had studied programming before we met. Sometimes she gets on the computer at home for hours at a time but I usually go down to the boathouse and play with an engine when that happens", admitted Farris.

"It's not much fun watching someone else on a computer", stated Linda.

"Its fun watching you snorkel", grinned Farris. He stole a glance at Phil who looked away while covering a smile with his hand.

Linda noticed. "What the Hell is going on?"

Finally Judy spoke up. "I suspect that our horny, immature, loser, childish men have been watching the somewhat provocative manner in which you snorkel, humped over the side of the dinghy".

Suddenly Linda realized what Judy was saying. Immediately she blushed almost to a crimson. "Oh my God! Why didn't you say something?"

Phil spoke up. "You have been so afraid of the water for so long. When you started to show such interest we thought embarrassing you might throw off your learning curve."

"I saw you staring", stated Judy. "It wasn't Linda's learning curve you had in mind".

"Phil. Have you been watching my wife's ass?" laughed Farris. Linda glared at him until he recanted. "Darling, I think we're all happy as clams that you are seeing what we see, underwater. As soon as we get back to shore I am sure I can rig up a float with a windsurfer or something that will be more comfortable for you."

Linda was still embarrassed but her blush had faded. "Judy, you can deal with Phil as you see fit but Michael, be prepared. If you want to stare at my ass you can damn well pay for the privilege! This is going to cost you the most expensive designer wetsuit I can find in Nassau."

High overhead a small plane flew over the Zara. Linda glanced up. There was a momentary look of concern on her face, which she quickly covered up. The others noticed nothing. It was only her experience as a pilot that had enabled her to see an anomaly in the flight path of the intruder.

"Now, what about these bones?" demanded Farris.

"We have ourselves a hull" answered Phil. "It's barely visible, buried deep in the sand. But it is a hull."

"Is it Rebecca's ship?"

"It could be, but somehow, I don't think so. We won't know for sure until we pump out the sand. I'll want to study it for at least a week before I jump to any conclusion. Maybe it will tell us a secret. It's a long way from the beach."

"What's the next step?"

"Blipper has been busy finding stuff on the other site. We haven't found anything big yet, but there has been a lot of small stuff. It's all logged in. I think we should keep our time split like before. Mornings at "the bones", afternoons at "the dirty beach". Do you want to see "the bones" now ?"

"I'll wait until tomorrow if we're going to do "the dirty beach" this afternoon" answered Farris.

Judy spoke up. "Why don't we sail over "the bones" on the way back? That way we can get some film footage and Mike can see the site right now on DVD. It will also give Linda and me a chance to review it this afternoon."

"Good plan", said Farris.

Phil reached over and started the diesel engine.

"God I wish we had the equipment back on board", mumbled Judy. "It's so frustrating working with one hand tied behind your back."

"How be Phil and I circle past here on our way to the other side this afternoon. Then tomorrow if you three go out in Zara, I can pretend to meet you later with the big Zodiac. That way we at least get some coverage of this site", suggested Farris.

"Sure, that will be a big help", said Judy.

As the Zara slipped over the ship's bones Judy got a bit of footage on video. The quality was poor but there was enough to point out to Michael exactly what they had seen. Only a few of the ship's ribs protruded from the sand. The rest had broken away or disintegrated in the ocean atmosphere.

"Someone was sharp to pick up a hull from those few pieces", said Farris appreciatively.

Linda saddled over and put an arm around Farris' waist. "That would be me, darling."

"You're kidding. You were the first to recognize it?"

"I think it was because I was on top looking straight down. All I had to do was connect the dots", Linda explained.

"For that, I'll throw in a divers watch with your new wet suit. Wow ….. You done good! What's next, Phil?"

"Tomorrow we will make a grid over the site like an archeologist would do. We will log every scrap of data and take lots of photos. I don't know which is the bow and which is the stern but one thing I do know. The hull lies along the same direction as the anchor chain. That means one is connected to the other. Not physically, but I would bet the anchor belongs to the bones. The problem is, that gives us the direction of drift. It seems impossible that Rebecca could have drifted the opposite direction toward shore." Phil's summary was followed by silence. Despite the biggest find of the hunt, a somber mood hung over the Zara as she returned to Normans Cay.

After lunch Phil and Michael left harbor in the Zodiac. They took two quick passes over the "bones" and circled the spit. As they approached the area off Rebecca's beach they rigged their fishing rods in the holders attached to the stern. Another fisherman might have suggested they let out more line but then again, another fisherman would not have lowered "Blipper" into the water. As soon as they started to move the computer was clicked on and as the GPS signaled the path the Zodiac followed, the computer recorded the information on a map, programmed into the database. Phil hit a couple of key strokes and previous paths showed clearly. The center of the map was a clutter of criss-crossing lines. The area they were in was free of any previous search.

Almost immediately the "fish" sent a signal indicating the presence of metal on the ocean floor.

Immediately Phil switched on the video recorder fastened securely to "Blipper's" belly.

"Bring her about and try to pass directly over the same spot" ordered Phil. Farris swung the Zodiac around in a tight circle and backtracked about two hundred feet. Coming about a second time, Phil watched the map. "Right on". He watched the screen as Michael studied a rock on Normans Cay and tried to keep it directly over the bow. "Just a tad to port. That's it. Steady ……"

There was another blip from the "fish". The Zodiac passed directly over the previous signal and kept moving forward. The beeper signaled another hit. Then another and another.

"That's the strongest concentration we have found so far", said Phil.

"Can you see anything on video", asked Farris.

"Looks like junk. Nothing I can recognize".

"Blipper" began to squeal again.

"We sure hit a hot area. It could be garbage someone dropped overboard, but it seems too strong for that."

There was silence for another two minutes followed by more activity. In the following half hour three more hits occurred. By four in the afternoon Phil and Farris had recorded twenty-seven hits within an area no more than a quarter mile square.

"The girls are going to have a field day with this" said Farris.

"And we'll be spending three hours watching "Jacques Cousteau un-edited", quipped Phil.

"I have a bottle of scotch that might ease the pain", grinned Farris. "Let's head in".

Farris turned the Zodiac and cranked the throttle. The shallow draft boat cruised over the coral heads that made up the spit only turning occasionally when a particularly shallow head appeared. Ten minutes later they were tied up in front of the Zara. Removing only the laptop and the DVDs before locking down the plywood box, the two men trudged wearily up the stairs to the patio.

⊰§⊱

Ricky lay sprawled out by the pool. He had been talking to one of the girls when his phone rang. He waved her away before answering.

"There were four on the sailboat this morning. The two broads and the two guys. This afternoon the two guys go out fishing in their rubber raft."

"Anything special".

"Naw, just the normal. They always go out to almost exactly the same spots. They must be looking for something", said the pilot. "Or, it's a good place to fish."

"I know what they're looking for Fuck Head. You just tell me when they find it, asshole".

Ricky clicked off the phone and threw it at a lounge chair where it landed without breaking. At the other end of the line the pilot cursed and muttered "God I hate that bastard. I should never work for him .... But I need his money! The bastard!"

Chapter 18

Over a week had passed since Gino had broken into Mrs. Gibson's home. During that week Mrs. Gibson had not had a single night of restful sleep. Her nerves were frayed and she had even snapped at Tessy on two occasions. Her neighbor, Doris, fearful for Mrs. Gibson's health, had repeatedly suggested that one of them should call the police.

"You have got to get this off your chest! I see the light on in your bedroom at all hours. Frankly you look like Hell!"

That had been the last straw. Mrs. Gibson, who had invited her neighbor over for tea, firmly suggested that her neighbor should mind her own business. The two elderly women never spoke to each other in that tone. Doris had promptly picked up her coat and gone home.

Now Mrs. Gibson was rummaging through a dresser drawer. She found what she wanted and carried it down stairs to the kitchen. A new roll-down blind was pulled down blocking the view from her neighbor's watching eye. There was an identical, brand new roll down in her neighbor's window. For both elderly ladies, the cost of the blinds came straight out of grocery money.

She poured a cup of tea from the pot on the table. The hand knitted tea cozy had kept the tea warm. Sitting down, Mrs. Gibson unfolded a single sheet of paper. "Thank God for photocopiers", she mumbled. "Mr. Windrow may have checked the counter on his photocopier and caught me red handed … but he didn't do the math." Proudly Mrs. Gibson spread out another copy of the letter.

This time she read the letter with more concentration on the content. For a while, after reading, she stared at the design on the wallpaper, not seeing it at all.

Finally she picked up the old rotary phone. When her neighbor picked up the phone Mrs. Gibson disregarded their argument and simply stated, "Doris, it's not the letter. It's the gold. You better come over right away."

A few minutes later the two women were discussing first David Windrow's visit and then the mysterious men in the Buick, one who had waited outside while the other had broken in the side door.

"Do you think Mr. Windrow sent the men in the Buick?" asked Doris.

"Oh no! Mr. Windrow already had the letter. Why would he break in again?"

"Then maybe you should tell Mr. Windrow what happened. Let him decide if the police should know."

"Perhaps you are right, Doris. I am certain that Mr. Windrow had nothing to do with the break-in. Yes, that's what we'll do."

Doris's heart sped up at the way Mrs. Gibson had said "we". She suddenly felt ten years younger.

❈

"Mrs. Gibson on line two" called Ginny through the open door. When there were just the two of them in the office live conversation was easier than technology.

Ginny could not help but hear David's side of the conversation. It was short, even abrupt. She could hear concern… or worry, in David's voice. David had told her at lunch, on the previous Saturday, about the letter and Mrs. Gibson. The only part he still held back were the contents. When David got off the phone Ginny entered his office and sat down across the desk from her boss.

"Someone broke into Mrs. Gibson's house", stated David.

"Oh my God! Is she all right?"

"She's fine. She wasn't home at the time. She saw the whole thing from her neighbor's window. It was a week ago, not long after I was there".

"Wow, she must have peed her pants!"

David looked up at her sharply. Ginny didn't back down. "I would have", she stated.

"It must have been frightening. But I don't think Mrs. Gibson frightens easily. The intruder went directly to her photo album with the old documents. He went through the pages, one by one. Then he left."

"He must have known the letter was in the album".

"Next you're going to tell me how he knew about the letter," said David. He stared directly into Ginny's eyes.

Ginny responded, not even a blink. "El Creepo".

"You mean Harry Gibson".

"The man with the saucer sized eyes. David, he's the only one else who is connected to this in any way."

David picked up Ginny's line of thought. "He could have seen the letter during his stay at his mother's house. But why would someone else break-in to Mrs. Gibson's."

"Suppose El Creepo read the letter. You never said anything directly but I figured out its some sort of treasure map. That's why you've kept it hidden in the safe. El Creepo must have made a copy of the letter. Now he wants to make sure there are no other copies."

"First his mother makes a copy. Then her son makes a copy of the copy?"

"Like mother, like son" said Ginny, with an exaggerated smile.

"He wouldn't break into his own mother's house. Besides, it wasn't him that broke in. Unless he sold the damn letter. This speculation is getting thinner and thinner."

"It's not that thin, David. El Creepo is too lazy to go after the treasure himself. He'd be just the type to sell a treasure map."

"Good point. Let me mull this over. You have obviously been thinking about this quite a bit".

"Of course I have. You have to admit it is exciting!"

"It's a little too exciting for Mrs. Gibson, right now".

"Maybe I should send her a card or something from you. Maybe some chocolates?" questioned Ginny.

"Hey, she stole that letter from me. Now you want me to send her chocolates!"

"She's a little old lady who has just watched someone break into her house. Be nice! You buy the chocolates and I'll bring you back a café latte, on me."

David relented. He knew when to quit.

꿍

Twenty minutes later Ginny deposited a café latte on David's desk and quickly showed him a box of chocolates.

"Hey, that box is huge. What did you pay for that?"

Ginny was already out the door. "Nothing, I put it on your credit card", she called back over her shoulder.

"Get back in here and sit down", ordered David.

When Ginny was seated David pushed back his chair and folded his hands across his stomach. "I've been doing some thinking while you were out. Let's suppose that Harry did copy the letter and then sold it, as you suggested. Remember the weird call from Judy. She didn't sound frightened … it was more as if she was angry with me. There was concern, of some sort, in her voice. Do you think it's possible that the letter could have reached the Bahamas and be in the wrong hands?"

"My female intuition says exactly that!"

"How did you get there so fast?"

"Female intuition. You don't have it!"

"Obviously not. While you were out I checked my schedule. I'm considering a quick trip to Florida. Have a little chat with El Creepo."

"And you want me to come along", suggested Ginny, flirtatiously.

"The Hell I do", snapped David. Inwardly the thought excited him but he covered up as best he could. "You just hold down the fort." David could feel a blush on his face. He hoped his golf tan covered it up.

"I'll book a flight and a rental car. I still have your card in my purse", answered Ginny.

"You always have my card in your purse".

"That's just so you don't have to leave petty cash lying around the office."

"OK. Tomorrow we have court and on Monday we close that real estate deal. Things should lighten up by next Tuesday. Go ahead and book me a hotel for Tuesday night. I'll leave first thing in the morning. Bright and early. But I think I'll put the roof down and drive."

Ginny returned to her desk. David swiveled his chair to look out the window. The thought of Florida pleased him. The idea of Ginny going with him stimulated him. He knew he was getting too close to such an adorable creature and he knew his professional demeanor was cracking at the seams. If she weren't working for him he would jump at taking her on a business trip. He considered the possibilities. "Tempting… but its not going to happen", he thought.

Chapter 19

When the morning broke, the sea was calm and there was only a hint of breeze. Excitement was high. Although there was a general consensus that it was unlikely that the hull was Rebecca's ship, it was, nevertheless, an old wooden ship which mankind had lost. The four people at the breakfast table were planning to discover her story. Her name, her age, her crew and her cargo were all mysteries. The only known fact about her fate was her final resting place.

Phil had dug deep into the holds of the Zara and came up with a thousand-foot long roll of polypropylene, quarter inch rope and a bundle of tiny marker flags from a building supply store. On the first dive of the morning Farris accompanied Phil and the rope was stretched around the perimeter of the hull and measured off to form a one hundred by two hundred-foot rectangle. The balance of the rope divided the rectangle into four quadrants. Zara had towed the Zodiac out to the site and Judy and Linda maneuvered the inflatable back and forth a dozen times over the acre of water, with the video rolling and the magnetometer cranked up to it's highest reading.

Phil and Michael found new debris spread around but it was difficult to identify any of it at first glance. With their second set of tanks they selected the northwest quadrant and began a detailed search, flagging and photographing everything that was not coral. To alleviate the tedious job of crossing back and forth across the grid with the hand held magnetometers, on the third dive, Phil and Michael began measuring the exposed ribs of the sunken hull.

The bow and stern had long since vanished, either buried in the sand or drifted away. Phil suspected either the keel or ballast would hold the few visible ribs in place, although with all the sand there was no indication of either. Phil placed tiny flags on each of the ribs, numbering them carefully. Then he and Farris measured across the beam wherever they could find a pair and from one rib to the next along the length. They were almost out of air again by the time they had finished. Phil was sure they had collected enough data to estimate the approximate size of the vessel. Before surfacing they swam along the length carrying the handheld magnetometer. Close to what Phil guessed would be the bow, the handheld magnetometer began to scream. Phil looked over at Farris and they gave each other a thumbs up. A good guess would be that somewhere below a layer of sand they would discover the chain locker. If that assumption proved correct, then they had determined the bow of the ship.

Phil checked his air. He was well into the red zone. Farris was doing the same. To Hell with it! Farris took one end of the tape measure and began to swim back to the first visible rib while Phil hovered over the place where the magnetometer emitted its strongest signal. As soon as he touched the rib he dropped the tape and began to surface, blowing a steady stream of bubbles as he drifted upward. "He was low!" thought Phil. He rolled up the tape and began his climb. Michael was drifting just below the surface having changed his regulator for his snorkel. The Zara bobbed up and down a hundred yards away.

"That's it for me today. Three dives! I'm done in. Time for a beer, a sandwich and another beer!" called Farris.

"The girls will be so busy collating this data that I'm spending an hour in the hammock", answered Phil. "Come on, let's get back. This tank is starting to dig a hole in my left kidney".

Phil switched to snorkel and the two, tired divers swam slowly back to the boat.

As the two men helped each other out of their tanks Phil handed his underwater notepad to Judy.

"Wow!" she exclaimed. "This is a lot of data".

"By the way, it's forty feet from the last rib to what we think is the chain locker," said Phil.

"That gives us the bow". Judy was bubbling with excitement. Linda was more subdued.

"Hun, something wrong?" asked Farris.

"You noticed we haven't seen Ricky?" asked Linda.

"Figured he was too lazy to continue and gave up. Screw the bastard".

"Not so lucky, dear. Consider yourself as under aerial surveillance."

"No kidding. That bastard knows something. He's hanging on like a moray eel."

Phil spoke up. "I promised myself an hour in a hammock but we can't afford to break our pattern. "I'll go fishing off the beach for at least an hour this afternoon."

"Phil, I'm going to bail out this afternoon. But what I will do is go back to the beach on foot with a hand held compass. I'll take a reading from the foundation to the white rock. We keep working close to the reef but maybe the ship sank further out. Look at this hull we've been diving. We are at least a mile and a half from the anchor, and five miles off shore."

"Good point, Mike. Hey, you still want that beer?"

"You bet I do! Anyone else?"

"Everyone else", answered Judy.

❄❄

Phil awoke in the hammock on the patio. He peeled off a bandana he had worn over his eyes and looked around. He wandered into the bedroom hoping to find Judy but she was nowhere to be seen. He wandered back to the kitchen and poured himself an ice water from the cooler, sat down at the kitchen table and stared out at the ocean.

A tiny smirk appeared at the corners of his mouth. He raised his glass toasting the ocean. "To great lethargy", he said out loud.

For ten minutes he did absolutely nothing, but finally rose and wandered down to the docks. He started the engine on the Zodiac and gave it a minute to warm up before leaving harbor. The breeze invigorated him enough to turn on the computer, the magnetometer and the underwater camera.

Coordinating the GPS with the computer he began a search in a new part of the grid off Rebecca's beach. In the next hour there was no excitement at all except for one brief moment when the magnetometer howled. Phil circled back and received the same signal. He was in only twenty-five feet of water and the sun was frying him. He shut off the engine and picking up a mask and snorkel, dove overboard. Using a frog kick he dove toward the bottom enjoying the freedom of diving without restrictive wet suits and heavy tanks. It was nevertheless hard work to stay down and he blew out a mouthful of air to decrease his buoyancy.

A few feet away on the ocean floor lay what had set off the signal on the magnetometer. Encrusted with green and brown barnacles, lying on its side rested an old Mercury outboard.

Phil grinned and his mask leaked. "Someone must have been really pissed off at that engine", he thought before surfacing.

He climbed back into the Zodiac and looked back to shore. Michael was standing on the beach. He was pointing at something. Phil scanned the horizon and saw nothing. Finally he realized what Michael was doing and started the engine. Michael was pointing at the white rock although from this side it looked like any other piece of coral. When Phil was in line Michael waved his arms in acknowledgement. Phil quickly checked the compass. Three hundred and seventeen degrees. Subtract one hundred and eighty and you have one hundred and thirty seven. Phil swung the Zodiac around and after a quick wave over his shoulder puttered out along that bearing at five or so miles per hour.

At that speed he was taking about twelve minutes to cover a mile. He set his stopwatch to zero and marked a way point on the GPS. He maintained his bearing for twenty-five minutes. He was in roughly sixty feet of water, long past any outcroppings of coral close to the surface. The sun was beating down on him and he was growing sleepy in the intense heat. The magnetometer, towing along behind the

Zodiac had been as quiet as the sea it swam through. Phil switched the laptop and GPS to a Map and Track program. He swung the small craft around one hundred and eighty degrees and then began a zigzag pattern on either side of the base line, traveling a hundred yards in either direction. The magnetometer made a faint squeal and Phil punched the co-ordinates into the computer with a quick note. A few minutes later there was another minor occurrence.

It was now late afternoon and Phil was fed-up. He shut off the monitor, cranked the throttle and motored back to the harbor at full speed. Farris was on the dock with Victor and George who helped tie up the Zodiac. Victor handed Phil a beer from a pail filled with ice and Phil gratefully accepted it.

"Anything?" questioned Farris.

"A couple of blips. Oh yah, and an old Mercury."

"You found the Mercury!" exclaimed George. "Man, I was hoping that old clunker was lost forever".

Victor piped in "Deep six was too good for that engine. We probably should have buried it under the shop… 'cause that's where it spent most of it's time".

Farris interrupted. "That engine was nearly twenty years old. You told me the transom assembly broke when you were in reverse."

"Sure boss. We didn't lie. It's just that we were hitting the assembly with a ball peen hammer when it broke. That's all."

"Admittedly, it was old…. But we could have fixed it" said Farris.

"Man, we did fix it", laughed George and slapped Victor's hand.

"OK. Just don't mention this to Linda, Phil", cautioned Farris. "She won't let us throw a beer can overboard."

On the way up the stairs Phil said casually. "You're pretty close with Victor and George, aren't you?"

"We've been in a few scrapes together. If things get tough I'd trust those boys with my life. They have their own houses over the shop".

Phil was sure that "their own houses" didn't carry the legal status it would have in the USA but he felt equally confident that in Farris' mind their property rights were as secure on Normans Cay as title was on any house in New York City. Phil was glad that the element of trust ran deep between Farris and his men. What he didn't know was how soon that trust was to be tested.

⊰⊱

After supper Judy and Linda announced that they wanted to show everyone their model. Farris looked at Phil and shrugged. Linda led the way down a hallway into a small bedroom in a part of the house that Phil had never seen.

The room was free of furniture except for a computer work station and a ping pong table. On the table, glued together with a lot of scotch tape was the map of Normans spit. This map was nearly twice the size of the earlier version. It included the sea stretching out from Rebecca's beach. A square on the shore marked the ruins of the foundation and a line made with a pink highlighter stretched from the foundation, over an outcropping marked "white rock" out to sea for five miles before it reached the end of the map. There were a number of red and gold stars speckling the map which gave the display a bit of a high school science project look, but each star was carefully numbered. Another pink line started at an anchor and ended at the hull, five miles off the coast. The line did continue a bit before the anchor as a dotted line.

Judy began to describe what she and Linda had concluded. "Somewhere in this area the ship suffered serious damage. It's a good guess to assume it lost its masts or lost its steerage. Or it was taking on water so fast that the captain guessed his ship was doomed. It probably drifted to about here when the captain ordered the anchor dropped." Linda pointed to the anchor drawn on the map. "We followed the anchor chain to there", said Judy, and Linda's hand followed the path along the pink line to a small notation. It was interesting how surrounding the line were a number of the gold and red stars. You could almost feel the ship breaking up, leaving a trail of debris in its path.

Phil was a bit mesmerized by the movement of Linda's hand. On her wrist she wore one heavy gold bangle and a number of thinner, delicate ones that seemed to accent the larger one. Three of her fingers carried elaborate gold rings, each with huge rubies. Her fingernails matched the color of the rubies but there was a sprinkling of gold dust applied over the wet polish which made her entire hand glisten in the light. A simple gold thumb ring completed the ensemble. All Phil had to do was follow Linda's hand and he was sure where it stopped would be a treasure trove the likes of which no man had seen for centuries.

He caught his breath. Linda knew how to play to the crowd. He glanced up and caught Judy's eye. Judy moved around to the other side of the map.

"Either the ship was breaking apart and became disconnected from the anchor or the line was cut.

The ship drifted on and sank, there." The jeweled hand slid gracefully across the map and came to rest on the drawing of the hull. The ship's deck separated and drifted off to some place unknown. Linda's hand came off the table and she folded her arms beneath her bosom, covering the gold and rubies in the process.

So far there had been no new revelations. Still the show was entertaining. Phil noticed for the first time that both women were wearing silk blouses, different colors but both showed ample cleavage. "The girls planned this well," he thought. He nudged Michael who also seemed to be caught in a spell. "I have a feeling this is going somewhere else" he mumbled.

"Now over to Rebecca's beach". Linda turned the demonstration over to Judy.

"To date," said Judy, "we have restricted our search off Rebecca's beach to magnetometer and video from the Zodiac. Today, Michael gave us a compass reading from the foundation to the white rock. Phil followed that reading and gave us a couple of blips here and here. Linda pointed to two stars on the map. Over here we have another group of readings of debris. Now let's connect the dots. Linda picked up a yardstick from the corner of the room and lay it out, stretching from a dozen stars indicating debris, across the stars where Phil had picked up readings today. The yardstick continued past that point until it crossed the pink line about three miles off shore. Phil had motored along the pink line but not quite as far out as the intersection with the yardstick.

"There is the point where we will locate Rebecca's ship." Linda pointed with a long ruby fingernail to the intersection. Then, with a flair that would make a Hollywood producer drool, Judy reached into her own blouse and plucked a tiny, ornate pill box from between her breasts and placed it beside Linda's finger. "There is where we will find Rebecca's gold", she concluded dramatically.

For a moment there was complete silence. Then Farris began to clap his hands. Phil followed and the two men clapped as the two women bowed appreciatively.

Linda wandered over to the computer desk and plucked a piece of cloth from behind the monitor. She gracefully picked up a tray containing a bottle of red Cinzano and four glasses. She placed the liquor on the corner of the ping-pong table and poured drinks.

Phil and Michael had circled the table and were staring at the map off Rebecca's beach. Linda handed a drink to Phil and Judy but held on to Michael's. She placed it on the map itself, not far off shore.

"And that's where you are going tomorrow to pick up that outboard motor", she said directly to Michael. "And make sure Victor and George are there to help", she added.

"Busted!" said Judy, dramatically.

Farris looked at Phil.

"Sorry, Mike. I forgot to erase it from the computer."

Chapter 20

The morning was gray and overcast. Rain pelted the tin roof with the familiar tatatatatata sound. Phil and Judy lay sprawled in bed half an hour past the time they normally got up.

"I remember my parents talking about the sound of rain on the tin roof at some place they lived before I was born. I think I now understand what they were talking about. It's funny, though. I've been in farmhouses and cottages with tin roofs before when it was raining and always wondered what my parents found so magical. I didn't notice much difference from other roofs. What do you think that means? I mean, it must mean something."

Phil grunted but said nothing.

Judy poked him hard in the ribs with her elbow. "Come on, Wonder Boy. Tell me what it means".

Phil reached over and put a hand on Judy's belly. Judy sprang over top of him, straddling him and began to tickle his love handles hard, digging beneath the soft flesh to the muscle below. Phil grabbed her wrists. Judy, grinning, ground her hips into Phil's.

Judy now picked up on the Meatloaf hit saying, "Come on, boy, tell me, tell me what it means, come on". She thrust her hips down hard, throwing back her head. "I got to Know Right Now, before we go any further."

Phil was grinning. He was also getting a good view through Judy's baby doll pajamas. He rolled over, toppling Judy in the process. "Let me sleep on it", he responded. Picking up the rhythm but talking, not singing, he continued. "Baby, Baby, let me sleep on it." He put a pillow over his head and mumbled from underneath it. "Let me sleep on it, I'll give you my answer in the morning".

Judy jumped on top of him again. "I got to know right now. Before I go have a shower…" She ran out of words. Phil rolled over. They were both laughing. He reached for her but she slipped away, sprang from the bed and glided into the bathroom.

Phil rolled over and gave Judy a few minutes. When he heard the shower running he entered the bathroom and poking his head into the shower stall answered: "Insulation"

"What?"

"Insulation…. Your parents probably were in an old house with little or no insulation. That's why the sound of the rain was so much louder. We have the windows open and we hear the sound of the rain on the overhang, where there is no insulation. That's why rain sounds better in the Caribbean."

Judy was not impressed. "That's a lousy explanation…. Even if it's right. Are you coming in here or not?"

※

Phil and Judy were finished breakfast and on their second coffee when Michael entered.

"You eat yet?" asked Phil.

"About three hours ago!" answered Farris. "So what are the plans for today?"

"I've got a ton of work to do on the computer", answered Judy.

"I'm going down to the shop to build Linda her raft", interjected Farris.

"I'm going to take Zara to Rebecca's beach", answered Phil. "I'll check out the coordinates the girls gave us last night and check out a little theory of my own".

"It's pouring rain. Not the best day to go sailing", said Farris.

"What better time?" answered Phil. "It's raining, not a storm but the wind is from the east. Look, your coffeepot drift theory worked pretty well. Suppose I set up nicely off shore. Then I drift until I line up the beach on three hundred and seventeen degrees. There is probably no reason to search west of that line. That should give us a corridor where we should find the ship."

"What you're saying is that the ship started breaking up east of our coordinates?" questioned Judy.

"Right. We have debris readings there already. Let's say that your coordinates are right on and that's where the ship lies. She started to break up before she went down. By the same token if the wind was the same as today, but stronger, then the ship broke up as it moved from East to West. So, there is no point searching west of that line. At the same time as I drift west I am also being pushed up on shore. If my drift line runs close to your projected line we will end up with a neat little square in which to search. High tide will be around three o'clock. I want to drift through both the ebb and flow. Remember that Rebecca ended up on the beach… but she started on a sinking ship. If we get out too far the tide wouldn't carry her all the way in…. not with her still alive.

"Not bad thinking" remarked Farris.

"Not bad at all", said Linda.

Phil was pleased his theory had been accepted. Besides, he wanted a day off. His original plan had been to work alone, live aboard the Zara and have plenty of time to himself. Suddenly Judy had appeared. Next Michael and Linda had become almost like next of kin. Phil was happy with the outcome but he was still his old self. Today was a day for Phil to work alone, do next to nothing, and enjoy it. It was a good day to drift.

An hour later Phil was heading out of the harbor channel. In the Zodiac he would have cut right across the spit to Rebecca's beach. In the Zara this was not possible because of the coral heads. Phil would have to sail north a bit, then about five miles off shore, circle around the spit and come back in from the south-east. Going out to the anchor or the hull was a much shorter distance and Zara always motored out to that location. Phil had much further to sail today. Michael watched him from the covered portion of the patio. He was not surprised when he saw the jib begin to unfurl. There was little wind on shore but a few whitecaps indicated stronger winds at sea. Michael watched, there it was. The main sail was being hauled up.

"You had better reef it", Farris cautioned from his garden chair.

A mile away the main sail stretched taught short of the top of the mast.

"Good move", congratulated Farris. He watched for another ten minutes before putting on a jacket

and hat and jogging down the staircase to the shop
in the boathouse.

⁓⁂⁓

Phil was enjoying himself. With the main reefed
Phil felt he was under all the sail he wanted. The Zara
cut through the water making excellent time. Under
the awning Phil was staying reasonably dry although
a strong gust of wind could wreck the awning
without warning. The awning also prevented Phil
from having a constant view of the sails but there
was a certain sensibility to staying dry. The awning
stayed.

He had moved the computer equipment from
the Zodiac back to the Zara. He was beginning to
dream about having two of everything. He poured
himself a coffee, dried off the cushions on one side
of the cockpit and sat down to enjoy the sail with
the autohelm mechanism doing most of the work.
He glanced at his instruments and realized he was
already in fifty feet of water. That would be his
minimum depth for the next few hours. Having just
got comfortable he grumbled to himself, got up and
reeled out the "fish". Now he could relax and sail for
the next two hours.

It was noon. Phil climbed below and began to
prepare a can of pea soup on the alcohol stove. Judy
had made him a huge chicken sandwich. He was
cool enough to want both. The cabin felt cozy with
the heat coming off the stove. When the soup was
prepared Phil went topsides and checked the sea and
his boat before going below for his lunch. He glanced
at the nav station as he passed it. The screen showed
he was very close to where Linda had placed the

ornate little pillbox, meant to represent the treasure. The "fish" was silent.

Suddenly the winds increased and the boat heeled over. Phil grabbed for his soup and caught it in time, spilling only a bit of it. "Damn" he swore. He wolfed down three spoonfuls and a bite of sandwich and then placed the pot in the sink where it wouldn't skid. He put the sandwich back in the plastic bag and hurried topsides. The wind was turning fierce. Phil scrambled to let down the awning, which he succeeded in saving. Although he was in no immediate danger he opted to haul down the main sail. Sailing under the jib alone the boat felt immeasurably more comfortable with only a negligible difference in the speed. He was now about five miles East of Judy and Linda's coordinates. Turning Zara into the wind and began to furl the jib. He disengaged the autohelm, locked the rudder and with only a patch of sail out, let his boat drift. He punched his time and position into the computer. Zara continued to turn her nose into the wind. She was buffeted to port, back into the wind and then to port again.

Phil's plan was to ride out the storm, monitoring his drift for three hours. It was much less pleasant being tossed around by choppy seas than sailing through them. For the most part, he stayed below or stood on the companionway steps where he could keep watch from underneath the dodger. By the time his three hours were up, Phil was checking his watch every five minutes, gritting his teeth. The second his stopwatch said three hours he immediately unfurled the jib and set his course around Normans Spit. Zara responded immediately, carving through the water instead of being bounced around by it. One thing he had confirmed without doubt. For three hours he had drifted west and had closed in on Norman's Cay. The course of his drift took him directly toward Rebecca's beach. The ebb and flow of the tide had pushed him around a bit, hardly worth mentioning.

And now the wind receded to a comfortable breeze. A bit of sun poked through the clouds. Phil stripped off his clothes and put on fresh dry ones. Suddenly he felt ravenous. Some soup remained in the pot in the sink. He rejected the thought of re-heating it and flushed it down the sink, out the through-hull fitting where it immediately became fish food. He rinsed out the pot and stowed it away before checking the contents of the plastic bag. The sandwich was little worse for wear and tasted good. He up-graded his sandwich rating to damn near perfect when he was washed it down with a mouthful with rum and orange juice. He took a towel up to the cockpit and wiped everything dry. Sailing downwind with just the jib was far too pleasant to ignore. He made a twenty-degree correction to the autohelm and sat back, drink in hand to watch the late afternoon sun play on the low hills of Normans Cay.

The magnetometer had been silent during the entire drift. That meant nothing. Phil had shut off the volume, immediately after passing Judy's pillbox co-ordinates. The system he and Judy developed recorded every blip automatically. The only difference of having it on manual was that one could add notes. He considered checking the computer for the day's activity but declined, preferring his current state of inactivity. The Zara, the late afternoon sun, the rum and orange juice and the gentle Caribbean breeze worked their soothing magic. Phil checked his watch. He would be back in harbor right at sunset. This was the way he had pictured hunting for treasure. It had been good to go out alone, today. It would also be good to tell the rest of the party about today's work. Phil could not remember a time in his life when he felt more satisfied.

Chapter 21

The day of sitting around the house had been therapeutic for Judy as well. Linda had joined her in the morning for a workout in the well equipped gym but after lunch Judy had gone into her room with a novel and read as the rain pattered on the roof. Now, supper over, and the weather once again perfect, she wandered down to the boat just to stretch her legs.

Without thinking she climbed aboard and opened the main hatch. Phil had mentioned that he had sailed over her pillbox co-ordinates but had shut the volume off following that. Judy turned on the computer. She entered the program she had written and entered today's date. Immediately a new screen appeared.

12 Low Level Magnetometer Readings
17 Medium Level Magnetometer Readings
21 High Level Magnetometer Readings
50 Total number of magnetometer readings
"Holy Shit!" Judy exclaimed, out loud.
She began typing furiously.

A large map that extended about ten miles in either direction appeared. There was a button at the top of the screen labeled Map and Track. Judy clicked on that button and a yellow line appeared against the blue background of the map, showing the course of Phil's journey.

Judy moved her mouse to the top of the screen and typed in her pillbox co-ordinates. A small mark appeared just a hair off the yellow line. She moved the cursor back to the top of the screen and clicked on the icon for the magnetometer.

Fifty tiny crosses appeared. Twelve were purple, seventeen were red and twenty-one was green. Only three were along the course Phil had sailed out on and each of those was a low-level reading.

Forty-seven readings appeared in a cluster less than half a mile from Judy's pillbox co-ordinates.

"I can't believe you had the volume off."

Judy hammered on the keys. A screen came up listing the sightings and giving the exact time of each blip. Phil had crossed over an area Judy was already naming "the motherlode" for a period of twenty seven minutes from the first hit to the last. The first hit had taken place at one eleven PM. Judy turned on the second computer whose sole purpose was that of a DVD player, interfaced with magnetometer readings. Judy typed in today's date and one eleven PM. It was after ten minutes of watching seabed and seeing absolutely nothing, despite an indicator that the magnetometer had picked up metal, that Judy witnessed something she had only dreamed of ever seeing. Rebecca's ship, it had to be Rebecca's ship, rested on the bottom, right side up, leaning to starboard. Judy stared at the screen as Zara passed over the wreckage. When she could see only seabed again she re-entered the time and replayed the video.

Judy stood up, dazed. What should she do? She was positive she had found Rebecca's gold. The next thing that happened took her completely by surprise. Gold fever set in. Judy paced around the cabin thinking, "It's mine... all mine!" She justified it to herself. It was her map. She had developed the computer programs. Phil would never have discovered anything with his primitive equipment. Michael and Linda were just taggers-on. Judy had, within her grasp, enough money to last her forever. All she had to do was store the data on disk and erase today's findings. "Funny" she thought. "I even built in a security system that allowed me and only me the privilege of deleting information. I have the password. No one else even knows I can do that! Not Phil, not Michael. They don't even know computers. Linda could probably find the program but without the password she could never activate it."

The clouds in her mind began to clear. Phil, Michael, Linda. She had to tell them at once. They were all partners.

It was Phil's accordion shaving mirror that saved her sanity. Judy saw herself in the mirror. Her face was twisted and wrinkles showed in her forehead. "Oh my God" she stammered. "What have I been thinking?" Judy spun around to the nav station. Her hand shot forward.

The movie was just reaching its climax. Linda had gone off to bed fifteen minutes ago and Phil and Michael reclined in Lazy-Boy chairs sipping drinks and munching on peanuts when the sound of an ocean liner exploded in the harbor.

"What the Hell!" shouted Farris over the drone of the horn.

Phil was on his feet, knocking over his drink and the peanuts. "Zara" was all he said as he bolted for the door. He raced across the patio and down the stairs to the dock. Michael was only a few feet behind him. As Phil raced toward Zara he saw the door open in the boathouse. The harbor exploded with lights. Victor and George came out of the doorway. They were both carrying something. The sound of the fog horn had ceased. Judy was poking her head out of the main hatch. She was grinning sheepishly. Phil slowed up as he reached the boat and saw nothing wrong. Farris stopped at the beginning of the finger dock surveying the harbor. Linda was in a bathrobe and half way down the stairs. Victor and George stood halfway between Farris and the boathouse. They too were staring into the well-lit harbor. Both carried short barreled automatic weapons, slung over their shoulders. Judy had not noticed Victor and George, or the sub machine guns.

"Sorry, didn't know it was so loud. You guy's have to see this. Hurry", she exclaimed excitedly.

For a second everyone stood still. Michael looked behind him and saw Linda glaring at him from the stairs. Quickly he motioned for Victor and George to put away their weapons and turn off the security lights. Phil looked over and saw the guns for the first time. Judy seemed in a daze, oblivious to every thing that was going on around her. She ducked back into the cabin. Phil looked back at Farris and shrugged. He called to Linda. "Judy has something to show us. It must be important."

Linda wrapped her robe tightly around her body. Phil climbed on board. Michael waited for Linda. Linda was fuming. As she approached Michael he lifted his arm so that Linda could link her arm in his. It was a gesture he wished he had never made. Linda's hand shot out and gave Farris a sharp upper cut in his left kidney.

"This is my house too and if I ever see machine guns on my dock again it will be the last you sleep with me for a good long time!"

Farris swallowed both his pain and his pride and quietly led Linda toward the Zara. As they entered the cabin Phil looked over and saw Michael's shirt had blood on it.

"Hey Pal, you're bleeding", said Phil.

"I caught the table as we left the TV room", lied Farris.

Linda looked down at her right hand. She was wearing her ruby ring. She caught Michael's eye and mouthed "Sorry" behind the backs of Phil and Judy who were hunched over the computer.

Chapter 22

Four people sat at the breakfast table.

"You start," said Farris, nodding at Judy.

"OK," she paused. "We found it…. At least we think we did. Let's explore it, pick up the gold and come back home…. I mean here… and celebrate! Simple, right!"

"Phil".

"First we have to explore the ship. It may take a sand pump…. That's almost a given… to retrieve the gold. And we don't know if there are any other goodies aboard. The flicks show a pretty reasonable hull, but it may be hanging together by a thread. We have a GPS position, so it shouldn't take long to find it. If we have what we think we have, its time to take some security measures. We agree that we don't want to advertise this operation."

"Linda, what about you?"

"I haven't dwelled on it but I believe we are under surveillance. At first we had Ricky with his sport fisherman, every day. Then just the sport fisherman. Now, for nearly a month there has been nothing."

"So what's the problem?"

Linda surveyed the room making contact with each pair of eyes. "Nothing except that damn plane that has flown over here two or three times a day, watching our every move. Ever notice how he always turns counter clockwise. That's so he gets a good look out the pilot's window. Besides, I recognize the plane. The owner is an old US navy pilot. He may have a pension but it would hardly support his bar bill. He couldn't afford to fly over here as often as he does unless someone, say Ricky, was paying him to spy."

"Could he be taking out tourists or student pilots?" asked Phil.

"Sorry, luv. I asked around the hanger. He always goes out alone. Funny, huh."

"Mike, it's your turn", said Phil.

"I say no advertising. First let's find out what we have. Then we deal with that. In the mean time I suggest we continue to dive the number one site. Just to keep Ricky, or some hot shot government taxman, off target."

"It's your decision, Phil", said Michael.

"I count three to one against moving too quickly. Sorry Jude. We are going to go slower and quieter. I think we should keep up the diversion on site One."

"No problem …I can fight gold fever with hard reason", grinned Judy. "Owe, ooh, uugh… Take that!" Her little pantomime made everyone grin. "OK under control."

"Good eyes, Linda", thanked Phil.

ঞ্জ

Phil was warming up the diesel and filling the scuba tanks onboard the Zara. Farris casually slipped inside the boathouse. He walked through the side door that connected the boathouse to the house where Victor and George lived. Victor was reading the news on the Internet and George was sitting at the kitchen table playing with a digital camera.

"Yoh, Mike. Wha' happen, mon", said George.

Victor looked around. When he saw Michael he moved from the computer to the table. Mike sat down.

"Has there been anything unusual lately?" he asked.

"No, boss. Some tourists. We gassed up at Highbourne, yesterday. Everything was cool."

"Ever look up", asked Farris, casually lifting one finger off the table.

"I looked up an angel the last time I was in Nassau", said George. "She looked fine from underneath".

Farris and Victor pointedly ignored George.

"No, boss. Not any more", answered Victor seriously.

"Time to start, again."

"What are we looking for?" asked George. George liked to goof around but when it was called for he was all business.

"Some ex-navy fly boy from Nassau. Linda knows him from the airport. See if you can find out whom he's working for. Quietly."

"No problem. Say, how's the treasure hunt?" asked Victor, grinning.

"Fun."

"No shit!"

"Honest, Vic." Farris was already getting up to leave. "Be kind to that angel, George."

"If he was kind he'd have to tear up her number and set her free!" said Victor as Michael left the house.

☙❧

Phil and Michael motored out to the Number One Site. They dove for forty-five minutes with hand held magnetometers, criss-crossing the grids laid out with the rope. They found a bit of junk but what was needed next was to blow away some of the sand that buried the wreck.

"I've been thinking," said Phil as they rested in the cockpit and drank some bottled water. "Suppose that we can extract the gold from Rebecca's ship. If we blow the sand out of this wreck and find nothing we have pretty good cover from both Ricky and the tax man."

"You mean report this wreck? Do it by the book? That's not a bad idea. I bet the girls would go for that!"

"I would want to be sure about the gold first", clarified Phil. "Let's not stake a claim here until Rebecca's ship is emptied.

"Makes sense."

"Furthermore I'm not real keen on the four of us being out over Rebecca's ship, this afternoon. If we are being watched from the sky four of us would be a dead give away."

"Suppose we took out one of the cigarette boats instead of the inflatable. It would look more like a party than a diving trip. Especially with Linda's rig in tow. We could even bring a sea-doo. Hell, I have a patio style umbrella that we could rig up."

"OK, this sounds like a plan. Just fun in the sun. With an umbrella up no one will even suspect that half the party is underwater." Phil was satisfied this was an adequate diversion.

"Speak of the devil" said Farris cocking his ear and hearing the drone of an aircraft. "There he is at ten o'clock. Do you want to stay here or move?"

"Let's stay put. We'll play up these co-ordinates and hide the other ones."

⊰⊱

The pilot took off his radio headset and replaced it with a cell phone headset. He called Ricky and reported in.

"They are in exactly the same location again. Two men diving, no women. They must be over something because they keep coming back to the same spot."

Ricky spat out a string of curses. "I'm sending divers this afternoon. I'll find out what's so fucking exciting about that piss-ant piece of the sea." He clicked off without the courtesy of saying goodbye.

"Asshole", said the pilot as he closed the connection. This had been a strange assignment but the pay was good so who cared about an SOB like Ricky. In the navy he had taken orders from lots of people he didn't like, he rationalized. But he had watched Linda take off and land and heard her on the radio. She had even given him an old set of tie down straps that were in almost perfect shape. She was a good pilot, and coming from him that meant a damn good pilot. For that reason alone he hated spying on her. Not enough to stop…. He just hated to do it, especially for someone like Ricky.

⊰⊱

Ricky wasted no time in rounding up four men and four divers for the afternoon. Something made Michael Farris go back to the same spot day after day and Ricky needed to know what it was. He was confused by the events. He re-counted the course of events.

"I had bought the letter from a cokehead, Harry Gibson. He got it through a nigger, Prince, who had been a reliable dealer, even if he was black. The letter led him right onto the doorstep of Normans Cay. That was bad! It smelled of a set-up! He had sent Gino to the States to check out Gibson's source for the letter. Gibson had lied about the source. His mother collected old stuff but the letter wasn't in her collection. That meant Gibson got the letter from the lawyer. Why? Then all the diving activity was indicating the letter was *real*".

Ricky had not yet given orders to Gino to take care of Gibson. Gino had had a grand old time with his friends in Florida, at Ricky's expense. Now, at least, he would be back tonight. Nothing added up! Perhaps this afternoon would shed some light on the situation.

⊰⊱

At two thirty PM, one of Normans Cay's cigarette boats was stationed exactly over the GPS co-ordinates for Rebecca's ship. Scuba gear hung six feet below the water line. Linda's dive bed floated on a tether and Phil, who had followed the cigarette boat out, showing off by playing in Michael's wake on a powerful sea-doo, was preparing to dive. Adding to the "tourist" look was a large, colorful umbrella over the cockpit of the cigarette boat. The umbrella made it impossible for aerial surveillance to verify anything.

Phil and Michael made the first dive. Linda watched from her floating bed. Judy tried to sit and wait in the cockpit but finally put on a mask and snorkel, dove off the stern and surfaced from under Linda. The men had swum out of sight and Linda was glad for the company. Judy had less patience.

"We are within a few hundred feet. I'll circle the cigarette boat. You can stay here in the bed."

"Are you crazy? You want me to water ski around behind a thousand horsepower boat", demanded Linda. "Not on your sweet life!"

Judy grinned. First Linda lying on a giant floaty with her face in the water constituted diving. Now she was calling being towed at idle speed "water skiing".

"No water skiing. I won't go faster than one mile an hour. I promise", returned Judy. "Besides, you have to tell me when you see the wreck."

"Are you sure you can drive that monster", asked Linda.

At that Judy snapped back, "Are you sure you can fly a plane, all alone, honey".

Linda's face hardened. Judy saw the strength and determination that Linda strove to hide most of the time. "Sorry Jude, but for Christ's sake toss me another life jacket. This is the closest thing to water skiing I've ever done."

Judy softened. "I promise I'll just idle. If you keep your face in the water and snorkel along, you are going to see Rebecca's ship before me and maybe even before the men".

"OK. Go ahead. But don't forget the life jacket. Two, if you think it would work better." She smiled weakly.

Judy swam back to the boat and Linda thought, "I wish I could swim like that." Then it dawned on her. She had never wished she could swim before. She had never dreamed that she would ever "want" to swim.

Forty feet below Phil and Michael were startled by the sound of the boat starting but decided to continue a sweep around in a circle, a couple of hundred feet from the anchor. The bottom was at sixty feet but the sea was still a bit murky from the storm and visibility was less than a hundred feet.

Judy touched the switch for the windlass and as the boat was towed over the anchor Linda got her first taste of water skiing. She was wearing a life jacket over a thin neoprene "shorty" suit that Michael had dug up in the boathouse. She wondered if she would float if she did fall in. "I'd have to", she rationalized, "wouldn't I?" She placed the mask over her face and the snorkel in her mouth. She waved apprehensively at Judy and put her face in the water. The bottom was gliding by. She could see it clearly. There were fish, and rocks and coral. Everything took on a greenish hue, less colorful than shallow water but not less beautiful. She watched, fascinated as the boat was pulled directly over the anchor by the windlass and amazed how the anchor lifted off the bottom, stirring up a cloud of sand, and rose to the surface. She heard the change in the motors as Judy eased the powerful engines into gear. The speed picked up. The motors were on idle but to Linda they were cruising at the speed of light. She took a gulp of air. She had instinctively been holding her breath. There was a slight tug on her mask as she was towed along. She took a few more breaths. If she wasn't so frightened she knew she would be enjoying herself.

Then she saw it. A hull, or part of it. It was just like the video but different. This was no movie. It was real. Linda was the first person to see Rebecca's ship in two hundred years. They had almost passed the hull when Linda remembered what she was supposed to do. She sat up in her floating bed and waved frantically to Judy. Judy immediately released the anchor and it sank to the bottom landing thirty feet off one end of Rebecca's ship. The cigarette boat drifted back and settled directly over one end of the sunken vessel. Linda was startled when Judy revved the engines, just a bit, but then she shut them down and silence prevailed. Linda was studying Rebecca's ship when Phil and her husband appeared from stage right, swimming into her field of vision. They stopped to wave. Linda put her hand in the water and waved back. Michael swam directly underneath her and deflated his buoyancy device. Linda watched as the bubble rose toward her but was shocked by their cold temperature and jerked her face out of the water as the bubbles hit her. She recovered quickly and put her face back in. She shook her fist at Michael but he signaled back to her first pointing at himself, then making an L sign with his finger and thumb and then pointing at Linda. It took a second to register. "I love you". Linda felt herself blush. She signaled back in the same actions finishing with two fingers. "I love you 2". Michael waved and followed Phil over the bones of Rebecca's ship.

The sight was amazing. At least two thirds of the ship remained visible. It was impossible, though, to tell the bow from the stern. Most of the ship's upper deck had disappeared. Some of it had it broken off and drifted away, the rest had caved in? One side had crumbled away but the other side appeared in tact though pieces of the copper sheeting had fallen away. There was no sign of masts or rigging. The ship must have sunk quickly, dragged below by its own keel and ballast. Entering the ship would be dangerous. What remained could easily crumble at the touch of a feather. It was like a house of cards. Phil unclipped a camera and began to photograph every aspect of the wreck that caught his attention, no matter how trivial.

Michael poked around trying to determine how best to enter the wreck. He poked around what he thought was mid ship and entered a small cave, covered by timbers, but only far enough to turn around. He had no light. The interior of the ship had not experienced light in two hundred years. He swam over top of the hull and over the rail. Funny, the opposite rail was gone completely. He wondered why. There was a large area where the copper had fallen off. Taking his divers knife from its holster on his leg he poked it at the exposed planking. The plank crumbled with just a gentle push. He made the hole a bit bigger. It would be easy to enter the hold from this direction.

He swam toward one end. There was damage here, and a good deal of sand had accumulated burying the ship. There was an odd shape protruding from the bottom not far from the ship's side. Michael swam toward it, studied it for a minute then poked at it with his knife. He pried off a handful of barnacles and found rust. He dug a bit of sand away. Suddenly he knew what he had discovered. It was a fulfillment of a childish boyhood dream, as valuable as any gold could ever be. He swam up on deck and found Phil photographing everything. He pulled Phil's arm indicating for Phil to follow. He raced over the end of the wreckage and toward his discovery with Phil ten feet behind. When he got to it he proudly displayed it like a vacuum cleaner salesman showing off his wares. Phil hesitated for a minute, studied it. He made hand signals pretending he was lighting a match. He mimed setting fire to something and swung his arm in an arc suddenly opening his clenched fist at the end of the arc. Farris grinned and his mask leaked. He nodded violently. Then he pretended someone had punched him in the stomach. The clown at the circus who is shot by the cannon. Phil indicated a "photo op" and Farris proudly accepted.

On the surface Judy and Linda watched. Linda from her floating bed and Judy snorkeling nearby. Judy gave Linda a "thumbs up" and the both raised their faces from the water.

"They're acting like idiots. Can you see what it's all about", asked Judy.

"Maybe they have *Rapture of the Deep*". Linda wasn't exactly sure what that meant, though.

"More like *Rapture of the Depraved*. They aren't deep enough for "Nitrogen Narcosis". I think they may just be idiots". She poked her head back under water. "They're coming up. Let's get back in the boat."

Phil and Michael took off their tanks underwater and hung them on the ropes hanging off the boat. When they surfaced any observer would have said they were only fooling around on the surface.

"What made you guys act so strange down there?" asked Linda.

"Nothing Babe, just furniture shopping. Got a nice piece for the patio".

"What the Hell are you talking about", demanded Judy.

Phil began to repeat his mime but as he followed the arc of his hand with his eyes he stopped abruptly.

"I repeat. What the Hell is that!"

Farris looked at Phil for permission to explain but found him staring at the spit.

Ricky's boat lay exactly where Phil and Farris had been that morning. Farris grabbed a pair of binoculars and studied the scene. "Divers going overboard", he reported without lowering the glasses. "I think we should get over there right away".

"Plan B", said Phil. "We get into Nassau immediately and hire a sand pump. What we need now is a diversion. This is Rebecca's ship. I'm willing to bet on that. If they find the other ship, so what? It will end up working in our favor".

"Not bad thinking, Phil. Not bad at all! But they found it all right. They can't miss all that polypropylene rope. For sure they have a radar fix on where we've been."

"To bad your patio furniture wasn't delivered yet", said Phil.

"You can say that again", replied Farris.

Linda cut in. "Enough is enough. What is all this talk of patio furniture?"

"One day soon, Little Darling, we are going to be defending our harbor with true "canon power".

"You found a canon … that's great!" said Judy. She looked at Linda. "Isn't it?"

"Its OK, I guess. Why is it men love guns so much?"

Farris looked at Phil and answered, "Lots of power".

Phil replied, "Lots of noise". He repeated his mime. "That was a cannon ball being shot from a bronze cannon. Hence, Michael's new patio furniture".

"Oh Baby. I'm happy. I really am. It's great!" cooed Linda. "We can put flowers around it. It will be beautiful".

They both shrugged at Linda's lack of understanding then hurried to bring up the tanks and lift Linda's dive-bed on top of the motor cowling. Farris maneuvered the powerful boat through the spit at a minimum of thirty miles an hour. "High tide

… it's pretty safe", he acknowledged when he saw Phil's nervousness.

It took less than an hour to shower off the salt, pack overnight bags and climb into Linda's plane. Ricky had left the area half an hour earlier.

Part Two

Chapter 23

At one time the harbor had been a shallow tidal reservoir and spawning ground, with a sand and coral bottom and plenty of sea grass, for food and protection. Eggs hatched and young sea life learned the game of hide and seek. It was the games original version. Hide from anything bigger and seek food. Before long, the youngest sea life grew up and became strong enough to catch an outgoing tide and enter the deeper water of the channel. Some of it followed the channel to Exuma Sound or other exotic parts of the Caribbean. The odd creature found its way beyond the sea to the Atlantic Ocean.

One day someone rowed their old wooden dory into the inlet and beached it on a patch of sandy shore. The inlet was easy enough to enter during high tide and safe in the event of a storm. Others joined him and soon, a small community of oared fishing boats developed. Years later, after countless discussions and still placing bets on the outcome, a pair of men planted dynamite in the coral breakwater during low tide. A half a dozen explosions later, a trench, accessible at both high and low tide was cut through the barrier.

Larger boats began to use the reservoir. More dynamite was set off. A dredge was employed. More dynamite. The dredgings were piled along the shoreline and stone retaining walls were built from the coral chunks. At first the piers were wooden, then they were replaced with steel. The new steel pilings were strong and easy to work with but after a short period, rusty and flaky. Nevertheless, as rusty as they were, they seemed to last forever …almost forever. The next generation wanted to dredge the harbor more, anyway. New steel piles were driven in, adjacent to the old ones. Concrete was poured, garbage accumulated on the shoreline. Conch divers cleaned their catch and thousands of conch shells added to the land fill that surrounded the man-made harbor. A couple of buildings were built. More clutter accumulated. It too became part of the land fill. The shoddy buildings could not survive the salty air. They were abandoned but new ones sprang up.

Two trees desperately clung to life on the piece of ground at the extreme end of the harbor that Steven Ray called home. The remainder of the space was piles of scrap steel and old machinery. Off the back end of one of the warehouse structures was a two room cement block, shack, rugged on the outside but surprisingly clean and cheerful within.

A burly, heavyset black man with arms that looked like tree trunks, closed the door to his home and padlocked it shut. He trudged up a rusty, oily path toward the streets of Nassau with the walk of a man who preferred a rolling deck to solid ground. His mother had named him Steven Ray although she had been the only one he could ever remember calling him by that name. Someone else had called him Sting Ray as a child. Perhaps it was a pet name his father had used.

Regardless, the name had stuck. Now middle aged and owner of a marine tugboat and salvage yard no one knew him by any name other than Sting Ray.

He turned another corner onto a pleasant secondary street. It was off the main drag by a block. Just far enough off the main traffic flow, that the street was part of the black community. White people were welcome and well treated. Somehow, though, white people preferred the main drag, a block away.

Halfway down the block was an attractive restaurant and bar named The Coconut Tree. The establishment derived its name from a large, healthy coconut palm that stood in the center of the property. A well built roof structure cantilevered out on all sides from this solid tree, protecting the center of the courtyard from the rain. The perimeter of the courtyard was either an eight-foot high, cement block wall, or a hodge podge of small, narrow buildings, each of which had a single purpose. The bar, the kitchen, a storage building and the washrooms in the corner. The entrance doors to the washrooms were screened by another block wall. The cement walls were painted a light blue, the roofs were red and doors and trim were a myriad of bright, friendly, tropical colors. The front of the property, facing the road, was a stone wall extending down to the sidewalk. The entire property was elevated about three feet above the road so that the small patio overlooked the street. The patio ended at the bar. That was as far back as most white folk ventured. The bar, on the right hand side, with a large overhanging roof, protected another grouping of tables. The small kitchen, opposite, on the left, helped form an isthmus beyond which lay the main courtyard with its namesake, the coconut tree, standing proudly in the middle. There was no one on the patio, a couple of people sat at the bar, but the courtyard was half full of small groups of black men, drinking rum and beer, laughing and enjoying the last daylight of the late afternoon. There was a noisy game of dominos going on in the back corner.

Sting Ray climbed the five steps to the patio and walked through the isthmus joining a group of six already seated at a round table beneath the cantilevered roof. He was greeted with a chorus of mumbled "Wha' happen, mon?"

A half minute later he was seated and a bottle of beer was placed before him by strikingly beautiful black woman of twenty-nine or thirty. She was wearing skin-tight designer blue jeans with openings in the legs held together with a lattice work of denim. A colorful silk blouse, knotted at her waist and unbuttoned low at the neckline, showed the curves of her body. Her black, curly hair hung to her shoulders. Red highlights caught the late day sun. Her smile was perfection, all white teeth and dimples and her voice had a sexy, throaty sound that purred out her Bahamian accent.

As she bent over to place the beer on the table, Sting Ray caught the scent of her perfume.

"There you go Sting Ray", she said in a low voice that made Sting Ray feel as if he was the only man in the world and this beauty was talking to him alone.

"Well, Samantha, thank you, but maybe I didn't come here for a beer this afternoon," he answered cordially.

Samantha straightened, crossed her arms beneath her shapely breasts and responded seriously, "Well then, what did you come here for?"

"Darling, I didn't come here for a beer, because, I came here to ask you to marry me."

Sting Ray's statement was met with a chorus of "oohs" and "awes". He was not looking at the beautiful woman but staring into space, across the table, a contemplative expression on his face as he waited for her answer.

Samantha was silent for a long ten seconds. Every eye in the bar was glued to her. No one moved, waiting to hear her reply. Slowly and gracefully, she sat down on Sting Ray's lap, put her arms around his neck and pulling his head forward planted a wet kiss on his balding forehead. Sting Ray's nose was inches from her cleavage and her perfume overwhelmed him with its musk fragrance. She shook her shoulders, just enough to move her breasts before straightening her arms and holding his face at arm's length, staring into his eyes.

"Sting, Baby, you know you old enough fo' me". She paused dramatically. There were a few groans from the bystanders. "And Lord knows you pretty enough fo' me." She paused again while a second, louder series of groans subsided. "But Sugar, you just ain't rich enough fo' me."

With that she stood up and hips swaying strode back to the bar to loud laughter and applause from the entire bar. There was an old black gentleman sitting at the end of the bar sipping a rum and water. Samantha took his glass and topped up his drink from a bottle she kept under the bar. Drinks from that bottle were on the house.

Sting Ray reached for his beer and downed half of it in a single gulp.

As the sun set, the men bantered back and forth, drinking and enjoying life. Occasionally they questioned how Samantha could have said the burly, balding, overweight tug boat operator could possibly be "pretty enough for her".

Just before seven o'clock a white limousine pulled up directly in front of the patio. Four well-dressed men stepped out and climbed the stone steps. From behind the bar Samantha straightened involuntarily. Her face hardened. One man seemed to be leading the way, the other two were a step behind, forming a wedge. The fourth man, following two steps behind, was Ricky. Drug lords did not frequent "The Coconut Tree". An eerie silence swept through the bar as the phalanx of evil marched through. The wrong place at the wrong time. Fear. The four men, dressed like modern day Al Capones, proceeded directly to Sting Ray's table. The point man zeroed in on the tugboat operator, then nodded at Ricky.

"The boss wants to talk with you", said the point man.

Sting Ray's eyes drifted around the courtyard, now silent, and settled on an empty table in a corner by the storeroom. Without speaking he got up and moved over to that table. Ricky and his men followed.

Behind the bar Samantha was regaining her composure. There was a small mirror on a post. She puffed up her hair. Reaching for her perfume she added fresh squirt from an atomizer bottle. Demurely, she loosened an extra button on her blouse. Loading a tray with five Heinekens, hips swaying, she strutted to Ricky's table.

"Heineken OK, or would you gentlemen like something else?" She purred out the word "gentlemen".

Ricky looked up. So did the rest of his party. As much as Ricky hated blacks he viewed Samantha as a choice specimen. "Heineken's fine."

Samantha passed the beer around but made a point of stretching over Ricky's body, giving him a bird's eye view of her breasts, and a sniff of her perfume. Her hand brushed his shoulder as she turned back to the bar.

"I think she likes you, boss", one of the bodyguards said.

"Fucking nigger bitch!" muttered Ricky.

Sting Ray felt his heart surge with intense hatred as he heard the crude comment, but his face remained fixed in deadpan.

Back at the bar Samantha put down her tray and nodded to her helper. She circled the courtyard ignoring drink orders and entered the storeroom from the far end. She moved quickly between the cases of drinks and empties to a small table and chair at the end opposite the door. This was her desk where she sat at when ordering supplies or paying bills. Without hesitation she climbed on the table and stood up. She was directly behind Sting Ray's chair. She could hear every word through the open soffit.

One of Ricky's men explained to Sting Ray that Ricky required a boat equipped with a sand pump to clean out a shipwreck. He wanted Sting Ray tomorrow. Sting said "No, next week".

The same man spoke again. Ricky would not lower himself to negotiate with a black man.

"We'll pay you double your daily rate but be at our dock at seven o'clock or don't plan on having a next week."

That was the end of negotiations. Samantha climbed down from her table and hurried around the courtyard back to the bar. On the way out one of Ricky's men slapped a fifty-dollar American bill on the bar and waited for change. Samantha hesitated, ignoring the money, and pretended to wipe off the bar. The money covered the beer and tip by more than double but Samantha wiped around it, smiled sweetly and began to talk to Ricky's bodyguard. The man glanced toward the limo and realized Ricky was already climbing in. He glared at Samantha and leaving the money on the bar, hurried away so as not to keep Ricky waiting.

Samantha then did a strange thing. She reached for her purse, took out some red lipstick and marked the bill with an "X" before jamming it her pocket. Only the old man at the bar observed the unusual occurrence.

Linda had driven them from the airport to the hotel in her Grand Cherokee. The foursome settled into their rooms and met a bit later for an exquisite supper of steak and lobster. The girls decided to test their luck in the casino while Phil and Michael went off in search of a sand pump.

Michael knew where Sting Ray's wharf was. They found a road leading in but it was barred with a heavy chain. Leaving the Grand Cherokee outside the gate they walked into the boat yard. There was only one small light bulb serving as a yard light but it lit up the area enough to determine where Sting Ray lived. There was a padlock on his door.

"Either he's not home or he climbed in through a window. Should we knock?" joked Phil.

"Sting Ray might have fit through that window about twenty tears ago", laughed Farris. "That's his tug, he won't have gone far. Let's leave it until morning."

They wandered back toward their jeep, prepared to go back to the hotel and try their own luck at the tables. A young kid, about twelve, was leaning against the bumper.

"Sting Ray's not home", he stated.

"So we discovered. Know where he is?" asked Phil.

"Over at The Coconut Tree."

"Where's that?" asked Farris.

"Just around the corner. I'll watch your car for you if you want to see him."

"Sure, hop in" said Phil, ignoring Michael's nasty look.

The kid climbed in and immediately began to play with the power windows. When they were parked and the jeep locked, Phil gave the kid ten dollars. His eyes lit up.

They climbed the stairs and walked directly to the bar. Samantha looked up. Tonight was full of surprises. First Ricky and his thugs, now a couple of decent looking white men.

"Excuse me, we're looking for Sting Ray", said Farris, politely.

"He's in there, around the corner, on the left. What can I bring you?"

"Two Heinekens and whatever Sting Ray's drinking, please," answered Phil.

Sting Ray had not joined his cronies but continued to sit alone. He drank his beer plus another one that Ricky hadn't touched. He knew who Ricky was and wanted nothing to do with him. He also wanted to stay alive.

When Farris pulled up a chair beside him and Phil came around the table to the other side he looked up, surprised. "Mr. Farris. It's good to see you. Long time, mon. How's that dock holding up?"

Sting Ray had driven in new piles, welded up the steel frame, and built the dock on Normans Cay for Michael Farris, ten years earlier. Farris had paid him promptly with a small bonus for a good job. Sting Ray never forgot him.

Samantha arrived with three beers.

"I'm looking for a tug boat with a sand pump, Sting Ray", offered Farris.

"Christ" muttered Sting Ray. "You and everyone else in Nassau. Ricky was here an hour ago. I'm supposed to be at his dock at seven tomorrow morning or settle my affairs before next week."

Samantha placed the beer on the table and quickly circled around to the store room door.

Phil looked at Farris but Farris ignored him.

"Did Ricky say anything else?"

"He didn't say nothin' 'cept calling Samantha "a fucking nigger bitch". One of his dogs tol' me what he wanted … the sand pump and all."

On the table, behind the wall, Samantha was fuming. "He called me what?" she whispered.

"Why is everyone looking for a pump all of a sudden?" asked Sting Ray.

"It seems we have a treasure hunt in progress", answered Phil.

"Oh, so that's what it is. Mr. Farris, you know I'd rather work fo' you but I got a business. If I don't show up tomorrow I'm likely to have a sunken boat and a yard full of ashes. That's if I'm still alive."

"That's OK, Sting Ray. We'll still need you in a couple of weeks. Ricky will be finished with you by then. Don't count on striking it rich while you're on Ricky's payroll", warned Farris.

"If the two of you are after the same thing I could arrange to slow down that Italian blood clot. You know, burn out a bearing on the pump, or something."

"That won't be necessary, Sting Ray. You just appear to co-operate. We'll provide whatever we need to slow down the job." Farris glanced at Phil who steadfastly returned his gaze. "I appreciate your offer, though."

Samantha climbed down, straightened her clothes. She left the store-room and wandered back to the bar, taking an order on the way. Sting Ray seemed to know one of the two white men and somehow this was connected to Ricky. What did they mean by a treasure hunt. Was that code for a drug deal? Samantha was determined to discover the nature of this unusual business. As she prepared the order she looked over at the old man sitting at the end of the bar.

"Kingsley, you know who those white men are?"

He beckoned her closer and almost whispering said, "Sure do know one of them. That's Michael Farris from Normans Cay. Don't know the other".

"Normans Cay! What the Hell is going on?" responded Samantha.

"None of my business and none of yours either".

"It is too my business and you know why."

"Sammy, you put those thoughts out of your mind right now, hear?"

"Uunh, uunh. Not this time." Samantha changed her tone of voice. "Kingsley, tomorrow I'm going to be at your beach at sunrise." She reached into her pocket and withdrew a bundle of Bahamian money, neatly folded in half. She peeled off a hundred dollars and gave it to the old man. "That's for fuel".

"No Sammy, don't do this, child". He pushed the money back at her.

"Either you take me or I'll get someone else." She smiled sweetly. "Come on, you know you need the money."

"Yes, you would get someone else", pondered the old man. "Someone young and stupid who might just get you killed. OK. I'll do it, but I don't feel good about it." The old man climbed down from the barstool, reluctantly took the money and left the bar, grumbling to himself.

ಭಿ

At five o'clock, after only a couple of hours of sleep, Samantha rose, showered, and entered her kitchen. She made a large pot of coffee and poured herself a cup. The balance she dumped into a thermos bottle. She made half a dozen sandwiches of tinned ham and chicken and wrapped them in foil wrap. She collected a variety of fresh fruit from her counter and put the entire package into a soft straw bag. As an afterthought she took a half bottle of Rum.

She arrived at the beach in the pre-dawn. There was Kingsley, already rowing an old dinghy to shore from the decrepit wooden Bahamian fishing boat that he called home.

As the dinghy touched the beach, Samantha plunked her straw bag into the bow gave the boat a strong shove, stepped in, and sat down. Kingsley pulled on the oars and the boat swung neatly around. They headed out to the fishing boat.

"I brought coffee," said Samantha.

"Coffee, that's good. I haven't had a coffee in the last month", answered the old man.

"I brought rum too."

"That's good. I haven't had a rum since last night." The old man rowed slowly but his strokes were strong and the dinghy neared the ancient hull. "Sammy, why do you have to do this?"

"You know, Kingsley. Darren was my only brother. Ricky poisoned him with coke and fancy clothes and then blew his head off when Darren screwed up. I think a deal went bad and someone didn't pay. Darren was caught in the middle. He paid, all right. With his life! Execution style!"

"Darren was playing a dangerous game, Sammy."

"He was only seventeen! He didn't even know what he was doing." Samantha was half angry, half crying.

"I know, I know", Kingsley quietly consoled her.

"Look, all I want to do today is follow Sting Ray and find out what is going on." They were approaching the boat. The boat looked worse close up than it did from the beach. "Are you sure your boat is going to make it?"

"The only thing wrong with my boat is the paint. Other than that she's as shipshape as they come. Paint is expensive, is all."

When Kingsley turned the key the diesel started immediately. They let the motor warm up while they drank coffee.

"That's Sting Ray leaving harbor," the old man said, pointing. "He'll be running across the channel to Ricky's dock. If we just keep on heading out the channel it won't take long before he catches up with us. If you keep your pretty little head down it'll look just like I'm going fishing."

"What if he heads out the other end?" asked Samantha.

"He won't do that because this is the way to Normans Cay. I don't know what is going on but I'll tell you it has somethin' to do with Normans Cay."

"What do you know about Normans Cay" asked Samantha.

"Just about what everyone knows. Stay away! Michael Farris is the best smuggler in the Bahamas. Haven't heard much about him in the last five years or so, but no one ever did hear much about him either. He's not like Ricky. Ricky wants it all. They say he has a whole organization in Florida. Farris just smuggles like his pappy did. He lies low and never makes trouble. I never hear about big parties or carryings on like Ricky. But he didn't get his big house and his cigarette boats smuggling tomatoes either."

"Sting Ray seemed to like him", said Samantha.

"I've heard that sometimes he brings back a new engine for someone's boat or a transmission for their car. Such things are a whole lot cheaper in Florida than here. His daddy did the same. I knew him a bit. But that was before cocaine gave smuggling a bad name. My own grandfather was a privateer. A regular pirate on the King of England's payroll. Now go up on the bow and cast off that mooring line."

Kingsley's prediction was correct. An hour and a half later as the old fishing boat passed the point and entered Exuma Sound, Sting Ray's tug passed and set course for Normans Cay. Samantha, wearing a loose jacket and a baseball cap looked like any other fisherman from three hundred yards away.

Chapter 24

Phil and Judy anchored the Zara along the outer edge of the spit about a quarter mile from where they had located the wreck. They waited nervously drinking coffee, as Sting Ray's tugboat approached. A half a mile away, and closing fast, Ricky's Sport Fisherman was catching up to Sting Ray's tug.

"What if he rams us?" asked Judy.

Phil tried to make light of the imminent danger. "You're right, Babe. Better kiss me now before it's too late!"

Judy pushed Phil away but had a sudden change of heart and clung to him with her head buried in his chest.

"Phil, I don't know if I'm up to this."

Phil held Judy tightly and stroked her hair. Over her shoulder he could see the approaching tug. Beyond the tug he could see Ricky's boat throttle back.

The tugboat bore down on them until it was about a hundred feet away before slowing and swinging broadside. Sting Ray picked up a loud hailer and called out "Hi folks."

Phil and Judy watched as a runabout with a powerful outboard was lowered from davits at the stern of Ricky's boat. Four men climbed aboard and it sped over to the tug and tied on. As Ricky climbed aboard the tug he ordered Sting Ray to pull closer to the Zara. Working at dead slow, Sting Ray maneuvered the tug but didn't end up much closer at all.

"All right, let's go!" commanded Farris. The cigarette boat shot out of the harbor at Normans Cay and raced toward the tug at full speed. Victor was at the controls and Linda sat calmly in the passenger seat beside him. Farris, completely dressed in diving gear crouched down below the gunwales, out of sight. George also remained low and out of sight. Linda looked at Farris, kissed her fingertips and reached down to touch his face.

"You're going to hit awfully hard, sweetheart. Be careful! Good luck!"

Farris grinned. "You're the lucky one. You'll get to see Ricky's face."

The cigarette boat came in wide and swung hard toward Ricky's boat leaving a huge rooster tail that obliterated it for a few seconds. The tugboat was in a direct line so it was screened from seeing the cigarette boat. No one on either boat saw Farris bail out over the far side and sink beneath the surface. Linda offered a quick prayer that he had avoided hitting one of the props or losing consciousness as he hit the water. She stabbed at the digital watch on her wrist setting the stopwatch into action. She had to keep Ricky occupied for five minutes. The cigarette boat circled Ricky's boat and then headed closer to the tug and slowed to a stop between the tug and the Zara. Linda, clad in a bathing suit with a muscle shirt overtop, sat up on the back of the cigarettes boat's front seat and picked up the microphone which was set to hailer mode.

"Normans Cay seems to be a busy place this morning."

"Linda Farris", answered Ricky through his hailer. "I expected to see Michael."

"You can. That's him on top of the hill." Linda pointed toward shore and then waved. The figure on top the hill waved back. Ricky squinted and looked towards the hill on Normans Cay. There was a figure that looked like he was watching through binoculars and waving with one hand but it was too far to distinguish more detail.

"Well he can keep on watching until we raise the gold from the seabed", sneered Ricky through his mike.

Linda appeared exceedingly relaxed. "We seem to disagree on whose find it really is, darling."

"It's my find, bitch. I have the letter that led me to it."

Judy glanced quickly at Phil. It was now confirmed.

"But Ricky darling, it's on the reef off Normans Cay."

Ricky was amply aware of that circumstance. He hesitated for a second. He was unable to think of a sagacious comeback so he resorted to a rude order.

"Get the fuck out of here, bitch, and take that stupid fucking sailboat with you. Why isn't Farris out here, anyway?"

"I had to talk him out of it, darling. He said if he got within range he would blow you out of the water. I dislike violence, so I said I'd ask you to leave."

At that Ricky laughed. "This tug is a lot stronger than your little glass toy", he sneered. "And I like violence. You would be the one blown away!"

"Oh yes, the tug is stronger." Linda checked her watch. Four minutes had passed. "I'm sure you will find it very useful, too."

"Just get the fuck out of here or you'll be swimming back to your precious little island", cursed Ricky. The three men from his boat had already picked up their weapons. A sub machine gun was handed to Ricky. Linda checked her watch again. It read four minutes and thirty-four seconds.

"Darling, isn't your sport fisherman getting awfully close to the reef?

I may be wrong but it seems to be drifting."

Ricky looked back over his shoulder and realized his boat was, indeed, drifting dangerously close to the reef. What had happened to the anchor? Ricky raised his machine gun but as he looked back he was staring into the barrels of two sub machine guns in the hands of Victor and George. In addition both Phil and Judy on the Zara had weapons trained on him. Ricky threw down the mike and yelled at Sting Ray.

"Radio the man on my boat and tell him to get the fuck away from the reef. The anchor line must be cut!"

Everyone kept his or her weapons up in a traditional Mexican standoff posture. Ricky held his gun on Linda and Victor while he watched Gino come out of the cabin and start up his boat. Instead of the normal purr of the engines the sport fisherman howled like a banshee as the engines hit red line almost immediately. Furthermore, the tall powerboat continued to drift onto the reef despite the screaming engines. Ricky watched as Gino tried to engage the gears on both engines. Each time he added throttle the engines red lined immediately.

"I believe you've lost your props, mate", said Sting Ray. "We should get a line on board before she ends up on the spit."

Phil had already switched on the windlass and was pulling up his anchor and backing away. Victor hit the throttle and swung the cigarette boat around to the other side of the tug two hundred and fifty feet off it's bow and out of accurate range of Ricky's guns but where it could run interference if Ricky decided to fire on the Zara. Off to Victor's left, a bright orange ball broke the surface of the water shooting up ten feet in the air before plunking back into the water. Victor hit the throttle and sped toward the ball. When Farris heard the engines cut overhead he surfaced and climbed quickly aboard.

"Get back closer to Phil and Judy", Farris barked. "How did it go?"

"Like clockwork," answered Victor.

"You OK, Linda."

"I'm fine, a little overwhelmed by the testosterone, but OK".

"She was great, boss" said George. "A real Viking".

On board the tug Ricky had lowered his weapon and was screaming orders like a madman. Sting Ray was ignoring him and maneuvering into position to heave a line aboard Ricky's fisherman. Not wanting to create a wake that would push Ricky's boat onto the coral the tugboat moved at dead slow. Ricky screamed at him to go faster. Sting Ray ignored him until Ricky entered the wheelhouse of the tug and slapped the back of Sting Ray's head with an open palm. Sting Ray shifted into neutral and turned to Ricky. No one could hear what was said but after half a minute Sting Ray handed Ricky a clipboard and made him sign something. Ricky stormed out of the cabin a few seconds later. Just then Ricky's boat lurched as it hit the coral causing the lone man left on board to pitch forward to the deck. Sting Ray went out on deck and taking a coil of rope threw it perfectly onto the stern deck of Ricky's boat. Gino scrambled for it but missed and the loose end slithered across the deck and dropped overboard. Sting Ray began to re coil the rope while Ricky screamed at his men.

Another dozen waves had pushed the bow of the fishing yacht up further onto the coral before Sting Ray could secure the line.

"They'll do more damage getting off the reef than they did getting on", commented Farris.

The Zara was now alongside the cigarette boat and the troop of saboteurs sat back and watched the show from a safe distance.

It took another ten minutes before Ricky's boat was clear. Sting Ray pulled the sport fisherman along side the tug and with no regard for Ricky's deck or paint began throwing tools and hoses onboard the luxury boat. Then, carrying a portable bilge pump with a three-inch nozzle he climbed aboard. Ricky's boat was listing badly by the time the pump was hooked up and a gusher of water was being pumped over the side. Sting Ray secured a heavier towline to Ricky's bow and after raising his own anchor eased away with Ricky's boat in tow.

Ricky stood on the deck of the tugboat and watched his boat listing and under tow. He took the submachine gun he was still carrying and blasted away indiscriminately at the Zara and the cigarette boat. Both vessels were well out of effective range and neither was hit. Nevertheless everyone ducked down. Phil, from his vantage point in the Zara's cockpit, calmly picked up a high powered rifle with a scope. Using the cabin roof as a rest, he carefully sighted in and placed a shot so close to Ricky that it hit a steel winch he was leaning on and ricocheted, whining, as the bullet tumbled. His second shot, ten seconds later took out the glass on Ricky's bridge. The third, fourth and fifth shot were aimed at the hull, just above the waterline.

Linda put a hand on Farris shoulder and he called to Phil to ease up. Phil stopped his target practice with a grin. "I enjoyed that, but you're right. Enough is enough!" He glanced at Linda.

"Nice shooting, cowboy", said Farris.

Ricky knew he was a sitting duck at that range. His sport fisherman had no props and had been holed on the reef. Sting Ray's tug had Ricky's boat in tow. Furious and frustrated he waved his machine gun over his head but ceased firing. He was incensed by the additional damage to his boat.

"A million bucks, you motherfucker! That boat's worth a million bucks!" Ricky screamed. No one on either the Zara or the cigarette boat could hear the remark but Sting Ray did and a thin smile appeared at the corners of his mouth. "Not any more, asshole. You got just what a son of a bitch like you deserves", he mumbled to himself. "Now just wait for my bill!" Sting Ray would tow Ricky's boat to an honest shipyard that would pull it out of the water immediately. According to salvage law and the standard Lloyds of London salvage contract Sting Ray could bill for a percentage of the boat and he would ensure that the shipyard did not release the boat before the bill was paid.

"Just do your job and for Christ sake don't smile again", the old tugboat operator mumbled to himself.

※

Samantha and Kingsley were still three miles or so from Normans Spit when they heard the machine gun fire followed by five rifle reports. Kingsley increased speed to near maximum which, for his displacement hull was about ten knots. Five minutes passed before he spoke.

"She...eet! Would you look at that?"

Samantha jumped up from the wooden bench in the cabin and grabbed the binoculars. Kingsley quickly handed her the hat and jacket which she put on with one hand while holding the binoculars with the other.

"That's Ricky's boat being towed by Sting Ray."

"All right, Sting Ray! Ricky must be some peed off!"

Samantha grinned. "Isn't Ricky's boat listing?"

"Sho looks that way to me", Kingsley grinned back.

Samantha continued to watch as the two boats passed a quarter of a mile off Kingsley's port side. When they were well past she gave Kingsley a playful hug to which he responded by just plain starting to laugh. Soon Samantha was laughing too letting the tension unwind out of her.

"I bet he has to walk around his boat like this," said Samantha leaning over until she was almost off balance and then dancing around the tiny cabin. She reached over Kingsley with one lithe, graceful arm and turned on a small transistor radio that was propped up on a shelf. Putting one hand against the cabin wall to support her weight she planted her feet in the middle of the cabin. Leaning at a crazy angle, bracing herself with one hand on the cabin wall, she started to gyrate her hips and snap the fingers of her free hand in rhythm with the music.

"I call this dance the Ricky list!" she laughed.

Kingsley locked the wheel and slapped his knee, laughing and watching Samantha dance. He put a hand on the cabin wall and tried to imitate Samantha but having obtained less than half the angle lost his balance and fell gracelessly seat first onto the plywood bench. Samantha tried to catch him on the way down and both ended up half falling half sitting on the bench with Samantha's arm wrapped around the old man. They were both laughing raucously and Samantha put her other arm around his neck and planted a huge kiss on his forehead.

As she kissed him, Kingsley's old and wrinkled face was forced down and he found himself staring directly at Samantha's magnificent breasts. He felt a stirring in his loins he hadn't felt in years.

"Sammy", he said, unashamedly watching her breasts, "I would court you 'til I won your heart and soul if I was just say...forty years younger". He looked up into her eyes.

Samantha gave Kingsley another kiss on the cheek and then holding his worn face in both her hands and staring him squarely in the eye said "Kingsley, I'd make love to you, right here and now, right down on this bench, if you was just, say... thirty years younger!"

They both broke out into fits of laughter again.

When the tug was out of sight Kingsley turned the fishing boat around and they putted back towards Nassau.

"Kingsley, I think I know how to get Ricky."

"How's that, babe", the old man answered gently.

"Ricky is going to have one giant hate-on for Farris. Maybe I can do something to lead Ricky right into a trap."

"Sammy, you're talking dangerous stuff. Why don't you just drop it?"

"I can't Kingsley," answered Samantha quietly. "It's been two years now but I can't forget. I even prayed in church to give up thoughts of revenge but I can't. I got to do it. He was my little brother and Ricky killed him."

Samantha dropped her head onto the old man's shoulder and began to cry. He kept one arm around her as he steered with the other and comforted her, quietly saying "O.K. Sammy.... O.K".

⁂

The closer Ricky got to Nassau the more incensed he became. Usually he liked the attention his sport fisherman received from passing boats and tourists. He would sit high on the fly bridge and never wave back to anyone. Coming in under tow and listing the way it did was embarrassing, degrading him far beyond his shallow sense of endurance.

"Gino", he called from the bow of Sting Ray's tug. "Get over here."

Gino walked over briskly.

"We were set up this morning! A few motherfucking heads are going to roll."

"Who told us about the letter in the first place?"

"Prince."

"Right! Where did he get the letter?"

"From Gibson, boss."

"Gibson is first. Annihilate the little prick. Send in Susie."

"Sure, boss."

"Prince knows more than he has told us. Squeeze him but don't kill him.... Not yet, anyway. See what you can find out about the fucking lawyer", spat Ricky.

"What you going to do about Farris, boss?"

"Leave Farris and his bitch to me. He wants to pull up the gold.... Let him do it. It's easier that way. We'll keep tracking his boats. Make sure that bastard pilot never misses a flight. I want to know where everyone of Farris' boats are ... all of the time."

"Sure boss."

Ricky took out a gold box he always kept in his pocket. Gino watched as Ricky snorted some cocaine using a gold spoon that hung around his neck.

"The fucking lawyer knew that Gibson would give the letter to Prince and that Prince would give it to me". The anger in his voice was abundantly clear.

"How do you figure he knew that, boss?"

"How the Hell do I know?" screamed Ricky.

Gino caught a depraved look in Ricky's eye, and involuntarily, backed up a step. He was never sure about Ricky. The mood swings were getting worse. This one was as quick and as deadly as he had ever seen. Ricky lived in such a state of paranoia that he would turn in a flash, threatening even his most loyal people.

"Get back to Miami and ask around about Prince. See if he's making any new connections. If you hear one word that links him to Normans Cay, that black motherfucker can kiss his ass goodbye. Maybe there is no gold. Maybe Farris is trying to take over my territory. Fuck! Now get going! Tell one of the boys to bring the runabout alongside. I'll go back to Nassau in it. This fucking tugboat smells like a rotten cunt."

As Gino turned he felt a wave of happiness. He was going to enjoy getting away from Ricky again for a few days. He rode back to Paradise Island with Ricky in the runabout and within half an hour he was sitting in the passenger seat of the chopper headed for Miami. He wasn't carrying a gun. Ricky forbade that on international flights and Gino would go through customs just like any other businessman. Once in Miami, however, Gino would be well armed. There was plenty of hardware in the apartment he maintained there. Gino thought about that apartment as "his second home". Things were looking good. He might even get a chance to get a little heavy with Prince. That thought pleased him. He hated Prince ... he too, hated Negroes.

❧❦

"Well it's confirmed. Ricky has a copy of the letter", said Michael as the foursome sat on the patio recapping the morning.

"I just can't believe it", responded Judy, her voice hollow.

"There wasn't much doubt about it," said Phil quietly. "Let's face it. There is only one source from where that letter could have originated. Your friend and mine, David Windrow. Liar and lawyer. Strange how those two words sound alike. He must have sold the letter outright or become a partner in a salvage operation."

"Why would he choose a partner like Ricky? That doesn't make any sense", said Judy.

"Then he must have sold the letter outright. The deal he had with you was ten percent of your share. That's only five percent. He might have figured that was too thin."

"What you say makes sense. But I still don't quite believe it."

Judy was pouting but at least she wasn't denying the logic.

Farris spoke up. "Look, all that happened this morning was we had a good first round. We bought a day or two while Ricky re-organizes. I think we can be pretty sure when Ricky returns, its going to be with both guns blazing."

"That's a comforting thought", said Linda.

"I think we ought to go back to Nassau and see if Sting Ray is available to go on our payroll instead of Ricky's", said Phil.

"Suppose Sting Ray is available. What next? Do we go after the wreck on the spit or off the beach", questioned Farris.

"Both" answered Phil.

"You're kidding, right?"

"How long will it take us to excavate the shipwreck off the beach?" asked Judy.

"A week at most. That's to clean out the hull enough to find the gold. That's assuming that the gold is within the wreck itself. Remember, if the ship broke up before going down the gold might be a mile away in any direction. If part of the deck separated from the hull, as often is the case, the hull would have been dragged down by the keel and the ballast. Let's say the gold was kept in the captain's quarters, not in the hold. The deck may have separated and drifted away Lord knows where. What we saw was most of a ship. Not, all of it!"

"That's really depressing. You mean we could find the ship and not the gold?" asked Linda.

"You got it!" said Phil.

"The wreck off the beach appears to still be together. The deck seems to have caved in, into the hull. That's good. There is no sign of a deck on the wreck on the spit."

"We are the only ones who know about the wreck off Rebecca's beach," said Linda.

"Sure, until we show it to Sting Ray and Ricky sees us working over there", said Judy.

"Unless we don't show it." Phil had a plan formulating. "Suppose we pumped out the spit wreck by day. The eye in the sky is never going to notice anything except the fact that we are always on the same location. The same one Ricky knows about. But night time is different. The pilot will have his usual half a dozen drinks and go to bed. We slip over to Rebecca's beach and work until daybreak. Then we move back to the spit. The only question is can we trust Sting Ray?"

"I'll vouch for Sting Ray. Do you think we can excavate both wrecks in one week?" asked Farris.

"We shouldn't have to do full excavation. Once we get inside the hull our handheld magnetometers should work through a foot or two of sand. Besides, I have a feeling that I can speed up the job, if Sting Ray is as cooperative as you suggest. It may delay the start of the job but it will pay in the end."

Farris leaned back in his chair. "When we begin isn't really very important. Rebecca's ship has been underwater for two hundred years. What is important is moving quickly once the salvage really starts. Is there anything we need to speed things up?"

"Three things. A good gen-set. Good underwater lighting and a mailbox".

"A mailbox?" questioned Judy.

"Not your typical mailbox. Leave that part to me. It will be a surprise", said Phil.

"The generator won't be a problem. Sting Ray has a huge one on his tug for arc welding. Underwater lights should be available in Florida, off the shelf. Linda can fly over and get them. No one navigates anywhere near Normans Cay at night because of the spit. There's no way that Ricky would tell Fly Boy to keep an eye on us after dark. I like the plan!"

"Me too", volunteered Judy. "I hate sleeping!"

Everyone looked at Linda. "Oh all right. If everyone else is convinced. But how are we going to defend ourselves from Ricky? We certainly rained on his parade today. Today was the first time in my life anyone pulled a gun on me, and I wasn't exactly thrilled about it."

"Well you sure looked good standing up to him. He was certainly at a loss for words", praised Judy. "It was a first for me too".

"First time I ever shot a boat. And I love boats!" grinned Phil.

"Not bad shooting, either", said Farris. "And Darling, you did do great!"

"Ricky is a mad man, a thief, a murderer and a drug lord. Up until today he was just a name but when I saw his eyes… well… he has earned the status of an "enemy". If he ever enters our harbor I'm going to relax my mandate of "never seeing a gun on my dock, again". I think I've been bitten by the lure of sunken treasure every bit as much as the rest of you, but I wasn't fully prepared to have to fight for it with machine guns."

"I admit it wasn't quite what I envisioned two months ago", answered Judy.

"To tell the truth, me neither", admitted Phil.

"I want everyone to come out of this in one piece", cautioned Linda. "Let's not lose sight of that."

Three days later, two hours after sunrise, Sting Ray eased his tug through the channel into Normans Cay. Phil and Michael, Victor and George awaited his arrival with boxes of equipment piled on the dock. As Sting Ray maneuvered toward the dock, Victor and George received lines and tied the tug off. Most of the equipment was obviously diving gear but Sting Ray was sure that there was also a good supply of firepower being stowed on board. He was surprised by the dozen underwater lights. You didn't need that on board to pump out a wreck in thirty feet of water.

He remembered how insistent Phil had been about electrical supply.

The men on the dock were also surprised by the stern of the tug. Bolted in place was a huge, strange looking, metal box hinged to the deck so that it could be lowered to extend over the propeller housing. Phil was standing off to one side, smiling to himself.

"So that's your mailbox," Farris called to Sting Ray as the tugboat operator stepped out of his wheelhouse.

"Yes sir, it sure is. I welded it myself. It's a helluva lot better than just the pump."

Michael had climbed on board and was studying the strange contraption. "Explain it to me?" he asked politely.

Sting Ray beamed. "It's the opposite of the sand pump. You see, when you are looking for treasure the sand pump works good if you know exactly what you are looking for. If you set it fast it moves a lot of sand but it can also damage artifacts. If you slow it down.... Well, it's slow. The mail box, on the other hand, swings into place over the prop and directs the water straight down toward the bottom. This blows the sand away but because it takes in water from the surface where it's clean, even as you are blowing up clouds of sand, you are blowing the sand away with clear water and your visibility is still pretty good as you are working. Artifacts are heavier than the sand. Blow the sand away and the artifacts remain on the bottom. No chance of chewing them up in the pump, either."

"Why didn't you have it when you were here a few days ago with Ricky?" asked Farris.

"Ricky just asked me for a sand pump.... So that's what he got! Mister Phil here, seems to know a lot more about this kind of operation than that crazy eye-talion. He asked me about a mailbox. Said he'd seen it in my yard the night you came looking for me at the Coconut Tree. Not many people would have recognized it. You got a pretty smart partner there. I dug it out and greased the hinges. Only used it once before. I copied the design right off the one Mel Fisher used when he discovered all that silver off Key West. Had it stored in my yard for over ten years just rusting. Now you can see it work just as soon as we can get out of here."

Linda and Judy arrived on the dock and were already climbing on board. Sting Ray was tipping his hat to them.

"We talked about this, already. There could be more trouble out there," said Farris to his wife.

"I also talked to Judy, privately. We decided that we had better be in all the way or all of us should get out."

Michael looked at Phil for support but Phil just shrugged.

"O.K. cast off," shouted Sting Ray.

Victor and George jumped onto the dock and untied the mooring lines. When Sting Ray was clear they boarded the cigarette boat and led the tug to the location of the hull on the spit.

Phil wandered into the wheelhouse once the tug had cleared harbor.

"What's with the underwater lights?" asked Sting Ray.

Phil stared straight ahead. "Overtime", was all he said.

Chapter 25

David Windrow had become distracted and was watching addresses and reading store signs instead of watching the road. He found Harry's bar at the same time that traffic slowed down and he had to brake hard to avoid running into a delivery truck. He found a parking space, walked back to the bar and entered through the glass door. It was only eleven AM but there were already a few patrons who looked like they spent most of their time hanging around the place. There were a couple of people playing pool and another, sitting alone at a table. A waitress was vacuuming and an attractive bartender, with an unnaturally large chest, was loading beer into the cooler. The tables and chairs were wooden and the atmosphere acceptable if unimaginative. The whole place looked like it had been nice, ten years ago.

David went up to the bartender and asked to see Mr. Gibson.

"Harry's in the office. Sit down and I'll tell him you're here. Do you want a drink?"

"Just a coke, please."

"Sure. Coke's on the house if you're here to see Harry."

"Thanks."

David sat for five minutes nursing his soft drink. The bartender returned and continued to fill her cooler, counting bottles and writing quantities on a clipboard. Finally a man came up behind him and said, "I'm Harry. How can I help you?"

David turned expecting to see the Harry Gibson whom he had met in his office a month earlier. Instead he saw a man who looked like he had come through a war. His face wore a fresh scar and was still a bit puffy on his right cheek. His wrist and hand were encased in a plaster cast. His eyes were bloodshot and he looked like he hurt all over, which, in fact he still did.

"I recognize you. You're the lawyer from up north. At first I thought you were selling something or other."

"That's right. Good morning, Mr. Gibson. Can we move to a more private table?" asked David.

"Sure, over there. Lisa, bring me a Coke."

The two men sat down and said nothing until the bartender left.

"My mother is all right?" Gibson questioned.

"Your mother is fine and the estate is almost settled. I'm here on another matter."

"What's that?"

"You seem to be in some serious difficulty, Mr. Gibson." David was bluffing but he thought he could pull it off.

"Hold on, Mister." Harry was obviously shaken by the comment. "Who told you that?"

David smiled so that if anyone were watching they too would take him for a salesman.

"Were you in a car accident, Mr. Gibson?"

"Yah, car was totaled", lied Harry.

"It seems that your mother removed a copy of a letter from my office." David watched as the color drained from Harry's face. "That in itself is going to be largely overlooked by the courts who will undoubtedly close your bar, revoke your license and send you off to a state institution for a couple of years. Her motives were not malicious and she is, after all, a senior citizen. Your intention was quite different."

The approach was working. Gibson was obviously a weak man of little resolve. It was amazing, he thought, how quickly Ginny had pegged his personality. David watched as Harry slumped in his chair and mumbled something.

"What was that?" asked David.

"You sound like a cop", said Harry, sourly.

David chose not to answer. "What did you do with the letter?"

"I should be talking to my lawyer."

"I am your lawyer, Gibson. Talk to me and I may not have to involve the police. Mess me around and Johnny Cochrane couldn't save your sorry ass".

Harry sat in a morose silence for a few moments, weighing his options. Finally, he made up his mind. "O.K. Here's what happened. I didn't mean to harm anyone."

He recounted everything, how he had seen the letter, made the photocopy, and returned to Florida. He told of the loan he had, saying that it was with a loan shark. He blamed his inability to repay it on heavy weekly interest. He had offered the letter in repayment for the loan to a man named Prince who had accepted the deal. Then, a couple of days later Prince had come to his apartment with three other guys, at eight o'clock in the morning. Harry didn't know the other men but they had worked him over pretty good, breaking a couple of ribs, his fingers, his face. They had kept asking questions about the source of the letter.

"Mostly, they kept asking questions about you!" Harry blurted out. "I wish I knew what was going on. Hell no ... I wish I had never read that damn letter", he concluded.

"Where can I locate Prince?" demanded Windrow.

"He cruises the bars on Spanish Boulevard. He's got a few girls there. He's never without a broad and a piece."

"Does he still come in here?"

"Yah, sometimes. Mostly on weekends."

David got up to leave.

"What are you going to do?" sputtered Harry.

"Gibson, two of my friends may be in serious danger because of your light fingers. You deserved to have them broken. If anything happens to my friends I guarantee you will spend a couple of years working for the government, in one of their finest establishments."

Windrow walked out leaving behind a weak man with stinking, nervous perspiration dripping from his armpits. "Ginny was dead on about him. What a pathetic jerk", he thought.

He drove two blocks before reaching for his cell phone. On the second ring a man's voice answered "Jason's Detective Agency"

"Jason, that you?"

"Sure is. Your voice is familiar. Who's calling?"

"David Windrow. How are you doing?"

"Davey boy ... it's great to hear from you. What's up?"

"Jay, I need a favor. Can you meet me in Fort Lauderdale?"

"I have clients coming in tonight. How about breakfast, tomorrow?"

"That's fine."

`   "Meet me on the south pier where we met a couple of years ago. Eight o'clock all right? You remember the place?"

"Yes, I remember. In the meantime can you dig up some information for me"?

"Say the word, man. I owe you one!"

"See what you can find out about a Harry Gibson. He owns Harry's Bar in Fort Lauderdale and also a guy by the name of Prince who runs some girls on Spanish Boulevard."

"You got it. Anything else?"

"That's it. See you tomorrow."

The line went dead. David decided he was tired and hungry and drove his BMW convertible toward the beach hotel that Ginny had booked for him.

As soon as he had entered the room and thrown down his bags, David picked up the phone and called his office.

"Hi, any news from the north?"

"David, where are you? It's been a zoo here."

"I'm in my hotel. Nice room, overlooking the ocean. I just had a meeting with Harry Gibson."

"Harry Gibson! David I just got off the phone with Mrs. Gibson. I had a long talk with her."

"What about, Ginny?" David could hear the strain in Ginny's voice.

"Mrs. Gibson wouldn't talk to me the first five times she called. Finally I told her you were out of town. Then she told me about you finding a copy of the Simpson letter and the men in the Buick coming looking for it. I told her I knew about that."

"I guess she just wanted to apologize again. Did she get the chocolates?" said David. He was starting to open a suitcase.

"Damn it, David. Listen!"

David sat down on the corner of the bed. Ginny had never spoken to him in that tone of voice before. Hearing her angry was.... Almost pleasant.... Not that he wanted her to be angry.... It was another side of Ginny that he didn't know. Now he concentrated, smiling to himself.

"O.K. I'm listening. What is it?"

"Mrs. Gibson described the man who broke in. He was wearing a suit and a topcoat. He wasn't your average thief. She made him sound more like the Mafia. I'm worried sick about you."

"Easy there, Ginny." David paused to collect his thoughts. "I just spoke with your favorite person and can confirm that the Simpson letter has, definitely, fallen into the wrong hands. But, I don't want to alarm an aging widow any more than is necessary. I also don't want to tell her that her son stole the letter from her. I have no idea who the intruder was. Try to convince her to spend a few nights at her friend's house. Can you do that, Ginny?"

"David, you're in some sort of danger, aren't you?"

"No, not yet anyway." David thought about Harry Gibson's battered body. "Right now I'm more concerned with Phil and Judy!"

"David, be careful... and phone back often. You remember my home number." Ginny really did sound concerned.

"Sure, it's "star 19". You know that, you programmed it in", joked David, trying to lighten the mood.

"Don't be silly. Do you remember it?"

"Of course I do. I've had to call you often enough on week-ends."

"Call again soon. I kind of miss not having you around the office."

David was on the verge of saying, "I miss you, too", when he caught himself. "I will, bye now, Ginny." He placed the phone gently back in the cradle. Moving the suitcase to the floor he flopped on the bed. He tried to think about the two men in a black Buick and what their connection was with all this but his mind kept wandering back to Ginny. It felt good that she really was concerned for him.

⚜

Jason Saunders stood six foot three and weighed in at a muscular two hundred and twenty pounds. There was not an ounce of fat on his body. He wore a sports jacket and a shirt with an open collar and leaned casually against a concrete abutment at the beginning of the south pier. There was no noticeable bulge where his thirty-eight caliber automatic rested in a shoulder holster under his arm. He turned his back on the parking lot as the BMW Z3 pulled in and came to a stop.

"Morning Jay", came a voice from behind him.

It was obvious that there was no attempt to avoid watching eyes so Jason turned but automatically scanned the area. Extending a huge right hand he clapped David on the right shoulder with his left as they shook hands.

"Nice car", he commented, wishing it was still his.

"It's getting a few miles on it but it still purrs like a kitten."

Jason admired the car from a distance. He remembered the pleasure he had taken from the shear power as he used to manually shift the gears through countless turns, then push it to the max on the straight a ways. He had given it to David in lieu of a legal fee two years ago. It was worth it. He had been exonerated of all charges, but left the state, anyway. Now he had a new life, a wife and a baby and a new career that was beginning to go somewhere.

"Come on, I'm starved and I bet there's some place that serves a good breakfast in this part of town." In one smooth, quick motion Windrow flipped the keys up in the air. Jason's oversized paw reached out and snatched them. Both men grinned and headed toward the car saying nothing.

Jason did not head for the nearest restaurant. First he put the car through its paces expertly maneuvering around traffic and occasionally leaving rubber in second gear. Finally, after a good ten miles he pulled into a truck stop.

"Good food here", he said casually.

"Nice and handy, too", replied David. Jason didn't so much as blink.

The waitress brought coffee without being asked and took their order without providing menus or writing anything down.

"What you involved in, Davey Boy?"

"Let's say I'm trying to help out a couple of friends."

Jason took a sip of coffee. "I checked out those two names you gave me. Prince is a pimp slash pusher. He has a reasonable network and turns a fair amount of coke in Miami and Fort Lauderdale. Harry Gibson is one of his outlets and rumor has it, a major consumer."

"Any idea as to the source?"

"Does the name Ricky mean any thing to you?"

Windrow shook his head.

"Everything in Eastern Florida comes through the Bahamas. Ricky controls over fifty percent of it. Maybe more. He's Italian out of New York but he lives in a mansion in Nassau, right on Paradise Island. They don't come worse."

"Keep digging. Just keep an ear to the ground, especially, if you hear anything about sunken treasure."

"Treasure? That's Mel Fisher's department. I've even seen his museum in Key West."

"I read about that. Mel might have some competition that's not so scrupulous. Harry Gibson sold Prince some information that pinpoints an old shipwreck. Later Prince and a few other guys came back and worked over Harry Gibson good. That was at least a week ago and he is still hurting. The document originated in my office."

"A treasure map?" questioned Jason.

"You might say that", answered Windrow without committing.

"Man, you branching out!"

⚜

It was about ten o'clock, Wednesday night. The bar was moderately busy. Harry Gibson sat at the last stool at the far end where he could keep an eye on the bar and the cash register as the waitresses on the floor ordered drinks from the bartender. Tonight though, he was more concerned with getting through to closing, attempting to kill the pain with rum.

"Fuckers!" he thought. "I did those bastards a favor and look what they did to me." He downed another rum. Even drinking hurt.

"Anyone sitting here?" asked a silky female voice.

"Go ahead. It's yours", answered Harry without looking up.

A hand brushed over his thigh as the woman sat down. That made Harry look up. What he saw was stunning. She was blond but even first impression said dye. That did not detract from the way her hair contrasted to her dark tanned face and body that was barely covered by a canary yellow dress. Her eyes were fastened on the bartender and she was ordering a Singapore Sling. That gave Harry a moment to admire her. Her elbows were on the bar partially covering her breasts but what he could see revealed a healthy bosom. The yellow dress narrowed to a tiny waist and then flared out into a pair of hips that covered the barstool. The dress was so short it barely covered her panties. Her deeply tanned legs were pressed tightly together and on her feet were a pair of bright yellow patent leather pumps. Harry looked back up at her face. It was beautiful, heavily made-up, but perfectly applied. Sexy. A fragrance drifted into Harry's nostrils.

"I don't know what kind of perfume that is but it smells great", thought Harry.

He looked at her hands as the bartender slid a drink across the bar. She wore gold bangles on her wrists and no shortage of rings on her fingers. Real stuff, too! It was her fingernails that put the lid on the ensemble. They were also bright, canary yellow like her dress and shoes.

"That's the sexiest broad that's been in this place in years and here I am trussed up in Band-Aids and wearing my arm in a cast. Shit I've got bad luck", thought Harry, taking another swallow of his drink and turning away.

The hand reached along the bar and closed on Harry's wrist. All he could do was watch in awe as his wrist was twisted gently to the right. Bangles, rings and yellow fingernails captivated him as his arm was drawn out straight. Finally, moving slowly she looked at Harry's watch.

"Eleven, hunh", purred a voice in his ear. "Thanks." The hand released the grip on Harry's arm and reached into a handbag extracting a gold cigarette case.

Harry regained conscious thought, and reached into his pocket for a lighter. The cigarette case was pushed along the bar in his direction. He extracted two long cigarettes that seemed thinner than usual. Working with one hand, he gave one cigarette to the woman and placed the other between his lips.

The woman turned towards him on the barstool. The front of her dress was cut deeply revealing plenty of perfectly tanned cleavage. She leaned closer as Harry lit her cigarette.

"You look like you've been through the war, soldier."

"Car accident", lied Harry. "My name's Harry. What's yours?"

"Suzie."

Harry's eyes glued to her chest as she put her head back and took a deep drag on her smoke. He could feel himself swelling in his pants. For the next fifteen minutes they talked, Susie often emphasizing her words by reaching out and touching Harry's arm or leg.

"Want to do some coke?" asked Susie, flashing a wide smile and running the tip of her tongue between her teeth. "My car is outside." She slid off the barstool letting her dress climb until Harry could see her yellow panties. Looking over her shoulder and giving a "Come on" signal with her eyes, she walked to the door. Harry followed not even giving any instructions to his staff about closing up. They knew what to do. Parked outside the door of the bar was a canary yellow mustang convertible with the roof down. Susie moved to the passenger door and slipped in dangling the keys for Harry. He took them and moved around to the driver's side.

"Let's go to your place", Susie commanded.

Harry entered traffic with a squeal of rubber that made Susie laugh and throw back her head letting the wind ruffle her hair. She inched closer to Harry but the console got in the way. Harry's hand slid off the gearshift and pushing her dress up high, tucked into the warm flesh between her thighs. Susie let it linger there for a moment and then took Harry's hand in hers and placed it back on the wheel. But not before spreading her legs slightly and pushing Harry's hand hard against her crotch.

"Better watch the road", she breathed and let her hand settle on Harry's erection, which she caressed first and then gave it a firm squeeze.

Harry pulled into his parking spot and hurried around to open the door for Susie. She had her yellow handbag open and he dropped the keys into it before taking her hand and helping her. Her yellow panties showed again as she climbed from the car. He hurried her through the back door of the building and up the elevator, fumbling for his keys at the door, and ushering Susie into his apartment.

Once inside the door Harry wrapped his arms around her and kissed her on the mouth. Her tongue darted out at his. Harry lowered his hands so he could squeeze her buttocks then slid them up over her waist and breasts. He began to loosen the shoulder straps of her dress when she gently pushed him away.

"Let's have a drink first. Do you have any bubbly?"

Harry had some cheap sparkling wine in the fridge so he led her to the sofa and hurried into the kitchen. As he poured the drinks Susie got up and moved to the bar cut into the wall, separating the living room from the kitchen. She reached into the yellow handbag and pulled out a vial that resembled a lipstick container. Spreading the white powder into six neat lines she plucked a straw from a cocktail glass on the bar and snorted a line. Lowering her shoulder straps she turned to Harry who was coming with the wine and coyly said, "Your turn."

Harry plucked a straw from the glass and did the next line. Susie did the next and lowered her shoulder straps a little further. Harry grinned and after running a finger along the top of her dress snorted the next line. With each line Susie lowered her dress a bit more until the fabric was hooked on, only by her nipples. Harry was getting very high and very horny. Susie reached for the vial and her dress slid off one breast.

"Oops" she giggled. She squeezed the naked nipple making it swell and demurely hooked her dress back on it leaving half the areola exposed. Then she dumped more coke on the bar and made six more lines. She reached over and undid Harry's zipper.

"Do another line, Hun."

Harry did as instructed while Susie loosened his belt.

"My turn". As she leaned over the bar her dress fell away to her waist. Harry reached out and touched her breast but again she pushed him away. This time she only did half a line. She turned toward Harry and pulled her dress up until he could see her frilly yellow panties. Tucking a finger in the elastic on the leg she pulled the panties back revealing her pink lips. She caressed herself for a moment then slid one long graceful finger into her vagina. After a couple of slow strokes with her finger she pulled it out, wet with her clear white juice. She picked up the balance of her line with her wet finger and placed it in Harry's mouth rubbing the coke over his gums. The smell and taste almost drove Harry wild but he let her repeat the process with another entire line. Each time he tried to touch her she inched back. Finally she moved a bit closer.

"You do it but be gentle."

She slipped her panties off and let them fall to the floor, moaning as Harry's finger entered her. After a few short seconds she clutched his wrist and gyrating her hips alternately pulled and pushed on Harry's wrist. Then she pulled his hand out, rolled his finger in the remaining coke put it up to his mouth telling him to rub the coke on his gums. Meanwhile she dropped his pants to the floor and stroked him.

"Let's go to the bedroom", she suggested.

She slipped completely out of her dress. "Lie down on your back."

She climbed over him and after licking her fingers sprinkled more cocaine on them and rubbed them on her nipples and clitoris putting a liberal dose on the swollen head of Harry's cock.

"I've got something special for you", she purred, removing a capsule from her palm and breaking it open. "Hold this up to your nose and snort it hard as you go inside." She pulled back the soft skin that covered her vagina and placed the tip of Harry's swollen cock inside her. For a few moments she gyrated back and forth until she could feel Harry's hips tighten as he arched to thrust himself deeper. Harry was ignoring the capsule in his fingers and she pushed his hand toward his nose, still gyrating her hips.

"Get ready, Hun. You're going to come like there's no tomorrow. Now!" she commanded.

As Harry snorted the amyl nitrate Susie plunged her hips downward taking all of him inside her. She closed her eyes and climaxed again and again as Harry squirted hot semen and cocaine into her vagina. Finally she collapsed on his chest and lay there trying to catch her breath. She lay still for an entire minute listening. There was no other sound. She straightened up. Harry was still erect inside her. Susie looked down at his face. He lay there, eyes glazed and staring.

"I hope it was as good for you as it was for me, Harry", she said tenderly. She dressed quickly and after wiping down the bar and making sure the apartment door was locked, left the building.

Chapter 26

The tugboat rumbled toward the wreckage off Normans Spit. Once anchored, Sting Ray spent an hour in his dinghy with Judy reviewing the site map and inspecting the bones of the ship through a glass bottomed bucket. Linda was thrilled to see someone else using an observation technique that didn't require swimming.

"Judy has a good site map. It is set up real nice," praised Sting Ray as he climbed on board.

"Sting Ray has told me that he hasn't used the mailbox for a long time, and even then it was on a different boat", said Judy. "We talked about anchoring about a hundred feet away from the ship, on the path it went down, and testing the bottom."

"That's right", said Sting Ray. "The wreck is shallow enough that the mailbox will direct the flow of water behind the prop straight down. We'll have to experiment a bit as to how much throttle I give. We want to blow away the loose sand but not blow away artifacts. Judy tells me you're photographing everything where it sits. That's good. Now before we start work, how be someone tell me exactly what we are looking for!"

"You're the boss, Phil. You tell him," said Farris.

"He's the boss. I thought you were", said Sting Ray, a bit confused.

Farris simply shook his head and eventually Sting Ray looked at Phil sizing him up, looking thoroughly over his muscles, his hands and finally his eyes locking on Phil's. Phil was tall and good looking but as Sting Ray surveyed him more closely he saw a hardness to Phil's physique and a small scar on Phil's hand that came from time spent at sea and hard work. Phil was not at all shy, but he had let Farris do most of the talking. That was a good quality, too. Sting Ray dismissed braggarts quickly. His eyes were steel blue, capable, trustworthy, yet hard to read.

"He's a tougher critter than your average pretty boy", he thought.

"This is going to take a few minutes. Let's all have a beer and talk this through. The only way we can make this whole thing work is if we are all on the same page", said Phil in a matter-of-fact voice.

"A beer sounds fine," answered Sting Ray. His tone of voice was non committal.

Judy opened a cooler and passed around four beers.

"This isn't the wreck we are really interested in," said Phil. "But we are going to work it, regardless. Let's start right at the beginning. I was coming down to the Bahamas to search for a wreck off Long Island. Meanwhile, Judy found an old letter that pinpointed a ship going down. I changed my plans and Judy and I became partners. The letter confirmed that the ship carried a small quantity of gold. Well, that small quantity is worth a few million at today's prices. The ship was not a Spanish Galleon or anything like that. It was a passenger and cargo ship from the early eighteen hundreds. We believe that we have found it but that's not yet confirmed. In the meantime, we found this wreck which we know nothing about.

We had proof that the ship we were looking for went down off Normans Cay. Judy and I came here and met Michael and Linda. The four of us formed a new partnership to raise the gold. Somehow, through our lawyer in the States, Ricky got hold of the letter that led us here. He has watched us for a month, waiting for us to locate the wreck, and the last time we saw you, he jumped our claim. You know what happened next."

"That was some fine marksmanship, and it sounds like it was well deserved", interrupted Sting Ray.

"The funny thing is, we are pretty much convinced this is the wrong ship. Fortunately, this is the only ship Ricky knows about. We have located another wreck. What we planned, is to work this ship by day and the other ship by night. The question is "are you prepared to work double shifts with us?"

"What about the archeologists and the government?"

"If we can get the gold first, the archeologists can spend as much time as they want studying the bones. No one knows about the other ship except the five of us."

"Double shift means twice the expense of running this old tug. I'd have to charge double pay", said the shrewd tug boat operator.

"We are OK with that. We'll add in a bonus if we find what we are looking for."

"What kind of a bonus?" asked Sting Ray.

"How about a quarter of a million?"

Sting Ray grinned. Phil had just passed the test. If Farris trusted him, well that was good enough for Sting Ray. Nobody wanted to argue about the bonus.

"Double shift it is! Night dives elsewhere. Back on this site by dawn! Everything sounds fine by me. Now, I'm curious as Hell as to how that mailbox is going to work. Let's get at it!"

"We'll only really work a shift and a half. We don't really care much about this wreck," added Judy.

"No problem, mon."

With that, the new group started work. Phil and Judy were in the water a hundred yards before where the ship found its final resting spot. The tugboat was anchored with two anchors and the mailbox was lowered behind the propellers. Phil and Judy stayed a respectful fifty feet away as Sting Ray pushed the throttle forward. At first there appeared to be a gentle breeze blowing sand and silt off the ocean bottom. Phil was wearing a mask that covered his mouth as well as his nose and eyes. This gave him full voice, radio connection to the surface.

"Add throttle", he ordered.

Sting Ray added five hundred RPM and almost immediately six inches of sand was blown from a ten foot circle on the bottom.

"Stop!" called Phil.

The engine noise subsided.

"The hole is six inches to a foot deep. The cloud of sand is drifting away more quickly than I thought with the current. We are going in to take a closer look."

Phil and Judy swam over the hole and studied the edges. There was nothing of interest. They swam a safe distance away and radioed back.

"Give her another shot for about a minute".

Phil and Judy watched as the tugboat's powerful propeller forced a stream of water straight downward through the mailbox. The hole deepened to about two feet before Sting Ray shut down his engine.

"Give her another minute, and another five hundred RPM."

Judy held Phil's hand as the ocean bottom blew away. When the noise subsided they waited for a few minutes before swimming into the hole.

"We have a hole here about ten feet wide and four feet deep. There are no protrusions on the sides". Phil drove his knife at the bottom. "We appear to be down to bedrock. There is nothing of interest in the hole…... But it was sure interesting watching it being dug."

"How's your air?"

Phil checked his gauge and Judy did the same. She flashed ten fingers at him.

"Ten minutes".

"Get out of the hole and stay off a safe distance", ordered Sting Ray.

Phil and Judy swam away but stayed on the bottom in stead of hovering close to the surface.

"Go ahead"

"Roger"

The powerful diesel revved up and the sand blew, slightly increasing the diameter of the hole. Then there was a new noise. It startled Judy and she clutched Phil's arm. The hole began to grow in one direction. The noise was the windlass pulling the boat toward its anchor but the effect on the bottom was bizarre. Instead of a hole, a ten foot wide trench evolved. In five minutes the hole was twenty five feet long. Sting Ray throttled back and shut his engine completely off.

"You still have five minutes of air. See what you see and come on up," commanded Sting Ray.

"I see a trench, twenty five feet long".

"Check the sides and bottom".

The trench revealed no anomalies but when Phil and Judy surfaced their excitement was evident from the grins they both wore. As they climbed up the ladder Phil grinned at Sting Ray.

"We have the technology!" he exclaimed, slapping Sting Ray's hand.

"Yah, mon."

Farris was already suited up and ready to go.

"Not without me, you don't," warned Linda.

"I'll get your diving gear," said Phil. Referring to Linda's raft as her diving gear was a stretch of political correctness but to Linda it *was* diving gear.

Sting Ray leaned back against the wheelhouse as Phil lowered the colorful raft over the side and handed Linda a mask and snorkel. Farris towed her out fifty feet from the side of the boat and dropped a small anchor. Then, after giving her hand a quick squeeze sank below the surface with the radio headset on.

"We are going to have to watch for surface turbulence", Sting Ray cautioned. "I've never seen anyone snorkel on a raft before."

"Yah, it is a bit unusual. We'll keep a close eye on her. We're ready when you are. Take it slow."

"Roger". Sting Ray called to Phil and Judy. "If she starts to drift toward us you make one Hell of a racket. Better still…." Sting Ray ducked into his wheel house and emerged with an air horn. Tossing it to Phil he shouted, "If I hear that horn I shut down immediately."

"Got you! Good thinking!"

Linda seemed oblivious to the precautions being taken for her benefit. She was calmly studying a fish that seemed to have found a food source in the newly dug hole. Farris gave her a thumbs up which she responded to in kind.

"Go ahead Sting Ray. Bring up the revs slowly until I say stop."

Keeping one eye on the surface and one eye on the bottom Farris heard the engine rev. Linda's face popped out of the water. The engine shut down immediately.

Linda appeared a bit embarrassed. She waved to Phil and Judy.

"Sorry, I didn't expect it to be so loud under water." With that she put her head back in the water to watch. The system seemed to work without creating too much suction.

"I think her ass looks good, even with the new raft," said Phil, seriously.

For that he received a formidable punch in the shoulder from Judy which he pretended to ignore despite the fact that it really did sting.

Fifteen minutes later Farris radioed to the surface to stop the engine. Sting Ray immediately shut down while Phil quickly suited up.

"There is something in the trench", called Michael as Phil jumped into the water.

Together they swam to the start of the trench and swam along it studying the walls. The trench was already thirty feet long. The water was murky but clearing quickly. At the end of the trench, half exposed were three round pieces of iron strapping. Phil photographed it and placed a red flag nearby, before he even touched it. He signaled for Farris to radio the surface for an exact GPS reading. Then he began to carefully dig sand away with his hands. A piece of wood, so rotten that it crumbled at his touch appeared. He fanned at the water to blow away the sand. The shape and size were undeniably that of a wooden barrel with iron hoops. Whatever had once filled the barrel had long since drifted away. It might have been water, or rum, fruit or salt cod. The two men carefully worked around it. Finally a piece of wood that had been buried deeper in the sand or had come from a stronger part of the tree, emerged. It was still fastened to the strapping. Phil took more photographs. This barrel would be of interest to an archeologist. It might help date, or even name the wreck. Michael was low on air and the two men surfaced together.

"What should we do with it?" asked Judy.

"Good question," answered Phil.

"At first I thought this was all about treasure hunting. But suddenly we're all concerned about history", observed Farris.

No one denied his statement.

"We better think this through," said Phil. "We can leave it and move on, or we can excavate it and find out what else lies close at hand. The more wreckage we catalogue the better the chance of finding the real treasure".

"Follow the bread crumbs", said Farris.

"First of all we have no idea what kind of a ship this is, how old it is, or what it was carrying. We don't think it is Rebecca's ship… but it might be", said Phil.

"I vote that we concentrate on finding the gold and salvaging it. I don't care what the Bahamian or any other government says. Rebecca wrote my great grandmother and I think that entitles me to finding the gold and keeping it. This wreck has been down here for a couple of hundred years. If we report it a year from now the archeologists can have a field day with it. But first we find the gold and remove it." Judy was clear about her position.

"That works for me", stated Linda.

"Me too", said Farris.

"Finders, keepers", added Sting Ray.

"You're the final vote, Phil," said Farris.

"I've probably thought about this more than the rest of you all put together. I've been reading about treasure salvage all my life. I don't want to bury history but I also don't want to give up a small fortune on pseudo intellectual, moral grounds. I say we work carefully, document everything we can, but go after the motherlode for ourselves. That barrel came off the ship on the way down. There is probably a trail from the anchor to the hull and probably beyond. Let's go back down and blow away some more sand. We'll leave the archeological pieces on the bottom, mark it with a flag, but put the booty in our pockets."

"Spoken like true privateers", said the burly tugboat captain.

"We'll work the trench for another hour. Then we should get some rest. Night shift begins at eleven o'clock."

The next hour realized three more barrels, one almost complete. It was impossible not to think about the last few minutes of the doomed ship's life as its deck slowly sank beneath the waves. The masts would undoubtedly have broken and thousands of feet of rigging would have tangled on the deck or dangled from the masts as they lay in the water, still attached to the crippled ship. The sea would have crashed over the gunwales, ripping the lashings that tied down deck cargo to shreds. Barrels and crates would have rolled and skidded around the deck crushing anyone in the way. Hundreds of items of all sizes, not to mention a few unfortunate sailors, would have slid over the side, scattering the contents of the ship in a trail of evidence that stretched for miles along the bottom. The masts and rigging floating off the lee side of the ship would have acted like giant sea anchors, turning the ship at right angles to the wind, making matters even worse than before.

Did she roll and capsize? Did the waves rip the hatch covers from their hinges and fill the holds? Did debris in the water puncture the ship at or below the waterline? The answers died two hundred years ago as probably a hundred souls drowned. Nevertheless, fear, panic, heroism and calm stoicism almost certainly accompanied this ship to the bottom.

Sting Ray had insisted on staying anchored out, over the wreck. He argued that no one would leave the gold unattended if that were what he was after.

Victor and George picked up the two couples, in the cigarette boat. Victor passed a huge, hot meal of fried fish, dumplings and vegetables that the young girls had prepared, to Sting Ray. They agreed to meet at ten thirty and start out at eleven.

Judy trundled down the stone stairs that led from the patio to the dock carrying a casserole dish filled to the brim with fish and rice and an assortment of vegetables. The glass top and towels, meant to keep it warm, were not enough to keep out the delicious smell of Caribbean spices that drifted upwards, permeating the air with a sense of home, love, safety and permanence.

She was dog-tired from the day's dive and her body's clock was telling her to go to bed and stay there, rather than to get up and dive until dawn. She was not alone in her tiredness. The alarm had woken her first and she had shaken Phil and listened to his groans of protest for a good five minutes before giving up, going into the bathroom and having a quick shower.

While toweling off, she had pulled the covers off him and listened to him mumble curses at her and all other wicked members of her gender. She had to admit that she had never been happier. Nevertheless, even the thought of the "midnight" boat ride failed to give her enough adrenaline to wake up. A worrisome thought entered her tired brain, posing the question of what would change, and by how much, when they finally did find the gold. It seemed a certainty that they would find it. She smirked at that thought. It had taken Mel Fisher sixteen years and millions of dollars to find the wreck of the Atocha and it's vast cache of gold and silver, yet each day he had encouraged his diver's, saying, "today's the day!"

Well if it was going to take sixteen years Judy was content to stay with Phil and see it through. She imagined Michael and Linda would sign on for extended duty as well.

Below she could see Victor and George loading air tanks into the cigarette boat. They were working without talking, using only the low voltage patio lights instead of the overhead floodlights. As she approached, Victor stepped politely aside and she handed the casserole dish to George who accepted it with out a word.

"You look tired, mon. Go have another coffee. We need another five minutes before the boat is ready", said Victor quietly. Judy liked his quiet manners.

"Thanks, Victor. You want me to bring you anything."

"No mon". It was the standard reply.

Judy slowly climbed the stairs again, thinking her legs were stronger from all the swimming than they had ever been before. The kitchen was busy with Phil and Michael waiting for a fresh pot of coffee, Linda talking quietly with the one of the Bahamian girls, while the other wrapped a second casserole dish in towels.

"Is the boat loaded?" asked Farris.

"Five more minutes. Victor told me I looked like Hell and needed more coffee, anyway".

Farris grunted a short laugh. Linda looked up and observed that everyone looked tired. Phil courteously handed Judy a coffee.

"Thanks, does this confirm Victor's assessment", she asked impishly.

Phil wisely did not respond.

Farris maneuvered out of harbor with neither harbor nor running lights. Two hundred feet from the mouth he accelerated bringing up the speed to thirty miles an hour. He made a long slow turn that took him out a quarter mile and then made a beeline for the tug.

The trip out to the tugboat was eerie. There was a light breeze and a bit of chop. Without the sun, the air had a chill to it. Farris steered expertly, in the pitch black, without even a moon for guidance. There were no running lights turned on. The lights on the dashboard were turned to the lowest level. Sting Ray was waiting for them with white bumpers hanging from his old rubber tires on the lee side of his boat. "Right on time", he said as the four climbed aboard. His diesels were rumbling at an idle.

"I already moved off the hull, about a hundred yards. One anchor is up so we can winch in the second one and start right on schedule."

The only light on board was an old, kerosene hurricane lamp that Sting Ray carried about with him. However, along the front of the wheelhouse were four lawn chairs. The chairs, complete with cushions, were brand new and perfectly normal except in one aspect. They were securely bolted to the deck.

"Can't have the young ladies sitting on oily machinery", Sting Ray proclaimed.

Judy and Linda thanked him for his consideration and each planted a kiss on one of his cheeks. The men were less demonstrative in their thanks.

The men pitched in and loaded the diving gear on the tug. Linda took over galley duty and dished out a huge plate of food for Sting Ray. Everyone else was served coffee, preferring to dive on empty stomachs. Judy sat in one of the lawn chairs with her laptop wired through the cabin window to the tugboat's cigarette lighter. She was totally absorbed in what she was doing. "Computers have that effect on some people", thought Phil.

Sting Ray wanted to raise the anchor immediately but Linda stood firmly in the doorway to the wheelhouse, a plate of fish and rice in one hand and a coffee in the other.

"We can spare ten minutes. We don't move until you've finished eating."

Sting Ray finally acquiesced but ate sitting on a winch cover, refusing one of the lawn chairs. Occasionally he grunted or hummed with pleasure as he downed another mouthful.

The anchor lifted and Sting Ray's boat swung around to skirt the reef and then swing back toward Rebecca's ship. Running without lights was not difficult although finding your way around the deck in the dark was. The lantern hung in the wheelhouse, it's yellow flame giving just enough light by which to watch the instruments. The deck itself was in total darkness and the lawn chairs served their purpose well.

After a while Sting Ray set the boat on auto helm and walked out around the front of the wheelhouse where everyone sat in his or her new chair. He had previously laid out all equipment needed for the night dive so there was nothing to do but sit and bide the time. In addition to the scuba gear Sting Ray had laid out an array of underwater lighting equipment.

"We have twelve lights that we wire up just the same as you would in your back yard. Plug 'em in and turn 'em on. They are connected back to the generator on the boat with a big extension cord. At first you will have to work with the big flashlights, while you get set up. It shouldn't take more than an hour to set up lighting all around the wreck. Tomorrow night all we have to do is plug in! Sound OK?"

"You are way ahead of us. Did you get any sleep?" asked Phil.

"Nope".

"Well we have sandwiches, drinks and a few thermoses of coffee to see us through the night", volunteered Farris.

"You tell them cooks that that was the best plate of fried fish I ever ate".

"They like the extra work so they are giving it their best effort. I can pretty well promise that you won't go hungry at Normans Cay", said Linda, kindly.

"That's the truth", laughed Judy. "Some of those lights look used. How did you know to bring the lighting equipment, Sting Ray?"

"I didn't. Carry it all the time. I've had to do salvage inside a couple of big steel hulls where lighting is a must. Can't say I planned to use them this trip!"

"Linda flew over to Miami and bought eight lights. A few extras will help for sure', said Phil.

"When it comes to salvage you won't find much that I don't already have on board," stated Sting Ray, "including a case of rum, so we can either celebrate or drown our sorrows".

"Gotta keep the bases covered", laughed Phil.

That got a grin out of Sting Ray. He was definitely warming up to Phil.

The tugboat slowed to a crawl as it neared the co-ordinates. Sting Ray's finger hovered over the windlass release. Phil and Farris were over the side at the same time. The women peered over the rail. As soon as the divers turned on their flashlights it became easy to track their movements. The hull was located almost immediately but Phil and Michael swam all around it before calling for the fixed lights. Another hour and the lights were located and plugged in. On deck the noisy generator was pounding away. Phil called topsides for power and Sting Ray pulled the switch.

With a depth of sixty feet of clear water, the bottom lit up like a swimming pool. Sting Ray lowered a huge glass bottomed bucket over the side on a davit. Sixty feet below the men were as clear and visible as they would be across a busy intersection. Many fish had been attracted by the hand held lights but many more came to inspect the portable spot lights.

"I need my raft", said Linda.

"Ma'am. You can't go swimming at night. I've been told you can't even swim!" said Sting Ray.

"Sting Ray. It's true that swimming has always been a challenge to me but I'm quite good on the raft. I'm one of the partners in this adventure and I expect to do my share of the diving".

Sting Ray looked to Judy for help but found her a step behind Linda, holding in a laugh with her hand over her own mouth. Referring to Linda's raft work as diving was a joke with the others but to Linda it was not. Sting Ray's shoulders slumped and he looked down at the deck.

"Yes, ma'am."

A few minutes later, as the men changed tanks, they too were surprised to see Judy in full gear and Linda in her wet suit. Linda was wearing a life jacket that Sting Ray had insisted on, over her neoprene wet suit, and was climbing down the ladder to her raft.

"I'll keep a close eye on her", said Judy, quietly.

Sting Ray paced the deck, first peering downward to the soft green color that emanated from the underwater lights. Then he looked to the shadow, barely visible on the surface, Linda, floating on her raft. The divers were indistinct although their bubbles were clear. He determined to mount a small light on Linda's raft.

Occasionally he peered into the glass bucket to catch a better view of Phil and Michael. The only light he had on deck was the hurricane light. He longed to throw the switch that would light up his powerful, halogen deck lights but with only the underwater lights they were virtually invisible to anything but an airplane. Even an airplane would pose no security risk. They would assume fishermen were using lights to attract fish.

Below Phil and Farris explored the remains of the hull.

"Sting Ray, you there", came a voice over the radio.

"Go ahead".

"Send down the hand held magnetometers. We'll try to pick up something big".

"Roger that".

Sting Ray tied a rope to the hand held units and lowered them to the ocean floor. He held the rope until he felt a sharp tug indicating the units were untied. He paced for another half hour before Judy tossed her flippers onto the deck and climbed back on board. He helped her with the tank and both stood guard as Linda stepped off her raft onto the ladder.

"The men will be up soon. They may have found something but they don't seem too sure."

A few minutes later everyone was on deck.

"We are going to have to blow the sand off the hull", said Phil.

"Too deep for the mailbox", said Sting Ray.

"In that case we use the portable blowers or start sucking the sand up."

"Blow as much off as you can. It will go slow but the sand pump is even slower", said Sting Ray.

"I propose we start right in the middle of the ship and work aft. It's unlikely that the gold would be stored before the mast. If we don't find it, we rethink everything", said Judy.

"Makes sense to me", agreed Phil. "Which end is the bow?"

"Good point".

Hand held blowers were lowered over the side. An hour later the lights went out. Sting Ray reeled in the main power line and shut down the generator. Working only by the light of the moon and the hurricane light, bringing the magnetometers and blowers up was hard work. Phil stretched his back when everything was on board.

"It's an old ship, not much left of her", said Phil when the heavy lifting was finished.

"Did you find anything at all?" asked Judy.

"We did see some ballast stone, about the size of softballs."

"It's already four o'clock. Let's get back to the first site. We can talk as the sun comes up", said Farris.

Sting Ray was winching in his anchor and within five minutes they were underway. Everyone was exhausted. Farris called Victor on his cell phone and the cigarette boat was running and waiting for them as they maneuvered over the first site. As soon as Sting Ray had anchored they agreed to meet again at ten thirty and piled into Victor's boat. All, that is, except Sting Ray. He would sleep on deck and pretend to be waiting for slow risers to begin diving the wreck, if anyone approached.

"We won't start diving until you have had plenty of time to enjoy your breakfast, after we arrive. Is their anything special you like", asked Linda, kindly.

"Seeing as you asked, those were mighty fine dumplin's", answered Sting Ray.

Linda smiled warmly. "I'll pass that on. Extra dumplings".

"Thank you, ma'am".

Once back on the dock everyone trudged off to bed while Victor and George dragged the air tanks into the boathouse and filled them. Then, they too slept as the morning sun rose.

The second and third night on Rebecca's ship was spent doing hours of grunt work that yielded few rewards. A grid of fifty feet by two hundred feet was constructed of polypropylene rope held down with wooden pegs, driven into the sand. The advantage of wood was it had no effect on the magnetometers although it was difficult to work with. The grid was centered over the largest pile of debris. Everyone looked for clues as to how the wreckage lay.

On the third night, while stretching out grid lines Michael discovered a smooth, rounded object. He pushed away a bit of sand and discovered he had found a glass bottle. Phil cautioned him not to move the bottle until they had completed the grid line and taken a measurement as to the exact location off the centerline. Once that was completed they took a portable blower to the location and blew away a foot of sand. Another bottle and a cooking pot emerged as the sand drifted away. The two friends had discovered the galley of the wreck.

By night four the exploration was becoming much more exciting. Each dive seemed to bring up another clue. Judy catalogued them and stored them in tanks of sea water on board the tug. Linda was proving to be a bigger and bigger asset to the team with each passing day. She had quickly learned Judy's program for mapping the finds and was entering them as quickly as they were being brought to the surface. Phil and Farris did the majority of the diving spending about three hours a night on the bottom. Sting Ray was the sole deck hand, always ready to send down a piece of equipment or haul up an artifact. Their first guess appeared correct, that the ship lay the length of the grid, based on the location of ballast stones, the galley and what was assumed to be ribs of the ship. The best news was that only a couple of feet of sand had accumulated.

Oddly it was Linda who was developing the best sense of how the ship lay. On the tug she continued to insert findings into the grid pictured on the computer. When she lay, belly down on her raft she observed the same grid, this time depicted with yellow rope. From her vantage point, looking down toward the floodlit bottom she pictured the shape and design of the ship better than those on the bottom. Late on the fourth night while the men were taking a break she donned a radio mask and Judy did the same. Then with remarkable accuracy she directed Judy to a spot, twenty feet to the north of the centerline and two thirds of the way down the grid.

"That's the bow, Judy", she stated.

To Judy, on the bottom, there was no visible indication of anything but sand. The hand held magnetometer, however, concurred with Linda indicating a weak signal of something metallic. Phil and Farris, who had been listening in on the conversation, arrived with a blower and began to blow away the sand where the magnetometer indicated a metal object.

A large iron bolt, probably part of the wooden bowsprit was soon discovered. If the hypothesis was correct, the four treasure hunters had determined the direction and starting point of the hull. Slowly they were closing in on the treasure.

On the dark journey back to the first site, Judy's program and Linda's understanding of it were toasted with weak rum drinks under the pale glow of the hurricane lamp that shone through the window from the wheelhouse. If this wreck was that of Rebecca's ship, and if the gold had gone down with the main hull, then the treasure hunters were within two hundred feet of their target. In a big ocean two hundred feet was a very short distance indeed. On the more pessimistic side, if the deck and cabins had separated from the hull, and drifted away, the gold could be anywhere. Some parts of the deck had obviously caved in. What parts were missing was the mystery.

Nevertheless, the mood on board was a happy one. A very tired, happy one.

"To Hell with an eleven o'clock start. Don't expect us before one in the afternoon, Sting Ray."

"Suits me, fine. I'll radio or phone if I have any visitors", answered Sting Ray. Sting Ray had had less sleep than anyone and it was beginning to show, even on the hardened old sea captain.

"Tomorrow is Saturday. Let's take Saturday night and Sunday off. We'll start fresh on Monday", suggested Phil.

"You take the time off if you wants, but the tug stays right over top of that wreck", stated Sting Ray.

"I'll put Victor and George in the tug. You go home and rest up. Everything will be safe", said Farris.

"That's OK by me. You sure?" questioned Sting Ray.

"He's sure", answered Linda. "We all need rest!"

"Just make sure that Victor picks me up at seven AM on Monday."

Chapter 27

David was in the process of rolling up his beach towel when his cell phone rang. He had enjoyed a relaxing day that started with buying a new summer suit. While leaving the mall, on impulse, he had purchased an expensive tropical weight cotton blouse, for Ginny. David was a bit unsure if it was Ginny's style, but he liked the blouse, and working on the premise that "if clothes are expensive, women appreciate them" completed the purchase. The sales girl had complimented him on his good taste. He thought she was sincere but he wouldn't know for sure until he had seen Ginny wear it twice. She would wear it the first time to say thanks. The second time was the test.

"Damn women are complicated", he thought.

Lunch was an excellent lobster salad. Then he bought a six pack of beer and a cooler bag and wandered out of his hotel onto the beach that stretched for miles in both directions. He walked for a mile or so until he found a pleasant spot, rolled out his towel, had a beer and fallen asleep for over an hour. The rest of the day had been spent swimming and sun tanning. Now he fumbled through his beach pack for his phone, which was playing its six-note melody again and again.

"Davie boy.... it's Jason."

"Any new developments, Jay."

"A minor one.... Were you aware we are investigating a dead guy?"

"No.... who, Prince?"

"Would you believe, Harry?"

"Impossible.... I met Harry yesterday morning." David was shocked.

"I guess he wasn't dead yet when you met him ... but he is now!"

"How did he die? What happened?" asked David.

"It looks like an overdose. He was with some floozy but no one knows doodley squat about her and she ain't around anymore."

"Jesus".

"This broad was something else according to one of the guys at the bar. Harry wasn't a real ladies man. Sometimes he'd go home with your typical bar fly but this broad was a real looker and just oozing hormones. The police are writing this up as a drug overdose but listen to this. A friend of mine on the force tells me that one guy is working on a different angle. There have been two other cases similar to this and he's trying to put together a case for murder. I don't think he has a clue as to who he is looking for but in each case the guy has gone home with a beautiful, extremely sexy broad and has later been found dead of an overdose. This guy thinks we are dealing with a very kinky hit man, female variety. She's got to be smart, too. If it is the same woman she changes her appearance enough that her description never coincides. The only common denominator is she is always gorgeous. Then, even if the cops did track her down, it would be impossible to prove that the victim didn't take the drugs of his own, free will... which he did!

Here's how she does it. First she picks up the mark and takes him back to his own house. They have a few drinks and she loads him up with coke. She gets him into bed and hands him amyl nitrate. The mark snorts the amyl from his own hand just as he comes. The dose is too much, and the mark is dies immediately. All this in his own bed, with her on top of him. What a way to go!"

David fought to gain composure. "You had better meet me right away. I'll be in the coffee shop at my hotel."

They had been sitting in Jason's non descript Chevrolet on the bar strip in downtown Miami for two and a half-hours. David finally put his head against the headrest and closed his eyes. Soon he was fast asleep.

In his dream someone was pulling his arm.

"Come on Davey boy.... Wake up."

"Yeah.... Oh yeah" David mumbled.

"That's him!"

There was little need to be more specific. Prince was wearing a silk shirt and quality dress pants, all neatly pressed.

"It seems that our man likes to be noticed, even in a crowd," said Windrow as he returned to wakefulness.

The silk, multi colored shirt seemed to light up under the neon signs. He was with two, scantily dressed hookers, one on either arm.

"They are going up to his apartment. We'll give them twenty minutes. By then they will all be higher than the Goodyear blimp."

One of the girls stumbled. "It looks like they already have a head start."

"Just stay in the car, David", said Jason as he climbed out.

"No way!" retorted David.

Jason had no problem picking the lock at street level. It took no longer than someone fumbling with the wrong key. David stood by quietly amazed at Jason's ability. The broadloom on the stairs was thick and soft and the wallpaper tastefully chosen. At the head of the stairs there was another single door. Prince obviously had the second story all to himself. Music with a heavy bass beat pounded through the locked door.

"Your choice", said Jason. "We break our way in, shoot our way in, or pick our way in."

"My guess is they're in the bedroom.... Pick our way in."

"O.K. but stand to the side, just in case bullets start pouring through the door.

Windrow's intuition paid dividends. No one saw or heard a thing as Jason and David slipped into the apartment. Voices could be heard in the bedroom.

"Stay out here facing the door unless you hear real trouble. Don't let anyone see your face. Here, put on this ball cap and put your sunglasses on", whispered Jason as he clicked the safety off his gun. In three quick strides he crossed the room. The bedroom door that was only half shut shattered under the impact of his foot.

Prince was on the bed totally naked. Both girls were dressed in their underwear. All three were crowded around a tray on which lines of cocaine had been neatly arranged. A plastic bag containing at least a thousand dollars worth of coke sat in the corner of the tray.

One of the girls screamed but Prince backhanded her, sending her flying off the bed and into the corner, with a curt order to "shut-up". He stared at Jason, concerned but unafraid.

"Ladies, go home.... Now!" ordered Jason. If you are not out of this apartment in ten seconds my friend at the front door will begin shooting. He began a slow count."

The two hookers grabbed their clothes and purses and ran for the door, still in their underwear. David heard them coming and opened the door timing it so they would see only his back. One of the girls looked back from the hallway but David sidestepped smoothly and was already and closing the door. He locked it immediately. He could hear the girls scrambling to put their clothes on, in the hallway.

Prince rolled his legs over the side of the bed and began to reach for his pants but Jason took a step forward landing a vicious kick to Prince's groin. Prince collapsed unconscious.

A pot of cold water from the kitchen woke him up. He tried to move however his arms and legs had been tied to the four corners of the four poster bed. A blanket had been tossed over him but his pain was excruciating.

"You must be quite a kinky dude", said Jason Saunders.

Prince glared at him with disdain.

"Interesting how those two girls tied you up good and whipped you with leathers and chains before you O.D'd on cocaine. Remember? Sort of like the way Harry Gibson died. Except for the whips and chains."

"Shit man, I heard about that but I didn't have anything to do with it."

"Who did?"

"I heard he O.D'd. That's all I know."

"Wrong answer, my man." Jason laid a vicious judo chop with the side of his hand across Prince's stomach. Prince would have doubled over, sitting up in bed if he had not been tied down. He groaned with the pain and swallowed to prevent throwing up.

"Try again", ordered Jason.

"Ricky, man. It was Ricky?"

"So tell me why?"

"It was the letter. Gibson's letter. I sold it to Ricky. It was like a treasure map, man. At first Ricky was all happy and excited but the letter directed him right to the island where his competition lives. The island is called Normans Cay. He must have figured it was some kind of trap."

"Keep going."

"Maybe it was a trap, maybe it was coincidence that the letter led to that island. Ricky still figured the letter and the gold was for real 'cause the people on Normans Cay seemed to be looking for the same thing. Ricky sent down divers and found an old shipwreck. But when Ricky tried to get the gold his boat was wrecked by the gang on the island."

"What gang?"

"Normans Cay, man. They are Ricky's competition. Shit man, you know that. Who the fuck are you, anyway?"

Jason Saunders mind raced. "I'm from out of town. Ricky just sent me to take care of you. He's very pissed."

"Fuck man, I didn't know the letter was a fake ... or a trap ... or real... or whatever it was? It looked real to me. Shit! Tell Ricky he can have his money back. Please man!"

"Not good enough", said Jason reaching for the bag of cocaine. "He's pissed about his boat. I guess it's a write-off. I heard it was worth a cool million. I got orders to waste you." He dug into his pocket and extracted a plastic case containing a hypodermic needle.

"Don't do me man. I'm begging you. There's thirty thousand under the bed. Take it. I'll blow town. Tell Ricky you got rid of me in some swamp."

"Then you pop up again and I'm toast... for thirty thou .... Can't do it. Sorry, but you have to leave town permanently. This way is as good as any." He held up the syringe.

Jason disappeared into the bathroom with the cocaine from the tray, and the needle.

"I have sixty thousand in the bank. It's yours, man", called Prince from the bed. I'll go to Mexico and disappear, forever. Shit man. That's ninety thousand dollars. And you still get paid by Ricky."

Jason poked his head out the bathroom door. "Ninety, you said? That's better than thirty."

"That's all I got, man. Money ain't no good to me if I'm dead. You can have it all!"

Jason had poured the cocaine down the sink and filled up the hypodermic needle with water. As he walked back into the room he gave a tiny squirt out the head of the needle.

Prince tried again. "OK. So you spend the night here. In the morning we go to the bank. Then you drop me off at the airport. I'm out of here, man." Prince was begging.

"Ninety, hunh. You got me thinking. I'll have to talk to my partner."

"You talk to him. Go ahead. I won't go anywhere."

That got a snort of laughter out of Jason.

"We would have to go somewhere private to talk. My partner likes doughnuts. But, you know, he's kind of a company man ... he does exactly like the boss says. And you know what the boss wants." Jason paused and pretended to ponder his next move.

"Come on, man. Ninety thou!"

Jason played along. "I don't want you screaming. If I leave you alone while I talk to my partner, I'd have to tape your mouth shut. I'm not going to die for ninety thou, either."

"Sure, man. No problem. There's tape in the medicine cabinet."

"What a putz", thought Saunders. "He's offering me his tape to tape a sock in his mouth. That's weak."

"Thanks", said Saunders and casually returned to the bathroom.

Jason checked the knots and left Prince with a sock in his mouth, taped in place with half a dozen wraps of adhesive tape wrapped round his head. As he left Prince tried to mumble a "thank you" but only a hum came out.

Once in the hallway David sputtered, "Let's get the Hell out of here!"

They were in the hallway going downstairs. There was a bra on the floor. Jason reached forward and placed a hand on David's shoulder.

"Not so fast, Davey. Slow down. We really are going to go to a coffee shop and have a little talk."

"Are you nuts....? I have to get to Nassau to warn Phil and Judy."

"Davey boy.... We are going to do just what Prince suggested. We are going to go to the bank with him tomorrow and then take him to the airport. We'll leave him some 'get out of town' cash and buy him a one way ticket to Mexico."

"You're fucking crazy. I'm a lawyer ... not an extortionist."

"Can you think of a better way to keep Prince from talking… without actually killing him, that is. He thinks we are hit men. If we walk away, sooner or later he'll slip out of the ropes and his first call will be to Ricky."

"Jesus Christ and Mother of Mary", answered David as he began to understand Jason's point of view.

As they walked down the street towards the nearest coffee shop Jason regretted involving David in tonight's business. Hell, David had insisted. After walking two blocks and not finding a coffee shop they decided on a quiet bar.

Jason had a beer but David ordered a double scotch. He downed it quickly and then sat back morosely playing with his water glass.

"Who's Ricky?" he asked.

Jason was pleased. David was starting to think again.

⊰⊱

At nine AM Prince and Jason caught a cab and drove to the bank Prince specified. David followed behind in Jason's Chevy.

"My partner says if you even take one peek at his face the deal is off, and you end up shark bait. Keep your eyes front and center. You got that", cautioned Jason.

"That's cool, man. Front and center."

Jason shook his head in disgust wondering how Prince would look if he had "Yes Man" tattooed across his forehead. Probably not much different. Yet Prince had kept his cool. You had to admire him for that.

Jason entered the bank with Prince and waited while Prince went to the safety deposit boxes. As they left the bank Jason directed Prince to place the briefcase in the back seat of the Chevy, which David had parked, ahead of the taxi. All Prince saw was the back of David's head. Next, they returned to their cab and drove to the airport. David followed and parked in the long term parking section. He pulled the brief case into the front seat and made a cursory count of the money to which he added the other twenty five thousand from under Prince's bed. Jason had agreed to give Prince five thousand dollars to help him disappear. Briefcase in hand he headed toward the Air Mexico counter.

Jason and Prince were talking away like two buddies, one of whom had driven the other to the airport. Jason saw David from across the terminal. When their eyes met David gave him a quick nod and turned away. An hour later Jason sat down beside David at the Air Bahamas section.

"I already have my ticket", said David. "Take the briefcase and buy your own. I'm not saying another word to you until we meet at the Holiday Inn, in the lobby, at five this afternoon."

"Good work". Jason stood up and taking the briefcase went to the ticket counter.

Ricky was sprawled out on a lounge chair by the pool. There was the usual amount of activity around him. There were four young women, dressed in the tiniest bikinis yet invented and half a dozen men in open necked shirts displaying gold chains, and all wearing hardware in either shoulder or belt holsters.

"There's a call from the airport boss. The pilot says there is a cigarette boat coming in from Normans Cay."

"How many people?"

"Three, boss."

"Somebody get upstairs with the telescope and watch them as they go by."

A few minutes later one of the goons came up to Ricky and said, "Boss, it's two of Farris' men and that fat tug boat operator."

"Keep an eye on them."

Ten minutes later he returned. "They dropped off the fat guy at his dock. Farris' men are headed back to Normans Cay."

"Wait until after dark. I don't like the way that fat nigger worked for me one day and a three days later is working for Farris. It ain't loyal. Make sure he gets a good lesson in loyalty." Ricky strutted back into the house.

George and Victor dropped Sting Ray off at the end of his dock, promising for the umpteenth time to pick him up at seven o'clock Monday morning.

Sting Ray's home was his boat yard. The dock was solid concrete and the bumpers were braided rubber tires, more suitable for work boats than for sleek, white fiberglass hulls. Victor had been careful not to touch the tires not wanting to have to spend an hour cleaning dirty black streaks off his hull as Sting Ray stepped out of the cigarette boat.

There was a heavy marine travel lift at the deep water end of the harbor. Machinery, barges and a couple of derelict hulls lay scattered over the acre of land. The tool shed looked old but the door and the windows were protected with steel strapping welded into a grid work. On second glance one might notice that the walls themselves were made of plate steel, salvaged from a grounded cargo boat. Once locked nothing short of cutting torches would allow any one to break in.

In the corner of the yard was a shabby hut, built with concrete block. The door was locked with a padlock that looked as if it came from the First World War. The door itself was old and wooden. There were security bars on the Venetian windows. But once inside the shack, the mood changed dramatically. The walls were plastered with concrete and newly decorated with fresh white paint. The floor was red tile that shone as if it had been waxed yesterday. The furniture in the tiny house was Spartan, yet friendly. A sofa with wrought iron and glass end tables, a television, a table with three wooden chairs. The kitchen area was no more than a small counter with a sink, but it sported a new gas stove and fridge, and a free standing china cabinet. The bedroom area held a double size bed, neatly made up with an attractive bed spread. The interior wall at the rear of the house had a single door. Through the door and to the right was a small bathroom with a modern glass shower stall. To the left, was a walk in closet. It was all meticulously clean and sparkling.

Sting Ray dropped his bag of dirty laundry outside the door. One of the laundry lady's kids would soon pick it up without being asked. The next day it would be delivered back cleaned, ironed and immaculately folded. If a button were missing there would be a new button in its place. Delivery was always be made by a child of about eight or ten years old, sometimes a boy, sometimes a girl. Sting Ray would give them a few dollars and it would always be the right amount but how the price was arrived at was always a mystery. It was never discussed. In fact the children seldom said a word to him.

He reached under the kitchen sink and pulled out a bottle of rum. He sat down at the table and drank two glasses of rum and water. Then he got up, showered, shaved and dressed in clean clothes. He was getting ready to leave when he saw headlights pull into the yard. He poured another glass of rum and sat back down at the kitchen table.

Ricky's two gunmen entered without knocking. A third man followed. Sting Ray recognized him as one of the men who came on board the tug with Ricky. He remained seated, his burly arms resting on the table.

"Working hard these days", snarled third man.

Sting Ray said nothing. The two goons sat down at the table on either side of Sting Ray while the third, who appeared to be the boss, remained standing at the head of the table, opposite Sting Ray.

"Better answer", suggested the first man, removing an automatic from a shoulder holster and laying it on the table in front of him.

"Hard enough", answered Sting Ray.

The second man reached out and slapped Sting Ray hard with his knuckles in a backhand motion. Sting Ray absorbed the blow ignoring the pain and continued to stare belligerently at the leader.

Slowly one of his hands came up off the table. After rubbing his chin both hands dropped to his lap.

"Ricky ain't thrilled with your choice of employers, asshole. He told me to give you a short lesson in loyalty, but I'm willing to be lenient and not break you up too much provided we have a little understanding. You let us know as soon as you find the gold and we'll leave you in one piece, a bit of minor denting just for show."

Sting Ray stared back at the leader silently. The second goon moved to strike him again but suddenly the table flew up, off the floor, as Sting Ray exploded into a standing position. In Sting Ray's right hand was a short machete, one that had been taped under the table for years. Just a precaution in an unsafe world. It now arced towards one goon's hand as he reached for his gun, catching him hard on the wrist and slicing half way through the bone. Clutching a table leg in his left hand, Sting Ray up ended the table and holding it in front of him, he hurled his sturdy frame forward. The table, acting as a battering ram knocked one man over backwards in his chair and sent the boss man flying towards the kitchen cabinet. In one fluid movement, with all three assailants on the floor or injured Sting Ray dropped the table and hit the electrical switch plunging the room into darkness. In that darkness he slipped out the door.

The first Italian recovered and followed Sting Ray out into the night. But he was slow in the dark. A piece of two-inch steel pipe aimed at shin level broke his leg as he crossed the threshold. He screamed in agony and crumbled to the ground, blocking the doorway. It took a few more seconds before someone found the light switch.

"That fucking son of a bitch", screamed the man who had been in charge. He looked at his two goons, one with a broken arm gushing blood and the other with a broken leg writhing in pain.

"Get in the car, fast", he ordered.

"Fast. I got a broken leg! Help me up!" whined one man.

Sting Ray was nowhere to be seen. The three men helped each other into the car with a great deal of cursing about their pain.

"You gotta drive, boss!" said one of them.

The car, a white limousine, was now covered with blood. The two injured men struggled into the back while the boss, swinging his gun left and right covered them. In a state of mad fear he searched in vain for Sting Ray, in the blackness. Taking a last glance around, he slid behind the wheel and started the car. Slamming it into gear, his tires spinning, he started out the lane. The car moved about fifteen feet when there was a crash of steel bending and the car stopped instantly.

"What the fuck?" screamed the driver. A piece of pipe crashed through the rear window. The driver, beginning to panic, restarted the car and once again, slammed it into gear. The pipe crashed across the hood.

The windshield gave way into a thousand shards of safety glass. Something was holding the limousine from going forward. He jammed his foot hard against the floor. The motor and tires screamed in unison and what ever it was gave way. The limo careened out the lane. The driver saw the heavy chain draped across the opening onto the street. It had not been there when they entered. Realizing his dilemma too late to stop, he jammed his foot to the floor and slammed into the chain that had been welded to the steel post on one side and fastened by a padlock onto a post at the other end. The padlock was the weakest link and the chain gave way, but not before it had demolished the entire front end of the limousine.

Sting Ray stepped out of the darkness, bent over, and hand over hand began to pull in a length of chain that stretched down the lane. At the end of it were a large hook and a twisted chrome bumper.

"God Damn General Motors. Could have built it better than that!"

Before leaving for The Coconut Tree, Sting Ray pulled the mattress off his bed, and after throwing down a piece of canvas, lay the mattress on the tool shed floor. He carefully locked his buildings.

Sting Ray entered the Coconut Tree and quietly sat down at small table close to the bar.

"What'll it be, Sting", said Samantha.

"Rum", he answered without looking up.

As Samantha approached the table she saw the welt below Sting Ray's eye.

"That looks like a shiner starting up on yo' pretty ol' face" said Samantha. She had a dozen questions about his being at Normans Cay and now she had a reason to talk to him.

"I'll get some ice on that, right away." Samantha hurried off returning quickly with a few chunks of ice wrapped in a cloth. She pulled up a chair and began to administer the ice pack. Sting Ray tried to stop her but without much conviction. Samantha pampered him as if he had just returned from a war, ignoring her other patrons.

Few men could resist attention by someone as attractive as Samantha and Sting Ray was no exception.

"It's OK. It'll be down by morning". He took a long swallow of rum.

"You get a winch handle in yo' face?" Samantha persisted.

"No.... something dumber than that. One of Ricky's Italian stallions got in a lucky swing."

"Ricky did that to you. I thought you were working for him".

"Not for the last week."

"That's something.... You must have sure pissed him off if he sicked one of his dogs on you."

"Three of his dogs", corrected Sting Ray.

"Three dogs", said Samantha admiringly. "But you look pretty good. Just a black eye. I hope you did a bit of damage yo' self".

That made Sting Ray smile, although the smile made him wince. "I broke one man's arm, the other man's leg and reduced a hundred thousand dollar limousine to a demolition derby contender."

"You joshing me, Sting."

"No ma'am, I'm telling you the truth".

"Well I'll be!"

Samantha rose and picked up Sting Ray's empty glass. She walked back to the bar and filled the tumbler with rum. Returning to the table she placed the glass in front of Sting Ray and sat down beside him. She took the ice pack from his hand and wrung out the cloth on the cement floor.

"You drink all you want. Your money's no good here tonight," said Samantha, with a wicked smile lighting up her face. "But you want to tell me all about this."

One of the regulars called to her for a drink.

"You can see I'm busy. You got legs. If you want a drink you walk over to the bar yo'self. Gladys, will serve you," was her tart reply.

Samantha's touch was as gentle as a butterfly's as she nursed Sting Ray's face. She spoke to him in a husky voice not much louder than a whisper. "You know, anyone who does damage to that peddling bastard is a friend of mine... but I thought you was working for him."

"I worked for him one day.... And he ain't paid me yet. You remember those two white men that talked with me the other day."

"Sure".

"Well those two men, with a bit of help, mashed up by Ricky's boat pretty nicely. Not just the two men, either. Their wives were in it, thick as thieves. See, Ricky had me working on a salvage job on the edge of Normans Spit. He'd driven out in that big fishing boat of his. The one he says has the tallest fly bridge in Nassau. Anyway, Mrs. Farris comes out in a cigarette boat driven by Farris's men. Farris must have been hiding in the boat. Somehow he went over the side with dive gear on. Mrs. Farris, she distracted Ricky while Farris unbolted Ricky's props and cut Ricky's anchor line. And that fancy, ol' fishing boat of his just drifted right up on the coral. I had to drag him off. Can't say I was overly careful about it, either." Sting Ray grinned at the memory and continued. "Ricky got all pissed off and starts shooting at Farris and the other guy from the deck of my tug, but they was smart and had backed up, out of range. The other white man is standing by with his woman in a real nice sailboat. Well he puts a high power rifle up to his shoulder and sends a shot right beside where Ricky is standing. The bullet ricocheted off a winch just like in the movies. Weeerrrr! Ricky jumped about a mile. Then the white guy aims at Ricky's boat and picks off Ricky's windshield. If that ain't enough he let's off a few more shots, right at the waterline. Nice shooting, too! Between the bullet holes and the coral head Ricky's boat would have gone straight down if I hadn't put a three-inch pump on board. Ricky was so pissed. But with no boat of his own he had to call off the week's work. Then Normans Cay hired me and they paid a week in advance so I been working fo' them ever since. That pissed Ricky off even more and he came gunning fo' me tonight, but I outsmarted the rotten wop bastard."

"What happened, mon? Tell me everything. I swear I won't tell a soul." Samantha drew a line across her lips and then drew a cross over her left breast. She reached across the table touching Sting Ray's burly forearm.

"OK Samantha. I'll tell you but you keep it to yo self, hear!"

Sting Ray downed half of his drink and collected his thoughts. "There's some salvage work being done over at Normans Cay. I won't say more about the work but both Ricky and Farris, who owns Normans Cay, want what's on the bottom. When Ricky showed up there, the Normans Cay gang blew them right away like I tol' you.

Ricky's boat is finished. I hauled it to a dry dock boat yard, but that boat is mashed up bad."

"I heard it came in all tilted over on one side. Everybody in Nassau is talking about Ricky's boat!"

"Yah, it was tilted over some, weren't it".

"Sort o' like this." Samantha leaned way over sideways and grinned at Sting Ray.

Sting Ray laughed and continued his story; "See, Farris and that other dude had tried to hire me the night they was here. Only Ricky had hired me first. Ricky wasn't exactly "offering" to hire me, neither. Then, when Ricky's boat gets all broke up, Normans Cay gets hold of me and offers me at least a week's work, payable in advance, and possibly more work after. So I go. Them people on Normans Cay are real fine people... not at all like Ricky's. They all been working hard.

"Anyway, tonight I come home to rest up for a couple of days. See, the folks on Normans Cay even gave me a ride back in their fancy cigarette boat. Ricky must have seen the boat in the channel so just after dark he sends three of his men over to pay me a little visit. Well Samantha, that's where he went wrong. My boat yard gets mighty dark when the sun goes down but me.... I knows every inch of her. So while they was stumbling around in the dark I had the upper hand. I managed to break one guy's leg and another guy's arm."

"Ricky will be seeing red when they get back," said Samantha smiling.

"You ain't heard the best part. Ricky might be seein' red, but he ain't goin' to be seeing much white limo color. See, the third little wop was just pissing himself to get the hell out of there. His two goons are too broken up to drive so he has to drive himself. Well, when they was piling into the limousine, I took a length of chain and hooked it onto the limo's bumper. The third eyetalian drives away about ten feet before the chain comes tight. The bumper is hanging down on the ground when the limo finally stops. I pick up an ol' piece of pipe and mash up the rear window, then the front window. The driver hits the gas again and after leaving half the rubber on his tires in my lane, the bumper breaks off, an' he shoots out the lane like a slingshot. Only problem is, I put the chain back across the gate. He hit it at about forty miles an hour. The chain broke but I got a whole collection of twisted limousine parts scattered up and down my lane."

Samantha was listening in awe. Nobody on the waterfront would have denied that Sting Ray was tough. He was no braggart, either. She suspected he would hang Ricky's bumper in a place of honor somewhere in his yard.

"I sure would have liked to see that," said Samantha. "You must have looked like Rambo." She knew she was laying on the flattery a bit heavily but she also knew that Sting Ray was enjoying her attention and would respond to flattery like a sponge to water.

"I just wish I'd have got that third guy better. Busting into my house like that.... Who does that little wop think he is, anyway?"

"You take care of yourself, hear! Ricky won't forget tonight."

"I already moved my mattress into the tool shed. Dynamite couldn't hurt that building. It's mostly built of scrap steel."

"You be careful anyway!"

Sting Ray became serious. "How come you hate Ricky enough to give away free booze, Samantha?"

Samantha looked down at the table without answering. A few minutes later she got up. She fetched a bottle of her best rum from the bar and returned to

Sting Ray's table carrying a clean glass. She topped up the tug boat operator's glass and poured herself a healthy shot.

"Ricky and his cocaine is the reason my kid brother is in the hands of the Lord. That man is a curse on paradise! He's worse than the devil himself. Sting.... You be careful, hear."

"I suspected something like that. I'm sorry, Samantha."

"I swore I'd get back at him some day." Samantha paused. "But I thought Normans Cay was drug dealers too!"

"Maybe they are, maybe they ain't. Farris is a smuggler, all right. So was his Daddy. And he didn't build that island of his without the kind of money that cocaine buys. But I'm going to tell you something. He's not the same kind of person Ricky is. No way! And I'm going to tell you something else. I hear a lot of gossip on the waterfront. But ever since Farris got married I haven't heard much about him. He still guards his little piece of the Caribbean with his cigarette boats and lives mighty private, but if I was a gambling man, I'd say he was retired. Now don't go repeating that."

Samantha topped up both drinks and sat back absorbing what Sting Ray had told her. Farris and the other white guy had certainly acted like gentlemen and treated her a lot differently than Ricky had. Questions began forming in her mind.

"You said that this is all about salvage work at Normans Cay?" she asked.

"I've been hired to do some salvage work but that's all I'm saying on the subject."

Samantha sipped on her rum. She was starting to formulate a plan. She just wasn't sure what the objective was. Other than revenge.

Chapter 28

Samantha drove her battered-up Toyota across the bridge to Paradise Island. She turned right and staying close to the water entered the domain of the very rich. It wasn't far to Ricky's house. A mansion, overlooking the channel between Nassau and Paradise Island. She knew her beat-up old car was conspicuous in such a glamorous setting but that couldn't be helped. Besides, it would be dark in another fifteen minutes.

She drove past the house and followed the road as it swung around the tip of the island and on toward the hotels and casinos on the ocean side. She pulled into a parking lot and turned around. Night was setting in quickly. By the time she returned to Ricky's house it would be pitch black. A few drops of water sprinkled on her windshield. A bit of rain would make it that much darker.

The automatic lights were on but they were neither particularly bright nor well placed. Samantha saw a route where she thought she could slip through, undetected.

"You don't even know what you are looking for, girl", she muttered out loud.

She pulled off the road and parked against some bushes.

"Don't let there be dogs, Lord. Please, don't let there be dogs."

Samantha had no problem jumping over the wall despite the broken glass embedded in the cement cap that topped it. Wearing dark clothes and tennis shoes she sprinted the hundred yards to the house. She took a minute to catch her breath with her back pressed tight against the stucco wall of the mansion. Her luck was holding. She managed a quick peak in the window. The room was large and seemed to be some kind of games room. There were six or eight chesterfields and a dozen or so easy chairs scattered about. A billiard table was the most prominent piece of furniture although a Wurlitzer Juke Box glittered in one corner. In the opposite corner was a big screen TV.

There was no sign of Ricky but one of his henchmen was playing pool with a girl in a blouse cut so low it seemed impossible that she didn't fall out as she leaned over the table.

"So what happened to Ricky's boat?" the girl asked.

"It's finished. Ricky told me to sell it. I bought a forty-foot Scarab for him today. The guy told me it would do a hundred miles an hour, plus. Personally I felt a lot safer on the fishing boat. It was OK on deck. I hated that damned ladder, though. Ricky liked it all right. He thought he was King Shit, sitting in that chair, four stories high."

"The Scarab sounds hot!"

"Ricky will need something fast if he takes on Normans Cay. They really screwed him good. You can bet your ass that Ricky wants to do some damage there."

The girl lined up another shot. She sank that ball and moved on to the next, sinking it too. Each time, she leaned low over the table, displaying her breasts and wiggled her behind just before shooting. The last ball hung an inch from the pocket. She stood up and stomped her foot.

Gino moved around the table to set up his shot. He put it down cleanly and moved quickly through four more. "Ricky told me he had ordered up some Colombians to help out at Normans Cay."

"You mean 'hired guns'."

"Those Colombians have been at war with each other since before you were born. They are frigging military. They've been wear army uniforms and carrying grenades in their pockets since they were six years old. I figure Ricky is planning some sort of commando mission. I hope he knows what he's doing." Gino's voice did not sound too convinced.

Samantha had heard enough. She waited until it was the girl's turn to shoot, then sprinted back to her car. She was soaked to the skin but feeling good about her reconnaissance. Next she had to decide what she would do with this information.

Kingsley sat in his favorite barstool at the corner of the bar. Samantha had hurried home and changed into dry clothes. She was now back at work. The rain had let up and the courtyard was busy. Samantha spoke to Kingsley, excitedly, while piling drinks on her tray.

"This is what I know. Sting Ray is working for Normans Cay on what he calls a salvage job. I think it's something valuable but he won't say much. Ricky is after the same thing. Seems like Farris and that other white man, who was with him, are partners. The day we saw Ricky's boat doing 'the List' Ricky had tried to claim jump on the Normans Cay find. Michael Farris cut the anchor line on Ricky's boat. Ricky's man tried to save the boat from being grounded on the reef… but when he gave it gas it had no props. The motor just spins Whirrrr! Then CRASH onto the reef. Sting pulls it off… yank! Yank! YANK! The boat gets mashed up coming off the coral. Ricky gets all pissed and lets go a few rounds … rattatattatta. The second white dude takes out a rifle and Bang…. Pitooowww … right beside Ricky. Then Bang again and Ricky's windshield goes … Scrunch. Then Bang, Bang. Bang, again, right at the waterline and … Blub, Blub, Blub …Ricky's boat starts to sink. Sting Ray puts a pump on board, Buhdoom, Buhdoom, Buhdoom, and pretty soon Kingsley and Samantha are doing "the Ricky List" and Ricky's fly bridge starts looking more like the Leaning Tower of Pizza. Samantha put one hand on the bar, and leaning at a crazy angle hummed a little ditty while moving her hips.

The old man laughed heartily "Those are some sound effects, girl".

"I gotta deliver these drinks. Soon come back, Mon".

Kingsley was still chuckling when Samantha returned.

"I was just over at Ricky's house. Ricky is planning a commando raid, with Colombian mercenaries, on Normans Cay."

"You was where?" Kingsley's laughter turned to bile in his throat.

"I snuck into his yard and listened at the window. That's why I was late."

"Them's dangerous people. You can't go sneaking around their house."

"Well I just did! Now we got to tell Normans Cay what to expect."

"What do you mean "we"?"

"I need your boat, Kingsley".

"Lord Jesus."

Chapter 29

With Rebecca safely lashed to the mast and floating away, over half the crew already dead, and the Captain drowned, it took only ten more minutes before sea claimed its prize and the ship's bow dipped into its last wave. The forward hatch cover gave way and the ocean rushed in. The bow failed to rise as the next wave approached. More water flooded in. The sturdy hull set a course it was never intended for, entering the third dimension rather than the two in which it had performed so valiantly. The stern section, already flooded did not rise dramatically. It was merely the last part of the ship to go down. The descent was far more peaceful than the last few hours on the surface. Even the impact on the sandy bottom was relatively gentle. The ship settled upright on the bottom, her keel still in tact.

Rebecca's sea chest skidded forward, snapping the wooden legs of the narrow bed, like matchsticks, as the ship came to a halt. A few minutes later a needlefish inspected its new home. A day later a plethora of sea life had arrived to scavenge on the food supplies and dead crew of the sunken ship. Crawfish or spiny lobster crawled everywhere in numbers that defied the rational thought of anyone who knew their habitat. Small fish pecked at the myriad of floating particles and bigger fish dined on a variety of meat and organs they had never tasted before. The large predators came and dined on everything, sometimes their own.

A month later the more voracious eaters had come and gone but the microscopic creatures stayed, content to nibble on a piece of wood for generations.

Iron hardware and tools slowly rusted until they were completely disintegrated or at least, beyond recognition. Larger items rounded out and lost their square edges. The cannon balls survived well. The two bronze cannons, which had sat proudly on the bow until they broke loose with the final impact on the bottom, resisted the sea admirably. The silver cross, which Rebecca had nailed above her bed, turned black and began to change its shape, losing its filigree and fine lines. The iron nail that held it in place gave way one day and the cross spiraled downward another two feet to the sand that floated into the hull, whenever the sea was angry. A while later, a piece of the hull fell on it and bent it. The leather hinges on the sea chest remained strong for fifty years, helped perhaps by the layer of sand that mostly covered it. But slowly, they too lost their integrity and gave up to the salt water and organisms that surrounded them. The sides of the chest still held but the top gave way and most of the contents, dresses and books and two fine linen table cloths, which Rebecca had treasured, failed to last long after that.

But the gold, impervious to nature, waited patiently, refusing to tarnish or give up its detail. Two hundred years later, when the wood and iron, cloth and leather had drifted away, enough to let in a stream of light, emanating from an underwater flashlight, it responded. Its untarnished surface shone in the light as it had eons ago, when the hand of God and evolution, had formed it. And as it shone again when an ancient miner's hammer had pried it from the rock that had been its home for a million years.

Phil stopped breathing. For a full twenty seconds he hovered, involuntarily holding his breath and staring. He reached down and touched it. It was so pure and clean. Looking up he saw Farris blowing a hole in the sand twenty feet away. A cloud, backlit by the powerful perimeter lights, drifted away from him. Phil swam over and touched his friend's shoulder. Farris looked up but continued to work. Phil shook him and he released the trigger on the blower. He seemed annoyed to be disturbed and pointed at the hole he was working on. Phil focused and shone his light into the pit. There was a distinctive shape of a chest, similar to the one Phil had just left. But it was heavier construction and had resisted the sea better. Phil ignored it and pulling Farris' arm dragged him back to his find. Farris too, caught his breath, then, with a reverence reserved for the past, for death and for history, slowly fanned his hand over the gold, blowing off bits of sand and sea life, but not touching it.

Phil signaled that they should surface and the two men began their ascent.

Without much ado, other than a conspiratorial wink, they climbed on board the tug and helped each other out of their tanks.

"See anything?" asked Judy.

"A few pounds of gold … nothing much", answered Phil, casually.

Judy bent over at the waist and jutted her jaw forward. "So why didn't you bring it up so we could all see it?"

"Thought you might want to see it "in situ". After all, Rebecca was your granny's friend."

Linda was carrying a towel for Farris. She stopped. Judy slowly straightened. The two women studied their men for telltale signs of humor.

Judy was the first to speak. Her voice was cautious and her demeanor uncertain. "You're not serious by any chance, are you?"

"Ask Michael", responded Phil, non-commitally.

Judy looked at Farris, then toward Linda.

"Well", demanded Linda.

"Just like Phil said. Better suit up."

"Linda, have you noticed anything strange", asked Judy.

"Not really. What?"

"These two guys haven't loosened their wet suits yet. Maybe we should put on our equipment."

"OK", said Linda uncertainly.

Sting Ray had appeared and was standing by. Suddenly he erupted. "Where's my glass bucket".

With that pandemonium broke out with everyone scrambling for equipment. To all the men's delight, including Sting Ray's, both Judy and Linda, who were still dressed in clothes, stripped to their underwear and donned their wet suits. For some reason, ladies underwear is sexier than bathing suits that cover even less. Maybe it's because it's thinner. The men unabashedly admired each other's wives undergarments while Sting Ray stood wide eyed, watching both.

In a beautiful ceremony, intended to show disdain for male immaturity, Linda, having put on her wet suit, turned toward the men. Her zipper was undone an inch below her naval and the tight fitting suit stretched open revealing a silk and lace brassier. She thrust her hips forward, took the zipper in her right hand and ever so slowly, pulled it toward her neck, covering her bosom in the process.

"Enjoy the show, boys", she asked sarcastically.

Judy stood watching in awe but quickly changed gears.

"Could you help me with my zipper, Lyn honey", she cooed.

"Sure, Hun".

Judy took a sideways pose with her hands on her hips and Linda reached down and slowly and tenderly raised Judy's zipper.

Judy slid close to Linda, pursed her lips, and planted an imaginary kiss, two inches away from Linda's puckered mouth.

Then both women stared at Phil and Michael's crotches to see what kind of reaction they had generated. Even through the neoprene wet suits the reaction was evident. They turned in unison and strutted toward the stern with arms laced around each other's back. After a few steps Judy planted a gentle slap on Linda's butt and then squeezed a handful of ass. Linda responded in kind and they marched off, holding firmly onto each other's asses.

The men stood, stupefied.

"You gotta love finding gold", said Phil.

"I ain't never seen anything like that", stammered Sting Ray.

"Jesus H. Christ!" muttered Farris.

Phil and Judy descended, with Farris hovering above, towing Linda's raft directly over the find. Once in position, he descended and the three held hands in a circle and looked up toward Linda. She waved down at them. Phil snapped a few pictures of the site but Judy was bent over, caressing one of the gold bricks. There were three of them, just as the letter had stated.

Michael had drifted off. Phil looked up when he heard the sound of the blower. Michael seemed intent on digging out that box he had discovered. Judy and Phil swam over to where Michael was working. Michael raised the blower and blew horizontally, pushing the cloud away. Using his dive knife he pried away the top of the chest which was already, all but disintegrated. He gave another shot with the blower and shone his light into the hole.

In front of their eyes the Captain's sextant appeared. It had been stored in a leather case, little of which remained. Beside it was a large gold cross, studded with emeralds. Beneath the cross, lining the bottom of the chest lay a layer of gold coins. It was the Captain's lifetime savings and working capital. And it was a foot deep.

Michael reached in and extracted a single coin. He showed it to the others and then carried it up to Linda, presenting it to her outstretched hand from underwater, then slowly curled her fingers around it.

Phil looked at Judy who returned his gaze. For a half minute they drifted, slowly sinking to a kneeling position, each holding the others hands and staring into each others eyes through their masks. Finally Phil gave an almost imperceptible tilt of his head in the direction of the gold bricks. Judy nodded firmly. Holding hands they swam back to the gold. One at a time he lifted out the gold bricks and handed them to Judy. The weight of them made her sink but she resolutely held on and braced her feet on the bottom. When Phil had extracted the third brick he looked up and saw Judy standing awkwardly. He grinned and reached over toward her. Gently he squeezed her buoyancy control device and a burst of air inflated her vest. Adding a quick shot to his own BC, holding on to one brick in one hand and Judy's harness in the other, the two slowly began their assent.

Sting Ray was standing on the ladder and proudly received the gold bricks.

"Michael wants me to send down buckets for the coins", he instructed Phil and Judy.

"Good idea!" Phil checked his gauge. "Mike and I will need fresh tanks."

"Got 'em ready for you. But we have to be out of here in an hour if we want to be back at the other site before dawn."

It took nearly two hours to fill three pails with the contents of the Captain's trunk.

Sting Ray poured on the steam as the tug sped back to the first site. Everyone, except Sting Ray drank rum and fruit juice and talked excitedly, reliving each moment. So enthralled were they, that they failed to notice a small Bahamian fishing boat that sailed past, a quarter of a mile away.

Samantha, wearing a man's shirt and a baseball cap, watched Sting Ray's boat approach through the powerful binoculars.

"What's Sting Ray doing way out there, at this time of the morning", asked Kingsley.

"I don't know. The two men and the two women are sitting there. They keep pointing at the plastic buckets in front of them. Wait a minute, Farris is reaching into the bucket. He's pulling out something. It seems heavy. It looks like a box. He's handing it to one of the women."

At that moment a ray of sunshine peaked around the corner of the wheel house and sparkled off the gold brick.

"Oh my God! Oh my God! Oh my God", stammered Samantha.

"What is it, child?" questioned the old man.

"Baby, it's gold. It's solid gold. That's why it's so heavy!"

"You keep your head down, girl. If they have gold on board they don't want nobody watching them through binoculars!"

"OK, mon. OK! Now one of the women is reaching into a bucket. She's got something. She's passing it around. It's too small. I can't tell what it is."

"Put those glasses away, now. We're too close. I'm moving away. No need to warn them about Ricky right now".

Kingsley put the boat into a slow turn. When a mile separated him and Sting Ray he completed the turn and headed back to Nassau.

Chapter 30

"Kingsley, would it be alright if I slept for a few minutes?"

"Sho thing, babe. You just put yo pretty li'l head down. If anything happens I'll wake you up."

Samantha stretched out on the forward deck resting her head against a rolled up towel. She thought back about Ricky coming into the bar, surrounded by his hired flunkies. Even in his designer clothes he had looked pathetic. His get up impressed half of Nassau, but the other half knew the real story. She thought about her brother, only in his teens. He had not been an angel. That was for sure. First he had mixed with the wrong people, then he had mixed with cocaine. Ricky's cocaine. A tear dribbled out of the corner of her eye. She took a corner of the towel and wiped it away. She was determined to live to watch Ricky fall. That was her promise to her kid brother.

"Sammy .... Sammy.... Wake up!"

Kingsley was calling softly from the wheelhouse. Samantha rolled over so as to see him but he was standing behind the glass, pointing out off the bow.

"Looks like we got company coming. You got better eyes than me, babe. What you make that boat out to be."

"That's a Scarab. Oh Lord. What if it's the one I heard talk about? What if it's Ricky's new boat?" she answered, moving back to the cabin and reaching for the binoculars. "Ooh man. They look like they have enough hardware to take on the US navy."

"It looks like they're coming this way. You get below and I'll pretend I'm not the US Navy."

"They're already beat, Kingsley. We saw Farris with the gold."

"That's right Samantha. Now get below like I said."

Minutes later Ricky's speedboat pulled alongside. Kingsley remained at the wheel.

"Out fishing, old man?" called one of Ricky's henchmen.

"Not fishing today. Just looking for a place that might have some conch." His voice was calm but he made no attempt to patronize.

"Better take a look", said Ricky, distractedly. The boat was coming from the direction of Normans Cay and that was the only justification Ricky required to be suspicious.

One man climbed the rail. He carried his sub machine gun. Almost immediately he saw Samantha in the cabin.

"Well lookee here. Hey boss, we got some high class cargo on board."

"Let's see", replied Ricky.

Gino was the first to recognize Samantha. "Hey boss, that's the broad from the Coconut Tree!"

Ricky stood and then climbed aboard the fishing boat. "So what did you say you was doing here, old man?"

"Looking for conch fields. Sammy came along for the ride."

"I never heard of anyone looking for conch with binoculars", sneered Ricky. He grabbed the binoculars, still around Samantha's neck and pulled hard on the leather strap throwing Samantha off balance before the strap broke. The strap left a nasty welt on Samantha's neck.

"What else have you been looking for? You're coming from the direction of Normans Cay? Seen any gold lately?"

Samantha started to say something but Ricky lashed out at her with a quick backhand.

Kingsley stood perfectly still. Samantha straightened up, defiantly.

"You OK, babe?" asked Kingsley quietly.

"I'm OK Kingsley." She turned to Ricky. "This little piss ant just likes to hit women, is all."

Ricky ignored the banter. "So you're looking for conch. Seen any "golden" conch, old man? They say you find it off Normans Cay".

"No such thing as *golden* conch", answered Kingsley.

"I say there is such a thing", said Ricky. The years of having cocaine and yes men around him had turned a spoiled brat of a kid into a powerful, young psychopath. He oozed arrogance and evil in almost equal quantities. "Bitch, you ever seen golden conch?"

"Of course I have, sugar," said Samantha smoothly. "All hissing and sputtering in a deep fryer. The same way you going to look when you leave this earth and go to Hell where you belong!"

For a second there was a stunned silence. Kingsley broke it with a sharp "Hah!"

The first man on board lashed out with a fierce kick, catching Kingsley in the shins. Kingsley began to fall but the man's left hand clamped around his throat and he rammed the side of Kingsley's head against the cabin wall. Samantha watched, terrified, as Kingsley's face began to turn blue.

Kingsley was everything to Samantha. He would treat her like a daughter, sweet talk her and flatter her like a lover, and be there for her like a friend. Watching the old man's face turn first blue and then a deathly gray was more than Samantha could stand.

"Farris already found the gold. You're too late, you cocaine peddling bastards!"

Everyone turned to Samantha at the word "gold". Samantha stared into Ricky's eyes. The young punk released his grip on Kingsley's throat.

"That's right! We saw it!" Samantha was buying time but she had no plan beyond that. "Farris found the gold. You got nothing, you dope peddling piece of shit!"

Kingsley took one last look at Samantha. Blood oozed, from the corner of her mouth where Ricky had hit her. He felt the adrenaline pump into his aging heart. He and Samantha had no cards left to play. Ricky's next move would be to slit their throats and leave them for the sharks. He was certain that his life was over. Drawing a deep breath he sprang from the cabin wall and snaked behind the wheel with an agility that amazed everyone on board. A slim bladed fishing knife appeared in his hand. He launched himself at Ricky. Perhaps his knees buckled, a result of the kick to his shins, as he sprang forward. He wasn't sure what went wrong but even as his tired old body sailed through the air he knew he had misjudged and was falling short of his mark. He saw the blade fall short of Ricky's chest but with a valiant second effort he stretched his body forward and felt the knife dig deep into Ricky's leg. He caught a glimpse of the butt of the automatic rifle as it came towards him. In a final act, with an iron grip developed through a lifetime of fishing, he squeezed the knife handle and twisted the knife. The butt of the rifle made contact. The old black man was dead before he hit the deck. Ricky fell backward against the rail, the knife buried to the hilt in his leg.

"That miserable old nigger stuck me!" he said in shock as he looked down at the blade. The pain had not yet registered, a result of the cocaine he had recently consumed. The flow of blood, however, brought vomit up the back of his throat.

Samantha flung herself at Kingsley, cradling his limp body in her arms.

Ricky was sitting on the deck, his back to the rail, pressing down on the wound that was beginning to spurt blood ferociously. "Jesus Christ! Look at this". He stared at the knife. He looked up and found himself staring into Samantha's eyes. Forgetting his wound for a second he spat out "What the fuck did you see, you bitch". His face was that of an angry child who had been beaten up and hurt.

"I saw you lose your precious gold, you miserable little prick", said Samantha venomously.

She knew Kingsley was dead and all the pain of her little brother and now Kingsley welled up in her. Hatred surged through her body. She lunged toward the rail of the decrepit fishing boat, toward Ricky's face, unthinking, wanting only to tear him apart. Her hands were clenched like a tiger's paws, her fingernails aching to gouge out Ricky's eyes.

The guard saw her move and stepped in front of her, blocking her path. He followed through with a powerful uppercut that lifted her upwards sending her crashing over the low rail of the wooden boat. She tumbled, bouncing off the deck off the Scarab, into the narrow space between the two boats. Only the cold splash of the water kept her from slipping into unconsciousness.

The guard aimed at the water where Samantha had fallen and let loose half a clip from his machine gun.

"Let the bitch drown. Sink this boat and get me home. Now!" screamed Ricky. "I'm bleeding bad".

Gino climbed aboard the fishing boat and without warning pulled the knife from Ricky's leg. Ricky screamed and collapsed, unconscious. Gino wrapped his belt around the wound. The guard fired two more bursts into the water before lending a hand to Gino, as the two men passed their semi-conscious boss across to the speedboat.

Samantha was underwater when she heard the machine gun and saw the bullets leave a trail through the water and peter out. The second burst did the same thing. She looked around and decided to surface close to the bow on the opposite side. If she stayed close to the hull, she could catch her breath and avoid being seen. Another two barrages of tiny torpedoes penetrated the surface. She watched as the bullets lost their momentum, slowed, and then simply sank in the clear water. She surfaced under the bow and held onto the start of the keel. She was slowly regaining her breath when the head of an axe penetrated the hull inches from her hand. She fought the urge to scream and instead ducked underwater. The hull shattered again a foot away from her face. This time she did scream but the water muffled the sound. Surfacing just in front of the bow she could hear Ricky moaning and swearing at his men as they tried to help him into the Scarab. The fishing boat was sinking fast but Samantha kept it between her and the Scarab. She ducked underwater again as she heard the speedboat's twin engines rev. She stayed under until she could hear it a long distance away.

Within minutes Samantha was holding onto the gunwale. She could see Kingsley's body stretched across the deck. The boat was sinking quickly and she didn't want to hold onto it any longer. She pushed away, hoping some debris or maybe even a life vest would stay afloat. Anything that she could hold on to.

The wreck started to roll towards her. The motion was slow and clumsy. Each second the list increased. She looked at Kingsley one more time and muttered a hurried prayer for him before he was taken down. Then she watched in horror as the boat listed and Kingsley rolled over on the deck. As he rolled one arm flopped over his dead body and seemed to point, in a deadly and sinister gesture. Samantha looked over her shoulder following the direction of Kingsley's hand. On the horizon, miles away, was Normans Cay. Samantha knew what she had to do.

"Thank you, Kingsley. If that's your last request, that's what I'll do. I love you, old man. I pray that the angels are taking you to a better place. You sure got Ricky good!"

Samantha started out doing a slow, steady crawl. At first each stroke hurt her rib cage when she lifted her arm and she remembered falling and bouncing off the Scarab as she fell overboard. She thought about Kingsley and the pain seemed to go away. She felt guilt about having dragged him into this mess. He had died defending her. He had been as true to her as any knight in shining armor had ever been. Now the only way she could pay him back was to save herself. She remembered his face. Even dead he had looked contented. He had died bravely. The crest of a wave coincided with her steady stroke. She looked up at the horizon. Normans Cay would be a long, long swim. It would be her penance for letting the old man die. Her pilgrimage. It was the only way she could forgive herself.

⊰§⊱

At three o'clock in the afternoon, Phil and Judy, Michael and Linda, tied up to Sting Ray's tug. Linda handed Sting Ray a casserole dish and his face lit up like a kid's at Christmas. The four sat in their lawn chairs and Sting Ray took his place on the winch cover.

"You look tired, Mon," said Farris.

"I got about three hours sleep", answered Sting Ray, between bites.

"Well you have the night off! We all do!" said Linda.

"That's just fine by me", answered Sting Ray.

"Why don't you come back and stay in the house", asked Linda.

"I prefer to sleep on board. This ol' lady don't like to be left alone".

"Well at least come back to the harbor".

"I thought about that, ma'am, and I do appreciate the offer, but look at it this way. Ricky thinks we are sitting right over top of the gold, right now. If I lift anchor, Ricky would know something was up. Either we found the gold, already, or we're getting careless. Ricky would be here in a flash and set up right where we are. It wouldn't take him long to see we ain't done much work on this site. Then he'd be bustin' into

Normans Cay, guns a-blazing, cause he'd know you duped him."

"You can't stay here forever!" said Judy.

"After a while, he'll just think we gave up. That's all."

"You make a good point", said Farris. "Just keep your radio on. We'll keep an eye on the radar from shore. If anyone approaches we'll ask you if you want "Fish soup". If you say OK, rest assured that the cavalry is on the way".

"You going back to the other location?" asked Sting Ray.

"Not for a while. There is probably more treasure to be had, but first we have to decide what to do with what we've already brought up", answered Phil.

An hour later the four climbed into the cigarette boat and headed back to Normans Cay.

"Will Ricky really attack, if he thinks the gold is here?" asked Linda.

Farris looked over at her and nodded.

Judy looked directly into Phil's eyes. Phil stared back, sensing Judy's fear.

⊰❦⊱

It was an hour before sunset. Samantha had been in the water since ten AM. Her body, exhausted though it was, still functioned. Her mind drifted lazily. She was cold.

Hours ago she had heard a sound that she was sure was the sound of powerful boat engines. Now land was closer but she was very, very tired. She had looked up from her sleepy breaststroke. She had long since given up her crawl, unable to lift her arms out of the water. From the top of a wave she saw a speedboat. "It's not going very fast", she thought. "It's not a speedboat, it's a "slowboat". In her state, approaching delirium, she thought that was very funny. It seemed to be a hundred yards away. She called to it but even in her fuzzy state she suspected she was barely whispering. She tried waving but that didn't work either. Another wave lifted her. She saw something black. She could no longer see the boat. She waited for the next wave. At what she thought was the critical moment she lifted her head.

"Land", she thought.

Kingsley spoke to her. "You ain't there yet, babe. Keep going."

"Yes Kingsley".

Samantha would not have made it if the sea had been unwilling. But the tide began to flood, pushing her gently toward Normans Cay. The sun had already set when Samantha looked up and saw a rock, looming above her head. She stopped her slow breaststroke and treaded water, trying to take in her surroundings. Something was different. There were no waves. She was surrounded by blackness but the nearby rock was the blackest of all. She was certain she was in a cave. She recognized the way the sea had undercut the rock. She had found land but she could never climb onto it. Slowly she turned in a circle.

"Over there", Kingsley called. "Look over there".

"It's a light, Kingsley. It's just a light."

"Go to the light, Honey! Go on."

Samantha took a weary stroke toward the light. Then she forgot what she was doing and simply repeated the action. Something bumped into her. It woke her and made her slightly angry. She opened her eyes. Reaching out she touched something. It was slimy but she thought it was wood. She looked up. There was a light, right above her head. She was certain it was heaven calling but she was disappointed that the light was so weak. "Heaven has little lights, Kingsley. Ain't that something!" She reached out for the wood but it bit her. The pain was sharp but not intense. Her dreary eyes opened and she looked at her hand. Nothing seemed wrong with it.

"Just a splinter, Babe", said Kingsley. "Stay awake, now."

She looked around a bit more.

"Is that a ladder?" she thought.

Her face went under water but she fought back with a weak stroke. It took two more painful strokes but she finally was holding onto a ladder. She placed a foot on the lowest rung and pushed. Her torso rose above the dock and she flopped forward, her legs still in the water.

The two couples stood on the patio at Normans Cay. Phil's arm was draped casually over Judy's shoulder. He felt the muscles tighten in her neck as she picked up the gold bar from the table.

"I can't believe it's so heavy", she exploded.

Just at that second there was a loud pop as Farris uncorked the champagne. Glasses were passed around and Farris did the honors.

"Here's to Phil and Judy ... two of the craziest people I know who were just crazy enough to put it all together."

"I'll drink to that", echoed Linda.

"Here's to new friendship and to our two, very successful business partners", responded Phil.

Phil took Judy by the hand and walked over to the patio wall overlooking the ocean. "We owe it all to you, babe", he said seriously.

"Your boat was already loaded, it was David that put us together, Mike figured out where to look when we went wrong and Linda has kept us all together .... But you're right! It was my letter ....you owe me a big kiss."

As the two embraced Linda snuggled up against Farris. She nodded at the couple and Farris grinned. "Young love", he whispered in her ear which he proceeded to nibble at.

"I never knew that finding gold stimulated hormones", she said coyly.

"You're going to find out what a good aphrodisiac it is, a little later."

"Ummm" she said and squeezed Farris.

The telephone rang and Michael picked up the cordless phone sitting on the table in front of him. He got up and walked down the steps toward the dock, out of earshot. After a brief conversation he depressed the button to disconnect. A slight frown passed over Linda's face but Michael returned to the party and poured champagne all around.

"If you two lovebirds will let go of each other long enough I'll get a photo of you holding the gold. Linda, get in there too!"

"Michael" she answered. "Put the camera on delay and get in this picture with us." She knew that Farris always avoided having his own picture taken, but there was a hint in her voice that forced Michael to comply. She gave him a disdainful look as he pulled his sunglasses out of his pocket and pulled the brim of his sun hat down. Michael balanced the camera on the edge of the table which meant that everyone had to kneel. The three gold bricks sat on a towel in front of the group.

"Just make sure the IRS never gets a copy of this photo", said Phil and everyone laughed.

"Good thinking, Phil." Michael removed his Panama hat and placed it over the front edge of the gold. "Now we can all hang copies of this picture in our living rooms."

Michael pressed the button and hurried around to join the group while the camera purred Linda reached up and pulled Michael down knowing he would try standing above the focus line as the camera clicked.

As Phil handed Michael back his hat he admired the gold bars.

He picked up one gold bar and stone-faced, said "When I was young we were so poor my parents used to wrap up empty boxes and put them under the Christmas tree".

Farris picked up the second gold bar and replied "When I was young we were so poor that we couldn't afford empty boxes." He put down the gold back on the table and shoved a hand deep into his pocket. "Why we were so poor that one year for Christmas my mother just cut holes in my pockets and told me to go ahead and play with it."

"Michael!" chastised Linda but Phil and Judy were laughing so hard that she had no choice but to join them.

The party was going strong but everyone had been caught yawning at least once. Finally Michael and Linda went inside. Phil and Judy were both tired.

"Want to go to bed?" asked Phil.

Judy slid her arm into Phil's and hugged it while laying her head on his shoulder. "You bet I do. But I'm still wound up. Let's walk down to the dock, first. I want to look at the stars."

Phil assumed there was some logic to that. His legs were tired enough that he would have gladly avoided both the stairs and the stars, but apparently Judy's muscles were impervious to lactic acid.

"What's that by the ladder?" asked Judy.

Phil disengaged himself from Judy's two handed arm hold and hurried forward.

"It's a woman. She's half drowned. Help me get her on the dock", urged Phil.

"Yoh, Farris!" he bellowed. If Michael or Linda didn't hear him Victor and George would.

Farris appeared on the patio at the same time that Victor appeared at the boathouse door.

"We've got a visitor! Get some blankets", Phil barked.

Samantha had been lying face down on the dock, her legs still dangling in the water. When Phil moved her she coughed and seawater drooled down her chin. Phil rolled her over and slapped her back hard with the heel of his hand. That brought up a bit more water but at least Samantha was breathing. Judy cradled her in her arms as they rolled her into a more comfortable position. Judy calmly detached a few pieces of seaweed from Samantha's hair and flicked them into the water.

Linda arrived with blankets. Victor and George arrived with semi-automatic pistols but quickly concealed them as they took in the scene. Farris stood back, supervising. His eyes scanned the horizon for a telltale sign of trouble but saw nothing.

"You're safe now. It's OK", cooed Judy, gently. She could feel Samantha shivering. Her lips were blue with the cold.

"I saw the white light", said Samantha. "I guess I thought it was the pearly gates". She mustered a weak smile.

"It was just the patio lights on the dock. Better luck next time", answered Phil.

"Oh." said Samantha. There were a few seconds while no one spoke.

"Kind of mistake anyone could make, hunh" said Samantha.

The tension broke. Everyone laughed quietly until Samantha started coughing again.

"You're going to be OK. If you can laugh about it, you're going to be just fine", said Farris. "Is there anyone else out there with you?" It was a question no one else had thought of.

"No.... do you remember me, Mr. Farris."

Farris studied her face. Until now she had just been someone needing help. A wet, limp woman, drooling seawater. "The Coconut Tree", he said, not sure what her response would be.

"Um hum" She looked at Phil and Judy. "Thank you for saving me. I'm Samantha". She closed her eyes and rested on Judy's shoulder. Linda tucked the blankets tighter.

"We've got to get her upstairs and warm her up before she goes into shock," said Judy.

"I'll carry her", said Phil. By the time he reached the top stair he was seriously chastising himself for volunteering. The living room was the closest. Kneeling down he laid her on the couch and stood back to catch his breath. Judy and Linda moved in with more blankets.

"What the Hell was Samantha doing out there, anyway?" muttered Farris six inches from Phil's ear.

"Beats me! Hey Mike, think we should put a blanket over the gold?"

"Jesus, yes". The dining room table was covered with a plastic tablecloth. The centerpiece was a stack of gold bars and there were piles of gold coins. Judy's computer sat closed on the corner of the table. She had tried diligently to log the find though no one had let her work. The bicycle bar was beside the table and empty glasses were scattered around. Farris had driven his "bicycle" right through the patio doors into the dining room after a few too many drinks.

Farris looked at the display. "Yah. OK. You know I'd forgotten about it for a minute."

David Windrow sat at the writing desk in his hotel room at the Holiday Inn on Paradise Island. Jason had come to the hotel in a separate cab and they had reunited in the lobby.

"We have got to contact Phil and Judy", said Windrow.

"OK. We'll check in separately. I'm going to deposit this money in the Casino's bank. It's safe there from everyone.... Including the IRS. I'll keep a few thou for pocket money. How be I meet you in your room in an hour and we'll make our plans."

David unpacked his toilet kit, washed up and brushed his teeth. He still had a half-hour to kill and decided to call the office to retrieve his voice mail.

"Mr. Windrow's office".

"Hi, Ginny, it's David. What are you doing there on a Saturday?"

"David, where the Hell have you been." Ginny was obviously upset.

"I'm in the Bahamas, in Nassau. What's the matter, Ginny? Ginny, are you crying?"

"Yes I'm crying. It's been a nightmare here. The FBI has been here ... I don't know where you are. What is going on?"

"The FBI?" asked Windrow, incredulous.

"Only I'm not sure they were the FBI. They had badges but they acted more like hoodlums than police".

"Sometimes it's hard to tell the difference. What did they want?"

"They wanted to see the Gibson file.... So I showed it to them. They had a warrant but they wouldn't leave me a copy of it. Not only that, they were all Italian. That could be a coincidence but three FBI ... all Italian. Fake warrant. I'm scared, David. Something is wrong!"

"OK Ginny, settle down. Tell me more about the FBI."

"David ... they weren't FBI. I'm not making this up. I'm scared to go home. Those guys were really creepy. Last night I went down to the corner for something sweet. I'm sure someone followed me. Then this morning I went shopping. I thought I saw him again. I was close to the office so I came here.... At least there is an alarm on the door. Then the frigging FBI show up. I wanted to tell them to screw off but I was afraid that you might get in trouble if they really were FBI agents."

David had never heard Ginny act like this. One thing he was sure of, though, was her instinct. She had a way of sizing up people at first impression that was too often correct for his logical mind to fully understand.

"Then, when they asked for the Gibson file I knew they had nothing to do with FBI. I decided I could play along and co-operate. Better still, I had them fooled. It seems like everyone wants Judy's letter, so I figured these creeps did too. Well it's not in the Gibson file. There's nothing in the Gibson file that the Pope wouldn't approve of. So I gave it to them."

David snorted a quick laugh. "Smart girl!" He collected his thoughts. What if the "FBI" did come back? Ginny might be in danger. Someone was on to his office. Gibson was dead. He reviewed his options quickly. "Ginny, here's what you do. Go to the bank and withdraw two thousand dollars. Buy a few essentials and go to the airport. There will be a room here at the Holiday Inn on Paradise Island, booked in your name. I'm in room 606. I may not be here when you arrive. If I'm not, don't worry. Enjoy the sun and the beach. Before you go, leave some kind of a message on the phone that the office is closed for a few days. Don't go back home. Got that!"

"Sure I got that. David, what is going on?"

"I'm not sure myself but it has something to do with Mrs. Gibson swiping the Simpson letter. Ginny, before you leave, seal up anything connected to the Simpson file and put it in the vault."

"O.K. David. Are you sure about this...? What if I'm over reacting?"

"In that case you get a free holiday. All expenses on the office. I hope that's the case, but I'm not taking chances, all right?"

"The Bahamas, hunh. David, you sure know how to cheer a girl up."

"Yah. See you soon. Take care!" He hung up the phone and sat staring at it.

"What the Hell am I mixed up in?" he asked himself. He checked his watch and decided to wait for Jason on the veranda. As he sat there he thought to himself that he was glad Ginny was coming to the Bahamas. He tried to push the thought away but it wouldn't leave.

⊰❦⊱

Linda walked into the living room and plunked herself down in a chair. She looked exhausted. Phil and Farris had been smoking cigars and drinking coffee.

"How's Samantha doing?" asked Farris.

"I think she's asleep by now. Judy is sitting with her but I'm pretty sure that Judy is asleep in the chair".

"It won't make me mad to crawl into bed either", said Phil.

"We kept Samantha in the Jacuzzi for nearly an hour. We were taking precautions to keep her from going into shock but I don't think she will now. At first she didn't want to get into the water but when she felt it starting to warm her up she liked it. She must have been swimming for ten hours."

"It's a miracle she made it. Thank God the tide was coming in. Otherwise she might never have reached shore. She must have been swimming in her sleep… if that's possible."

"It's a wonder she found the harbor. A lot of the island is undercut", commented Farris. "Did she say anything about why or how she happened to be out there?"

"Nothing much and I didn't press. I said we would talk about it tomorrow. After warming her up in the tub we got her into bed. There wasn't much time to talk. I made her a sandwich but she took one bite and put it down. She drank a little tea, though, with a ton of sugar in it", answered Linda.

"Well, the sun will be up in about twenty minutes. Let's all get some sleep", suggested Phil.

"How can anyone swim fourteen hours?" questioned Linda, with admiration in her voice.

Farris and Linda headed off to their room and Phil moved off toward the guest suite. He poked his head in the room where Samantha was recuperating. Judy was curled up in a big chair beside the bed sound asleep so Phil quietly shut off the light and went to their room alone. His head was spinning with the events of the night but he too was soon sound asleep.

Chapter 31

Samantha stirred in bed. She woke up confused by her surroundings but almost immediately began to remember. She closed her eyes and said another silent prayer for Kingsley.

Pushing back the covers she swung her legs over the side of the bed. They felt rubbery and she tested them before putting her full weight on them. The ensuite bathroom door was open. Samantha wobbled into the bathroom and closed the door.

"Wow!" she exclaimed under her breath as she turned toward the room. Everything was laid out on the large vanity. There was a terrycloth robe, neatly folded with a small array of cosmetics and creams in a wicker basket sitting on top. A hairbrush, toothbrush and everything else she might need were laid out beside. There was a stack of fresh towels in an ornate rack hanging on the wall but what made the largest impression was a feeling that this room had been designed by a woman, with all the little things a woman likes in a bathroom, to make it look homey. There was even a little straw hat with bows and flowers hanging on the wall. At the other end of the vanity was a silver tray with a thermos carafe, a coffee cup and saucer, a sugar bowl, and a half dozen coffee creamers in their little plastic cups sitting in a bowl of ice cubes, mostly melted. On a small desert plate were half a dozen chocolates in fancy paper wrappers. There was a note on pink stationary with a bouquet of flowers in the top corner. It read:

"Good morning, Samantha. Hope you are feeling well enough to join us in the house or on the patio when you wake up. But if you're not up to it, that's O.K., just go back to bed. We'll look in on you from time to time." It was signed, Linda.

Samantha unwrapped a chocolate and took a tiny bite. It started to ooze a sweet cream and Samantha popped the rest of it into her mouth to keep it from dripping. She looked at herself in the mirror.

"Linda, honey, it will be a pleasure to join you in the house but not before I spend at least half an hour enjoying this bathroom!"

She emerged from the bathroom in the terry cloth robe feeling fresh though still sore from her long swim. On top of the dresser, neatly folded, were a pair of designer jeans and an embroidered blouse that she had not noticed when she went into the bathroom. She unfolded the clothing and held it up in front of her in the mirror.

"I won't mind wearing these threads at all!"

⁂

David spent the remaining time trying in vain to get a phone number for Normans Cay. He had reached Highbourne Cay and had learned from the dock master that Phil and Judy had been there. After considerable prodding he learned that they were now living on Normans Cay but no one would give him a phone number. David was totally frustrated. Finally he had given up and lay down for a nap.

There was a knock on the door. David walked over to the door but just before opening it, he decided to use the peephole. Immediately he recognized Jason and let him in.

After hasty formalities he said:

"I have tracked Phil and Judy as far as Normans Cay but no one will give me a damn phone number."

"Well sit down, Davey. I'll fill you in on what I've learned." Jason picked up the phone. "You eaten yet?" he asked. Not waiting for a reply he spoke into the phone "Could you send up a couple of club sandwiches and two beer?" He glanced over at David for confirmation.

"Get me a glass of milk instead of the beer", answered David.

"And a large glass of milk. Thanks", said Jason hanging up the phone.

David raised his eyebrows and glared at Jason. Inwardly he chuckled at how smoothly Jason had invited himself to a two beer lunch on David's tab.

Jason sprawled out in the easy chair. "Don't tell me I'm a married man cause I already know that, but there are some good looking babes in this hotel, my man."

"So what have you learned", asked David somewhat caustically.

"Nobody seems to want to talk much about Normans Cay. It's owned by a guy by the name of Michael Farris who lives with his wife, Linda. There are a couple of guys who live there and work for Farris. There is also a family that lives on the island. They have their own house way at the opposite end and they take care of the grounds and cook and clean. Farris is a smuggler, that part's clear, but no one knows anything about his operation. No one is allowed on the island.

There is another drug kingpin in Nassau. His name is Ricky Somethingini. In the last couple of weeks a feud has flared up between Ricky and Normans Cay. Apparently Farris trashed a million-dollar sport fisherman that belongs to Ricky. The story goes that Ricky apparently got too close to the island. Farris must have tricked him somehow because when Ricky's fishing boat was towed in, it had no propellers, no windshield and a half a dozen bullet holes as well as a big gash from a coral reef.

Ricky is one bad ass Mafia drug lord. That is for sure. He lives in the biggest house on Paradise Island. Right here! He sells his coke to the tourists, and to the locals here in Nassau, and to half of Miami. Big operation. He drives around in a big white limo and always has two or three bodyguards. He keeps a regular, ever-changing harem at his house and personally consumes huge quantities of coke daily. People are scared shitless of him but he pays good money and there is no shortage of Bahamians willing to run his drugs to Miami. He must pay the police here a small fortune because they just look the other way."

"So what about this feud?"

"No one knows much about it. It just started after about five quiet years. My guess is that Farris pirated a big shipment of Ricky's coke. Anyway, Ricky is out to get Farris. I heard that Ricky's limo came back over the bridge all mashed up on Friday night so whatever is going on, is going on right here in Nassau too. Ricky is out a limo and a boat. No damage report on the Normans Cay gang."

"You hear anything about sunken treasure.... Or gold?" asked David

"No", answered Jason. Jason looked surprised but covered it quickly.

"Anything else?"

"Maybe, I'm not sure. I heard a rumor that some heavyweights were being assembled in Miami. It might have nothing to do with this feud but then again it might. I have a man at the airport and another with a view of anyone coming in or out of Ricky's hacienda."

"What about the money?"

"I took out five thousand". He reached into his pocket and tossed a roll, tied up with an elastic band, at Windrow. "That's twenty-five hundred. The balance is in the Casino bank. When it comes out it will be as clean as a snowfall in Vermont. Don't be afraid to lose it either. It will look better if I use the money rather than just letting it sit."

"OK. New development. My secretary is arriving sometime soon. I just spoke to her. Three Italian guys with FBI badges, which Ginny thinks were fake, showed up at my office. My office! Can you believe that? They asked for the Gibson file and had some paperwork to back up their request. Ginny smelled a rat but was as cool as a cucumber. She willingly complied with their request and turned over the Gibson file. You see, the letter, that everyone is after, is in my personal safe. Ginny knew that. If those bozos were after the letter they sure didn't know where to look. So I figure they were just guessing. Anyway, Ginny was pretty upset. She may have been followed home last night. She's scared so I told her to get out of town." David tried to sound casual but he knew he could hardly wait to see Ginny. He also had a feeling his relationship with her was going to take a dramatic turn.

"This letter sure is "hot", what's your secretary like?"

David picked up a shoe from under the bed and threw it at Jason who nimbly caught it.

There was a knock on the door. "'Bout time" said Jason. "I'm so hungry my stomach thinks my throat's been cut."

❧

"So that's pretty much it." Samantha sat at the kitchen table with Michael and Linda, Phil and Judy. "I know now it was pretty dumb to say anything about the gold but.... I wasn't thinking."

"You were just trying to protect Kingsley", said Phil,

"He tried to talk me out of vengeance. He said vengeance was the devil's work, but I wouldn't listen", said Samantha.

Michael looked at Phil and cocked his head toward the door.

"Don't you dare, Michael Farris! Judy and I have as much stake in this as you do. If you have something to say, say it to all of us." Linda could be very assertive when she chose to be.

Michael shrugged his shoulders. "Can't get away with a thing!" he commented casually. He looked at Linda and spoke directly to her. "Ricky's next move will be a frontal attack on Normans Cay. Did you really want to hear that, dear?"

"Its true", said Samantha. "I heard someone talking about Colombians and grenades".

Linda sucked in her breath and Judy muttered, "Oh my God!"

"Am I to blame for this?" asked Samantha. For a second she sounded like a small child about to be punished.

"No. Not really", said Michael, calmly. "Ricky has been sitting back for over a week while we've been working with Sting Ray. He's had the same plan since we wrecked his boat. He wants us find the gold.... Then he wants to liberate it."

"What made you come out here yesterday?" asked Judy.

"I told you that Kingsley and I saw Ricky limping home doing "the list"." Samantha leaned sideways in her chair, hummed a tune and danced a bit, still sitting down. Everyone chuckled. "Then, when Sting Ray was attacked on Friday night, I knew that something serious was due to happen, soon. I drove over to Paradise Island and listened under the window of Ricky's mansion. I snooped around and heard he bought a new boat. A Scarab. That's when I heard about the Colombians and the grenades. I talked Kingsley into coming out here to see what was really going on. I'm not really sure. I guess I wanted to warn you. So you would be prepared".

Phil looked over at Farris. "Tell us about Sting Ray being attacked."

"He didn't tell you himself! That man! Well here's the story, just like he told me."

Samantha told the story exactly the way that she had told it to Kingsley. Crash, boom, wshhhh, pitoooow. Blub, blub, blub. By the end she remembered she had promised Sting Ray that she wouldn't repeat it.

But by then Phil and Farris were grinning like crazy and Judy and Linda's jaws were hanging down around their navels.

Samantha ended the story with "Where is Sting, anyway?"

"Just offshore, anchored directly over the wreck. I wondered about that eye of his but I thought he'd tell me if he wanted to. I'm glad we all heard the story," said Farris, appreciatively. "And thanks for wanting to give us the "heads up".

"Sting Ray's tougher than he looks", said Phil, with a touch of sarcasm in his voice.

"Yah, right!" said Judy. "As if anyone with eyes would think he's a putz".

"If Ricky's going to attack us here what we need is a platoon of green berets", said Phil.

"Already taken care of! I have one on hold", stated Michael. "I think we should notify them to arrive as soon as possible".

"How many is a platoon, Michael" asked Linda.

"Ours? Four.... Plus Victor and George."

"Plus you and me, Linda and Judy", added Phil.

"I was hoping that you might consider taking the girls for a little sail.... Say to Miami. According to our partnership this seems to be my part of the bargain, now."

There was a loud protest from all three. Linda was the most coherent. "If Ricky or any of his men try to set foot in my house I will personally blast off his ass with a shotgun."

"We agreed ... we're all in this together". Judy was not as determined as Linda was but neither was she backing down.

"God put me on this island for a reason and I'm staying too", added Samantha. "No arguments.... If Sting Ray is still here then I'll go on his team. He won't miss another crack at Ricky, and neither will I."

Farris got up and walked angrily out through the patio door. He walked directly over to the ice cream cart and pulled open a drawer. Extracting a package of cigarettes, and jamming one in his mouth, he walked to the wall overlooking the ocean. There he smoked the cigarette, staring out to sea.

"I think I better talk to Michael," said Linda quietly and getting up followed him to the edge of the patio.

"I knew you hid them somewhere," she said almost in a whisper as she linked her arm through his.

He grunted.

"This is what happens when you get married, dear", she said sweetly.

"Jesus, Linda. Ricky will be arriving with machine guns. This isn't a game. Phil and Judy aren't qualified. She's the least equipped to handle this. There is no reason for them to die here! Then what about Samantha?"

"Samantha is strong enough to swim five miles. She's passed the fitness test! Phil knows his way around a rifle… you saw that. Judy… well Judy's just stubborn. We couldn't drag her off this island with a tugboat. I know a few things about your former life. I guess I always knew it might come back to haunt you", responded Linda.

Farris looked hard into Linda's eyes.

"Victor and George could take Samantha back."

"Except that Ricky already thinks she's been drowned. He'd have her throat cut an hour after she arrived in Nassau."

"You've got a point there. Christ!"

"Now put out that filthy cigarette or I won't sleep with you for a week."

Farris took a long pull and flicked it over the edge of the wall. "Are all women as mean as you?" he asked.

Linda gave his arm a squeeze. "Only the good ones."

❦

Phil and Michael sat on the sofa, with a large chart of Normans Cay spread out in front of them on the coffee table.

"We have two priorities," said Michael. "One, we have to protect Normans Cay and two we have to get the gold into Florida."

"Agreed".

"I have four good men, who can handle themselves. It will be their job to protect the island. Victor, George and I will take care of transporting the gold to the U.S. The unfortunate thing is that, assuming an attack, it doesn't make sense for us to leave on our run, until after we have eliminated Ricky as a threat."

"We have three women here on the Cay who we obviously can't leave alone, while we make the run", said Phil.

"That leaves us all here until Ricky is out of the way", stated Farris.

"What happens when Ricky attacks?"

"He will likely attack with, say, a dozen men. What we have to do is cut off his retreat and close in around him."

"I can assume that you envision a mini "War in Iraq", here on the cay."

"Worst case scenario... yes. It won't drag on afterwards, though". Farris sat silent for a minute following his statement.

"What about heading off the attack before it reaches the island?"

"That's a good idea but it puts us in a crapshoot as to whether we can disable Ricky at sea or whether he disables us. It's risky. He probably has more boats and better firepower. It's a chance I don't want to take".

"What's your idea, Mike?"

"If he enters the cay at the harbor we have him cold. It's easy to close off the entrance and we have him trapped. He's not that stupid! That means he'll put a landing team on the island at one or more, of a number of different places, and attack by land. My idea is to wreck his boats so he can't retreat and to box him into some place, preferably, as far away from the house as possible. That's probably not realistic."

"If he gets by our defenses?"

"If that happens our only chance is to make a run for it.... With the gold. If we have disabled his exit route he's stuck on the Cay while we're headed, en masse, for Florida. That increases our risk factor of running into the US Coast Guard but at least we have avoided Ricky. If Ricky is chasing us, we'll stick out like a sore thumb."

"And what happens to Normans Cay."

"Ricky would burn it to the ground as soon as look at it."

Chapter 32

The next twelve hours saw Normans Cay a beehive of activity. Four men arrived, each one alone. One came in an old fishing boat, one by sea-do, one in a powerful, but far from pretty cigarette boat, painted in camouflage colors. The last came in an ancient bi-plane. Boxes of equipment were unloaded from both the plane and the cigarette boat. Each man, after conferring with Michael, set to work at a specific task. The two girls, who prepared the meals, were put to work preparing dozens of box lunches under the supervision of Judy and Linda. Samantha, despite being sent off to rest, returned an hour later. She quietly reorganized the kitchen and under her watchful eye, things seemed to go so much smoother. After that, all arguments about her resting, ceased. Each package contained water and chocolate as well as sandwiches and fruit. Granola bars were the first thing they ran out of but there was plenty of other food to substitute. When the job was done, Victor whisked away the two girls and their parents, to another cay, where they had relatives.

George remained cooped up in the communication hut. The man, who had arrived by sea-do, after setting up some equipment in the hut, had disappeared with

Victor in one of the boats, with twenty odd cases of various materials.

The man with the cigarette boat, a huge black man of about thirty five, with muscles rippling under military fatigues and a fishnet undershirt, set up six different camps at the main corners of the cay. In odd contrast to his military fatigues was a large gold cross which hung around his massive neck. Each camp was equipped with a sub machine gun, a handgun, a sniper rifle, night vision goggles, food and water, and sleeping gear. Liberal amounts of camouflage cloth made each enclosure nearly invisible. As each camp was completed the man took hold of a large cross and said a brief prayer, blessing each hideout.

Sting Ray had also arrived in harbor. He had already been briefed on the goings on by Phil and Michael and set to work with the man from the fishing boat welding steel plate over the windows of the cabin on his tugboat. Each sheet had a gun slit cut in it. At the bow of the old tug, an I-beam from a davit was welded out like a bowsprit. It would prove a formidable battering ram, capable of skewering any fiberglass vessel.

Phil and Michael packed the gold in a crate. A net with two strong rings was put around the crate and the entire assembly was taken to an easily definable spot between two coral heads outside the harbor and carefully lowered to the bottom.

As Phil and Michael returned to harbor the sea-doo crossed their bow and the beat up cigarette boat crossed astern.

They were just pulling through the harbor entrance when Phil looked over at Sting Ray who was waving from the bow of his boat.

"That looks more like a fortress than a tugboat," exclaimed Phil.

"Sting is our gatekeeper at the mouth of the harbor. Apparently he didn't appreciate the visit he got from Ricky the other night, in Nassau. He confided in me that he was equally angry with General Motors, for not making the bumpers stronger on their limos. I guess he thought he would stop the limo completely, so he could pound it a little more with his steel pipe. If the bumper had held, I doubt the limo would ever have returned across the bridge to Paradise Island."

Phil was looking at the Zara. She was the poorest boat capable of battle. Farris read his mind. "I think we should put her in the boathouse. Best protection is behind doors and out of sight."

"What about the mast?" asked Phil.

"Part of the roof is canvas. It can just fold back. Back her in. If you do have to leave in a hurry, just run for the harbor entrance. Sting Ray will move out of the way for you but will close the entrance again after you leave."

"I won't ask who your friends are. But I am curious as to how they got here so fast with all this equipment", asked Phil.

"Just old friends of mine, probably a little bored. They seem happy to be putting their former training back into action. I guarantee you won't find more competent people. When Ricky attacks he's going to get a few surprises."

"You're convinced Ricky will attack?" asked Phil.

"Positive... furthermore I suspect it will be tonight! He's been receiving mercenaries at his house for the past couple of days. It's close."

"Will we be ready by then?"

"We'll be ready. We will all meet at seven o'clock for supper and will go over our preparations. Every one of us, you and me included, has a job to do. If we all do our jobs then Ricky will have a very frustrating experience."

As they pulled up to the dock George came out to meet them. "We got a small problem, Mike."

"What's that?"

"We've got the walkie-talkies, six sets. That's you, the four new imports, and me. The only trouble is everybody seems to be set on a different frequency.... We've been working on it for an hour with no joy."

"Put Judy on it!" interjected Phil. "She'll have it working in no time."

"You heard the man, George. Judy's in the kitchen. Keep me informed", ordered Farris.

Ginny had arrived by early afternoon. David had again tried to reach Phil and Judy by phone without success. Jason had gone off on his own to talk to the men he had planted at the airport and near Ricky's house. Then David had taken Ginny for a walk along the beach and had filled her in on all the details he had not told her over the phone. They had stopped for rum drinks served in coconut shells at one of the bamboo bars on the beach. It was already late in the afternoon when Jason rushed up to them.

"David, I've got some serious news." He glanced at Ginny.

"Go ahead, Jason. I've told Ginny everything."

"You're the boss." A scowl crossed Jason's face indicating that he didn't approve but he got down to the facts without wasting another second on the decision. "Those heavyweights from Miami. They arrived in Nassau an hour ago. Where do you think they are right now?"

"Ricky's house".

"Bingo! But that's not the worst of it. There are another half dozen Colombian mercenaries that I didn't know about already there. They are setting up for some kind of action. There is a lot of activity on Ricky's dock. I think they are planning a raid on Normans Cay.... And it looks like it's going to be tonight."

"We have to get hold of Phil and Judy", said David.

"No luck by phone, hunh?" asked Jason.

"What about by boat?" asked Ginny.

"I asked around about that.... Word has already spread. No one in Nassau will go near Normans Cay! The only boat going out there is going to be a stolen one."

Ginny flinched but the expression on Jason's face was adamant.

"The hotel rents outboards," stated Ginny. "I saw it in the brochures. We could rent a ski boat."

"It's thirty miles to Normans Cay, Ginny. Thirty miles of open water in a ski boat?" said David.

"We could get there safely with a hand held GPS. David, what choice do we have?"

"If we're going to do it we have to do it now", said Jason. "Nobody is going to rent us a boat after dark. We can buy a GPS easily enough. And read the instructions as we go! We have got to tell the guys who rent the boats that we just want to tour around the island. They'll get worried at dark but if we phone them and tell them we're tied up in Nassau, having a few drinks, they won't want the boat back until tomorrow."

David took control of the logistics. "Jason, you rent the boat. Tell them you'll want it for a few days. Make sure you rent the skis too. Spin a yarn about picking up your friends in Nassau. When we phone in at dark you can pretend to be drunk. They'll be happy to leave the boat out overnight! Ginny, take a cab and find someplace that sells those navigators. There must be lots of boat and dive shops in Nassau. I'll keep trying to contact Phil and Judy by phone. As soon as you've done your job come back to my hotel room. Have you got enough cash, Jason?"

"Oh yeah, cash is no problem". He grinned.

David reached into his pocket and pulled out his roll of bills. "Take this, Ginny. Then get the best navigator you can find. Have you ever used one before?"

"Not really, but I can read charts."

"Let's hope I can get through by phone. If not we'll be reading the instructions for the navigator by flashlight."

"It's called a GPS, not a navigator, David."

Ginny studied the roll of cash and looked over at David suspiciously. "I've never known you to be so free with cash, David. No cards, no receipts?"

Jason glanced up.

"We had a windfall in Miami. I'll tell you about it later", said David. "Now go!"

An hour and a half later David and Jason were together again in the hotel room as Ginny came through the door. There was a porter with her, carrying her bags as if she had been shopping for a week.

"What the hell is all this!" David exploded.

Ginny gave him a look so frosty that it could have kept a ski resort open all summer.

"The navigator", she said coolly, extracting a small box. "Night time binoculars." She plunked another box on the bed. "A flare gun." She placed another box on the bed and then pulled out a large book about eighteen inches by twenty-four. "A chart book of the Bahamas. Two spare gas cans.... We might find them useful."

She stood proudly staring at the merchandise on the bed. The sarcasm in her voice had verged on being distasteful, but it suddenly changed to her normal, musical cheeriness. "Two flashlights and matching windbreakers for everyone." She held up a colorful windbreaker with a huge logo that said "Sun Divers" on the back. "And they threw in free Tee shirts... nice, hunh."

"O.K." admitted David grudgingly. "You done good. What do we owe you?"

"Another thousand" said Ginny cheerfully.

"Give it to her", David ordered Jason.

Jason kept peeling bills off his roll but when he had finished had something short of two hundred dollars left. "I better go to the casino and make another withdrawal", he muttered. "What's in that duffel bag?' he asked.

"I stopped by the grocery store and bought some emergency food and bottled water in case the boat breaks down", stated Ginny in her practical, efficient manner.

"All right." Jason looked over at David and with obvious admiration asked, "Is she always like this?"

David looked at Ginny and held her in his eye. "You ought to see her buy office furniture", he said, just before Jason left the room.

"Thanks, Ginny. You're a good organizer." Uncharacteristically David leaned over and gave Ginny a quick peck on the cheek. "Jason and I will be fine, thanks to you."

"Not on your life, David Windrow. You would have left here with a half a tank of gas and no drinking water. I'm not letting you get in that boat without a responsible person!" Again her outburst subsided, "Besides, the man at the store already showed me how to work the GPS. And I threw out the instructions!"

"The GPS? What does that stand for, anyway?"

"That's short for "Global Positioning Satellite". Ginny kissed her fingers and brushed them over David's cheek. She then strutted over to the bathroom and quickly closed the door.

⚜

The man who had come in by cigarette boat sat in a tent he had constructed out of camouflage materials and scrub brush on high ground overlooking Rebecca's beach. His trained ear had picked up a sound he thought might be an outboard. Using night vision glasses he scanned the bay.

"This is the Preacher.... Angels are arriving," he said into a microphone inches from his mouth.

"We hear you", answered George from the communication hut on the patio. "We have two inflatables and a larger boat offshore. The second inflatable is heading through the main channel and will probably land on the Atlantic side. Can you tell how many troops?"

"Not yet ... out."

The inflatable landed and the Preacher saw six men disembark. They dragged the boat up on the beach. Their movements were quick, but the Preacher noticed the lack of precision that came with highly trained troops.

"Six angels on the beach", he reported. "My guess is these are the Miami boys".

"Back-up is on the way", he heard in the single earplug.

The Preacher fingered the large cross that hung around his neck. The patrol was moving down the beach toward the trail that led past the old Negro's house. They would have to pass within thirty feet of him. As they came closer he could make out more of their features. Each carried an Uzi except for the last man. He was fat. Slung over his shoulder was an M16. He seemed to be breathing hard, even after a short trot of seventy-five yards.

"Doing fine, just keep on coming", the Preacher whispered silently to himself. He picked up a remote control device that was positioned on the blanket in front of him. He waited until the fat man had passed him. He depressed the button on the remote.

The patrol found itself in a fifty foot circle, lit by twelve-volt patio lights planted in the sand and covered with dry seaweed or hidden by driftwood. Every man knew that inside the patio lanterns they were sitting ducks. Their first reaction was to hunch down with their guns pointing to the perimeter searching for a target before they became targets themselves. The Preacher did not give them an opportunity to find a target.

He picked up a microphone that ran to a ghetto blaster he had buried in bushes and announced his presence through the speakers.

"I regret to inform you gentlemen that you have just entered the center of a minefield. In my hand I have a remote detonating device, that, if deployed, will leave God's seagulls and other scavengers happily fed for a week. To prevent detonation, I suggest that you start by piling your weapons ten feet in front of the fat man."

The men on the beach looked around. Two men had switched on flashlights mounted to their assault guns and were searching the bushes to no avail. There was nothing but darkness outside the perimeter. The lead man had instinctively pointed his gun in the direction of the ghetto blaster but the voice coming through the speaker had sounded artificial. Now he was looking around in all directions.

"Gentlemen, please do as instructed."

The six men looked at each other. Finally one man shrugged and lowering his weapon walked over to the place described and carefully lay down his gun. The others followed and did likewise. They returned to the center of the circle.

"Well done. Now please make a second pile, moving one at a time and leave jackets, boots, and any other hardware such as clips, handguns and knives about ten feet from the first pile. When you have completed making your deposit put you hands high in the air and turn slowly making a complete circle so that I can check you from a distance."

They came quietly, one at a time, each one finishing with a slow turn. The fat man was the last. He was also the most heavily armed. He had twin shoulder holsters with small handguns in each and four throwing knives in a belt around his waist. He almost lost his balance removing one of his shoes but once barefoot lifted his hands high above his head and did a ballerina style pirouette, followed by a deep bow to the bushes at the edge of the beach.

"The judges will take a few minutes to select a winner. Please join the others," said the Preacher into the microphone. He was smiling despite himself.

When the group had reassembled the Preacher stepped out of the bushes. He carried a machine gun on a shoulder sling and a small satchel. The detonator hung on a string around his neck. He was dressed in military fatigues and looked like the oversized leader of a swat team. His cross glittered in the light of the patio lanterns. The headset microphone was inches from his lips.

"Good evening gentlemen. The next task we are about to perform may cause some minor embarrassment and discomfort but I assure you it is a happy alternative to dying in an explosion. Please line up, shoulder to shoulder, with your backs to me, and bending over, Drop your drawers until they are around your ankles."

"Fuck you.... I ain't dropping my drawers for some damn nigger!" hissed one of the men.

"I can assure you I will take no pleasure in seeing your honky ass but I do have a bag of syringes. Your alternative to dying right now, is to simply fall asleep for the rest of the night. Your choice. But I'm afraid the decision must be unanimous." With that the Preacher closed his huge hand around the detonator.

"If he pushes that button he goes up in a million pieces too", said the loudmouth.

"Should I tell them?" asked the Preacher, cocking his head to the dark area outside the perimeter lights. He wiped the sweat off his face with his sleeve.

From outside the circle came the sound of a parrot's voice. "Tell them. Tell them!"

"What the fuck was that?" asked the fat man, incredulous.

"That's my accomplice. Talks like a parrot, doesn't he?" said the preacher conversationally.

"Tell us what?" said the loudmouth.

"Unfortunately dying makes little difference to me. I had the misfortune to end up with a very attractive young lady in a hotel room, after a night of carousing. Now I test positive for AIDS."

The entire group took a step back in unison. Being close to a person with AIDS was more frightening to them than any number of M16s.

Still holding the detonator in one hand the Preacher reached behind him and unclipped a canteen from his belt. Keeping his eyes on the group he lifted the canteen to his lips.

"Shoulder to shoulder, time to bend over!" came the squawking sound of the parrot.

The Preacher lowered the canteen. "I can assure you that AIDS is a terrible disease and I would not wish to inflict it on anyone. To that end, each of you will have your own, personal syringe. No sharing! Now, gentlemen, like the parrot said, bend over". There was a command in his voice with the last two words.

The men did as instructed and each bent over, with his hands on his knees, exposing six pairs of untanned cheeks.

The Preacher reached into the satchel with his right hand and extracted a syringe. While five men looked over their shoulders the Preacher squeezed a drip out of the needle and then stuck it into the first in line and depressed the plunger. Almost immediately the man slumped forward. The Preacher took a new syringe and repeated the procedure and continued down the line.

The third last man begged "Please don't give me AIDS! I got a wife and kids."

The Preacher reached back for his canteen and once again put it to his lips. The parrot in the dark spoke up.

"Get a new job. Get a new job!"

"I won't give you AIDS. Nighty night", the Preacher promised and quickly injected the sedative into the intruder.

The second last man just gritted his teeth and stared straight ahead. With the injection he fell forward, awkwardly. Only the fat man remained on his feet.

"How much do you weigh?" asked the Preacher.

"Three-twenty", answered the man over his shoulder.

The Preacher looked at the syringe. "I hope it works." He shrugged. He reached for his canteen again.

"Give him two…. Give him two", squawked the parrot.

He plunged the needle deep into the man's butt and squeezed. The fat man remained standing for a second before his knees buckled. He fell on his side but he was not totally knocked out. He looked up through sleepy eyelids and smiled.

"I got it! You're a ventriloquist. Hunh"

"You figured it out". The Preacher paused and then said conversationally, "Fat ass, but not a dumb ass like the others, right?" said the Preacher.

"Dumb enough to be here", he admitted.

"Sweet dreams", said the Preacher as he plunged a second syringe into the fat man's cheek.

The Preacher walked back to his tent. The man who came in by fishing boat was sitting back smoking a cigarette.

"A fine performance!" He grinned. "Are you going to blow them up now?"

"Might as well." The Preacher lifted the remote control that dangled from his neck. He pushed the button. The patio lights went out. Nothing else happened. "Guess I wired it wrong."

"Yah, sure." The man from the fishing boat took another long drag from his cigarette and stubbed the half-smoked butt in the sand. "There's another landing party on the Atlantic side and a boat hanging outside the harbor."

"Let's check with Mike and find out where he wants us." The Preacher touched his transmit button. "Six angels are sleeping. Willy is with me. We need orders, Mike."

"Good work! We don't know the status of the boat outside the harbor. Let's clean up the other landing party first and deal with the boat last."

"Roger that. Out."

The two men started off immediately at a jog up the hill and across the island. When they hit the beach on the Atlantic side they ran half a mile north until they could see the cliff at the northern point of the cay. Using the night vision glasses they scanned the hillside.

"I have one located," said Willy, pointing.

"Number two is over there. Should we try Jack?"

"Why not? He won't answer if he's inconvenienced."

The Preacher touched his shirt pocket again. "Jack. We see two on either side."

"There are six total. Two are close to me. Two are unknown. Sixty second countdown and we all fire at once."

"O.K. we're moving." The Preacher pointed to the man farthest away and moved out quickly along the bushes counting to himself as he moved. After thirty seconds he slipped behind a rock and set the M16 to single shot. With the cross hairs of the scope on his target, he waited.

"Five, four, three..." came the transmission on the walkie-talkie. The last numbers were not counted so that each man was holding his breath as he fired. Three shots rang out in unison. A second later there was a fourth.

"One down", said Willy.

"Two", answered the Preacher.

"Three, I missed four", answered Jack. Suddenly there was an eruption of machine gun fire from above where Jack was located. Willy and the Preacher began scrambling up the hill moving from one piece of cover to the next, converging on Jack's location. Half way up the Preacher spoke into his microphone.

"Jack, come in Jack." There was an awesome silence. After thirty seconds the Preacher heard Mike's voice.

"Bob, three coming your way. Be careful. Willy, Jack and Preacher are following."

The Preacher could see Willy. He motioned to him to move. Willy scrambled another twenty feet while the Preacher covered. Then the Preacher moved. There was no sound from above them, no shots fired. Willy was the first to reach Jack. His body was riddled with bullet holes and his eyes stared vacantly. Crouching on one knee with his weapon ready Willy scanned the area around the camp. The Preacher scrambled up beside him, weapon ready but expecting that whoever had shot Jack had already moved on. His right hand on his gun he reached across Jack's face with his left and closed Jack's eyes. "God rest your soul", he muttered and closed his own eyes for three quick seconds. Over his earphone he heard a quiet "Amen", from Michael.

Willy spoke. "They're converging on the house. To do that they will skirt the airstrip. Bob's well located but they know we're behind them." He lifted up his hand and put a finger across his lips. "That sounds like a chopper."

"I hope it has nothing to do with us," said the Preacher.

George, in the communication hut jerked forward staring at the radar screen. He hit a button on his console giving him private communication with Michael Farris.

"Mike, we got a chopper coming this way."

Mike digested the news his jaw tightening. Phil, Judy, Linda and Samantha stared at him. He had been standing behind his desk in his office while the others had spread around the room. They had all listened to the open communication over a speaker that Judy had hooked up on Farris' desk. His body language, however minute, told them the chopper was something he hadn't counted on.

Farris spoke.

"There is a chopper coming in. Just pray that it's not loaded. We have three of them and three of us out there right now and I like those odds. There is also their other boat, probably the Scarab, outside the harbor."

⋇

The Preacher and Willy, spread out by fifty yards, watched as the helicopter landed. Five men piled out and sprayed the bushes around the airstrip with machine gun fire before running into the scrub growth. The sixth man, the pilot, shut down the machine and then, he too moved toward the bushes. He was limping badly.

"Six more on the ground", said the Preacher into the mike. They headed into the bushes in the direction of the house. "Bob, don't give away your position until Willy and me are closer. We're moving."

It was a dangerous gamble but Willy and the Preacher both knew they had to race across the airstrip rather than waste the time it took to skirt the end of it if they were to provide help for Bob.

⋇

In Michael's office Farris wasted no time in making up his mind.

"Phil, Judy, Linda, Samantha. Head for the boat.... We just lost the advantage. I'm staying here on the cay. Victor will provide back up for the boat outside the harbor. Sting Ray will too once you're clear of the harbor. Now move.... Take the tunnel."

"With that he punched a code into what appeared to be a calculator on his desk and a bookcase, against the wall began to move. Shock registered on all the faces in the room but mostly on Linda's.

"I've been married to you for five years and you never told me about a tunnel!"

"Yah", Farris grimaced. "Sorry Hun. The tunnel goes right under the patio stairs directly to the boathouse. There is a lever at the end. The whole workbench rolls away."

"I'm staying," said Linda.

"No you're not. Nobody is varying from the plans we laid out." Michael's voice was firm leaving no room for discussion. Even Linda knew that it was best to follow orders according to plan.

"All right, but put on your flak jacket and don't be a hero. I want to spend our share of the gold together."

Phil was standing in the tunnel entrance. Judy and Samantha were already ahead of him prepared to move.

Michael gave his wife a quick kiss but she stood there, resolutely, until he put on the bulletproof vest. She tightened the Velcro strap around the waist, gave a quick but tender hug and stepped into the tunnel. The bookcase was already moving back toward her.

Phil passed out flashlights from a rack, inside the entrance.

"This house really does have everything", quipped Samantha.

Phil moved to the front of the procession and started down the tunnel.

Michael Farris switched off the ceiling fan. He climbed on his desk and tugged on the fixture. A four-foot wide circle of cedar that surrounded the fixture lowered, allowing enough room for Michael to scramble on top of it. Seconds later he emerged from what had appeared to be an air conditioning ventilator on the roof. He moved to a corner of the roof closest to the airstrip. It was also the easiest wall from the outside from which to gain access to the roof. Spread out on a blanket was an arsenal of automatic weapons, a rifle with a high-powered scope, and extra clips for the pistol that was strapped to his waist. There were also four hand grenades. Sensitive, motion detector spotlights would pick up any movement below him while still leaving him in a shadow of darkness, well protected by the parapet wall that surrounded the roof.

"This is Michael, I'm on the roof. George, if things get to hairy on the patio lock up the hut and move into my office."

"Got it, boss."

"Victor, you got any company yet?"

"Just arriving now."

"Willy?"

"Inside the airstrip"

"Preacher?"

"Same".

"Bob?"

"Just waiting for the bastards that killed Jack."

Ten minutes passed like it was ten years. Suddenly the spotlights came on and when they did they illuminated four men at the perimeter of the clearing that surrounded the house. Michael sprang up and began spraying the area with machine gun fire. Half a dozen other guns were heard from various angles. Then total silence. As Michael moved along the perimeter of the roof a single rifle shot cracked the night from the direction of Bob's foxhole. The lights, which were set on a short cycle, switched off. Once again silence and darkness abounded. Michael rested his back against the cement parapet. There was a soft clink of metal at another corner of the house.

"I want to hear from anyone near the west wall", whispered Michael. There was no response.

"George.... Anything on the monitor."

"No Mike ...it's clear."

"We have a grappling hook over the wall", whispered Michael.

"Mike, this is the Preacher. The hook must be too small to set off the motion sensor, or they shot it out. They're still in the bushes. Get over there with a grenade. George, stay on the monitor. When George gives the signal pull the pin. Count to five and then lob it out, away from the wall. Do it right and you use the wall to trap the blast and deflect it back towards the assailants. Do it wrong and you create a large breach in your wall."

Michael had learned years ago never to second-guess the Preacher. His movements were quick and precise. Keeping low, he moved directly underneath the grappling hook. He could see the hook was wrapped with black friction tape so it would make little noise. "Very professional", he thought. With his back against the parapet, he waited until George had the assailants on video.

Suddenly there was a huge eruption of gunfire from the patio. At almost the same instant the motion sensor clicked and spotlights came on.

George's voice came over the earphone. "They're all over the patio. Two on your wall, Mike. Hold onnn! Now, man, now!"

Michael pulled the pin. He counted to five and tossed the grenade backward over his head in a high arc. Suddenly he saw two hands above his head. Then a face appeared. Half the man's torso was hung over the wall and the man's eyes were staring into his own. Michael froze, pressing his own body, in terror, against the parapet that surrounded the roof. The explosion nearly ruptured his eardrums but he was sure it had done more than that to the man climbing over the wall. Suddenly the man fell top of Michael. Farris pushed and rolled over pointing his pistol at the man. His attacker was already dead. Cautiously he looked over the wall. There was another body on the grass.

"Two down", he said grimly into his microphone.

There was still sporadic gunfire around the patio as Michael raced across the roof. He raised his eyes just above the parapet wall. He could see the Preacher standing in the center of the patio. His gun was dangling at his side and he was standing perfectly still with his eyes closed saying a silent prayer. Michael stood up. First Willy came over the patio wall on the left. Then came Bob from the right.

"There are two down here. How many did you get Michael?" There was no pleasure in his voice.

"One on the roof and one outside the wall."

"Two still missing. Keep you eyes open, men", ordered the Preacher.

He looked around surveying the carnage. His eyes fastened on Bob.

"You hit, Bob."

"Yah, just in the arm. Must be getting old."

"None of us will ever get old unless we stop this kind of shit", said the Preacher, disgust strongly apparent in his voice.

George stepped out through the heavy door of the communication hut. Michael scanned the harbor. Suddenly remembering Phil and the women. He could see Sting Ray easing backward opening the entranceway to the harbor. Victor was in the cigarette boat. Someone was with him. Phil's boat was moving toward the gap under motor power.

"We've got to stop Phil. The harbor is now safer than the open sea. That boat is still outside the entrance! George call Phil."

"I can't Mike. Victor doesn't have a walkie-talkie. All he had was the intercom that Judy hard wired down to the boathouse. Once Phil and Victor leave the boathouse they've got no radio."

"I thought they could talk to Sting Ray", demanded Farris.

"Phil can... on his walkie-talkie. It's a different set-up from yours. No one will have their VHF on because everyone in the cays could hear the conversation."

Michael saw a movement on the path. "Watch out, the steps to the patio."

The three ex soldiers on the patio dove for the ground, the preacher landing spread eagled in the center of the patio while the other two rolled toward the edge. George ducked back into the communication hut and closed and locked the door.

"Don't shoot! It's me, Linda."

"Hold your fire!" shouted Michael from the rooftop. "Watch out Linda, there's still two bad guys missing", added Michael, half for his wife's benefit and half to caution his men that Linda might not be coming of her own free will.

Bob was the first to react and sprang over the wall that surrounded the patio.

"It's all right. I'm alone", shouted Linda as she ran onto the patio.

Michael stood up again and the others followed.

Bob was the last to climb back over the wall. He was holding his arm, which was obviously giving him a great deal of pain. "I damn near slipped over the ledge with this gimp arm", he muttered.

"Why the Hell aren't you with Phil?" demanded Farris.

"If you think for one second I was going to leave you alone on this cay, with a small army attacking it, then you don't know me well enough to be my husband!" Linda was clearly angry.

"We've defended the cay but right now Phil, Judy and Samantha and Victor are heading into a problem and we can't radio to stop them. I'm coming down. Meet me in my office."

George had reopened the door of the communication hut and Linda stormed through it and then through the back door into Michael's office. She was standing by the door when a four-foot section of ceiling lowered and Michael jumped down onto the desk. As soon as his weight was off the rig it raised back into the ceiling. Linda stood in shock and Michael simply looked up at the ceiling and smiled a crooked smile. George stood in the open doorway and drawled out,

"Shit, man. I didn't know you could do that!"

"Neither did I!" challenged Linda. "When this is over we have a few things to talk about!"

Michael ignored the comments and started giving orders over his headset.

"Preacher, take your boat and try to stop Phil."

"I'm moving but its way the hell down the cay. What about the sea-doo?"

"It's on the Atlantic side", answered Willy who took off at a run.

"Who was in Victor's boat"?

"Samantha", answered Linda.

"She was supposed to be with Phil, Judy and you!"

"I guess women aren't so good at taking orders in the new millennium, dear. God I'm glad you're safe". She hugged him.

Suddenly there was a loud roar as the helicopter started its engine.

"That's the one or two last men!" exclaimed Michael.

There was an eruption of gunfire out at sea.

"Christ, we've got no boat to lend assistance." Michael slammed his fist on his desk.

"What about our other boats?"

"We pulled the batteries for the perimeter defense. Willy has motion sensors and lighting in half a dozen spots on the island. They worked perfectly for the Preacher but it left us with minimal transportation."

"Come on, we'll take the Cessna."

Farris grabbed a sub machine gun and a handful of clips and raced after Linda, as she ran for the Cessna.

They approached the airstrip at a run until Linda suddenly stopped and stood in shock as she watched the helicopter hover over her Cessna, slightly off to one side. The pilot of the chopper emptied the clip of a machine pistol into the aircraft. A huge explosion erupted from the ground as the fuel tanks in the wings exploded.

"That's Ricky in the chopper", said Linda as Farris raced up behind her. "Now I'm pissed. Follow me!" Linda sprinted across the airstrip.

⚜

As soon as they had reached the boathouse Linda had stated that she wasn't leaving the cay. Phil and Victor had tried to argue with her but had succeeded only in wasting valuable time. As Phil started the diesel in his boat and Victor started the cigarette boat Samantha had decided that Victor could not both drive the boat and offer firepower at the same time. She had leapt into Victor's boat and grabbed a submachine gun.

"Shit lady, get back in the sailboat now!"

"How are you going to drive and shoot at the same time!" snapped Samantha. "Besides, this boat is faster." She smiled, wickedly.

"You've got a point there!" Victor decided arguing was a waste of time. "Ever shot one of those before?"

Samantha shook her head.

"That's the safety. Release it and pull the trigger. When it stops firing press that button to release the clip and jam another one in from underneath."

Samantha looked confused.

"You just keep firing. I have two guns here. I'll keep them loaded". Victor called to Phil.

"Everybody ready?"

"Go ahead Victor. I'm behind you going as fast as I can", answered Phil.

Phil gave full power and to himself seemed to shoot out of the boathouse and towards Sting Ray's boat. Victor barely touched his throttle to compensate for the slow speed of the sail boat. Sting Ray threw the tug into reverse and backed towards a buoy he had anchored which indicated as far back as he could go.

Victor crossed under his bow and as he put it in forward and turned hard toward Exuma Sound. Phil slipped by missing the battering ram Sting Ray had installed by only inches. Once out of harbor Victor had accelerated hard making a beeline for the boat drifting outside the entrance. Ricky's Scarab immediately accelerated swinging away, leaving a giant rooster tail.

As Phil passed through the harbor entrance a spray of bullets erupted from the cliff that formed the end of the harbor. Judy dove for the cabin but Phil was fully exposed behind the wheel. He grabbed the shot gun he had leaned against the binnacle and in one swift movement, shouldered it, flipped off the safety and pulled the trigger. Phil had aimed at the center of the man's body but shooting from a moving deck was not easy and the shot went wide. The man on the rock aimed directly at Phil as Phil pulled back the pump, chambering another shell. There was another blast from the shotgun and the man's face vanished. His body bounced backward toward the cliff and then tumbled fifteen feet into the water from its perch.

Judy had witnessed the entire scene from the companionway. Her face drained and she almost vomited. A second later she was in one of Phil's arms as he swung the wheel hard to complete his exit of the harbor.

⊰§⊱

"Don't fire till I say so. Then do it in bursts. Aim low", Victor shouted at Samantha.

The Scarab was approaching Victor's boat at full speed like a medieval jouster challenging his opponent.

Just when a head on collision had seemed imminent, Victor cut hard to starboard. Samantha had fired an entire clip but had shot over the head of the other boat. Victor assessed the Scarab. It was just as fast as his boat but he was sure he could out maneuver it. There appeared to be a driver and two others aboard. They too had fired high as the two boats crossed paths. He held hard on the starboard turn while passing another gun to Samantha.

"Go lower, sugar, go lower." The statement had heavy sexual overtones.

Samantha had grinned back at him but said nothing.

As the Scarab passed Phil's boat Judy had fired a clip from the portholes. That seemed to be enough to keep the Scarab back a piece from the Zara. Victor circled behind the Zara until he emerged between Phil's stern and Sting Ray's bow. Samantha fired another clip spraying water around the Scarab but doing no damage.

"One more pass Victor. I think I'm getting the hang of this."

⁓

Jason, David and Ginny could hear more than they could see. Jason cut the throttle of the single, two hundred and thirty five horsepower Johnson outboard ski boat they had rented. David had night vision binoculars in one hand and a hand held GPS in the other. He was standing up in the front passenger seat peering out into the blackness through his binoculars. Ginny sat in the back seat clutching the chart they had used to cross the sound.

"Well, you got us here with that little GPS, which I have to tell you, I didn't trust. But now we seem to be entering the gunfight at the O.K. Corral and a hasty retreat might be in order before someone starts shooting at us", drawled Jason.

"That's Phil's boat. I'm sure of it", shouted David.

Phil and Judy kept an unwavering course that headed out past the shallow water and into the channel to the Atlantic. Phil was almost ready to turn east into the ocean leaving Exuma Sound behind. The Scarab was turning to make another pass. Phil looked behind and saw Sting Ray's powerful bow less than fifty feet behind and gaining. Then Sting Ray pulled to starboard and began to pass on the right blocking Phil from turning out to sea.

"What the Christ are you doing?" shouted Phil as the tug pulled along side.

Both Victor and the Scarab were behind him on the left. Phil looked over and saw Sting Ray waving forward. Phil waved back and maintained a course parallel the tugboat. It soon became apparent that Sting Ray wanted to be out in front. Phil dropped behind but stayed as close as he could to Sting Ray's stern. The walkie-talkie squawked. Phil picked it up.

"Zara, go ahead."

"Can you see me in the cabin if I leave the light on and douse my other lights?" asked the tug boat captain.

All the lights went out on the tug until a tiny white cabin light came on.

"See you clearly", answered Phil.

"When the Scarab comes up behind, you turn hard which ever way I point. Understand?"

"Understood".

"If you head toward the Atlantic keep your lights off and get lost in the dark. If you head toward the Sound, then cut your engines. You might be in pretty shallow water so work your way back to the center of the channel. Now kill all your lights and watch me closely, mon."

⛤

David continued to stare into the binoculars.

"You got it figured out yet.... You know, who's the good guys and who's the bad guys," said Jason sarcastically as he sprawled out in the driver's seat with his hand draped limply over the throttle.

"David those two boats are firing at each other. One of them is running interference for Phil! Phil is following the tugboat. We have got to help Phil and Judy," exclaimed Ginny, sounding a bit naive.

David did not put down his binoculars. He pointed with the GPS in his left hand. "Good guy, good guy, good guy, bad guy!"

"People? This could get dangerous", questioned Jason.

"We have got to try. I'll drive. You man the gun", ordered David.

David quickly moved into the driver's seat and pushed the throttle forward. The small boat leapt out of the water. It bounced over the waves but at least it responded quickly. The Scarab was pulling up behind Phil. Phil could hear it but kept his eyes glued to Sting Ray's back. Victor's cigarette boat was behind the Scarab.

"Judy", called Phil. "Stay below. I'll tell you which side they're coming from."

"Just call it, left or right, O.K. Be careful, please."

Phil checked his shotgun and held it at his hip while he steered with the other hand.

"Get ready babe. They're passing on the ... Left! Left! Left!"

Judy swung the gun out the left porthole prepared to open fire on the Scarab. Victor was coming up from behind. Samantha was preparing to shoot over the bow of the cigarette boat as they came within range when he saw another small boat come in from the left and pull parallel the Scarab. Victor could see three people in the boat. One of them was clutching a handgun as they pulled up to nearly point blank range along the side of the Scarab. Victor had not noticed them before on radar and the Scarab had not noticed them at all.

The Scarab was traveling about sixty five miles per hour as it closed to pass the Zara, which was puttering along at full throttle, about eight knots. As the ski boat pulled parallel the Scarab Victor's first assumption was that it held more of Ricky's men but something was holding him back from confirming that in his mind.

"There's a woman in that ski boat," he yelled at Samantha. "They are shooting at Ricky's boat!"

In the cockpit Phil waited Sting Ray's signal. As the Scarab pulled up, behind and to the left of the Zara, Sting Ray pointed out to sea. Phil pulled hard on the wheel turning to starboard as fast as he could. The Zara responded. Simultaneously the tug boat swung to starboard and cut his engine. David had been running parallel to the Scarab, watching the ballet of boats, ignoring, somehow, the gunfire. Now he realized the plan as if it was a chess game and the little ski boat was one of the ponds. He was now fifty feet off the Scarab. Three heavily armed men including the driver were preparing to blast away, broadside, into the Zara as they passed at high speed.

"I'll stay parallel. Don't let them turn away. Block them!" ordered David.

One of Ricky's men was turning towards the ski boat having just noticed it for the first time. The Scarab was now almost alongside Phil's boat. Judy was firing out the porthole at the Scarab, and Samantha was firing at it from behind. Jason was emptying his semi automatic at the Scarab which was caught in crossfire from the Zara, the ski boat and Victor's cigarette boat.

"Block them, box them in", shouted David.

"Man, they're three times our size," shouted Jason. "They can drive right over us!"

"Block them!" shouted David from behind the wheel.

Jason was exasperated, not even understanding why he was involved in this battle on the high seas. He also wanted to avoid direct crossfire. But instinctively he realized that David had a plan. He didn't have to understand the plan but he was prepared to follow David's lead. Despite the fact that the small ski boat was bouncing like crazy, now a short twenty feet from the Scarab, Jason stood up behind David and pointing his automatic directly at the Scarab's driver fired three more rounds. The driver looked directly at Jason for one split second, missing the fact that the Zara had turned. He swung his own gun back into Jason's face.

Ginny, the unarmed observer, reached up and grabbed a handful of Jason's Sun Diver windbreaker with both hands and pulled with all her strength, dropping Jason back into the seat.

The Zara swung sharply to the right as the Scarab driver focused on the ski boat.

Victor, closing fast from the rear, realized the consequences of what was happening killed his throttle and turned hard left. The Scarab surged straight forward, passing the Zara by five or six times the sailboats speed. The driver of the Scarab did not realize, until it was two late, that he was about to broadside the heavy tug. David turned slightly left, missing Sting

Ray's stern by inches. Jason looked up just in time to realize what was happening as the Scarab shattered into a million pieces of broken fiberglass and steel in one horrific crash as it hit the heavy steel tugboat's hull. Phil watched the horrible collision as he powered out to sea. Judy had begun to scramble up the companionway and she too witnessed the mayhem over the stern of the Zara.

Victor was the first to turn on his running lights. Sting Ray poked his head over the steel wall that surrounded his control room and switched on his own lights. Phil slowed down to an idle and turned on his lights. David, unfamiliar with boats in general, was the last to turn on his.

Ginny was waving at Victor who was the closest boat. Victor and Samantha pulled alongside.

"I don't know who the Hell you are but thanks for your help", said Victor politely.

"Just tell me that Phil and Judy are in that sailboat," said Ginny.

"Yah man, that's their boat". Victor smiled a huge smile. His white teeth glistened against his black face, in the running lights of the two boats. "Now, who are you?"

David answered, "I'm David Windrow, Phil and Judy's lawyer. This is Ginny and my investigator, Jason."

Victor recognized the name. Michael had briefed him and he viewed Windrow as Ricky's partner in the treasure. He leveled his machine pistol at the ski boat but Samantha, staring at Ginny in the back seat put a soft but firm hand on Victor's forearm. Victor relaxed and lowered the weapon.

Sting Ray was checking for damage from the collision, determining whether he was in danger of sinking. He was taking on water, but he was equipped with powerful pumps. Phil was well past the swell where the two bodies of water, the Atlantic and the Caribbean, met. Sting Ray idled alongside.

"It took a while before I figured out your plan but it sure worked well", shouted Phil over the rumble of the tug's powerful diesel.

"Did anyone from the Scarab survive?" asked Judy.

Sting Ray just shook his head.

The small runabout pulled up on the other side.

"Ahoy", shouted David.

"David... Ginny, what are you doing here?" Judy was incredulous.

"We thought you might be in some kind of trouble. Guess we were right."

Ginny felt wet as water seeped into her shoes. She spoke up. "We have to get to shore fast. We're taking on water. Badly!"

"Probably a few bullet holes. Pull alongside Sting Ray. He'll winch your whole boat aboard", suggested Phil.

Victor came alongside. "Trouble?"

"We're taking on water fairly fast", repeated Ginny. She was already tying the anchor line to the ski pole.

"We've had a lot of trouble tonight. Mike wants Phil and Judy out of Bahamian waters and into the U.S.A. as fast as they can sail. I suggest the same goes for all the Americans here. Better get on board the Zara and get moving. Climb onto my bow and I'll take you over to the sailboat."

"Good advice", answered David.

"What about the rental?" asked Jason.

"We'll take care of it and return it for you. Sting Ray will pick up the ski boat and head back to Nassau. He will fix any holes and paint. You will never get a bill for it. Just get out of here fast!"

Within minutes David, Ginny and Jason were on board the Zara and she was pulling out into the Atlantic. Victor pulled alongside one more time. "I talked to Mike on the radio. He said that everything was O.K. on Normans Cay. He and Linda will meet you as arranged in Miami. He wants you to maintain radio silence and avoid radar if you can. Keep your lights and your motor off until you are in Florida waters. He sends his regards and wishes you a good sail, mon. Leave your radio and your own radar "off".

As Victor pulled away Samantha looked at him. "You didn't talk to anyone on the radio. Why did you lie to them?"

"The boss told me to do that before we left the cay. Now let's get back there and find out what has happened."

On board the Zara everyone was jubilant. Jason, who had never been on board a sail boat tried to help Phil raise the sails, while David tried to steer. Ginny went below to help Judy mix a round of drinks. Everyone was asking each other questions and gulping strong cocktails. They had been sailing for ten minutes and were two miles out to sea with everyone talking when Linda's Cessna blew up on the airstrip. They saw the flash of light behind them and heard the rumble of the explosion as the Zara slipped silently through the water, under full sail.

Ricky rose high above Normans Cay before switching on the radar. It wasn't necessary because he had already spotted the lights as the boats congregated around Phil's boat. He hovered motionless for a moment and then pushed the joystick just a tad forward. As he flew he reached into his pocket and pulled out a small vial of cocaine. He dumped a little on the back of his hand and snorted it. He licked off what he had missed. As the cocaine rushed to his brain he laughed out loud. The laugh was cut short by another mood swing.

"Now you miserable mother fuckers! Now you are going to pay." He jammed a fresh clip into his Uzi and rammed the joy stick forward.

⁂

Linda studied the controls of the ancient Bi-plane.

"The prop is clear," shouted Michael as he raced to pull back the camo netting that had been spread over the tiny craft. With a razor sharp knife he cut the tie downs on both the netting and the plane itself. Rolling the netting as he ran he soon had the plane clear for take-off. He climbed quickly into the open cockpit, behind his wife, with a bundle of camo netting in his arms. Linda had already started the plane and was running up the engine. In seconds they were airborne, far less runway than it took in her Cessna. She felt the exhilaration of the wind flowing over the open cockpit as she gained altitude, testing the controls, turning left and right, amazed at how responsive this antique was.

"Can you see Phil and Judy?" shouted Farris into her ear.

"That's them over there, a couple of miles offshore." She pointed. Then she searched the sky above her in the moonlight.

"There's Ricky. He's headed right for them!"

Phil was the first to recognize the sound of the approaching chopper.

"Judy, get the machine gun."

"The what... oh, O.K. It's empty anyway."

"Then bring fresh clips and break out every gun we have. There's a helicopter coming this way and I think its Ricky."

Jason was more familiar with guns than anyone else aboard. He pushed Judy aside and dove through the companionway. Instinctively he matched ammunition clips to weapons and passed them up to the others in the cockpit. David had shot a rifle once and was vaguely familiar with it. He gave Phil a handgun and another to Judy.

"Ever shot anything before?" he asked Ginny.

"My brother's shot gun", she answered.

"We have one of those. Nice gun case, Phil. I like the sheepskin lining."

He rammed the cartridges into the magazine. "It will kick like a mule and it doesn't have much range. Wait until the target is close." He handed the weapon to Ginny. Stuffing his pockets with clips for the automatic that Judy had been using, he raced topsides. "Spread out everyone".

Ricky's helicopter descended on them with a horrible roar. Water sprayed up from the spin of the rotors just fifty feet above the sea. The sails flapped horribly and the boat simply stopped sailing, dead in the water. Phil hit the starter switch for the diesel. It turned over a few times and started in its normal manner, unhurried by the imminent danger. Jason fired a short, ineffectual burst. Ricky returned fire. A spray of bullets hit the water just in front of the Zara. Ricky was having trouble both flying and shooting and backed off to reload.

He came in again and hovered just fifty feet to the side of the sailboat.

Jason, in charge of artillery, had ordered people into position around the boat and warned them to hold fire until they had a good shot. Ginny was in the rear of the cockpit. Jason and Judy crouched on the narrow deck on the starboard side with their backs against the cabin as the sails stretched to port. David, braced against the forestay stood on the bowsprit with his rifle ready. Phil stood resolutely behind the wheel his semi automatic dangling from his hand.

෴

The Bi-plane was four hundred yards behind and above the chopper.

"This will create a lot of drag, Linda. Get ready!"

"If this old bird starts to stall, cut her free", instructed Linda.

Farris began to unravel the camouflage net. The wind caught it and it let go all at once, stretching out behind the aircraft. It was tied on to a brace that went from the fuselage to the upper wing. The strut bent slightly but held as the netting dragged twenty feet behind the plane. The drag immediately slowed down the antique plane but Linda compensated with extra power and pulled the nose up.

"We're coming close. The draft will pull it in! Ready, love?" asked Linda over her shoulder.

"Just pray it doesn't pull us in, too! Here goes!" responded Linda.

Michael reached forward and squeezed Linda's shoulder. She reached over with her left hand and squeezed his tenderly. "Say when", commanded Farris.

"Four, three, two, now!" The Bi-plane pitched crazily as the draft from the chopper sucked the wind from underneath it. Farris yanked hard on the slip knot. The rope was yanked out of his hand taking away a layer of skin as it went. Linda who had dropped like a stone as she crossed over Ricky's stationary chopper was now pulling hard on the joy stick as the wheels almost touched the waves.

Ricky, who had not even suspected another craft, jerked, startled by the plane diving in front of him but he stabilized quickly. Flying with one hand he emptied a clip from his Uzi into the Zara out the open door of the chopper. A few rounds put tiny holes in the sails but the majority of the fire hit the water around the boat. The netting floated in the sky drifting downward assisted by the suck of the rotors. Then, with a terrific clap, it was sucked directly into the rotors. The nylon mesh wrapped around the moving parts, tearing and splitting but tightening with each revolution.

As the mesh hit the rotor the helicopter took on a life of its own and began to spin in a wild dance. Ricky dropped his weapon and tried desperately to control his craft. First the chopper veered up and away from the Zara. Then it circled and came straight towards the sailboat on a collision course. Jason let loose an entire clip. Ginny sighted in on the glass bubble and let loose two rounds from the shotgun. She watched the bubble shatter around Ricky but for the most part it held its shape. Judy blasted away with the handgun and David, aiming carefully popped three rounds into the cockpit. He was never sure if he had hit the chopper or not.

Phil had fired two shots with the handgun but as the chopper descended on a collision with the Zara he too had dropped his gun as he tried desperately to turn the boat.

The rotor finally seized. At almost the same time a barrage of gunfire erupted from the sailboat. Several shells pierced Ricky's body but there was no pain, or even fear, registering in his cocaine filled brain. Ricky focused on flying. As the netting choked the gears the chopper groaned and then simply stopped flying and plummeted into the sea, its rotors missing the Zara by inches. Ricky's first and only sensation of fear came as the helicopter literally stood on end, beginning it's head first dive and he found himself staring at the water, a hundred feet below him, through holes in the glass bubble. He was still screaming as the fuselage hit the salt water.

The crew aboard the Zara watched in awe as the fierce piece of machinery sank quickly into the ocean. Phil shut off the diesel. The wind filled the sails and the Zara, silently, under full sail left the oil slick of the wreckage in its wake.

Linda circled the Bi-plane and waggled her wings as she flew by. The crew on the Zara waved unenthusiastically, more shocked by the drama than excited by the triumph.

A mile away, Samantha, who had urged Victor to turn and follow the helicopter and Bi-plane as they left Normans Cay in the direction of Phil and Judy's boat, watched in awe as the helicopter silhouetted itself against the moon, for one quick second, before crashing into the sea. They saw Linda do her fly by and waggle her wings before they turned back toward shore.

Jason climbed down the companionway. He found a bottle of rum and poured a heavy shot into a glass, which he downed in one gulp. He returned the bottle to its place in the rack and stretched out on the settee staring at the ceiling. Judy stood beside Phil at the wheel, watching the compass and checking the luff of the sails. Ginny sat down in the cockpit and stared at the stars, silently. David went below and fetched a blanket from the settee. He sat down besides her, wrapping the blanket over both of them. She tucked her feet up on the cushions under the blanket and snuggled deeply into David's shoulder.

At exactly four o'clock in the morning Ginny nudged David gently.

The moon had sunk below the horizon over an hour ago and the night was as quiet and peaceful as any night Ginny could ever remember. The Zara was cruising at a steady six knots, without lights, leaving a gentle trail of phosphorescence in its wake.

"Hmm", he said contentedly waking from a light sleep.

"Time to get up. It's four o'clock." She stood and quietly walked over to where Judy stood wrapped in Phil's arms behind the wheel. "You two get some sleep. David and I will take over until eight."

She moved in front of Phil and checked the compass setting. Phil grinned as Ginny disengaged the auto pilot.

"Ginny, I don't know how to sail", said David weakly.

"Well I do. I'll show you how. We'll be O.K.," she said looking Judy squarely in the eye.

"Sounds good to me", said Phil. "Holler if you need anything".

"I'll make a thermos of tea before we lie down", volunteered Judy.

"That would be nice. Come on David. It will be light in another two hours and this is one sunrise I'm not ever going to let you forget."

As Judy made tea Jason rolled over. I guess I should get up and help for a while."

Judy looked over at him and grinned. "No need.... David and Ginny are on duty until eight this morning. You might as well sleep until then."

Jason smiled. He was happy to be absolved from duty. "Like that, hmmm".

Judy passed the thermos out to David, along with two cups. Jason had already rolled over and was snoring gently. Phil had wasted no time stretching out in the forward cabin. Judy joined him but on impulse, before lying down, closed the louvered door behind her.

Chapter 33

Phil rose shortly before eight o'clock and after making a bit of noise in the galley poked his head into the cockpit. David was sitting in the corner with Ginny's head on his shoulder. They were holding hands.

"She's right on course and sailing at seven knots", reported Ginny. "I've been playing with your toys. I love your chart plotting system. Between that and your auto helm I haven't touched a thing for two hours".

"And people say sailing is a lot of work. I think I could get used to this", added David.

Ginny gave him a quick hug.

"First a pot of coffee and then I'll take over", said Phil.

"Already brewing", called Jason from the galley.

"You might want to take a look at your life raft", said Ginny.

Phil climbed topsides and viewed the damage. The hard plastic case that held the folded up inflatable, had been hit a half dozen times. Phil began a survey of the boat. The jib sail had a number of holes and one life-line stanchion was severely bent. There were a few holes in the deck but nothing had penetrated the main cabin except in cupboards.

"It's not that bad", Phil mused as he returned to the cockpit. "We had better deep six the life raft and furl the sails before Customs come on board".

"I'd say we got off very lightly", said David.

At that point Jason came topsides carrying coffee. His shirt was bloodied although he seemed fine. Phil caught his eye.

"It's just a scratch. I wrapped it up last night but it did bleed on your blankets a bit. Sorry."

"Glad you're OK. I didn't even know you had been hit".

Judy appeared topsides. "Let me take a look at that, Jason".

"Deep six the shirt and blankets. We'll do our best to cover any damage before we hit Florida."

"According to your chart plotter that gives us about five hours", said Ginny.

Phil grinned, "Got it all figured out?"

Ginny beamed.

For the next hour everyone pitched in and scrubbed the boat clean. Phil unbolted the life-raft compartment and heaved it overboard. The bullets had penetrated the hard plastic case and then buried themselves in the folded rubber of the dinghy. Judy gave Jason a clean long sleeve shirt and when Jason appeared in it Phil joked, "Not that one. It's my favorite".

"Tough luck. It hurt like hell putting it on. Its mine now", came Jason's reply, followed by a display of white teeth.

"I can't find any news about the attack or the helicopter crash anywhere on the internet. Nothing on the radio either. Maybe we are the only ones who know what happened", called Judy from the cabin.

"Let's hope it stays like that", replied Jason.

"Your luggage is back at the hotel? Will that cause any problems?" asked Phil.

"Oh shit. My passport is back there", said David.

"Mmmm, mmmm", said Ginny with a twinkle in her eye.

"You're kidding. You really are one damn good secretary", said David.

"Looks to me like she's more than your secretary", teased Jason.

Ginny looked at David and held her gaze. David's face began to turn crimson.

"You are blushing, boy!"

David finally looked Ginny in the eye. "I think you're right about that", to which Ginny moved closer and rested her head against David's chest.

"Jason, I have your passport too", she said quietly as everyone turned away.

Jason was genuinely surprised. "Hot damn. You are a good secretary". They all laughed.

Phil spoke up, trying to focus on the immediate upcoming problem. "OK. There are enough bags on board that we can make up suitcases for everyone. Just in case. The story is that you all joined Jude and me for the sail back home. Everyone OK with that", said Phil.

Everyone nodded.

Five miles offshore Phil took in the sails and switched to diesel. The boat looked good. Most of the damage had been covered. When Phil docked at the customs house he put his undamaged side against the pier and reported in. The customs officer reviewed everyone's papers but took only a cursory glance at the boat.

As Phil moved the boat into a slip at the marina Judy served everyone a large glass of rum. Jason offered cigarettes and Judy took one.

⊰⊱

An hour later the entire crew headed out for the nearest restaurant.

Following a second round of drinks David finally brought up the question that had been eating at him for nearly twenty-four hours.

"Are you going to tell us what happened back there?"

Phil looked toward Judy and waited. Finally there was an almost imperceptible nod. Phil leaned his elbows on the table and everyone else drew up their chairs and leaned in.

An hour later, Ginny let out a breath. "Do you realize that your entire lives have changed and you are now fabulously wealthy because you followed a trail of bird shit?"

David leaned back in his chair.

"But after all that, you left the gold on Normans Cay?" he stated incredulously.

"Michael is the professional smuggler. Getting the gold into the States is his job", answered Phil quietly.

"And you think he's going to show up? He's a drug smuggler ...... you trust him with millions of dollars worth of gold?"

"We trust him", answered Judy defiantly. "He said he would be here and we'll wait until he comes."

"Count on a long wait."

Ginny put a hand on David's arm. He relaxed a bit and reached over with his other hand and took her hand in his.

"It was so beautiful last night ..... I mean after all the excitement..... Just the stars and the trail of phosphorescence in the water", said Ginny, trying to change the mood.

"Perfect sailing .... You were right on course at eight bells", answered Phil.

Ginny smiled.

"I think you ought to consider getting a boat, David", giggled Judy, knowingly.

"I never even considered it until last night", answered David. He looked into Ginny's eyes. "Maybe", he smiled.

Phil was in a pensive mood throughout the rest of the meal. He disliked the way David had suggested the gold would never leave Normans Cay. He considered Michael as a true friend. Yet the only way he could prove David's assessment wrong was for Michael and Linda to show up. They had arranged in advance to meet at the marina where Zara was tied up but no timetable had been arranged. A lot had transpired. The Bahamian police could be involved by now. Phil did not regret following Victor's relayed orders, to run for international waters and return to the States immediately. On the other hand, it did leave the gold at the harbor entrance. Leastwise, it did yesterday.

David and Ginny headed off to find a hotel room. They would drive home tomorrow. Maybe stretch the drive a few extra days. Jason was going home immediately. Phil and Judy said goodbye to the others in the lobby and walked back to their boat on sea legs that refused to walk in a straight line.

"Did you have too much to drink", teased Judy.

"Not enough", answered Phil.

The first couple of days passed pleasantly. Phil hung around the boat and fiddled with the hardware.

Judy went out and shopped. Most of their clothes had been left on Normans Cay and others had been shared. Phil was amazed that Judy could pick out clothes that he actually liked. He suspected that she paid more than he would have but the result was good and he was glad not to have to shop. He was aware that this was the first time in his life that a woman had ever purchased underwear for him and he acknowledged that he was giving up something. But whatever he was giving up seemed unimportant.

After a week he moved the boat from transient slips to monthly rentals in the same harbor. By the second week Phil was playing David's words, again and again in his head. He began to refer to their adventure on Normans Cay as their mis-adventure. One afternoon Judy arrived back at the boat with a bundle of developed photographs. One was an eight by ten of Phil and Judy, Michael and Linda standing in the dining room. Piled on the table top were the gold bars, hidden by a Panama hat. Judy had already framed it.

Phil looked away when he saw the photo but Judy grabbed his arm and spun him around.

"Look here, Phil. I still think Michael and Linda will show up. We couldn't find a peep about anything in the Bahamian papers so at least nobody ended up in jail. And even if we never see them again we went treasure hunting and found gold. That's an accomplishment very few people can admit to. So let's get over it! I just don't think it's over!"

"Do you want to go back to Normans Cay?"

"No. People died out there. Maybe the police are waiting for us. I'd rather be poor and free than rich and in jail."

"On that aspect, we both agree", said Phil. "Go ahead, hang up the picture. It sure is a memory".

Life steeled into an easy pattern. Living in a marina was an ongoing social event full of parties, cocktails and outings to watch a movie or rent a car and travel around Florida for a day or two. The coastal sailing was superb with an almost never-ending offshore breeze. Most mornings included a long walk on the beach and afternoons that were spent at the marina, usually ended up in the pool.

Summer slipped by and Phil's morose moods began to abate.

"We have three choices", he said one morning.

"What choices are those?" asked Judy.

"We can head north, head south or stay here."

"I'm not keen on spending the winter in Boston but I would like to visit there for a couple of days. I vote we sail up to Chesapeake Bay for a week or two, but come back here, or further south, for the winter. We can drive from Chesapeake to Boston."

Phil grinned. "I just asked you about three choices and you chose all three."

Judy smiled, turned and walked the three or four steps to the galley".

Phil just shook his head in defeat. Forty-eight hours later they were heeled over in twenty-five knot winds heading north.

The days were warm but the nights had cooled considerably as the Zara approached their destination in Annapolis. Phil radioed ahead to notify the marina of his arrival.

"We are doing some fall maintenance on the finger-docks and direct you to tie up on the main dock behind a large steel sailboat. Over".

"Roger that. Zara over and out."

Phil looked back over his shoulder to Judy who stood gracefully behind the large wheel.

"They want us to tie up on the main dock behind a big iron sailboat. I'll put out the fenders."

Ten minutes later the Zara eased into harbor.

"Wow! Is that the boat they want us behind? We'll look like their dinghy!" said Judy.

"That boat must be seventy feet."

"I'm guessing over eighty. Bet you a beer?"

"You're on."

As Phil and Judy got closer their level of admiration for their new neighbor increased. The hull was black with gold stripes at the gunnels and the waterline. The cabin was white with a lot of shiny brass trim. There was a handsome amount of bright work, gleaming with fresh varnish. Rigged as a ketch, with twin masts, her lines were perfect. She even sported a maidenhead, with long flowing golden hair, below the bowsprit.

Phil took the wheel and slid in behind her at dead slow. Two young dock attendants received the lines, tossed ashore by Judy. Once secured, Phil and Judy admired the stern of the boat in front of them. The aft cabin was lit by a large window in the stern, reminiscent of a Spanish Galleon.

"Nice neighbors!" said Judy.

Phil read the name across the stern of the steel beauty.

"Iron Pyrate. That's a helluva name for a steel ship."

"It means "Fools Gold", dummy."

"Yah right, "Fool's Gold". That's what we should rename our boat." The bitterness crept into his voice

"It's bad luck to rename a boat! And we agreed to forget about the past", warned Judy.

"Sorry, Hun. It just slipped out."

A couple appeared on the stern of "Iron Pyrate" looking down at the smaller boat below them. "Ahoy, Zara."

Phil and Judy looked up in awe at the stern rail. Michael Farris stood, dressed in white, with a broad brimmed white hat and a wide grin. His arm wrapped around Linda, dressed in white slacks and a dark blue silk blouse, accented with a heavy gold chain.

"You must be thirsty after your long sail. Martinis will be ready when you are", said Michael.

Judy was first to recover. "Five minutes to clean-up", she answered. Michael and Linda vanished.

"Jesus H. Christ!" stammered Phil.

"Put on some clean clothes." Judy was already rushing to the cabin.

Michael and Linda stood formally at the head of the gang-plank which was decorated with gold life-lines.

"Welcome aboard", said Michael as Judy stepped onto the teak deck. Phil was a step behind her.

"Welcome aboard, Captain", came a voice from the wheelhouse. George and the two Bahamian girls, all wearing crew uniforms of black shorts and white shirts with gold and black embroidery, stepped forward.

"George, Marcia, Yolanda", Phil stared at them as startled to see them as he was to see Michael and Linda.

Judy's jaw was hanging just above the floor. Linda opened her arms and gave her a big hug. Farris stepped forward with his hand outstretched toward Phil. He pumped it in an iron grip and clapped an arm around Phil's shoulder.

"Thought you'd never get here", said Farris.

"That ain't even close to what I thought", countered Phil.

Farris coughed. "Martinis?" He turned his back on
Phil and waited for his turn at a hug and a kiss from
Judy. Linda gave Phil a warm kiss and Phil and Judy
greeted George and the two girls in turn. It had only
been a few months but Marcia and Yolanda seemed
much more mature. Their hair was different and the
crew outfits made them look more like models than
maids. They both wore make-up, something they had
never done on Normans Cay. Phil held their hands.

"You girls look great!"

"New job, better pay, new clothes", answered
Yolanda. She even sounded more mature.

A few minutes later the four were sitting in the
spacious cockpit, sipping martinis from frosted glasses.
Chuck Mangione played from hidden speakers.

"So this is what you did with the gold?" said Phil
waving an arm at the luxurious surroundings. He was
pissed off about being kept in the dark for four months
and wanted Farris to understand that. Judy glanced his
way with a warning look. So did Linda but her eyes
were more understanding.

"No, the gold is right where I left it", answered
Farris.

"Outside the harbor entrance. Sure it is".

"No, that was a chest of scrap iron that we put
outside the harbor. The gold is right where I left it", he
repeated.

"Care to tell us where that might be or is that
another Michael Farris secret." Phil was making little
effort to be polite.

"Not at all". Farris picked up a remote control and
Chuck Mangione's trumpet played louder. Judy, Linda
and Phil leaned in a bit closer.

"You've been sleeping on the gold for the last four
months."

"What?"

"You've been sleeping on it. Remember how we put the Zara in the boathouse, the night before the attack. George didn't sleep much that night."

"You mean we smuggled the gold into the US and didn't even know it?" said Judy. She might have been angry about it but a strange sense of pride swelled inside her.

"It was safer that way. No need to tell lies at Customs."

"You bastard", said Phil although he wasn't sure if he was angry or congratulating Farris for his ingenuity.

Linda spoke up. "That's what I told him, too. Unfortunately by the time I found out you were already in Miami. Mission accomplished".

"What could go wrong?" asked Farris. "You even had your lawyer aboard!"

"That wasn't planned", said Phil. Farris shrugged.

Linda spoke up. "When I found out, Michael slept alone for a week! It would have been longer but we have always been able to work out compromises. I think you will agree this one was in your favor."

"Let me explain", said Farris smoothly. "It's like the test of fire. You never really join the smuggler's club until you smuggle something. We had a good partnership but deep down there were undercurrents of distrust. You felt them in the last four months".

Phil was still pissed off. "You're damn right I did. What … Did we smuggle a load of drugs in too?"

Linda's back stiffened but Farris shrugged. "No, I haven't smuggled drugs since I met Linda. That was a promise she insisted on. We compromised. I can smuggle emeralds or Mercedes Benz, but no drugs".

Phil relaxed and even grinned. "You told me you have known each other for five or six years."

"That's right. That's why Ricky and I were sworn enemies. I still had to pretend to be in the drug business. A few years ago I scooped one of his shipments. It became fish food and it cost Ricky millions. He had been waiting for a chance to strike back".

Linda piped in. "Well he's lost that chance now. Permanently. Michael won't talk about it but he funded a foundation for a half way house in Miami as a wedding gift to me. He never was a drug lord. Just a smuggler who I fell in love with."

"Getting back to the compromise, Linda thought I had put the two of you at undue risk. I thought it was fair because you might have done some work on your boat, one day, and discovered the gold. If that occurred, I would have to trust you to contact me. Regardless, if I wanted to sleep with a warm body next to mine, I had to do something. So I bought this boat in all our names. You each own twenty-five percent of Iron Pyrate."

"Yah, right. Good joke. We own half this boat". Judy's eyes fell on Linda's. "Holy shit!" stammered Judy. "You're not kidding".

"You are kidding, aren't you?" questioned Phil.

"No, the papers are in the wheelhouse. Everything is in order. How's your drink?"

Phil and Judy looked at each other and simultaneously, like synchronized swimmers, downed their drinks.

"Empty", said Judy.

"Are we all happy? Is everything forgiven? New tomorrow?" asked Linda.

When Farris had topped up drinks Phil raised his glass. "To a New Tomorrow".

"Oh, Mike. I like the name. Iron Pyrate".

"Bad spelling", said Judy. "Is it supposed to be Iron Pirate or Iron Pyrite?"

Michael looked at Linda and began to repeat Linda's phrase. By the end of the sentence everyone joined in.

"It was a com...prom...ise".

"It's good. Did you name the dinghy?" asked Phil.

"The dinghy? No." Farris looked unusually perplexed.

"Then as part owner I'm taking it on myself to Christen the dink. From this day forward Iron Pyrate's dink will be known as ....", Phil paused dramatically... "Ore Else".

It took a second to sink in. Finally Farris grinned and raised his glass. "To Ore Else."

After congratulations on another good name Judy finally asked. "Where's Victor, anyway?"

Farris looked at Phil and winked. Linda turned to Judy. "Samantha".

"Oooh".

⁛⁛

It was nearly two o'clock in the morning when everyone drifted off to their staterooms. Phil and Judy went into theirs and looked at the king-size bed. Judy jumped onto the mattress and rubbed the satin sheets against her cheek.

"I think I can get used to this, you know ..... Evolve", she said quietly.

Phil sat down in a tub chair, put his feet up on the footstool and looked out the stern lights at the Zara, below. "Comfy".

Without speaking another word the two left the room and walked down the gangplank to the dock.

As they climbed into the vee berth Phil hugged Judy and said. "Sorry to pass on the king-size bed but some nights, when I'm on my boat, my bed feels like a million bucks."

Judy snuggled close and they made love gently but quickly. They were both almost asleep when Judy murmured "I told you some smugglers were really very nice people."

"Ain't no delinquent ... just misunderstood", quoted Phil, from West Side Story.

"Deep down inside him there is good", responded Judy.

"What next? There is a second hull to explore on the Spit."

"And there is your lost ship off Long Island, then how about Polynesia ... then the Indian Ocean."

The waves lapped gently against the hull and the bumpers squeaked against the dock. Hidden beneath them the gold waited for a shaft of light to strike it.

"You decide, Jude. It all sounds good to me."

The End

About the Author

Paul Boardman's real life love affair with the sea, whether it be from the topsides of his boat or diving on a coral reef, is evident in his novel Normans Cay.

"My main goal in writing this book was for it to be entertaining … not too heavy … no need to save the world. Philosophically, when writing the book I often felt the need to escape the drudgery of day by day business. Remember Steve Martin's line; "Sorry, I just took a quick trip to the Bahamas". Personally, I accomplished that as I sat at my computer and dove into shipwrecks, love affairs, murder and battles with drug lords. My real goal, though, was to create an escape for the reader. When a good friend said he got half way through and couldn't put it down … well, that felt alright".

To Purchase copies
visit the Authorhouse website at
www.authorhouse.com
or call 888.280.7715

Made in United States
Orlando, FL
06 August 2022

20634483R00232